Looking up with a toothy smile splitting his beard, Ilbars saw a large group of shadowy figures approaching through the mist. At first he couldn't put his finger on it, but then it occurred to him that they were too tall, considerably taller than most dwarves.

"Elves!" he muttered in disgust. "I hope the king hasn't brought a bunch of elves along. He's too generous, really."

His warriors shuffled nervously. One of them cleared his throat and said, "Captain, I'm not so sure . . ."

His voice trailed off as the mist parted, revealing a rank of armored reptilian creatures with leering faces and loaded crossbows poised for firing.

The Age of Mortals Series

Conundrum
Jeff Crook

The Lioness
Nancy Varian Berberick

Dark Thane
Jeff Crook

DARK THANE

JEFF CROOK

DARK THANE

Cover art by Matt Stawicki
Interior Art by Sam Wood
First Printing: November 2003
Library of Congress Catalog Card Number: 2003100833

9 8 7 6 5 4 3 2 1

US ISBN: 0-7869-2941-3
UK ISBN: 0-7869-2942-1
620-17878-001-EN

U.S., CANADA,
ASIA, PACIFIC, & LATIN AMERICA
Wizards of the Coast, Inc.
P.O. Box 707
Renton, WA 98057-0707
+ 1-800-324-6496

EUROPEAN HEADQUARTERS
Wizards of the Coast, Belgium
T Hofveld 6d
1702 Groot-Bijgaarden
Belgium
+ 322 467 3360

Visit our web site at **www.wizards.com**

BOOK
I

CHAPTER

1

Tarn Bellowgranite hurried along the tunnel, surrounded by his personal guard of twelve dwarf warriors in jangling plate armor. A stiff, wet wind shrilled in his face, whipping his straw-colored beard over his shoulder like a scarf. Miles behind him now, King Gilthas led the last of the refugee elves away from their homeland of Qualinesti. Against the advice of his own Council of Thanes, Tarn and his dwarves had dug escape tunnels to help the elves avoid detection as they fled the green dragon Beryl. Somewhere ahead, Tarn's army of dwarves was battling Beryl and her legions of goblins, draconians, and human Knights of Neraka. Somewhere behind, the elves they had come to save were fleeing to safety.

For a moment, the thirteen dwarves slowed their steps as they listened to the wind blowing up the tunnel. Dwarves could tell by the sighing of an underground breeze what kinds of stone it had blown through, or so it was said. It was also said that a dwarf could hear a copper coin rattle in the shoe of a troll standing in a cesspit. What Tarn heard, though, were screams. Terror, pain, anger, and the rending of stone, the scream of the very earth as it succumbed to some great force.

The floor of the tunnel suddenly dropped from beneath their feet, sending the dwarves plunging down a slope of loose gravel and soil that had not been there moments before. The thirteen heavily armored dwarves crashed in a heap on a level twenty feet below, sounding as if a tinker's cart full of pots had been thrown down a well.

"What in the name of the Abyss!" Tarn swore as he rose, groaning and knuckling his back. The other dwarves climbed to their feet, battered and bruised, covered in dust and gravel, grumbling like the dead crawling out of their graves.

A wild-eyed dwarf with an unkempt beard jutting furiously from his mail coif leaned against the damp stone wall as though caressing it. "The very rock groans," he hissed after a few moments.

"I can feel the strain of the earth through the soles of my boots," Tarn said. "What I want to know is why?"

"The dragon," one of the other dwarves cryptically pronounced. The others nodded while dusting off their beards.

"Where are we now?" Tarn asked. The collapsed tunnel had dumped them into a deeper passage, one that crossed beneath their tunnel at right angles. All around them, they smelled the soft, peaty loam excreted by the monstrous Urkhan worms the dwarves had used to delve these tunnels.

"Urkhan holding pen," the first dwarf said. "If we follow this passage, it should lead us back to a main tunnel."

"You know these passages better than I, Captain Mog. Lead the way," Tarn said.

The other dwarves fell into protective positions around Tarn as they trotted off together. Mog ranged ahead a dozen yards to scout the way. The round passage led them along a meandering course through more worm pens and past the abandoned quarters of the worm wranglers. Several worm harnesses still hung from the wall of a chamber chewed from the earth by the worms' passage. All the pens in this area were empty, as the Urkhan worms had been moved into the tunnels beneath the city in preparation for the dragon's attack. Eventually, the tunnel led them into a wider passage.

"This is not the same passage as before," Tarn said as he examined their surroundings. "There's no wind here, and these walls are shored with timbers."

"This tunnel's not so deep as the previous one, m'lord Thane," Captain Mog said.

"Just so long as it takes us to Qualinost," Tarn grunted. "Lead on."

They hurried along the passageway, their iron-shod boots tramping the soft earthen floor. Soon, they passed several wooden support beams that had fallen across the tunnel, partially blocking the way, and these they had to scramble over or under as best they could. Each damaged section of the tunnel filled Tarn with a deepening sense of unease. The air stank of the forest just a few yards above their heads, and the tunnel felt close and dank. There was an unnatural silence, as though of the grave.

Tarn and his companions traveled without benefit of light from torches or lanterns. The long dark of the tunnel was no hindrance to them, for they were blessed with dark-vision. Not all dwarves possessed the ability to see in the dark—Tarn had it by his mother, Garimeth Bellowsmoke, a Daergar. His personal guard was made up of warriors from the Klar clan, who like the Daergar and Theiwar also had the gift. Tarn considered himself lucky to have been born with his mother's eyes. She gave him little else. He might have inherited his Hylar father's blindness to the dark, forcing him to travel in the deep places of the earth with torch or lantern light. Darkvision was a distinct advantage to those who dwelt underground.

The bends and turns gnawed through the earth by the Urkhan worms thus appeared to Tarn's eyes as though lit by bright moonlight. His companions were outlined in warm red, especially wherever their flesh was exposed to the open air. They wore iron-shod boots to hide their footprints from other creatures of the deep earth, who could track the residual heat left in stone by a person's tread. The Klar also painted their faces and caked their beards with white clay before battle, because white was the color of hiding among those with darkvision. To Tarn, their faces were blank masks in the dark, visible only by the heat of their open eyes; to their enemies, such faceless visages were terrifying.

Tarn guessed that they were nearing the city of Qualinost. He urged his guards to greater speed. They began to splash through muddy puddles where before there had been dry stone or moist earth.

"Are we near the tunnel entrance?" Tarn huffed as they jogged along.

"Not yet," Captain Mog answered from the front of the party. "This tunnel will slope down to join the main passage before entering the city. But we're close."

Tarn grunted in acknowledgement, hiding his anxiety under his customary gruff exterior of command. He feared the worst. The evacuation of the elves had been going as planned, with the last refugees escaping into the tunnels before Beryl's expected daylight attack. He and King Gilthas had been rounding up stragglers when a great blast of chill, wet air roared up behind them, from the direction of the city. The young elf king had wanted to return, but Tarn had urged him to lead the refugees to safety while he took his personal guard and investigated. Gilthas had reluctantly assented, marching off with his elves while Tarn turned back, the damp wind in his face speaking volumes that only a dwarf could read.

He dared not speculate as to the cause of the wind or the tunnel collapse that had dumped them into the Urkhan pen, but as he had said, he could feel the tension of the earth through his feet as he ran. The ground almost seemed to vibrate with the strain, the floor to hum like a harp string pulled to the breaking point.

They stopped at another partial collapse of the tunnel. Fallen beams crisscrossed the passage like the web of a spider, and sections of the roof had fallen, blocking the way. Captain Mog led the digging, clearing a path through the rubble for their king to follow. Tarn impatiently slapped the pommel of his sword while he watched them excavate. The Klar were not careful miners, but they were quick, strong-backed, and stubborn. They heaved beams aside or hacked through those too tightly wedged against the tunnel walls to budge. They clove through mounds of rubble with their hands, pushing, clawing, snarling, and cursing at the work. Earth, dust, and small pebbles sifted down from the unstable roof, threatening to bury them all, yet they pushed onward, needing little encouragement.

Soon, they cleared a path, but as they crawled through the last few feet of rubble, the beams around them groaned and cracked, pouring black soil, leaves, and twigs onto their heads. At the same time, something large and heavy struck the wall a tremendous blow. They clambered to their feet to find another section of tunnel collapsed not thirty feet ahead. Half-buried by tons of stone, an Urkhan worm was thrashing in pain and torment, its huge head hammering the walls, floor, and groaning roof. The monster was enormous, the largest and oldest in their stables. They had used it to burrow out the main passageways. Its tubular body was as thick as three dwarves standing on each other's shoulders. Its three jaws were large and powerful enough to shear through granite boulders. Two horns, each thicker than Tarn's wrist, sprouted from the creature's enormous head. With each blow, dirt and pebbles poured through ever-widening cracks in the ceiling.

"Kill that thing before it brings down the whole tunnel!" Tarn shouted.

Four of his Klar bodyguard rushed the monster, but their axes seemed to bounce off its rubbery reddish-brown skin. One dwarf dived beneath the creature's upraised body and stabbed with his dagger into the joint between two of its body sections. He disappeared with a sickening crunch beneath the monster as it flailed him to a pulp. Another dwarf managed to hack off one of the worm's horns, to which was still attached a length of broken harness rein. Writhing in agony, the huge worm spat a glob of clear viscous fluid. The glob splashed over the dwarf's upraised shield, coating his face and left hip. Immediately, his flesh began to hiss and smoke. Screaming in agony, he dropped shield and axe to claw at his dissolving face. Tarn jumped toward him and jerked him out of the way just as the worm's enormous head swept down, flattening his shield like the blow of an enormous hammer.

As captain of Tarn's personal guard, Mog leaped in front of his thane, sword raised. The blind worm seemed to sense his movement and lashed out. Mog ducked the blow that would have crushed him then jabbed with his sword into the creature's neck, just behind the huge misshapen skull. The worm flailed back, seeking to crush and destroy, but the Klar warrior rolled free, his sword dripping black blood that hissed on the stone. Another dwarf landed an axe blow between the creature's horns, and the blade stuck fast in the hard bone, jerking the weapon free of his grasp as the worm reared up in agony and bashed its head against the ceiling, vomiting corrosive spittle over the weakened roof. The force of the blow drove the axe blade deep into its tiny brain. Acid saliva dripped from its champing mouth as its enormous head wove uncertainly in the air.

Mog drove in again with his sword and stabbed behind the skull. This time, his sword found its mark. The creature collapsed as though struck by a thunderbolt. The floor, shattered by its death throes, opened in a hole that swallowed both the worm and the rubble that had crushed and trapped it. No longer supported by the rubble pile, the roof followed floor and worm down, widening the chasm. Tarn tried to drag the injured dwarf to safety but had to release his hold or be killed himself, as a whole elm tree dropped roots first through the roof and smashed to the ground, branches snapping, then toppled through the hole in the floor. He and his remaining band of dwarves scrambled to the other side of the tunnel as the last sections of the floor broke free beneath their feet.

After a few terrifying seconds, the collapse ended. Hazy yellow sunlight streamed down through gaping cracks in the tunnel's ceiling, sending dusty shafts of light probing the yawning black hole in the floor. The eleven surviving dwarves clung to the walls, staring down into the hole with eyes half-blinded by the sudden light. At the bottom of the hole black water swirled and churned like an underground river.

CHAPTER

2

We have to get out of here," Tarn shouted above the roaring of the water. A fine mist rising up from the hole began to wet the walls, making clinging to their precarious perches a treacherous affair. At the same time, the dwarf leader had noticed that the water level was rising.

Where was the flood coming from, and what of the dwarves in the deeper tunnels, what of the dwarves beneath the city? This was what Tarn had feared the moment the first damp breath of wind fingered his beard earlier that morning. Had they accidentally tunneled beneath an underground stream or lake?

There was no time to answer these questions. The water was already up to the crumbled edges of the tunnel floor. Tarn's bodyguards had worked their way up the sides of the tunnel toward the sunlight. He quickly followed. Climbing was no easy matter, even had the walls been dry, and his heavy armor only hindered his efforts. Mog was the first to reach the surface. He cut a branch and used it to pull the others to safety.

Tarn clambered out of the hole onto a leafy forest floor. Towering trees surrounded them like leafy columns in some sylvan feasting hall, marching in serried ranks in all directions. There was a strange, otherwordly beauty to the forest of Qualinesti. Leaf and moss were greener here, more vibrant, more alive. The light seemed to shine from another more ancient day. Even in war, there was peace here, so one could not imagine war ever disturbing such a place.

War there was, though, and war was near. This place was an garden, and nearby Tarn saw a house of rose quartz secreted among the trees, made to look like a natural part of the terrain. They were near the city; the hills rose behind them to the south. A haze hung over the forest, yellow and reeking with some familiar but unnamable odor. Yet there were no black pillars of smoke to be seen, not like there would have been if the city were burning. Perhaps the dwarves and elves had won after all. Perhaps Beryl had been driven off and Tarn's dwarves were waiting in the city with those elves who had stayed behind to defend their homeland, waiting to receive him with feasting and rejoicing.

Tarn's hopes leaped at the thought, but as he paused to glance back down at the water swirling up into the collapsed tunnel, he saw a sight that filled him with foreboding. A dwarf, ashen gray and purple-lipped with a jagged, white-edged wound splitting the crown of his head, had been twirled up by the stream. For a moment, the dead dwarf spun lazily in the water below, his beard and hair floating about his face like a dream, milky eyes staring up at a sun they could not long see, at a king they no longer revered. Then the water sucked him down again. As he sank away into the black gloom, his slack cheeks fluttered in a mockery of laughter.

Tarn looked away, his heart tightening in his chest. Captain Mog glanced up at the hazy sun to get his bearings.

"The city is that way," he said, pointing through the trees.

The other dwarves started off, fanning out through the trees to scout the way. Mog took a moment to sidle up beside his king and glance down into the water.

"Our warriors were down there," he whispered.

"I know," Tarn snapped.

He tromped off, kicking up leaves in his wake. Mog dropped behind him and warily scanned the forest for enemies.

The forest floor sloped gently downward as they traveled north toward the city. The lead dwarves stumbled and swore as they pushed their way through the woods, tripping over every root and snagging their clothes and armor on any vine or thorny creeper that crossed their paths. Tarn cringed at the noise of their passage, which seemed to echo through the eerily silent forest. He'd been to Qualinost several times in the past months, and he'd never experienced such a profound silence.

They had not gone more than a bowshot when the dwarves emerged from the forest and into the hazy yellow sunlight. They hung back in the shadow of the trees and gazed in wonder and awe at what confronted them. Tarn hurried forward, but even before he reached the edge of the trees, he saw. At first, he doubted his senses. He stumbled past the last tree and stood, gaping, from the margin of the forest.

The elven city of Qualinost was gone. In its place, a vast steaming lake hissed and bubbled with yellow vapors that reeked of chlorine gas—and something worse. Here and there, a crumbled crystal spire jabbed up through the haze hanging over the lake, proving that this was not a dream. It was a nightmare come to life. The entire city of Qualinost, wonder of the western world, was drowned in a hideous swamp of greasy black water.

The dwarves choked on the gasses rising from the lake as they stood on a forest hillock overlooking the site of the destroyed city. Water lapped along the flotsam-choked shore at the bottom of a steep bank some forty feet below. At first they wondered at what they saw. The waters were littered with debris from the shore to the edge of sight—

broken bits of furniture, shattered trees tossed up by the flood, and whole rafts of leaves and twigs that looked solid enough to walk atop. There were other things that they could not at first discern—low humped shapes that rode just beneath the surface of the water. Their horror swelled as the chaotic jumble of shapes began to resolve into the recognizable outlines of elves, goblins, and dwarves, floating in the water along with the other wreckage of the city, some facedown with their backs humped in the water, others facing skyward with milky, sightless eyes. By the thousands, they had drowned in the flood of water that filled the city, and now the bodies of enemies and allies alike bumped side by side in the greasy water. With tears streaming from his eyes, Tarn wrenched his gaze away from what lay below them and turned his attention to the sky. He half expected to see Beryl's hideous, bloated form circling overhead, reveling in the destruction of the city and all its occupants.

However, the sky, though hazy, was empty of dragon shapes. It was blue, peaceful, without even a dark cloud or portent.

Tarn crept back to the relative safety of the trees while he continued to scan the skies. He couldn't bear to look anywhere else. He half hoped that a dragon would materialize to attack them so that he could die an honorable death along with all those he had sent to their doom beneath Qualinost. He doubted now that any of his dwarves could have survived. The disaster must have come upon them without warning.

The dwarf king sagged against the bole of an enormous tree and glanced around at the horrified faces of his companions. Some stood as though struck blind, no longer even seeing what was before them. Others, like Tarn, could no longer bear to look and had turned away, beards trembling with the anger, horror, fear. Only Mog continued to stare out across the lake. The dwarf captain moved slowly up to the edge of the bank and glanced warily down at the shore. With a cry, he leaped. Tarn feared Mog had been driven out of his mind by the horror of the lake. He rushed after him, but as he reached the lip of the bank, he saw that Mog had only climbed down to the water's edge. Some piece of flotsam had caught his eye, and now he was dragging it out of the greasy water.

"Mog!" Tarn hissed. Even though there was no one around to hear, he felt reluctant to shout. "Let the dead lie. Come back at once!"

The dwarf continued to struggle with his prize. Finally, he wrested it free from an entangling mass that Tarn realized had once been a fine carpet in some noble elf's home. The object that Mog dragged from the lake was nearly as big as the dwarf and a dull olive in color. Its outer surface was pitted and cracked like weathered stone, but the underside was a soft pearly pink. It took a few moments for Tarn to realize what the thing was, but Mog had known as soon as he had spotted it at the water's edge.

"It's a dragon scale!" the Klar captain said as he struggled up the slope, dragging it behind him.

"It can't be," Tarn said. "It's too big." Even as he said it, he knew that he was wrong. It was, indeed, an enormous dragon's scale, many times larger than the scale of any dragon native to Krynn. Tarn had only seen a few loose dragon scales in his life, but none were anything like this one.

The captain clambered up next to him and flung the thing on the ground. Tarn knelt and ran his hand along the rough, cracked edge, feeling the stonelike texture.

"It must have come from *her!*" Mog hissed. He flipped it over, revealing the pink underside. A ragged bit of bloodless flesh clung to the upper flattened edge of the scale. Mog drew a dagger from his boot and sliced off a piece of the stringy, waterlogged flesh. He held it up to his nose then tested it with his teeth. He turned and spat.

"Dragonflesh!"

A hissed warning sounded from the trees. Looking up, Tarn saw one of the guards pointing across the lake. He crouched lower, peering through the haze rising off the horror-filled water. Something had crept out of the forest on the far side and stood at the water's edge. Something else joined it. The two began to creep along the shore, bending low as though sniffing the ground. Batlike wings rose from their backs, and long tails snaked behind them.

"Draconians," Tarn said.

"Looks like someone survived after all. Probably looking for something to eat," Mog growled then shuddered at the thought of the scavengers' banquet floating in the lake. "We should leave."

Tarn gazed around at the woods, the hills, the broken crystal spires rising from the lake. He was reluctant to depart without first discovering the fate of his army. Maybe some dwarves had survived. He couldn't allow himself to believe that everyone had perished. If any did survive, they would head for the dwarves' nearest stronghold, the fortress straddling the pass between the elven and dwarven lands.

"To Pax Tharkas, then," he said.

Mog nodded. As Tarn scurried back to the relative safety of the trees, Mog heaved the huge dragon scale onto his back. Staggering for a moment to balance its weight, he followed his companions up the slope into the wooded hills.

Tarn paused to wait for him at the edge of the trees. "Are you going to carry that all the way back to Thorbardin?" he asked grimly.

Mog nodded under his burden. "This is proof of Beryl's death," he said.

"You don't know that," Tarn said. "We can't assume anything."

"I'll make a shield out of it, then," Mog grunted as he started off, pushing his way through the forest undergrowth. "Dragonscale armor is worth its weight in steel."

"Reorx knows, we paid enough for that one," Tarn muttered into his beard as he stared back at the lake. More bodies than he could count filled the water as far as he could see.

CHAPTER

3

Crystal Heathstone paused and set aside her hammer, pushed down the leather mask protecting her face from the heat, and dragged the heavy leather gloves from her hands. Behind her, red coals pulsed and waned from the air pushed by a bellows pumped by a young male dwarf of her household. He leaned over to check the quality of her work then shook his head ruefully. He let the bellows fall, exhaling a last gasp into the forge coals.

She flung her gloves on the floor. "My forge skills never were much to brag about," she said, "but no one here in Thorbardin knows how to make a decent pair of shears. I promised Aunt Needlebone I'd make her some shears, but these will never work." She dragged a battered pair of tongs out of a barrel and lifted the still glowing but hopelessly warped shears from the anvil.

"This is pathetic," she said laughing as she plopped them steaming into a bucket of water. "How many is that I've ruined, Haruk?"

The apprentice thoughtfully stroked his wispy blond beard. "Eleven? Or is it twelve? I forget, Mistress. Why don't you just send me to the Hylar market to buy a pair?"

Crystal untied her leather apron and folded it lovingly before stowing it in a wooden chest. "Everything there is made for cutting leather, heavy wool, or mushroom fiber. Auntie needs something with a finer edge for delicate work. As she says, 'leave it to a mountain dwarf to chop wood with a battle-axe.' "

"What sort of delicate work?" Haruk asked. He shut the cover on the portable forge Crystal had set up, then he screwed down the damper to cool the fire within. The chamber grew dark, lit only by a single candle burning on a side table.

"Just some frilly things she wants to finish," Crystal answered quickly as she bent over and fished the cooled shears from the cooling bucket. She flung them onto a heap of scrap metal. "You know the kind of things she wears. It's not important. Her heavy shears will have to suffice until my forge skills improve."

"Aye, Mistress," Haruk said. He untied the leather cord binding his hair and shook out his full golden mane. Younger than Crystal by thirty years and not yet considered an adult, he was a fine specimen of dwarf youth, already come into his full growth and able to hold his own with more mature fighters in the sparring ring. He sighed and stretched, flexing the muscles of his bare sweaty arms. Crystal smiled appreciatively and crossed the room. In the corner by the door stood two stout lengths of ash wood, polished and ready for fitting with spearheads. She snatched them up and tossed one to the young dwarf. He caught it, his lips peeling back in a fierce grin.

"How about a few rounds before dinner?" Crystal asked.

"Gladly!"

Crystal stabbed the end of her staff into a pile of charcoal, coating it with thick black dust. Haruk did the same, then the two dwarves backed several paces across the chamber to give themselves room to work.

"Spear practice," Crystal said. "Black touch wins the round. How many rounds?"

"Best of five," Haruk said.

Grasping her pole at the low quarter, Crystal presented her blackened end, spear-fashion. Haruk dropped into a low guard, the charcoal-dusted end of his staff weaving tight figure eights in the air. Crystal stamped toward him three steps, her staff licking out in rapid feints, which he blocked effectively with the tip of his staff. The two wooden dowels clacked together in a brief staccato that left a cloud of charcoal dust hanging in the air between them. Crystal withdrew, smiling, then shifted to her left and took up a defensive posture.

Suddenly, Haruk bellowed a charge and leaped across the room. She quickly sidestepped his headlong rush, knocked aside the tip of his staff, and dragged her own weapon across his naked bicep as he passed, leaving a black streak across the bulging muscle.

The younger dwarf swore mightily as he returned to his position.

"You fall for that every time, Haruk," Crystal admonished. "An injury like that is as good as a killing blow. If that had been a real spear, your bicep would be severed and your arm useless."

"I know, Mistress," Haruk answered sullenly. He assumed a guarded stance.

Crystal advanced to within a spear's distance and presented her own weapon, crossing his at the tip. "Begin!" she snapped.

Slowly, they began to circle one another, staff tips crossed and touching at the axis of their circle. Their soft boots scratched on the dusty floor. Haruk lunged, but Crystal pressed the attack aside and countered, driving Haruk back to his original position. They crossed staves again and continued their circle. Haruk's green eyes danced in the light of the single candle as he sought some weakness in her defense. The tip of her staff dropped almost imperceptibly, and Haruk immediately seized the opportunity, thrusting past it. Crystal slipped below his attack and punched him squarely in the solar plexus with the end of her pole.

Haruk staggered back, gasping for air and nearly dropping his weapon. When he had gathered his breath, Crystal said, "I did that because I know you so well. We've practiced together many times, and I knew you would bite the bait I dangled before your nose. It's easy to draw you into a foolish attack with a simple feint, like a mother bird pretending to have a broken wing. Be still when you fight. Calm your emotions."

"Uncle Jungor says I should cultivate my emotions," Haruk said as he rested on his staff. "He says anger and fear will make my reactions quicker and my attacks stronger."

"Your uncle, the Hylar thane, is a great arena fighter, true," Crystal said, "but those he faces in the pit are his equals, at the height of their fighting ability, and there are few who could trick him into exposing himself. Yet a great warrior must respect every opponent. You must also learn to fight those who have little military training, for their movements will be unorthodox and unexpected. A great fighter might try to trick you with a feint, but a gully dwarf could do the same by accident and just as easily. Either way, you're just as dead."

"Yes, Mistress," Hurok said.

"Ready?"

Haruk nodded. The smile was gone from his face now. He circled her warily, and Crystal could see her lessons turning over in his mind. He was alert now but relaxed. His movements slipped fluidly from one moment to the next. He was no longer fixed, rigid in his stances. His eyes no longer darted nervously from her weapon to her face and her feet. When he attacked, he almost caught her by surprise. Only a slight shifting of his feet betrayed his intention.

What did surprise her was his method of attack—the same blind spear charge she had beaten a thousand times before. Slipping to the side, she blocked his jab and . . . a blow to her stomach staggered her. Haruk had reversed it in mid-charge, hiding the movement with a shouting leap. The charcoal-blackened end thudded against her belly even as she, once again, dragged her own weapon across his biceps.

"Mistress!" Haruk cried in surprise, dropping his staff and falling to his knees.

Crystal rubbed her stomach, momentarily frightened by what had happened. Haruk's blow hadn't been a hard one, but if it had been a spear, it would have spilled her belly's contents onto the floor. Haruk kneeled before her in abject apology.

"I never taught you that," she complained.

"My uncle, Jungor Stonesinger taught it to me. He said I should try it on you. Please forgive my impertinence," he said, head bowed almost to the floor.

"Stand up," she said, touching him on the shoulder. "No harm done, I think." She crossed the chamber and seated herself on an upturned keg. Haruk rose to his feet. "Shall I fetch Auntie?"

"I'm fine," Crystal sighed. "Come, tell me what your uncle said. You didn't even try to defend yourself. Yet what you did would have killed me, even as I killed you, had this been a real battle."

"That's what Uncle Jungor said," Haruk said, nodding. "He said that if you cannot defeat your opponent, you should consider sacrificing yourself in order to get close enough to kill him. Thus many a dwarf has bravely died in defense of his homeland."

"When he has no other choice," Crystal countered sternly. "When his sacrifice may save the lives of his family or companions. It is the height of folly to throw away your life needlessly. A good fighter also knows when not to fight."

"I understand, Mistress," Haruk said.

"I'm glad you do, Haruk. Your uncle is wise in his way, and I would not speak against anyone from your family, but he is a hard, uncompromising individual, and he holds with ancient ways and ancient traditions that are no longer always best. The world has changed, as King Tarn has said many times. New times demand new ways."

"Any word from the king?" Haruk asked.

"No word yet," Crystal sighed. "A messenger arrived from Pax Tharkas two days ago saying that the evacuation of the elves was proceeding well." She rose to her feet and picked up her staff. "Now, I believe the score is two to one in my favor."

"Are you certain you are recovered, Mistress?" Haruk asked in concern. "Perhaps it would be better—"

"I'm fine," Crystal snapped. "It is you who must beware. I intend to give you a good drubbing. On your guard, sir dwarf." With that, she gripped her staff and swung.

Desperately avoiding her blows, Haruk hopped across the dusty floor and retrieved his weapon just in time to block a thrust that would have unhinged his jaw. He tumbled across the floor, thrusting wildly at her feet to give himself time and room to maneuver. Crystal seemed to dance atop his weapon, nimbly avoiding his blows while shouting, "Good! Good! Just what I would do."

He rolled to his feet and began to backpedal as the blackened end of her staff flicked again and again in his face, mere inches from his nose. He blocked each thrust only by the most heroic effort, and he knew he couldn't keep up with her much longer. He tried to force the charcoal tip of her staff over his head so that he could step inside the range of her weapon and grapple. At that instant, she hammered his instep with the butt of her staff then leaped back, on guard once again.

Howling in pain, Haruk hopped on one foot while clutching the other injured one.

"A spear is but a staff with one end sharpened. The blunt end can be just as dangerous," she shouted. She twirled the staff humming through the air, passing it from hand to hand. Haruk noted that she wasn't even breathing hard. He shook his head in disbelief.

"You should fight in the arena," the young dwarf said with undisguised admiration.

Crystal laughed, tossing her staff into a corner. "The king would flay my hide and hang it from his wall," she said as she took Haruk by the hand and helped him to a seat atop a barrel.

"If he didn't, I surely would!" An elderly female dwarf stumped into the room and pointed one quivering finger in Crystal's face. "I thought I heard staff work in here. You should have better sense than this, Crystal Heathstone. Frolicking around like you are still a girl in your father's army!"

"Oh, Auntie, I was just teaching my pupil his staves and spears."

"Pupil? He's supposed to be your personal guard," Aunt Needlebone snarled then turned on Haruk. "And you, young fellow. What have you to say for yourself? Haven't you better sense? You might have injured your queen."

"No disrespect, Aunt Galena, but I doubt I could seriously injure Mistress. Not on purpose, anyway," the young dwarf answered sheepishly.

The old woman glared at him then back at Crystal, but there was a twinkle in her rheumy gray eye.

"You're probably right at that, lad," she cackled suddenly, slapping him on the shoulder. "Ouch! Hard as stone, that is. Why, if I was a hundred years younger . . ."

Haruk flushed a deep scarlet up to his ears, to the delight of both women.

CHAPTER
4

A lone dwarf strode up the earthen ramp to the towering outer gate of Pax Tharkas. The night was
dark as the deep earth, with not a star in the sky, and the
warriors guarding the ancient dwarven fortress had set up
dozens of torches along the ramp to illuminate anyone
approaching in the night. Huge stone walls rose more than
a hundred feet in the air before him, bone white in the light
of the torches lining the ramp. The walls stretched away in
a gentle curve on either side of the ramp, disappearing into
darkness long before they reached the stony slopes of the
mountain pass that Pax Tharkas guarded.

The dwarf wore a ragged assortment of plate and
chain-mail armor, heavily weathered. He stopped just
inside the circle of the torchlight and lifted his hands palm
up to show they were empty. He couldn't see the gate's
defenders because of the glow of the torches, but he knew
they were watching him, probably down the length of a
cocked crossbow.

After a few moments, he pushed back the chain-mail
hood covering his head, loosing an unruly mass of greasy
black hair and a jutting nest of beard. Flecks of some white
substance clung to the ends of his beard hairs, while the

deeper crevasses of his weathered face showed white with the same substance.

He thrust out his chest and shouted, "Open the gates!"

"Who are you, and what do you want?" a harsh voice answered from atop the battlements high above him.

"I am Mog Bonecutter, captain of the High Thane's personal guard. The thane desires entrance," Mog answered.

"If the king is with you, why doesn't he show himself?" the voice asked sharply.

"He doesn't want to be shot by accident in the dark by you night-blind Daewar dogs. I know your voice, Mason Axeblade, and you know me better than you'd like. So open this door before I hew it down!" Mog roared.

"It'll take more than one motherless iron-throated Klar to breach the gates of Pax Tharkas," the voice shouted in answer. "Open the gates! Wake up, you sluggards. The king has returned. Open the gates for your king, blast your hides!"

As Tarn and the remainder of his guards climbed the ramp to the outer gate of Pax Tharkas, one of the massive, ironbound valves slowly and silently swung open on its well-greased hinges. Torches appeared in the gap, held aloft by grim-faced dwarves dressed in mail. Half held loaded crossbows at the ready, the others clutched spears, and they all formed a lane to welcome Tarn into the fortress.

Mog led the way through the towering gate and into the first outer courtyard. Here between the first and second curtain walls, they were met by a hawk-faced dwarf bearing an enormous, two-handed warhammer. His meticulously groomed beard lay in a profusion of curling copper ringlets across his broad steel breastplate. As Tarn approached, the dwarf stamped down a narrow stair leading down from the battlements of the first wall.

"It is good to see you, Captain Axeblade," Tarn said wearily as he gazed around, taking in the arrangement of the fortress's defenses with a quick glance. Dwarves lined both outer curtain walls and stared down into the courtyard. Strict discipline held their tongues, but Tarn knew they were waiting to hear the results of the battle. He was not yet ready to speak openly of the disaster, though.

The outer defenses of Pax Tharkas consisted of two curtain walls that completely blocked the mountain pass. The two outer walls were too far apart to bridge, but narrow enough to provide a killing field for any attackers unlucky enough to become trapped between the first wall and the defenders on the second wall. The first gate was reached by a ramp leading up from the valley below. The second wall was higher than the first, as the road into the main fortress climbed up into the mountains. Beyond the second wall, the two massive square towers of Pax Tharkas rose majestically into the night sky, looming like black bulwarks with their narrow windows winking with torchlight. A third wall, taller and broader than the first two, was pierced by a massive iron gate and defended the pass between the towers.

The fortress was one of the wonders of Krynn. It had been built to guard a narrow valley through the Kharolis Mountains, which connected the high plateau of the elven woodlands with the wide plains lying before the dwarves' mountain home of Thorbardin. Dwarves and elves had built and garrisoned it together as a sign of peace between their two peoples, but that was long ago in another time. Now Pax Tharkas was a fortress on the northern frontier of dwarf lands, a buffer between Thorbardin and the troublesome north.

Captain Axeblade led Tarn and his party through the main gate and into a broad, paved courtyard beyond. The courtyard lay in a bowl-like valley, deep in the shadows of the gigantic towers. Here Tarn saw the preparations for war were continuing even at this late hour. Donkeys brayed beneath their loads, while the caves dotting the eastern slope glowed like red eyes from the forge fires within.

The dwarves guarding the walls watched the king and his party pass then turned back to their duties. Tarn's silence told them all they needed to know. They looked now to the north, their commanders quietly telling them to be on their guard for the attack most felt was sure to come. Tarn ground his teeth in his beard. He wanted to say something to dispel their fears, but he would not lie to them, and the truth was too grim, too fresh in his memory.

"I must see General Otaxx Shortbeard," Tarn said to Captain Axeblade.

The captain nodded and led them across the courtyard into the east tower.

"I don't like crawling in here like a whipped dog," Mog whispered harshly as he and Tarn waited in the general's study. General Shortbeard was one of Tarn's oldest and most loyal commanders, one of the few Daewar who had not followed Severus Stonehand on his mad quest to retake Thoradin in the years after the Chaos War.

The general's quarters were located on the second level of the east tower of Pax Tharkas, but his office was within the great shaft that had been built during the War of the Lance to house the dragon mount of the commander of the red dragonarmies. The shaft had once pierced the tower from its base to its top, but the dwarves had since roofed it over and divided it into its proper levels once more.

The general's office was spartanly furnished, as befitted an old campaigner. His desk had once been a door, looted from some ruin or dungeon during his youth. Fitted with iron bands and rivets, marred by axe blows that had since been lovingly polished, it sat atop a pair of wooden chests. An iron dragonhead ornament in the center of the door held an inkpot in its gaping mouth. A book lay open on the desk, the page marked with an ornate silver dagger.

A canvas-backed chair, much sagged in the middle, stood behind the desk, and trophies of old battles hung on three of the stone walls—an ogre's wolf-toothed club, an evil knight's broadsword decorated with skulls, an elf's delicate but deadly longbow. A pair of ancient wooden chairs dating back to before the Cataclysm completed the room's furnishings.

"No disrespect, Thane," Mog whispered, "but it was wrong of us to slink in here like gully dwarves. The lads on the walls were looking to you for encouragement."

"I've no encouragement to give them, Mog," Tarn snapped. "What did you want me to say? Half of them had friends or relatives in Qualinost. Shall I tell them how their loved ones were buried alive? Or drowned? I don't know which is worse. I can't get their faces out of my mind. I can't stop imagining all the ways they could have died."

"They're warriors. They knew what might happen when they chose their lot in life—to die and to see your friends die. We all learn to accept it. You should have told them the truth," Mog grumbled. "You owe them the truth."

"What? That their kith and kin died horribly for no good reason?" Tarn snarled

"You should have told them that they died honorably and their deaths were not in vain," Mog said as the door opened. He lowered his voice. "They won a great victory."

A stout dwarf stopped short within the doorway. "Victory?" he exclaimed. "Do my ears deceive me?" He entered, his round face flushing crimson above his spade-shaped beard. "They told me you'd been defeated!"

"Shut the door, Otaxx!" Tarn barked, glaring at the dwarves crowding the hall outside. Every word he'd said to Mog had probably been overheard and was already spreading like measles through the fortress. He gnawed at the filthy ends of his straw-colored beard while the general closed the door and locked it with an iron key.

As he turned and crossed the room, General Otaxx stared first at Tarn then at the Captain of the King's Guard. Mog only shook his head, while Tarn avoided his gaze entirely.

"What happened?" Otaxx asked he as he lowered his rotund bulk into the creaking canvas-backed chair.

When Tarn didn't answer, Mog hesitantly said, "We're not sure."

"We're sure enough that no one survived," Tarn said in a low voice trembling with suppressed emotion.

General Otaxx's breath escaped his lips in a long sigh. He leaned back in the creaking chair, which threatened at any moment to split apart at its canvas seams.

"We don't know that for certain," Mog amended. "There could have been survivors, but we never found any. We tried to get away—er, get back here as soon as possible. The woods were crawling with the remnants of Beryl's army."

"Remnants?" Otaxx's face brightened. "Beryl is dead, her army scattered?"

"So we hope," Mog said. He quickly recounted what had happened in the tunnels, their discovery of the drowned city. "I found one of Beryl's scales floating in the flotsam along the shore of the new lake. It was not some old dried scale that dropped off her body naturally. It was torn out of her flesh, by what force I cannot begin to guess."

"Whatever it was that flooded the city must have also killed her," Otaxx ventured.

"We don't know that for certain either," Tarn snarled. He rose to his feet and began to pace the small chamber. "She may only be wounded. In truth, we know almost nothing. We don't know why the city was flooded or what happened to those defending it. We don't know how many of Beryl's soldiers were killed or if they are still under any kind of central command. We don't even know for sure if Beryl is alive." He stopped before the door and slammed his fist into it so hard that the center wooden panel split down its entire length. He seemed not to even notice, for he immediately resumed his pacing. Blood dripped from his knuckles onto the flagstone floor.

"I cannot allow myself to hope that the Great Green Bitch is dead," Tarn finished.

"If you had no hope of defeating her, why did you aid the elves?" Otaxx asked with a frankness that might have been traitorous had Tarn been any other king. His commanders and generals knew that Tarn valued frank advice, even if it disagreed with his plans.

Still Tarn spun and glared at the portly general, anger flaring in his violet eyes.

"I had no other choice," he said, repeating the excuse he'd been practicing since they left the Qualinesti forest early that morning. He felt weary to the bone. He'd had no sleep in almost two days, but that was little more than an inconvenience. He'd gone far longer without rest in the days after the Chaos War, when the survival of his people had lain in the balance. He felt as though there were a palpable force trying to restrain him, to surround him and smother him, plucking at his elbows and tugging at his sword belt. Even now, he sensed it. It felt as though there weren't enough air in the room for all three of them to breathe, as though each breath were a struggle.

"I aided the elves because I had no other choice," Tarn repeated wearily. "To not aid them when they came begging at my door would have been immoral. Besides, since when has an elf ever begged aid of a dwarf? I could not pass up the opportunity to forge an alliance between our two people in this time of danger. And I wanted a chance to strike a blow at Beryl and her minions and also at the Dark Knights."

"Then you *did* hope to defeat her," Otaxx shrewdly observed.

"The elves' plan was a good one. It could have worked. For all we know, it did work," Mog said, a smile creasing his unkempt black beard.

"Their plan was foolish, and I should have seen it. Some madness blinded me," Tarn said, waving his hands in the air before his face as though he still felt his vision and his judgment clouded. "Aiding them in their escape was the right thing to do, but helping them fight Beryl with arrows and ropes, that was more akin to catching a bird in a snare." He shrugged. "I don't know what I was thinking. I wasn't thinking."

"You can't trust the elves, I always said," Otaxx murmured as his eyes strayed to the elven longbow hanging on his study wall.

"Elves!" Tarn growled huskily. "I wish to the gods I had never listened to them. If Gilthas himself were to stick his pointy head through that door, I'd chop it off." Snarling an oath, he slapped the pommel of his kingsword and resumed his seat in one of the antique wooden chairs. The chair looked like a sentimental attempt at a throne. There was distinct elven craftsmanship in its woodland motifs—oak leaves and acorns and unicorns passant. The sight of it made Tarn's stomach turn.

Yet it was unfair to blame his failures on the elves, and Tarn knew it. This only made him angrier. He had no one to blame but himself. How could he go back to Thorbardin and face those who had lost so much beneath the waters of doomed Qualinost?

"I must return to Thorbardin," Tarn sighed.

Otaxx clucked his tongue and shook his round head ruefully. "You know what you will find there, my king," he said. "The Hylar thane will seize this opportunity to challenge your authority. It's just the sort of event he's been waiting for."

Tarn stared darkly across the desk at Otaxx, but said nothing.

"Perhaps it *would* be better to wait . . . a couple of days, no more, of course. If there are survivors, we should give them time to find their way back here," Mog offered. "We can send out search parties. Maybe, with confirmation of Beryl's death, we can lessen the impact of the news."

"Lessen the impact?" Tarn asked incredulously. "Do you hear yourself? Thousands of dwarves died because I foolishly went against the will of the Council of Thanes."

"But if Beryl truly is dead—" Otaxx began.

Tarn silenced him with a look. "I can't put this off," he said. "I've failed, and thousands of dwarves have died as a result. Let no one speak of what happened to the elf city until I have spoken to the Council of Thanes."

"There are already rumors, my thane," Otaxx said.

"Deny them," Tarn ordered.

"Yes, my thane," Otaxx said, rising from his creaking chair. "When will you go?"

"At first light. Before I leave, I'll need to draw replacements for my personal guard from your garrison."

"I'll escort you personally," General Otaxx said. "Evil things will be roaming the plains, now that Beryl's army has been scattered. It isn't safe for you to cross alone."

The huge, vaulted cavern was carved in steps of concentric rings that climbed down to an oval stage at the center, but the air was so thick with smoke that it was impossible to see the opposite side of the arena and nearly impossible to see the stage from its topmost steps. Dwarves of every clan and family crowded the steps, some sitting, many standing and shouting, not a few snoring drunkenly on the rough stone floor. The acrid smell of sweaty unwashed bodies competed with the reek of pitch torches and the stomach-roiling odor of the heady alcoholic beverage known as dwarf spirits. The unmistakable rat-warren-stink of gully dwarves lay like an foundation beneath the other smells, pervading everything, much as the gully dwarves themselves lay everywhere, under everything, in the midst of everything and usually in the way, despite the curses (and worse things) hurled their way.

In the center of the arena, two dwarves battled. Stripped to the waist, their beards bound by leather cords, the pair exchanged bone-crushing blows as fast as their fists would fly. Heavy booted feet tore divots from the hard-packed dirt floor as they fought. Swearing and spitting teeth and blood, the two battlers parted for a moment to catch their breath, their pale, naked backs heaving for air and glistening with sweat in the smoke-dimmed torchlight. All around them, the crowd roared in approval, stamping their boots in thunderous applause that seemed to shake the very foundations of the cavern. The two dwarves stared at each other with hate-filled eyes for a moment longer.

Then one snarled, "Theiwar pig!"

"Daergar worm!" the other shouted, launching himself in a sudden wild leap that took the Theiwar by surprise. The first dwarf ducked, only to catch the heel of the other's boot under his bearded chin. His knees buckled and he sat down then toppled over nosefirst into the dirt.

Half the arena erupted in wild screams of delight. The other half, having lost their wagers, stared grimly for a few moments before demanding an opportunity to win back their money on the next fight. A door at the edge of the sunken arena floor opened, and several dwarves rushed out to drag the limp body of the defeated away and to help the victor stagger out, his arms weakly lifted above his head in victory.

"That should settle that old feud once and for all," Thane Jungor Stonesinger said to his morose companion. The thane of the Hylar dwarves sat in his personal box high above the arena, out of reach of the unruly, jostling crowd of common dwarves. With an amused smile creasing his luxuriously groomed beard, he extended his left hand, palm upward, and wiggled his fingers.

To his left sat a short, dour dwarf with skin the color of a fish's belly. His cinnamon-brown beard was plaited and rolled into two thick coils beneath his chin and bound with thin copper wire. His black cloak barely covered the vest of studded leather armor he wore. Snarling, he dug into a pouch at his belt and produced a fistful of steel coins. With obvious reluctance, he counted them out onto the thane's palm, and each clink of a coin seemed to stab him through the heart.

"Why do you always side against the Daergar in these matters?" he asked petulantly when the last coin was counted.

"I do not *always* side against the Daergar. I simply do not allow clan loyalties to cloud my judgment," Jungor said with a smile as his fingers closed around the untidy stack of coins. "Your Daergar cousin was overmatched. Anyone could see that, even you, Ferro. No one forced you to accept my wager."

He passed the coins over his shoulder to the tall, grim-faced dwarf standing behind him. "Hold these for me," Jungor said without turning.

"As you wish, my thane," the captain of Jungor's personal guard answered, quickly pocketing the coins.

Ferro Dunskull scowled at the tall Hylar warrior standing protectively behind his thane, one massive fist resting on the broadsword at his hip. Captain Astar Trueshield was from one of the most respected Hylar families in Norbardin, Tarn's new city. He bore the long golden beard of a high dwarf of that clan. He returned the smaller, paler Daergar's scowl with a haughty sneer.

In the arena below, two new combatants entered to a round of thunderous applause and roars of laughter. The first warrior bounded across the arena floor, a long sword twirling from fist to fist in a brilliant display of swordsmanship. The powerful muscles of his arms rippled beneath skin already glistening with sweat. His strong, white teeth shone in a fierce grin through his short-cropped chestnut beard. He wore a vest of mail over his broad back, and his stout legs were clad in leather greaves.

Behind him slinked a miserable creature clad only in rags and dragging a spear far too long for him to wield with any effect. At the sight of him, the crowd howled with laughter and shouted, "Ong! Ong! Ong!" the noise resounding like an iron bell in this deep subterranean cavern. At the sound of his name, the gully dwarf grinned

35

and waved, and he tried to heft his overlong spear in salute to the crowd, only to topple over with its weight. The unruly mob of spectators only howled more loudly than ever, and he seemed encouraged by their noise, jutting out the tangled nest of his filthy beard and strutting cockily a few steps before tripping over his own feet.

His smile broadening, Jungor leaned closer to Ferro Dunskull and shouted over the noise, "Ah, this ought to be interesting. Yon Daewar warrior is Uurk Straightbeard. He claims that his opponent, the gully dwarf named Shnatz Ong, cheated him at dice and refused to return his money. He has demanded an arena confrontation according to Tarn's Law of Redress outlawing unsanctioned revenge killings."

"Interesting?" Ferro Dunskull snorted. "I fail to see what could possibly be entertaining about watching some dull-witted Daewar lawfully slaughter a gully dwarf."

"You've already made up your mind who will win this battle then?" Jungor inquired with a taunting lilt of his basso voice.

Ferro started and stared at the Hylar thane. "You don't mean to suggest . . . " he cried. "That gully dwarf could never . . ."

"Of course not. He's only a gully dwarf, after all. I simply wanted to give you an opportunity to recover your losses from the previous battle," Jungor said quickly, finishing with another oily grin. His smile only deepened the impression of the predator in his hawkish features. His beard did little to hide the craggy angles of his face, the beaklike projection of his nose. Yet for all the fierceness of his imposing countenance, his taunting smile bore a certain charm.

"You want me to bet against that gully dwarf, don't you?" Ferro asked, his dark violet eyes narrowing suspiciously.

"I'll give you three-to-one odds," Jungor said solicitously.

Ferro glared down into the arena in time to see the gully dwarf nearly impale himself on his own spear. The Daewar warrior stood at the far side of the arena, respectfully waiting for the forms of combat to be completed. His bearing and demeanor spoke of supreme confidence, and his previous display of swordsmanship left no doubt as to his ability.

Ferro darted a quick glance at Jungor Stonesinger.

"Well?" the Hylar thane asked.

"It seems a sure thing," the Daergar began slowly, as though still pondering his decision. "Which makes me doubly suspicious."

"It's only a friendly wager," Jungor said innocently.

The Hylar thane's hurt tone only provoked the Daergar. "If I don't take the bet and your gully dwarf falls at the first blow, I'll look like a fool. So I'll take your bet, and this time I'll make you suffer for it! Five hundred steel coins is my wager! There! Ha!"

Astar Trueshield's eyes widened in alarm at the extravagance of the Daergar's bet, but Jungor's smile never wavered.

"Five hundred, then," Jungor said as he rose to his feet. Ferro shrunk back in his chair, worriedly gnawing the ends of his beard.

Jungor turned and faced the arena, and, seeing him rise, Uurk Straightbeard strode to the center of the arena and began to address him. The crowd slowly became quiet as the Daewar's words filtered through.

" . . . demand vengeance. This is my right! But according to the Law of Redress enacted by our high thane, Tarn Bellowgranite, blood feud and revenge killing outside the arena is forbidden. Therefore I ask the President of the Arena of Justice, Thane Jungor Stonesinger, to sanction this combat between myself and the Aghar dwarf known as Shnatz Ong."

"The council recognizes your right to redress, and I affirm the legality of this forum," Jungor answered, his basso voice resounding in the thick air. He spoke with a natural authority, so that even the most intoxicated dwarf in the crowd paused for a moment to appreciate the Hylar thane's command of the forms and procedures of law so dear to many a dwarven heart. "You have chosen weapons combat, knowing that your contest may result in serious injury or death. Let it be known that no one may claim the right of revenge for that which happens in the arena here today."

He lifted his hand in sudden invocation. "Let the spirits of our ancestors witness these events and be pleased by the honor and courage displayed by the combatants, and let them curse those who dishonor these rites."

Many of the dwarves in the crowd turned and stared up at the thane's box, for these words were not part of the official ceremony prescribed by law. Uurk Straightbeard seemed momentarily taken aback by this unorthodox departure from the recognized rituals. He shuffled uncertainly, waiting for the Hylar thane to finish with the usual invocation of a blessing from Reorx, the traditional god of the dwarves.

Without doing so, Jungor summarily completed the ceremony, and, dropping his hand, shouted, "Let the combat commence!"

For another moment, Uurk stared up at the box then turned and shuffled ominously toward his gully dwarf opponent.

With many eyes upon him, Jungor resumed his seat, his beatific smile unchanged. Ferro leaned close to the Hylar thane and whispered, "What in the blazes of Chaos was that all about? Did you forget the invocation to Reorx?"

"Not at all," Jungor said absently, leaning forward in his seat to watch the combat. "Ouch! Looks like you might win that bet after all."

At these words, Ferro's attention snapped to the arena floor, where Shnatz Ong was now fleeing for his life, shrieking like a murdered peacock. Ferro leaned forward and gripped the edge of the box, his eyes beginning to flame

with the bloodlust native to the dark dwarves of Thorbardin. Even if it promised to be a quick slaughter of a
lowly gully dwarf, the sight of violent combat stirred his
blood, as well as the blood of the crowd. They had quickly
forgotten about Jungor's departure from tradition in their
lust to see blood spilled onto the thirsty arena floor.

The hapless gully dwarf had long since abandoned his
weapon and was running in ever-tightening circles around
his opponent, his rags flapping about his knees as he ran.
Uurk Straightbeard continued to jab at his opponent and
close the distance, even as his fury exploded at the way
Shnatz Ong managed to stay just out of the reach of his
silver sword. Although in prime physical condition, the
Daewar couldn't match the dizzying speed of a gully dwarf
running in crazy circles.

Shnatz stumbled. The crowd roared. Ferro surged from
his seat. Uurk lunged, and the tip of his sword sank into
the gully dwarf's thigh just before the small fellow rolled
out of reach. Squealing in agony, Shnatz crumpled in a
quivering heap, clasping his wound with his filthy hands
and trying to staunch the flow of blood.

"Ha! I've beat you this time, Jungor Stonesinger," Ferro
exclaimed as he leaped onto the edge of the box. "Fifteen
hundred steel coins! That's what you owe me. Three-to-one
odds."

Jungor shook his head and smiled.

On the arena floor, Uurk Straightbeard hovered menacingly over his fallen opponent, his longsword raised to
strike. Meanwhile, he taunted the crowd, many of whom
were shouting for him to spare the gully dwarf. Suddenly,
two gully dwarves dropped over the wall and crawled
toward him, weeping and crying. Females, by the looks of
them, they begged him to spare their father's life.

Uurk threw back his head and laughed. Lowering his
weapon, he strode toward them, spitting insults and curses.
"Worthless Aghar!" he screamed, his voice rising even over

the tumult of the crowd. "I should kill the lot of you."

"Do it! Kill them all!" Ferro shouted, pounding his fist on the rail box. Suddenly, his voice stuck in his throat and his mouth dropped open in surprise.

Shnatz Ong rose quickly and silently while his opponent's back was turned. Streaking across the floor, heedless of his injury, he launched himself onto Uurk's broad back. One grimy hand whipped over the top of the startled dwarf's head, looping under his beard in one quick motion, before coming together with the other hand behind his neck.

Uurk's eyes started from his face as the steel garrote tightened around his throat. His longsword fell from nerveless fingertips, and he clawed weakly at the instrument of his murder even as his knees buckled and he sank, the fiercely grinning gully dwarf riding his back all the way to the ground.

Shnatz maintained his hold long enough to be assured of his opponent's death then slipped the steel wire free and turned grandly to accept the accolades of the crowd. The two female gully dwarves rushed out and swept under his arms, helping to support him on his injured leg even as they wantonly lavished kisses on his filthy face and beard.

Ferro turned and gaped at Jungor Stonesinger, his mouth champing soundlessly.

"They aren't his daughters, I assure you," the Hylar thane chuckled.

CHAPTER 6

Jungor bellowed with laughter at his Daergar companion's mute bewilderment. Ferro could hardly believe what he had just witnessed. Gully dwarves were universally stupid, cowardly, and craven, utterly worthless for anything but the most menial of tasks. As warriors, they were more dangerous to their allies than their enemies. The only thing that kept the gully dwarf population under control was their inability to maintain even the most rudimentary hygienic habits. If a gully dwarf infant somehow managed to survive his own parents through the first year, he was considered unusual. Many died within a few months of birth from a variety of maladies and accidents, from smothering in their family's communal bed to being devoured by the rats that shared most gully dwarves' warrens.

To see a gully dwarf defeat a skilled Daewar warrior in single combat beggared belief, even for Ferro Dunskull. Words evaded him as he glared at Jungor Stonesinger's smirking face. At the same time, a new dwarf entered the box and took the empty seat next to Jungor and opposite Ferro.

"Will these young fools never learn?" the new dwarf gloated as he rattled a bag of coins hanging at his belt. "I made quite a haul on that last fight, my thane."

"Uurk Straightsword won't be the last dwarf to underestimate The Flea," Jungor answered. He turned back to Ferro. "Isn't that right?"

"You fooled me!" the Daergar spluttered.

"You fooled yourself," Jungor countered seriously. The change in his tone was familiar to those who knew him well. The Hylar thane was fond of instructing those around him, and they did well to listen, for he was both wise and cunning.

"Uurk Straightbeard underestimated his opponent," Jungor continued, "because he was a gully dwarf. There are more than three thousand dwarves in this arena tonight, and if he had bothered to ask even one of them, they would have advised him to be wary of tricks and to never turn his back on The Flea.

"But Shnatz knew Uurk, knew the weakness of his arrogance, and he waited patiently to use it against him. That's why The Flea is one of the best fighters the arena has ever known. He's never lost a bout, and I've never lost money on him, while I've made a fortune on those who, like Uurk Straightbeard, believed that when they'd seen one gully dwarf, they'd seen them all."

"It only took once for me, my thane," the newcomer dwarf admitted with a rueful smile. Captain Trueshield snorted appreciatively.

Jungor nodded solemnly and peered from beneath his bushy brows at his Daergar companion. "Ferro, I believe you know Hextor Ironhaft?" he asked.

Ferro tilted his head in acknowledgement. "Everyone in my profession knows Master Ironhaft. He is one of Norbardin's wealthiest merchants, a scion of the Hylar families."

Hextor Ironhaft accepted this compliment by stroking his long, blond beard. "What is Master Dunskull's profession, if I may be so impudent?"

"Ferro is a merchant of information, shall we say," Jungor answered for the Daergar. "Though he bears the brand of the thief . . ."

Ferro unconsciously lifted his hand to cover the small scar above his left eyebrow.

"Still, he has recently turned his talents to more profitable ends," Jungor finished.

"Most commendable," Hextor said with undisguised conceit.

"Moreover, he is our eyes and ears in the court of Shahar Bellowsmoke, thane of the Daergar clans," Jungor added. "On our behalf, he spends most of his time in the service of his thane. Thus his knowledge of the arena and its most successful combatants was incomplete. I am confident he will not be so easily misled in the future."

Jungor clapped one large, heavily scarred hand on the Daergar's shoulder, drawing him closer in a gesture of friendliness.

Ferro bowed his head. "I am in the thane's debt. I fear I do not have the means at present to honor to our wager," he said.

"There are other coins of the realm," Jungor said in a low voice. "Now, tell me, what passes with my cousin, the thane? Is his loyalty to Tarn firm, or—"

His questioning was cut short by a bellowing roar.

"Jungor Stonesinger!"

The Hylar thane paused and peered through the smoke toward the source of the disturbance. The arena grew nervously silent as hundreds of bearded faces also craned to see. On the floor of the arena near the exit door, a lone dwarf stood with his hands on his hips and his pale face turned arrogantly toward Jungor's private box high above. His beard, split into two plaits, lay over his belly almost to his belt, and he wore a vest of fine silver scales over his barrel-chested frame. A heavy curved sword hung at his hip. His sallow, well-muscled arms were bare except for a pair of jeweled bracers protecting his forearms.

"I see you, Jungor Stonesinger," the Daergar warrior roared. "You can't avoid me any longer. I demand justice!"

"Vault Forgesmoke!" Hextor Ironhaft exclaimed. "What's he doing here?"

"If you are not a coward, come down here and face me!" the dwarf shouted in derision, eliciting an excited roar from the previously silent crowd.

"I should have warned you," Ferro said quickly as Jungor rose to his feet, "he's been talking about challenging you for weeks."

Seeing the Hylar thane rise, the crowd roared its approval. It wasn't every day that the formidable Jungor Stonesinger returned to the arena. A veteran of its bloody floor, he had never been defeated in the five years since its construction. He was its undisputed ruler, judge of all contests of arms under the council's laws. Almost a hundred warriors had tested his skill in the wild early days of the arena, before Tarn Bellowgranite usurped its forms and traditions in an effort to limit the clan battles and blood feuds that had reigned in dwarven society since the first dwarf carved stone.

"Allow me to deal with this rogue, my lord," Astar Trueshield snarled as he drew his sword and pushed toward the stair.

Jungor jerked him back. "In this place, I fight my own battles," he barked.

"But you are our thane," Hextor Ironhaft pleaded and clutched at the hem of Jungor's cloak. "If you should fall to this Daergar's treachery . . ."

Ferro glowered at the wealthy Hylar merchant, before turning to Jungor in concern.

"He's a dangerous foe," he admitted.

"Not as dangerous as I," Jungor growled obstinately. He pushed past his guard and tore free of the merchant's grasp, then quickly descended the stair to the arena floor, accompanied by the shouts and whistles and thunderous stamping of the gathered dwarves. As news of the challenge raced upward to the inhabited areas of Norbardin, dwarves began to pour into the arena to witness what promised to be a momentous battle. The leadership of the Hylar clan hung in the balance, and as its sworn protector, Astar Trueshield hurried down the stairs after his battle-fey thane, his face a blond-bearded knot of worry.

Jungor slid over the outer wall and dropped to the hard-packed dirt floor. He slipped out of his black, fur-lined cloak of office and stripped off the golden silk shirt, baring a back rippling with well-toned muscles. His frame was longer and narrower than that of most dwarves, which made him look weak by comparison to his stouter compatriots. One look at the whipcord muscles of his arms spoke of hidden energies and deceptive power, however. His movements seemed slow and fluid, almost languid, but when he struck, it was like the strike of an adder. His hands were narrow and long, like a magician's hands, with long expressive fingers. He preferred a lighter sword to the heavy metal weapons favored by most of his opponents—axes, hammers, heavy maces, and broadswords. Yet his great reach gave him a distinct advantage.

Unlike his opponent, Jungor wore no armor. He had not expected to compete in the arena this day, and in his anger, he had rushed to the arena floor without even bothering to grab a shield. Now he glanced quickly around the arena and shouted for someone to lend him a shield. A familiar face at the arena's edge greeted him—the Theiwar thane, Brecha Quickspring. Shouting his name, she tossed a battered steel buckler at his feet. Dented and worn, it was still a serviceable piece of armor.

Stooping, Jungor slipped the buckler over his left arm then drew his short sword as Vault Forgesmoke edged toward him, curved broadsword held in a guarded position, round shield pushed forward defensively. Nearly a foot shorter than the tall thane, the Daergar warrior respected Jungor's reach and skill well enough to make full use of his stout iron shield.

"Six months ago, you murdered my brother in the arena after he begged mercy from you," Vault Forgesmoke formally pronounced, following the rules of the arena.

"I offered your brother mercy, but he repaid my chivalry by trying to jab me with a poisoned needle as we clasped hands," Jungor responded.

"That's a beardless lie!" the Daergar warrior shrieked as he leaped. He drove his shield against Jungor's side, trying to force his opponent back while at the same time stabbing under it with his broad blade. The tall Hylar thane spun past this obvious tactic, his lighter blade flickering in a quick succession of lunges that Vault barely blocked with his shield. As the two fighters separated, the crowd screamed in delight. Usually, the arena saw only clumsy brutality—entertaining, to be sure, but nothing compared to the artistry of two skilled sword wielders.

The Daergar shook back his black mane of hair and dared Jungor to attack, taunting him by holding his shield aside and exposing his breast. Jungor circled grimly, his face expressionless, feinting half-heartedly at the proffered opening, while watching his opponent warily. The crowd grew restless and shouted for blood. An empty bottle sailed out of the stands and landed with a chink near the two warriors. For a split second, Vault's attention shifted, and as quickly Jungor launched his attack.

The Daergar leaped back in response, easily avoiding the sword blade licking at his throat and laughing at his escape, only to find that the leather strap of his shield had been neatly severed just above his forearm. The shield dangled uselessly from his fist. He angrily tossed it aside.

"Now we are more evenly matched," Jungor said to him.

"A lucky blow!" Vault Forgesmoke blustered, but a note of fear had crept into his voice.

The Hylar thane only smiled wolfishly and continued to circle. Now his movements were light and fluid, and his feet hardly seemed to touch the ground. He feinted untiringly, forcing his opponent to continually defend against a sword strike that never fell. The Daergar warrior's own movements grew desperate, his blows wild. Like most dwarf warriors, Vault sought to plant his feet and swing with all his might, to kill with a single blow, whereas Jungor's attacks were designed to chip away at his opponent's confidence and strength, to force him to wear himself out, to use his strength against him. He never remained in one place for long, moving east and attacking west, as the old military scholars liked to say.

"You fight like an elf," Vault Forgesmoke growled after missing yet another vicious sword blow.

Jungor darted in while the Daergar was still complaining, his right hand raised for a devastating overhead swing. Meanwhile, he switched his sword to his left hand and drove in low with the blade while Vault was lifting his own sword high in defense. The point scraped against the metal scales of the Daergar's vest and slipped harmlessly under his armpit. Jungor caught Vault's sword arm before he could counter the blow, and Vault trapped Jungor's weapon under his arm. Grunting furious oaths, feet stamping on the hard-packed floor, the two warriors grappled in a dance of death to howls from the crowd.

Vault was the more muscular of the two, but Jungor's height gave him leverage over his opponent. He began to force his opponent's sword arm into an awkward position over his head. In response, the Daergar spat full in Jungor's face. Blinking through the spittle, Jungor only bent his arm more pitilessly than before, muscles cracking and joints straining to the breaking point.

Suddenly, Vault's knees gave, and he dropped to the ground with a cry of agony. Normally Jungor would have followed up with a killing blow, but his alert senses detected deception in that bellow of pain. Vault had fallen before his strength had given out. Jungor released his grip on the Daergar's sword arm and leaped back.

At the same time, Vault scooped up a handful of dust and flung it in the Hylar thane's face. Jungor turned aside and threw up one hand against the cloud of dust, while slashing in a wide arc to prevent his opponent from following up on the blinding attack. Something wet and sticky struck him on the right side of the face and clung there like tar.

Immediately, the flesh around his right eye began to sting horribly. He clawed frantically at the burning substance even as he slashed blindly with his sword, desperately trying to hold back his opponent while he fought to clear his vision. Some clinging vitriol was even now eating away at the flesh of his face, sizzling in the wet tissues of his right eye. Jungor ground his teeth against the hideous pain and fought to see through the haze. In the gray blur of his vision, he detected movement and little else. He turned, his sword held defensively before him.

A sharp blow knocked the weapon from his hand, and he ducked instinctively as his opponent's blade whistled over his head. He caught up a double handful of dirt and flung it blindly upward. Hearing the Daergar splutter in rage and surprise, Jungor rolled free and came to his feet in a stumbling run.

He careened blindly across the length of the arena, blundering to a stop against the wall. Members of the crowd hung over the wall's edge, howling with fury and bloodlust, pounding the stone with their fists. He stared up at them, blinking through his ruined right eye. He felt the flesh on the right side of his face begin to sag, and darkness clouded his vision, but after a few moments, he was able to make out the individual faces of those leaning toward him. There were dwarves from all the clans. Some taunted him, more shouted encouragement.

Jungor glanced quickly around, still blinking furiously against the stinging pain. His right hand and wrist burned where he had used them to try to wipe away the clinging acid from his face. He searched for his bodyguard and found him, pinned to the second tier of seats by members of the crowd who wanted to prevent the captain from interfering in the combat. Across the arena, Vault Forgesmoke was shaking the last of the dust from his eyes and spitting curses that were lost in the uproar.

Jungor reached for the dagger he usually wore at his belt, but he had left it in the royal box in his haste. His sword lay on the ground on the other side of the arena. Weaponless, half blind, and weak with pain, he knew he had little chance of besting an armed foe as determined as Vault Forgesmoke. He had but one tactical choice—to accept a wound in order to come to grips with his opponent.

Jungor steeled his resolve and started to advance toward his opponent when something fell at his feet. At the same time, he heard a voice cry his name over the din of the crowd. He looked down and saw an ornate staff lying before him. He turned toward the voice and saw that once again the Theiwar thane Brecha Quickspring had come to his aid. She leaned over the barrier wall, crying his name and urging him to pick up the staff she had thrown to him.

Jungor had seen the staff in her hands at many meetings of the Council of Thanes. It was a wizard's staff, for Brecha Quickspring was one of the more powerful sorcerers of her clan. The Theiwar had an innate magical ability that allowed them to cast spells, unlike most dwarves, who feared and distrusted magic. The staff was made of some unidentifiable dark wood and mounted with a large round red stone set in gold.

Jungor reluctantly picked up the staff. Although he bore a natural prejudice against magic and doubted that it would prove much use against his Daergar opponent's heavy sword, he had few options. The staff felt surprisingly light in his hands, which only deepened his distrust. Surely it would shatter at the first blow. A staff was no weapon for a true warrior.

Vault Forgesmoke lifted his heavy curved sword and charged across the arena, bellowing a battle cry that eclipsed the deafening crowd. Jungor readied himself, still trying to blink away the last of the acid. Vault switched his blade to his left hand as he closed. Jungor turned to meet him. Out of the corner of his eye, he saw the dagger appear in the Daergar's right hand and dart toward his unprotected left side.

Jungor dived under the Daergar's sword, away from the slashing dagger. At the same time, he swung around, smashing the butt of the staff into his opponent's left leg. Vault Forgesmoke stumbled with the momentum of his own attack, crumpling from a shattered kneecap. Jungor turned the staff and swung it with all his might against the Daergar's back before he had even hit the ground. As the staff slammed into his back, a flash of scarlet light burst from the red stone. Steel scale armor shattered like glass, and his spine sank beneath the blow, a sodden pulp of bone, meat, and nerve. Vault Forgesmoke dropped like a poleaxed hog.

As he fell, he rolled onto his back, his arms thrown wide to either side. He lay before Jungor, panting, paralyzed, his dark violet eyes wide with terror as he looked up at the Hylar thane's acid-stained visage. The crowd fell silent at the suddenness and violence of the attack.

"Mercy!" the Daergar cried weakly.

Snarling, Jungor tossed aside the staff and picked up the dagger his opponent had dropped. He knelt on Vault Forgesmoke's chest and with a violence that shocked even the most hardened warriors among the crowd, plunged the blade into his helpless opponent. Not satisfied, he sliced open the dwarf's body, reached inside, and dragged out his red, still-beating heart.

Jungor rose and approached the silent, horrified crowd, the Daergar's heart dangling from his fist.

"You want blood?" he screamed. "I give you blood!"

With a wail of rage, he flung the organ into the stands. Blood spattered the faces of those in the front row, but they barely flinched. They sat mesmerized.

Jungor returned to stand over his vanquished opponent. His fists covered in gore, his right eye a milky ruin, he glared down at the dead Daergar warrior. "As thane of the Hylar, I bar your entrance to the Kingdom of the Dead, Vault Forgesmoke. For your treachery, your ghost shall wander the houseless mountains beyond the doors of Thorbardin forever!"

He turned and stalked toward the exit. As if released from a spell, the crowd erupted in wild cheers. Dwarves poured over the wall and into the arena, some to gather reverently around the Hylar thane, others to drag Vault Forgesmoke's body out of the arena. Astar Trueshield surged past them and raced to Jungor's side, Thane Brecha Quickspring following closely in his wake.

The Theiwar thane stopped only to retrieve her staff. To anyone who would listen, she cried, "I have *the sight,* and I saw Vault Forgesmoke's ghost obey Thane Stonesinger's command! I saw his ghost bow in obedience."

Those who heard her turned to Jungor with awe written into their features. "The dead obey him!" Thane Quickspring shouted over and over again, gleefully.

CHAPTER

7

Jungor slapped the doctor's hand away from his face. "Clumsy oaf!" he spat, then snatched the bloody towel from the doctor's grasp and clapped it to his ruined eye. "Must I do everything for myself?"

"The wound *must* be cleaned, my lord," the doctor insisted as he tried to pry the towel from Jungor once more.

"Just do it, then," Jungor snarled. "Stop pussyfooting around. I'm not some nobleborn fainting at the thought of a hangnail, whose brow you pat to cool his fevered brain. I won't have your head lopped off if it hurts. Just do your job and be done with it!"

"As you wish, my lord," the Daewar doctor said, bowing. He picked up a leather bag from the floor, set it on a chair, and began sorting through various gleaming metal probes, knives, pliers, and other instruments of torture and surgery. Jungor lay back on the examination table, sighing angrily while he pressed the crimson-soaked towel to his face. The table was as sturdy as a butcher's carving block. It had seen enough meat carved upon it in its day. The doctor's examination room lay one level beneath the arena at the bottom of a staircase leading directly up to the arena floor. Those wounded in the arena were usually carried here by orderlies, but Jungor had made the descent on his own feet, refusing to be coddled.

Hextor Ironhaft nervously paced the chamber, trying to oversee the doctor's work. Astar Trueshield stood beside the closed door, his hackles up and still angry at being prevented from protecting his thane. Jungor glanced at him and snorted. "You would have disgraced me," he said. "Interference isn't allowed."

"You are the thane!" Astar shouted angrily, forgetting himself for a moment.

"If I had been attacked in some alley of Norbardin," Jungor said, "I would have your head on a pike for failing in your duty to protect me, Astar Trueshield. But in the arena, there are rules—"

"Nevertheless, you shouldn't have risked your life in this wasteful manner," Hextor Ironhaft interrupted. "Rules be damned. There is more at stake here, my thane."

"Do not preach to me, Hextor Ironhaft," Jungor said in a low, dangerous snarl that brought the wealthy Hylar merchant to a stop. "My honor was at stake. What do you think would have happened if I had been dishonored by that Daergar?"

Cowed, Hextor shrugged and resumed his nervous pacing. "Those who prevented Captain Trueshield from going to your aid may have been part of the conspiracy."

"I assure you, they now regret their mistake," Astar said.

Jungor chuckled appreciatively. "Yes, I know. The doctor has already seen them in the other room. I expect nothing less from you, even though they were merely enforcing the rules of the arena," he said. "I'm glad you didn't kill them, though."

Jungor smiled grimly and turned his attention to the doctor, who was still rummaging through his surgery bag and laying out various instruments, the use of which was beyond guessing. "By the gods, how many knives does it take to pluck out one eye?" the thane snarled at him.

"I can do this quickly, or I can do it correctly, my thane," the Daewar doctor said, rising up with a pair of metal tongs in either hand.

"They're probably already saying I am dying down here," Jungor grumbled. He toweled his eye one last time and tossed the bloody rag on the floor. Though a veteran warrior of many battles, Astar winced at the sight of the thane's vitriol-scarred face. Hextor clapped a hand over his lips and turned away. The skin around the eye was hideously marred and bruised a dusky purple, like rotted meat, while the raw flesh showed through in places where the skin had fallen away entirely. The right eye was the color of watery milk, and a sickening wheylike substance oozed down the thane's face and into his beard. He seemed not to notice the pain, which must have been excruciating. He lay on the table as though waiting for the physician to remove a splinter.

Suddenly, the door banged open. Astar started out of his study of the thane's face, his sword already in his fist. Ferro Dunskull ducked aside as the captain of the guard came leaping around the door.

"It's me!" he shrieked, lifting his hands defensively.

"What do you want here, Daergar?" Captain Trueshield demanded harshly as he sheathed his blade. Outside the door, dozens of dwarves huddled in the hall, awaiting some word of Jungor's fate. Astar blocked their view with his body, filling the narrow doorway, but the look on his face discouraged their efforts as much as the breadth of his shoulders. Many turned away and pretended interest in the quality of the floor's stonework.

"Let him in, Captain," Jungor sighed from the table.

Astar closed the door and resumed his post. Ferro sneered at him and approached the examination table. When he saw Jungor's face, his sneer changed to a pained smile. He glanced quickly at Hextor, who merely shook his head as though still trying to recover from his bout of nausea.

"What passes above, in Norbardin?" Jungor asked. "Do they think me dying?"

"Quite the opposite, my lord," Ferro answered without looking the thane in his remaining eye. He couldn't pull his gaze away from that milky white orb resting in its bruised flower of flesh. "The testimony of . . . um . . . of Thane Quickspring . . . that is to say . . ."

"Spit it out!" Jungor barked impatiently.

"Does it hurt?" Ferro asked, edging closer. He reached out one hand and gingerly touched the ruined flesh of Jungor's cheek.

The thane jerked away as though touched by a snake. "Like the unholy blazes of the Abyss. Now get on with your report!" he shouted.

Composing himself, Ferro continued. "Thane Quickspring continues to spread word of her vision."

"Who asked her to meddle in this affair?" Jungor asked, his gaze turning to Hextor.

"Her staff proved quite useful," Ferro remarked. Jungor scowled at him, but then his face grew thoughtful.

"This vision of hers may prove more useful still," Hextor said in a soft voice.

Jungor nodded slowly and motioned for Ferro to continue.

The Daergar cleared his throat. "All known accomplices, acquaintances, and family of Vault Forgesmoke are being rounded up as we speak."

"Find them. Hunt them down to the last dwarf," Jungor said through clenched teeth. "I want to question them myself. Tarn Bellowgranite arranged this, mark my words. He arranged it to happen while he is away, to remove any possible link back to himself. That link is there, and I want you to find it!" In his fury, he sat up on the table, eliciting vehement protestations from the physician.

Jungor turned his rage against his healer. "Dig this thing out of my face or I'll have you replaced. Permanently!"

Shrugging, the doctor picked up a black pottery bottle and removed its stopper. He tipped its liquid contents onto a handkerchief. Jungor's nose wrinkled at the pungent aroma. "What is that?" he demanded.

"Something to make you sleep while I operate," the doctor said.

"Put away your potions. You won't use any magic on me," Jungor said. Shrugging, the doctor set aside his anesthesia and picked up a long, narrow-bladed knife and a pair of thin tongs from the table. Climbing up on the table beside the thane, he set one knee across Jungor's thigh and commenced probing the ruined orb's socket.

After a few moments of watching, Hextor's knees buckled. He sank beside a washbasin. Astar closed his eyes, but Ferro continued to observe the procedure with professional fascination.

Meanwhile, Jungor sat stoically under the doctor's ungentle ministrations. He said through gritted teeth, "The people love me, they look to me for leadership, not Tarn Bellowgranite—that half-breed whelp of a Daergar bitch, may his father's bones rot."

The doctor popped Jungor's ruined eye from its socket and dropped in with a wet plink into a bucket beside the table. The thane didn't even wince, but Hextor gripped the edge of the washbasin as though the room were turning over. Astar shook his head in disbelief, and Ferro giggled nervously. Jungor snatched a rag from the table and began toweling out the empty socket.

"I should cleanse the wound with dwarf spirits," the doctor said.

"I'll do it myself," Jungor growled.

"I'm sure you will," the doctor responded as he began to gather his instruments. "Have a care that you don't pour the dwarf spirits directly into your brain pan."

"Thank you. You've done quite enough," Jungor sneered. "You have other patients, I'm sure."

"The king couldn't have arranged this without the aid of Thane Shahar Bellowsmoke," Ferro said.

"What do you know of Vault Forgesmoke's family?" Jungor asked. "Is there a connection to the thane?"

Ferro tugged his chin whiskers in thought, slowly massaging his thick lower lip. "The Forgesmoke clan are cousins to the Bellowsmoke, so there is the familial connection. Thane Bellowsmoke is cousin to the king . . . but if Tarn ordered this, it will be difficult to prove. It is dangerous to challenge us Daergar at this time. Most of our warriors refused to go with Tarn on his mad adventure to save the elves, but Shahar is said to be loyal, if any Daergar can be called loyal."

"Present company excluded," Jungor interjected.

Ferro smiled, revealing a row of uneven brown teeth. "Of course!"

Somewhat recovered, Hextor said, "Thane Bellowsmoke has little love for you, my lord, and that makes him a friend of the king. If a confession were arranged, it could be used to overthrow Tarn Bellowgranite."

The doctor dropped one of his metal instruments in surprise, its sharp metal clatter punctuating the look of horror on his face. He quickly gathered it up and stuffed it into his bag.

Jungor leaped down from the table and accosted the Hylar merchant angrily. "Who said anything about overthrowing the king?" he shouted. "Did anyone here even mention rebellion? May the gods forgive me for saying so— if Tarn Bellowgranite is behind this murderous attack on me, the evidence will be presented before the full council, in accordance with the law. I am a loyal thane of Thorbardin. My well-known dispute with Tarn Bellowgranite is restricted to the Council Hall. Let no one speak treason before me."

"Forgive me, my lord," Hextor cried, bowing low, almost to the floor.

Jungor turned to the doctor, smiling with his face like a mask of death. "Again, I thank you for your services. Forgive me if I was impatient."

"Not at all, my thane," the doctor answered nervously. He clutched his surgeon's bag to his chest as Astar led him to the door.

When the doctor had gone and the door was shut, Jungor spun back to face Hextor. "Fool!" he hissed. "Do you want to give everything away? Leave us! Astar, clear those people away from the door and await me at the stair."

Grudgingly, the two Hylar departed, leaving the thane alone with Ferro Dunskull.

Jungor returned to the examination table. Kicking over the bucket that still contained his lost eye, he sat down wearily and leaned his head against the leg of the table. A few drops of blood trickled down his face like teardrops from his gaping socket. Ferro came closer and stooped beside him, his hand nervously fluttering over Jungor's shoulder as though he were afraid to touch him.

"Is everything prepared?" Jungor asked in a low, tired voice.

"It is, my lord," Ferro whispered eagerly. "My scouts on the plains report that Tarn has left Pax Tharkas with a small party of guards. Everything is in readiness."

"Be careful," Jungor cautioned. "If anything should go awry, you know what must be done. It cannot be traced back to me."

"Nothing will go wrong, Thane Stonesinger. Tarn Bellowgranite will not reach Thorbardin alive."

CHAPTER
8

Captain Ilbars Bleakfell stopped before the tent and muttered a curse as he scraped a clod of clinging black mud from his boot. Around him, half a dozen campfires burned wanly in the misty twilight, each with its company of five or six miserable dwarf warriors huddling near it against the damp and cold. Though still several hours before sunset, the sun had already been swallowed by the thick mist that hung perpetually over this place. Known as The Bog, this swampy region lay on the Plains of Dergoth north of Thorbardin, between the mountain and the ruined magical fortress of Zhaman.

"They call this a road?" Ilbars swore. "If this is a road, I'm a gully dwarf."

"You stand now on a wandering ridgeback of land that stretches from the plains in the north to Thorbardin in the south," Ferro Dunskull said as he exited the tent, wiping his mouth on the back of his dusky hand. The pungent aroma of dwarf spirits wafted before him, and he belched a contented sigh. Waving his hand at their gray, dripping surroundings, he continued, "To either side of this road stretch endless miles of sucking bogs, strangling mud, quicksand, and bottomless pools."

"Bah! Ridgeback of land!" the Daewar captain snorted. "There's a pool of water under my tent. And the flies!" He swatted the air about him, momentarily scattering the humming swarms of tiny bugs that hung perpetually around his head.

"You don't get out of Thorbardin much, do you?" Ferro commented in disgust.

"That's funny coming from a Daergar," Ilbars said with a sneer. "I thought you and your Theiwar were going to melt in the sun this morning."

"We suffer so that we may be the first to greet our king," Ferro answered dryly.

"An honor guard of Theiwar, led by a Daergar, come to welcome a Hylar king back to the mountain!" Ilbars laughed. "Why didn't they send gully dwarves and make a parade out of it?"

"You forget that Tarn Bellowgranite is half-Daergar by his mother," Ferro muttered as he pushed past the Daewar captain and edged close to their fire. Two Theiwar warriors grumbled as they made room for him.

"Now we Daewar, I can understand sending us to welcome the king," Ilbars continued, nodding his shaggy head toward a squad of the doughty warriors squatting around the next fire. "We're loyal and trustworthy. By my mother's beard, I wouldn't trust a Theiwar any farther than I could throw a spear."

Ferro spat into the fire and glanced at the two Theiwar warriors sharing their camp. They glared into the crackling flames, obviously holding their tongues firmly in their teeth. Because Captain Bleakfell had been ordered by the Council of Thanes to meet the king and escort him back to Thorbardin, they dared not challenge him directly. He was well known as a brash and arrogant commander of the Council Guard and a close friend of the Daewar thane, Rughar Delvestone.

"Well, at least we don't have any arrogant Hylar to deal with on this trip," Ilbars said, laughing.

"That is a blessing," Ferro agreed. The two Theiwar snorted appreciatively but continued to say nothing. Ferro picked up a damp stick and began to poke at the fire, stirring up a plume of sparks that rose a few feet into the damp air before they died. Ilbars pulled his cloak closer around his shoulders and shuddered.

"Is it summer yet?" he asked.

"It's hard to say," Ferro sighed.

"What a miserable place. I hope the king arrives before dark, if it ever grows completely dark here. I think it is never dark nor light, just this miserable interminable gray."

The mist seemed to have drawn closer, fading to ghostly outlines of the stunted trees lining the opposite side of the road. Wisps of fog crept along the ground like ethereal serpents, nosing into the scattered tents of the Theiwar and Daewar guards.

"Haven't we a Theiwar sorcerer who can dispel this fog?" Ilbars asked.

Ferro shook his head in exasperation then looked up as they heard a sentry shout in challenge. After a few moments, a Theiwar scout hurried toward their campfire. Long strands of dank gray hair hung over his face, and droplets of oily water clung to his beard. His boots were spattered with black mud, his cloak tattered and filthy. He knelt beside Ferro to deliver his report, ignoring Captain Ilbars for the moment.

"A large force is approaching from the north—" the scout said in a hurried whisper.

"I am in command here," Ilbars angrily interrupted.

The scout glanced disdainfully at the captain, but Ferro nodded his head. His lips curled in a sneer, the scout continued his report, now to Captain Ilbars. "They are not more than a league away."

"How many?"

"I could not tell in the mist. It was a large force, more than two score," the scout answered.

"That will be the king's company," Ferro said, rising from the fire and straightening the short sword hanging at his belt. "I anticipated his arrival within the hour."

"You might have told me that you had information as to the king's schedule," Ilbars said to Ferro.

The Daergar ignored him, instead dismissing the scout and ordering the Theiwar guards to prepare for the king's arrival. Before he had finished, several tents were already being collapsed and packed away.

Ilbars watched the activity in a confused fury. The Council of Thanes had sent him, after all. Ferro Dunskull was merely an advisor of scouts attached to his command by Thane Jungor Stonesinger. Yet ever since they had left the north gate of Thorbardin, the insufferable Daergar had acted as though he were in command. Ferro had chosen the location of their encampment in what Ilbars suspected was the most sodden and desolate part of The Bog, long leagues from Thorbardin. They might have awaited the king's arrival back in the foothills surrounding the mountain, high up above the stink of the bog and with good solid stone to rest their backs against. Against his better judgment, he had allowed the Daergar to lead them into this reeking morass, to make their camp amid the mud and the flies and the serpents.

Ferro reappeared from the mist, followed by Ilbars's personal guard of six Daewar warriors. The captain approached him angrily, thrusting out his curly beard.

"I am in command here," he said.

"Of course you are, Captain. I shall see to the arrangement of the Theiwar troops while you take your warriors to greet our king and show him the way to our encampment," Ferro said hurriedly. He ducked into a tent then reappeared wearing a steel helmet with a bronze nasal and silver rivets.

"I shall go ahead and welcome the king while you remain here," Ilbars said to him.

Ferro bowed deferentially then hurried off to continue his supervision of the packing. Satisfied, Ilbars ordered his six guards into line and marched off into the mist.

When they had gone, Ferro paused, listening. At a sharp word, the other Theiwar ceased their bustling activities and lined up in defensive ranks, hands on their weapons, faces staring grimly along the path Captain Ilbars and his guards had taken.

Ilbars marched at the head of his company, his heavy boots slogging through the muck, pleased to have left Ferro Dunskull behind. He didn't like sharing the glory with anyone, especially a Daergar—not that there was much glory to be gleaned from this ceremonial duty. Still, the king would probably welcome the sight of a friendly face appearing unexpectedly as if by magic out of the gloomy mist, welcoming him home from his long and dangerous journey.

He was within earshot of Tarn's company before he remembered why the king had gone in the first place—to rescue the Qualinesti elves. Ilbars reminded himself to be sure and ask the king how everything had gone. Not that it really mattered. The elves were no concern of his.

Hearing the clank of armor approaching through the fog, the captain stopped his company and searched the road for a dry spot in which to kneel before the king. There wasn't one, and he supposed that a sweeping bow would have to satisfy the demands of protocol. He planted himself in the center of the road, his warriors arranged in a line behind him, their weapons held in salute, while he twitched his cloak out of a puddle and tried to brush the mud from his leather vest.

Looking up with a broad smile splitting his beard, he saw a large group of shadowy figures approaching through the mist. Being Daewar, he did not share his Daergar and Theiwar cousins' ability to see the outline of heat that surrounded any living body, and at first he couldn't put his finger on it, but then it occurred to him that they were too tall, considerably taller than most dwarves.

"Elves!" he muttered in disgust. "I hope the king hasn't brought a bunch of elves along. He's too generous, really."

His warriors shuffled nervously. One of them cleared his throat and said, "Captain, I'm not so sure . . ."

His voice trailed off as the mist parted, revealing a rank of armored reptilian creatures with leering faces and loaded crossbows poised for firing. At sight of the dwarves, they loosed a volley, cutting down half of Ilbars's force in one swipe.

"Draconians!" the Daewar captain shouted, stumbling over one of his fallen guards.

He fell facedown in the muck as another volley of crossbow bolts shrieked over his head. He struggled to his knees and tore frantically at his sheathed sword. Suddenly, a silver-scaled, clawed foot sank into the mud between his knees. Ilbars looked up, his sword half drawn, blinking through the muddy water running into his eyes, as the screams of his dying comrades shrilled in his ears.

CHAPTER

9

Ferro turned and watched the faces of his Theiwar soldiers as the first cries of battle sounded through the thick mist. He was pleased to see sly grins spread across many of their faces, though a few looked as though they suffered a bad taste in their mouths. He had selected this band because he knew they could be trusted so long as they were sufficiently compensated. Among his own clan, Ferro couldn't be sure who might be on the payroll of their thane, Shahar Bellowsmoke. Shahar would not approve of what he was doing this day, not that the thane had a weak stomach for assassination. He was Daergar, after all, and Daergar drank intrigue with their mothers' milk.

No, Shahar would oppose it because Tarn's premature death would help Jungor Stonesinger. Jungor wanted to return Thorbardin to its old ways, to its old hierarchies of the clans. For centúries, the Hylar had been the lords of Thorbardin. With the support of their Daewar lackeys, they had relegated the powerful and ancient Daergar clan to an inferior status, even calling them "dark dwarves," along with the magic-using Theiwar.

Two things had changed all that. The Chaos War had so decimated the population of Thorbardin that no clan was powerful enough to rule over the others, and had any tried, they might have warred their race into oblivion. The Daewar revolt and exodus back to the ancient dwarf home of Thoradin, led by Severus Stonehand several years after the Chaos War, had left the remaining Hylar without their strongest allies. Historically, the Theiwar and Daergar had been too suspicious of one another to band together against the Hylar and Daewar. With most of the Daewar gone, the Hylar were left even more vulnerable than before.

After the Daewar exodus, Tarn had welcomed dwarves of all clans to join him in the new city he was carving from the ruins of the North Gate complex—the least-damaged portion of Thorbardin after the destruction of the forces of Chaos. Most dwarves had gladly accepted. The Chaos dragons that had attacked their mountain stronghold had so undermined the foundations of all the dwarven cities that they were literally crumbling around their ears. Even Hybardin, the great city of the Hylar, carved from a huge stalactite that hung over the Urkhan Sea, had been abandoned after large sections had broken off and fallen, taking hundreds of Hylar to their deaths—including Belicia Slateshoulders, Tarn's betrothed.

Ferro knew that his thane would oppose his actions on behalf of Jungor Stonesinger. He also knew that with Jungor Stonesinger as high thane of Thorbardin, there might be a new thane of the Daergar. He nodded to his Theiwar mercenaries and drew his own blade before turning back to the road.

In the misty distance, the horrible sound of slaughter gradually diminished. Soon, dark figures appeared on the road, crouching and slinking forward through the fog. In a low voice, Ferro ordered the Theiwar to hold their ground but take no further action. After a few seconds, the draconian scouts disappeared. Silent minutes passed, during which the dwarves could only hear the dripping of water or the sigh and gurgle of marsh gas escaping from the mud.

A shadow appeared from the mist, followed by another, then a dozen. Tall, gangly creatures, reptilian, with batlike wings and long, powerful tails, the draconians approached the dwarves' camp warily, curved swords in their hands and crossbows at the ready. They were a mixed group wearing a motley collection of armor, shields, and helms scavenged from a dozen battlefields. Their weapons represented nearly every race on Krynn, from a straight-bladed Solamnic broadsword, to a dwarf's heavy battleaxe, to a massive club once wielded by an ogre. A few even wore remnants of blue dragonarmor of a style not seen since the War of the Lance.

Their leader stood out among his lesser companions. Unlike the darker-scaled draconians, this one was covered in silvery-gray scales that looked almost white in the foggy twilight. He was taller than any of the others by more than a head, powerfully built, with the scars of countless battles visible on his arms and nightmarish reptilian face. He was dressed in black armor, with an iron-black breastplate covering his chest, but his armor had obviously been made at great cost to fit him snugly. Interlocking leaves of black steel protected his flanks and back while allowing full range of movement for his large silvery wings. He was a sivak, one of the most dangerous of the five races of draconians.

Ferro warily watched the draconian brigade approach, softly encouraging his warriors to hold their positions and to make no sudden moves. As they neared the camp, several of the smaller draconians disappeared into the swamp to either side of the road. Ferro guessed that they were good swimmers, as these wore no armor and carried daggers clamped between their razor-sharp teeth.

This rendezvous was extremely dangerous for the dwarves. The draconians outnumbered the dwarves by almost three to one, and Ferro had no way of knowing how many draconians there truly were. Perhaps there were many others out there in the bog watching them. The foul creatures might decide to go back on their agreement, in which case Ferro and his dwarves would likely be killed to the last dwarf for their armor, weapons, and clothes. Or one of his dwarves might speak something out of place, offend one of the draconians, and start a battle that had no end. He was thankful he'd had the forethought to hire Theiwar mercenaries, who did not share the hotheaded nature of their Daergar cousins.

The sivak leader of the draconians stopped a spear's throw from the camp and peered ahead with his black, soulless eyes. No one spoke, and the draconians made no move to approach closer. Finally, Ferro sheathed his sword and swallowed in a throat suddenly parched dry as the Plains of Dust then stepped toward the draconians, empty hands raised palms outward. At his movement, a dozen crossbows were turned to train their sights on him. His step hesitated for only a moment before he muttered, "Ah, to the Abyss with it," and walked boldly forward.

"Welcome, General Zen. I trust you had no trouble on the road," the Daergar said in affected friendliness.

The sivak hissed in amusement and stepped out to greet Ferro, reaching out one huge clawed hand to clasp the dwarf's smaller one. Ferro winced at the draconian's strength, but continued to smile through gritted teeth.

"It was as you said it would be," General Zen said in a voice that slithered like scales scraping over stone. He released the Daergar's grip and made a sharp motion with his hand toward his company of draconians. Ferro tensed until he saw them lower their weapons and appear to relax, though they remained well outside the camp. The ones who had slipped off the road still hadn't reappeared.

"I killed the loud one," Zen said as he stepped past Ferro and approached the fire near the Daergar's tent.

"Excellent," Ferro said nervously as he followed the draconian. Zen stopped near the fire and spread his huge powerful wings, stretching them out to catch the heat from the glowing coals. Ferro ducked under the draconian's wings and moved to the other side of the fire.

"Won't you come into my tent so that we may discuss . . . things," he said.

The lids of the draconian's eyes lowered, and his black eyes seemed to grow somehow blacker. Folding up his wings, he stooped through the low opening of the tent. Ferro squeezed in behind him and tugged a cord, loosening the flap and allowing it to fall over the opening, closing them in.

There was hardly enough room for the huge draconian to turn around. Zen crouched opposite the cot, his folded wings scraping noisily against the canvas wall every time he moved. An oil lamp sat on the floor, smoking heavily in the damp air. The only other furnishings in the tent were a large leather chest studded with silver rivets sitting in the middle of the tent floor and a long wooden coffer lying in one corner with the lid thrown back, revealing a variety of dwarf-made weapons. Zen eyed these with undisguised envy. His own troop's armaments weren't half as good as these extras that the Daergar had brought along out of habit.

Ferro sat on the cot and realized that he was closer to the draconian than he cared to be, but there was no choice now. In any case, he made an effort to keep one hand near his sword at all times. He'd never before had an opportunity to observe a draconian so closely, and what he saw only increased his nervousness. The creature's black eyes seemed to look at him as though he were some choice morsel that it might consume, its teeth superbly designed for ripping flesh. The sivak was easily twice his size.

Part of his warrior training had taught him how to defeat much larger opponents. Nearly everything on Krynn was larger than a dwarf. As dwellers of the deep earth, the Daergar had to learn how to defeat hobgoblins, ogres, trolls, giants, and any number of much larger and more powerful opponents. Ferro was no shabby swordsman. He had beaten opponents larger even than this draconian. Nonetheless Zen's draconic features, his scaly flesh and batlike wings, would inspire fear in even the doughtiest warrior. It was said that all draconians had hidden abilities, magical powers of a surprising nature, and that they could kill even after they were dead.

Ferro didn't have to wait for the draconian to begin the dialogue. Straight and to the point, Zen said, "You did not ask me to bring my gang here to kill that fool we met on the road."

Ferro nodded, appreciative of the draconian's businesslike manner. There was no guile in this creature, he could see that as plain as the end of his nose. The draconian was used to taking orders, a creature bred to the mercenary life, something Ferro could well understand, having dealt more often that he cared to remember with members of the Daewar clan—dwarves like Ilbars Bleakfell. Ferro wondered what had become of their hapless leader, but he thought it better not to ask. The draconian's fangs were not made for idle talk or chewing *quith-pa* (a form of elvish dry rations composed, according to the dwarves who had been forced to eat it, of bark and twigs).

"Indeed, I did not. My agents hired you for a greater purpose. I need you to kill a certain dwarf," Ferro said.

Zen glanced at the weapons locker lying in the corner. "I do not think you need our help just to kill a certain dwarf," he said shrewdly.

"Naturally, his death cannot be traced back to me," the Daergar amended.

Now the draconian nodded his great silver-scaled head. "I understand," Zen said. "Who is to be killed?"

"The king of Thorbardin, Tarn Bellowgranite," Ferro answered. He watched the draconian's face for any betrayal of surprise, but if the creature was taken off guard by the enormity of his task, it did not show. The draconian merely closed his black eyes and nodded again.

"And in return . . . ?" Zen said, his voice trailing off inquisitively.

Ferro leaned forward and threw back the lid of the leather chest sitting in the middle of the floor, revealing a treasure of steel and gold coins. Zen only looked at the coins for a moment, blinking with boredom.

"Money," he hissed as though he had swallowed something sour.

"If not money, then what?" Ferro asked sharply.

Without pausing, the draconian stated, "There is an abandoned fortress north of here. We passed it on our way from Newsea."

"Zhaman?" the Daergar asked in surprise.

"It looks like a human skull," Zen said.

"The humans call it Skullcap. It was once a Tower of High Sorcery, but it was largely destroyed during the Dwarfgate Wars. No one has lived there for hundreds of years," Ferro said, "except the ghosts."

"The spirits of humans and dwarves do not concern us," Zen scoffed.

Ferro asked, "What do you want with that haunted ruin? My masters will not agree if you plan to use it as a base of operations to raid dwarven lands."

"I have been wandering the face of Krynn since I left the egg," Zen explained, "always taking commands from others, fighting someone else's wars. Now I have a band of stout lads under my own command. I want a base, a place to defend. We will not raid to the south."

"If you'd rather have some tumbled-down old fortress than a chest full of coins, that's your business. My masters will see to it that you are not harassed in the fortress by dwarf war parties, so long as you do not raid our lands," Ferro said.

Nodding, the draconian extended his large clawed hand in a curiously human gesture, betraying the long years he had spent among them. Ferro reluctantly shook it, inwardly cringing at the scaly texture of the creature's reptilian flesh.

Withdrawing his hand from the draconian's grasp, Ferro closed the chest and pulled a scroll from his leather vest. He unrolled it and laid it atop the chest. It was a map of The Bog, with all its waterways and twisting paths and deathtraps precisely drawn to scale. Down its middle wandered a dark line that was the road. Pressing his finger against a certain spot, he said, "You will be able to ambush the king's party here."

A sudden burst of laughter interrupted his train of thought. Lifting the tent flap, he saw that the larger body of draconians had entered the camp and were now passing around a bottle of dwarf spirits that the Theiwar had produced. The brotherhood of mercenaries is universal, he thought.

Ferro turned back to the map and continued, "The road is narrow here, with shallow bogs on either side where your group can hide."

General Zen leaned over and examined the map, nodding. "I will approach the king alone," he said. "After I kill him, the others will attack and destroy their force to the last dwarf."

Ferro intended to ask how Zen proposed to get close enough to the king to kill him, but he froze, his jaws snapping shut, at what happened next. The huge, silver-scaled draconian suddenly began to shrink before his eyes. At the same time, his scales receded into his skin and his reptilian features transformed into the likeness of a dwarf. In moments, the Daewar captain Ilbars Bleakfell stood before him, identical in every way to the dwarf Ferro knew was dead, from the top of his shaggy brown head to the decorative tooling on his boots.

CHAPTER

10

The first half of the journey from Pax Tharkas had been uneventful.

An hour or so ahead of their baggage train, Tarn, Otaxx, and Mog had reached an ancient well near the ruined fortress of Zhaman, halfway between Thorbardin and Pax Tharkas. Otaxx had been collecting supplies for Thorbardin for some months, and their train of mules and ox-drawn wagons carried a small fortune in iron ore, Abanasinian grain, timber, and bolts of close-woven woolen cloth.

The dwarves did not approach the ruins any nearer than the well. Zhaman was said to be haunted. Long ago, it had been a fortress of the Conclave of Wizards, one of their places of study and training. Zhaman was far removed from human lands, and so the wizards found it a convenient laboratory for their more arcane and bizarre experiments, ones too dangerous to conduct near populated areas.

In the years before the Cataclysm, the wizards abandoned their fortress as they retreated from the persecution of the Kingpriest of Istar. For a hundred years after the Cataclysm, Zhaman had stood empty, until the archmage Fistandantilus led an army against Thorbardin during a time later known as the Dwarfgate Wars. While hill dwarves and humans battled the armies of Thorbardin on the Plains of Dergoth, Fistandantilus loosed powerful magic that not only destroyed both armies, but also Zhaman, and himself along with it. So mighty was this magical explosion that the plains had sunken and become The Bog, while the towers of Zhaman collapsed upon themselves and melted into the fearful skull-like visage that it now bore.

Tarn and his company had made camp an hour before sundown near the large ancient well in the hills north of The Bog. From their campfire, they could see Zhaman in the middle distance, while some distance behind it loomed the great profile of their mountain home. Even before they had finished setting up tents around the well, a runner arrived with news that the wagon train was under attack. The king and his company of more than a hundred dwarf warriors grabbed their weapons and arrived in time to drive off a party of goblin archers who had pinned down the trains in a narrow defile, killing most of the mules and oxen while the dwarves took cover under their wagons. Mog led a band of Klar into the hills and easily drove the goblins away without further losses, but the attack left them without the means to transport their supplies. Otaxx was loath to leave such valuable goods behind, but Tarn was moody and impatient to hasten his return to Thorbardin. He wouldn't allow the general to send to Pax Tharkas for more beasts of burden, and in the end, the dwarves themselves took the supplies and divided them up to carry on their backs. Only the timber was abandoned, along with the wagons.

This added burden severely slowed their progress through The Bog the next day. Tarn had originally planned to traverse it in a single march and arrive back at Thorbardin before nightfall, but storms had soaked the perpetually waterlogged ground and turned some sections of the road into an oozing morass. With their heavy burdens, the dwarves were forced to slog forward at a snail's pace, further deepening Tarn's black mood. They were still some distance from the foothills when the sun began to sink into the mists above the swamp.

Already deeply concerned about the risk of passing through The Bog, Mog watched the sun fade into the fog with growing alarm. He had no desire to make camp in the swamp, but traveling through this place after dark was more dangerous. With the majority of Beryl's forces still unaccounted for, there was no telling what might be lying in ambush on the road ahead.

Not for the first time that day, Mog said, "You run far too great a risk, my king. Let me scout ahead."

"We're almost home, Mog," Tarn growled. "There's nothing to worry about here. Soon there'll be good stone beneath our feet and you'll feel better."

"That is what concerns me," his captain said. "They always hit you just when your guard is down."

"They? Who are they?" Tarn asked. "You are paranoid, my old friend."

"It's my job to be paranoid where the king's safety is concerned. The road here is more muddy than any we've seen so far, and I wonder if perhaps some large force has passed this way already. We're almost home now, and if I were lying in ambush, this is where I'd set my trap. Look how the road narrows up ahead. At least allow me to scout there."

"There is no need. Someone has already scouted it for us." As Tarn said this, a lone dwarf emerged from the fog and strode briskly toward them. "Maybe this stranger knows who churned the mud," he said.

Mog called a halt to await the newcomer's approach. Because he was a dwarf, Tarn's guards kept their weapons sheathed but ready. Mog's axe, however, never left his hand. He held it at his side and watched the stranger struggle and stumble through the mud, curses exploding from his lips every time he nearly fell. Finally he was close enough for all to see his face.

"Ilbars Bleakfell," Mog said in surprise. "How did they get you to stick your nose outside the Gates of Thorbardin? This is a rare day!"

Ilbars nodded curtly to Mog and continued his approach. "I was sent to welcome the king back to Thorbardin and to ease his journey," he said to Tarn, stopping a moment to deliver a sweeping bow. "Our camp is not far ahead."

"Ah, very good," Tarn said. He extended his hand to the Daewar captain. Ilbars strode forward to greet him, but suddenly Mog stepped in front of him, blocking the Daewar's progress with his axe.

"Mog, what—" Tarn barked as the Klar seized him and pushed him to his knees. Ilbars stopped short, a snarl of anger forming on his face.

At that moment, bowstrings twanged from either side of the road, and Mog pushed Ilbars away.

"Draconians!" the Klar shouted as arrows and crossbow bolts clanged and pinged off the dwarves' armor and shields. Two of Tarn's guards dropped immediately, the swarm of arrows having found chinks in their armor. The others quickly formed into a circle around the thane, their round shields locked together, as more arrows poured into them.

Mog shielded Tarn with his own body, grunting as arrows pummeled his mailed back. Tarn swore and cursed at him to let him up, to let him fight, but the captain maintained his protective position. Another volley of arrows tore through their ranks, dropping three more dwarves. The others closed up the spaces, drawing back to tighten their circle around the thane. They hunkered behind their shields beneath the relentless rain of arrows. Scrambling to find protection, Ilbars picked up a shield from a fallen dwarf and crouched behind it, swearing furiously as he inched closer to the king.

Under cover of their missile fire, draconians began to climb up out of the bog onto the road, crawling up through the mud with their swords in their teeth. These were the smallest of their kind, known as baaz, a race of cruel and rapacious fighters. Without even waiting to form ranks, they assaulted the dwarves' defensive circle, throwing themselves into the chaotic fray. As the first baaz crashed into the dwarven circle of shields, the last volley of arrows fell among both friend and foe, and kapak draconians appeared from the swamp to join in the assault. This species of draconians poisoned their blades with spittle before entering battle.

Quietly, Mog loosed his hold on the thane, pointing. A dwarf to their right fell, his head split to the teeth by a draconian sword, opening a space in their ranks. With a nod to the king, Mog threw himself into the empty space, his axe flashing out, separating the draconian's head from its neck in one blow. Its body slumped to the ground and immediately turned to stone.

Tarn quickly clambered to his feet. A good head taller than any of the other dwarves in his company, he could see the whole battle from his protected position within the circle. Still, this made him an obvious target, and he knocked aside one spear with his sword, while trying to figure out his best move. All around him, his dwarves were battling furiously, some of them engaging two or three opponents at once. In one glance, he knew that they couldn't last for very long. More and more draconians were climbing onto the road, while his dwarves were slowly being cut down before his eyes. Ilbars Bleakfell rose up beside him, sword drawn, and eyes blazing.

Then a gap opened as a dwarf fell with a spear through his heart. Tarn grabbed Ilbars by the shoulder and rudely thrust the surprised dwarf into the gap. He turned and looked back the way they had come. There didn't appear to be as many draconians attacking from the rear. He might be able to slip out of this trap, but only if he acted swiftly, before the draconians cut off their escape route.

Tarn was about to shout orders that would shift his dwarves into a column when he heard words of magic being chanted.

"Wizard!" he shouted, seeking out the source of the eerie words.

Too late, he saw the bozak draconian standing at the road's edge, its brown robes caked with mud. The creature lifted its hands, and as it did so Tarn threw himself to the muddy ground. Crying in surprise and rage, nearly a third of Tarn's dwarves suddenly found themselves engulfed in thick sticky strands of web.

Tarn scrambled to his feet, brushing clinging fibers from his arm and beard. Mog was instantly at his side, pulling him away from the battle. Half the draconians attacked the entrapped and helpless dwarves, slaughtering them mercilessly. The other draconians surged toward Tarn and the others, who had fallen back in disorder at the actions of the magic-user.

Tarn barked a quick series of commands that brought the dwarves together in an inverted V shape just in time. The bozak came up, already casting another spell. Tarn braced himself and shouted for shields to be raised. Two bolts of white energy exploded from the draconian's fingertips and streaked toward Tarn. Brave Mog threw himself into their path, but the gesture was futile, as the bolts wove past him and the shields to strike Tarn full in the chest. They seemed to burn through both layers of his armor, searing into his flesh like gouts of molten metal. He sank to one knee, screaming in agony.

Mog stared in horror at his fallen thane then turned, his face flushing crimson. He knew that the bozak must be stopped, but the few dwarves who had been armed with crossbows had long since switched to axes or hammers. Casting about, he saw a spear lying half trampled in the mud. Jerking it free, he hefted it and rushed the advancing draconian line.

Those draconians who had shields lifted them to their shoulders, but Mog halted halfway and flung his spear. It sailed over their heads and thudded into the bozak magic-user's chest. So forceful was Mog's throw that the head of the spear burst out a good arm's length from the creature's back. Its eyes widened in surprise as it clutched the shaft and staggered forward.

Mog then dropped back, ordering the others to retreat. He quickly reached Tarn's side and lifted his gasping thane under one arm, retrieving his war axe with his free hand. Tarn struggled to stand on his own feet, even as the smell of his own burning flesh filled his nostrils. Nevertheless, he fought through the pain. He didn't have the luxury of hurting.

Meanwhile, the dying bozak, clutching the spear that transfixed its body, wasn't done. It half ran, half staggered toward the dwarves, its hideous reptilian mouth champing a bloody froth. The other draconians parted to let it pass, then closed ranks and held their ground. The dwarves at the head of the inverted **V** eagerly awaited the bozak magic-user, and, when the wounded creature got close enough, swarmed forward and hacked him to pieces. Strangely the other draconians merely watched their leader die under the dwarven axes. Blinking through the pain, Tarn watched, baffled. It almost seemed that the draconians were smiling.

As the bozak fell to the ground, its flesh instantly turned to dust, leaving behind a gleaming draconian skeleton. One of the dwarves stooped to retrieve Mog's spear, dragging it free of the hollow rib cage. At that instant, the bones exploded violently. The dwarf stooping over it vanished in a glowing golden ball of fire, his gore spattering the survivors. Others were flung back, their bodies riddled with bone fragments. The rest fell back in horror, utterly amazed and routed. With a shrill, inhuman cry, the draconians charged again. They fell upon the confused and dazed dwarves like wolves among thunderstruck sheep, slaughtering left and right.

Mog battled valiantly to keep them away from his injured thane. There seemed no end to the draconians. They swept around the surviving dwarves, cutting off their retreat. At last there were only four dwarves, drawn together shoulder to shoulder, Mog, Tarn, and two young Klar warriors barely into their beards. Their swords and axes wove a deadly net of steel that piled stony baaz corpses about their feet. Tarn thrust his blade through the chest of one and failed to withdraw it quickly enough. As the draconian fell, its body turned to stone, trapping Tarn's sword and yanking it from his grasp. He quickly picked up a curved draconian blade.

After the initial onslaught, the baaz draconians fell back a pace from the four dwarves. Then several kapaks came forward, armed with crossbows. Neither Tarn nor Mog had a shield, and of their two young companions, one's life was quickly escaping through a spear wound in his thigh. Yet this young one grimly stood his ground and raised his shield to protect his king with the last of his strength. Tarn gripped the unfamiliar sword, all the dark rage of his mother's Daergar blood rising in him. His chest wound forgotten, his neck muscles standing out like cords, he prepared himself for his last moments on Krynn. Unbidden, the memory of his wife, Crystal Heathstone, came to his mind. Her face seemed to float before him, smiling in that particular way of hers. He laughed suddenly, emboldened.

Mog joined him, a sudden bellow of unbridled mirth erupting from his lips, as though somehow he had shared Tarn's vision. Tarn looked at him as though the Klar warrior had lost his mind. Then he heard what Mog had heard, and now the king's laughter changed to a cry of challenge. The draconians paused and with furrowed brows, looked north.

CHAPTER

11

Ferro's face drained of blood, leaving his pale skin an even more sickly shade than before. He watched in utter horror, unable to tear his gaze away. The slaughter was terrible to behold.

The draconians had slain all but four of the dwarves—unfortunately not Tarn, nor his captain, and two Klar guards wearing the livery of Pax Tharkas. They had the four surrounded, and kapaks were just about to end the king's life in a hail of heavy crossbow bolts. But then . . . !

Disaster was too small a word to describe it. Ferro turned to the Theiwar scout who had just brought the bad news and, drawing his dagger, plunged it furiously into the scout's throat. The other Theiwar warriors shifted uncomfortably as one of their own was murdered before their eyes.

Ferro turned to the others, hissing, "Why didn't anyone warn me that Otaxx Shortbeard was following with half the warriors in Pax Tharkas? What do I pay you people for?"

There was no time for any reply.

The roar of the charging dwarves shook droplets of water from the surrounding trees. As quickly as Tarn's small band of dwarves had been decimated by the larger draconian force, now the draconians were falling back in disarray. Leaderless, baaz joined with baaz and kapak with kapak, fighting as two separate forces against the united might of Otaxx's Hylar and Daewar force. A wedge of dwarf fighters drove between the two groups of draconians. The baaz were forced into the swamp, where they were quickly slaughtered or drowned, dragged down by their armor. The kapaks managed to hold together and retreat along the road, directly toward Ferro and his Theiwar mercenaries.

"We're in a tight place!" the Daergar exclaimed in frustration. He removed his helm and ran his fingers through his oily black hair, pushing the dank locks back from his face before settling the helm securely on his pate. "If Tarn and the others catch us here, they're sure to suspect we were involved."

"We could run," one of the Theiwar said, voicing the opinion of his fellows.

Ferro looked at him as though he were a stone that had suddenly found its voice and spoken. The fellow shrugged nervously and glanced toward the fighting. "Or we could hunker down and try to hide here."

"Great god below, can you be any more stupid?" Ferro almost shrieked. "Be my guest, run for it. If you aren't seen, our campsite certainly will be found, whether we run for it or hide. They'll wonder who was camped there, and as soon as they reach Thorbardin, they'll know. The plan was for us to arrive too late to save Tarn and then to barely escape with our lives." He looked back up the road toward the fighting, which was drawing ever closer. "We're in a tight spot for sure," he muttered.

The kapaks were holding together, and they fought valiantly. Wherever one fell beneath a dwarven weapon, its body quickly dissolved into a large pool of acid, which slowed the dwarves' assault somewhat, since the road was extremely narrow here. Ferro and his band of Theiwar crouched in the underbrush at the road's margin, watching hopelessly.

"There's nothing for it," Ferro said. "We can't just sit here. When the draconians draw near, we'll rush out and attack them from behind. I'll deal with Tarn's questions afterwards. I should be able handle him. Make sure you leave no draconian alive. There can't even be one survivor to expose us. Do you understand?"

The Theiwar nodded, faces set in grim lines as they watched the retreating draconian line. Ferro glared at them, looking for any sign of weakness or second thoughts. He saw none but added for good measure, "I certainly hope you do understand. If Tarn finds out about us, I hate to think what his Klar will do to your families."

Ferro smiled to see the look of desperate determination on their faces now. The Klar clan had been fiercely loyal to Tarn ever since the days after the Chaos War, when he had forgiven the very people who had slaughtered so many of his father's clan. In the ruins of the war's aftermath, a great and lasting friendship had blossomed between Tarn and the Klar thane, Tufa Bloodeye. The new Klar thane, Glint Ettinhammer, had renewed that friendship when he took his seat on the Council eight years ago. The Klar were among Tarn's most resolute supporters.

As a race, though, the Klar were also known to be unstable at times. It was as though Reorx had formed their brains of different stuff than the other clans. Even Tarn could not control them completely. They were known to avenge him even against those he himself had already forgiven. The thought of their families falling into the hands of blood-mad Klar slayers caused the Theiwar mercenaries to take their task with utmost seriousness. An hour ago they had shared dwarf spirits with some of those draconians. Now they were ready to stab them in the backs without mercy.

Tarn's powerful voice rose above the din of battle, shouting for the surviving draconians' surrender. The kapaks continued to fight as they retreated. Ferro realized that the creatures might see the futility of their situation and throw down their weapons at any moment, something he couldn't allow to happen. Drawing his short sword, he leaped into the road, his Theiwar troops silently pouring out behind him. Ferro plunged his weapon into the nearest kapak's back and ripped upwards, shearing through muscle and bone. The creature fell and immediately began to dissolve into a pool of acid. Ferro jumped back as his Theiwar slammed into the rear ranks of the astonished draconians. In seconds, all met similar fates.

Ferro and his Theiwar warriors picked a path through the steaming pools of acid left behind wherever a kapak had died, slogging forward to meet Otaxx's surprised force. He saw Tarn at the rear being tended by a healer, and Tarn's captain, Mog Bonecutter, crawling through the mud and the bodies, looking for survivors. Other dwarves were busy clearing the road or retrieving weapons from the stony corpses of slain baaz draconians.

Then, to Ferro's amazement, Ilbars Bleakfell appeared, his shaggy hair and beard matted with white spiderwebs. Ilbars strode purposely toward Ferro, an axe dripping with draconian blood in his fist. Ferro stepped back in alarm, knowing the draconian general would be furious at his apparent double-cross. He hesitated, unable to figure out how to expose the sivak without explaining how he could see through the draconian's disguise.

"Ferro Dunskull!" Zen shouted in Ilbars's voice. Tarn looked up from the bandages being wound about his chest wound.

"What took you so long?" Ilbars demanded. "They very nearly killed the king!"

Ferro's eyes narrowed suspiciously. What kind of game was this sivak playing?

Mog hurried up, his face curious. "How did you survive, Captain Ilbars?" the Klar captain asked. "I saw you engulfed in webs and hacked to pieces with the others."

"I tripped as the spell was cast. Dead bodies piled on top of me before I could rise. The draconians must have assumed I was already dead. I only just managed to extricate myself," Ilbars said as he brushed spiderwebs from his beard.

"You were very lucky," Ferro said in a voice dripping with menace.

"Yes, I am blessed with an abundance of luck," Ilbars/Zen responded. "That's how I've survived this long in such a hostile world."

Mog watched this exchange with curiosity, but he had no time to give it deep thought. Day was swiftly turning to night, and the fog was growing thicker by the minute. He didn't know how many more draconians might be out there in the swamp, and he would shave his beard before he'd allow the thane to spend the night here. He hurried away, shouting orders for the bodies of the fallen dwarves to be gathered and prepared for transport home to the mountain. Otaxx already had a dozen dwarves lashing spears together to make stretchers for the dead and injured.

Behind his back, Ilbars and Ferro exchanged venomous glances. The draconian seemed to be daring the Daergar to betray him. Knowing there was nothing he could do, at least not at the moment, Ferro bit his tongue and stalked away.

CHAPTER

12

Tarn refused to be carried into Thorbardin, though Mog and Otaxx argued all the way to the mountain's door. The entrance into Thorbardin was made to look like the rock surrounding it, so that when it was closed, it was invisible to those who did not know its secret. The morning of Tarn's return, the massive valve, several feet thick, had already been opened. Hundreds of dwarves crowded the streets near the gate, awaiting their king. A drum and pipe band stood just within the entrance. Their enormous bronze kettledrums looked more like weapons of war than instruments of music.

But though they had come prepared for a celebration, the mood swiftly darkened upon Tarn's approach. Tarn had insisted that those slain in the battle with the draconians, and those too wounded to walk, should proceed ahead of him into the mountain. These long lines of litters dampened the spirits of the crowd, and so did the walking wounded. They were followed by the soldiers from Pax Tharkas, many of them returning home for the first time in years.

Last of all came Tarn, walking slowly and grimly, with Mog, Otaxx, Ferro, and Ilbars in attendance. Tarn's face was pale from the wound to his chest, but also from the deeper wound to his soul. The people had come expecting a triumphant return, with the king leading his army of thousands. Fewer than a hundred actually passed through the gates of Thorbardin, and most of those returning were either wounded or carrying some wounded or dead member of their party. Many of those waiting at the gate shook their heads in dismay. "So few?" some muttered. Others hoped that the majority of the army was still in the forest, helping the elves hunt down the last of Beryl's army. But most realized that to be a vain and empty hope. They began to grumble among themselves.

Once through the gate, the survivors entered a broad hall carved into the heart of the mountain. Streets, alleys, and doors opened into it at regular intervals, and windows lined the way, filled with dwarven faces staring down at them anxiously. Tarn ordered the gate closed, while the various groups quickly split up—the wounded toward the houses of healing, those bearing the dead toward the clan centers where their families were already gathering to claim them. Otaxx led the soldiers from Pax Tharkas to temporary guard quarters on the third level. Tarn, accompanied by Mog and a small squad of guards, followed the wounded. Ilbars stuck close to Tarn. Ferro was not far behind.

Tarn's new city of Norbardin was not so grand and humbling as the cities it sought to replace. Before the Chaos War, all the different clans had had their own cities scattered around the great cavern and underground sea that lay at the heart of the mountain. The Daergar had lived in Daerbardin, far to the south across the black Urkhan Sea, while the Daewar inhabited Daebardin on the sea's eastern shore. The Hylar, hereditary rulers of Thorbardin, lived in a magnificent city carved from an enormous stalactite that hung over the Urkhan Sea. Called the Life Tree of the Hylar, it had been one of the marvels and wonders of all

Krynn. But now the Life Tree was dead, most of it having broken off and fallen into the sea following the Chaos War. Chaos dragons of fire had burned tunnels through the solid rock, weakening it structurally until it could no longer hold its own weight.

Tarn had carved his new city from the area known as the North Gate complex. Once its halls and galleries had served to house those guarding the North Gate of Thorbardin, and for hundreds of years it had remained largely unoccupied except for a few soldiers, for once the massive gate of Thorbardin was closed, the mountain was virtually impregnable to assault. Under Tarn's direction, the dwarves had expanded the halls and houses, built shops and markets, and carved new tunnels into the stone. But most of the new construction consisted of filling the vast area known as the Anvil's Echo with new warehouses, barracks, strongholds, residences, and butteries. The Echo had once been a vast pit crossed by a narrow bridge. But the dwarves' immediate need following the Chaos War was for living space, and the Anvil's Echo had first served as a refugee camp, then gradually the temporary structures were replaced with permanent ones. The soaring bridge had fallen during the war and was never rebuilt. The Anvil's Echo was now the location of the Daergar and Theiwar quarters of the city, a dark region with close alleys and narrow streets, and high defensive walls separating the people of the two clans. The son of a Daergar mother, Tarn felt as much or more at home here as in the lamplit, glittering marble-paved boulevards of the Hylar section.

There was a new Council Hall to replace the one lost in the ruins of the South Gate complex. New mines had been sunk, providing the dwarves with the metals they needed for their crafts, new caverns opened and cultivated with the mushrooms that were the staple of the mountain dwarf diet.

Such as it was, it was home, but it wasn't Hybardin, and those who lived here knew it. They knew that they were living in a diminished age, in a time when glories of the past were becoming fading memories. They were comfortable, they were safe, and after the terrible destruction of the Chaos War, that was enough for most.

There were dwarf children playing in the streets as Tarn made his way toward the new Council of Thanes, after seeing that his wounded soldiers were being properly settled in the houses of healing. He refused medical care for himself, for he had one final duty to perform before he found the rest he so sorely craved. But the sight of the children made Tarn smile, for here was the future of his people. Traditionally, dwarves were slow to reproduce; some dwarves never even married—not because of a shortage of mates, but because their standards were often above their stations. In the past, dwarf marriages had been conducted like business dealings, the merger of two families arranged for mutual profit, and no dwarf wished to marry below his or her station, as this was seen as a loss, both of wealth and honor. Naturally, this system produced a disappointing number of marriages and therefore few children, though no one had ever seemed to mind. It helped to keep the dwarves from outgrowing their mountain home.

But so very many dwarves had died in the Chaos War; whole extended families were destroyed in the breath of one dragon, whole clans and all memories of them annihilated by the touch of the horrid shadow wights. Tarn's mother and father had died, fighting on opposite sides of the battle—Garimeth Bellowsmoke was slain by the daeman warrior leading the forces of Chaos; Baker Whitegranite had been consumed by the magical gem he used to destroy the Chaos armies invading their home. Even after the war, the dying and destruction had continued, as Tarn led the surviving Hylar and Klar back into the mountain and found it held by the survivors of the Daergar and Theiwar clans, who were not ready to quickly give up what they felt they had won during the war.

And then, the damage wrought by the chaos dragons continued to take its toll on those still living in the cities. Walls collapsed and floors gave way, killing dozens. Tarn lost that which he held most dear. His fiancée, Belicia Slateshoulders, had died when a section of Hybardin that she and several hundred workers were trying to restore broke off and plunged hundreds of feet to the Urkhan Sea below. It was this incident that prompted Tarn to abandon the old cities and start building a new one out of the North Gate complex. He called his new city Norbardin. Norbardin was everyone's home now, dwarves of all the clans, but at the same time it never really felt like home, not even after forty years.

So many had died that in the years after the Chaos War, the clans could no longer afford the luxury of hating and distrusting one another. They needed one another just to survive, especially after Severus Stonehand led most of the remaining Daewar on a mad exodus to the ancient dwarven homeland of Thoradin. Now, after nearly forty years, the population of Thorbardin was finally beginning to grow. Dwarves had continued to marry largely within their own clans, but many dwarves were glad to find any eligible mate. The realm had begun to prosper.

There was a whole new generation of young dwarves who had never known the former glory of Thorbardin, however. They experienced it only through the tales of their parents and grandparents. They were strong, having been forged during a time of great hardship, and they were eager to win new glories.

It was this generation that Tarn had led to disaster beneath the elven city of Qualinost. Once more, as he approached the Council of Thanes, the enormity of his failure descended upon him. A generation lost, all because he had been too eager to win honor and glory, too hasty to build a new alliance between the elves and the dwarves. He had abandoned caution when caution might have served him best. He had accepted the swiftest course as the wisest, decided that he who hesitated was lost, for this philosophy had served him well in the past. He had agreed to help the elven king because he was eager to forge new ties with the elves.

He wished now that he had listened to the Council of Thanes and waited to see how the elves' conflict with Beryl and the Dark Knights would shake out. He had argued that they could not afford to wait, for if the elves were defeated, there would be nothing standing between Thorbardin and the green dragon Beryl. Yet he had never had much hope that Beryl could be stopped. So why had he aided them?

That was the question revolving in his mind as he climbed the broad marble stairs leading up to the old temple of Reorx. His wound bothered him little, if truth be told, but he found the climb arduous. The North Gate's old temple had been converted into a new Council Hall for the Council of Thanes. Its steps were as broad as a dwarf is tall and rose over forty feet to the columned portico that surrounded it. Six marble walls white as milk rose up to form a towering hexagonal structure, which supported a dome of rose quartz from Qualinesti—likely the last standing structure of that material left on Krynn, now that Qualinost was drowned and destroyed. Each of the six walls contained an entrance into the Grand Gallery, which, like the portico, ran the entire circle of the structure, but on two levels. In the portico and Grand Gallery, dwarven philosophers had once expounded on the mysteries of creation and the nature of law; now they were crowded with dwarves awaiting Tarn's arrival at the Council of Thanes.

Word had spread quickly through Norbardin. There were no celebratory cheers or derogatory jeers at Tarn's arrival. The citizens watched in silence as Tarn climbed the steps. Tarn had led them successfully for forty years and the people had trusted his judgment. Without widespread support, especially the support of the younger generation, he couldn't have mounted such a large operation—delving tunnels beneath Qualinost to aid in the elves' evacuation from their city. He had betrayed his supporters.

Tarn seemed to have aged a century in the fortnight he had been away from Thorbardin. Though his footsteps never faltered, they were slow, as though each boot were soled with lead. Behind him walked his captain of the guard, Mog Bonecutter, grizzled and wary, with bloodshot eyes staring out of his half-mad Klar face. He bore some large, disk-shaped object wrapped in a travel-stained blanket. The two were accompanied by a strange pair—the Daewar captain of the Council Guard, Ilbars Bleakfell, and a Daergar that most recognized as the master of scouts, Ferro Dunskull. Captain Ilbars seemed oddly nervous, searching the silent crowds as though expecting to see an enemy awaiting him, while Ferro walked slightly behind with his dark eyes glued to Ilbars's back.

As Tarn reached the top of the stairs and passed into the torchlit portico, the crowd parted, opening the way to the Hylar door into the temple. Each of the clans had its own door—Hylar, Daewar, Daergar, Theiwar, and Klar. The sixth entrance was not an entrance at all—it was actually a false entrance meticulously carved to represent a partially opened door. So cunning was its craftwork that even dwarves often felt compelled to touch it just to disprove the illusion. This door was for the Kingdom of the Dead, and through it only the dead could enter. The door faced the Road of Thanes, a road that led directly from the new Council Hall in Norbardin to the Valley of the Thanes, where the dwarves of Thorbardin buried their dead.

The Aghar, otherwise known as gully dwarves, merited no recognized entrance of their own, though some said that the entrance to the catacombs beneath the temple counted as a seventh door. Certainly, gully dwarves came and went from the Council Hall at will, and through no door that anyone could observe.

Tarn entered the Grand Gallery from the portico and found it thronging with restless dwarves of every clan. The new Council Hall was considerably smaller than the old hall at the South Gate. That place had been built to house thousands of dwarves, while the new hall did well to contain more than five hundred. Those who were too poor or of too low a rank to obtain a seat within were forced to stand in the Grand Gallery or the portico outside and there they could listen to the Council's proceedings from afar. Tarn had started a new Council Hall beneath the first level of Norbardin near the Shaft of Reorx, but it was not yet complete; in majesty and scope, it was intended to eventually rival the old Council Hall.

The hall was constructed like a great bowl, with six sets of stairs leading down from each entrance to a circular dais at the center. Concentric rings of benches surrounded the dais, climbing up the bowl's sides. The six stairs divided the Council Hall into sections, and each section was occupied by the most important members of the six clans. Wealthy merchants and craftsmen, generals and captains, guild leaders and dwarves who had won fame or renown filled the benches. The Aghar section, however, was first come, first seated.

Eight chairs were arranged in a broad circle around the edge of the dais, facing inward—six for the thanes of the six clans, one chair for the king, and an empty chair for the unseen representative of the Kingdom of the Dead. Each of the six thanes' chairs faced their own clan's section across the dais, and each thane sat with his back to another clan. From the highest to the lowest: the Hylar thane, Jungor Stonesinger, sat with his back to the Aghar section of the audience. Looking like an old bag of dirty laundry, the Aghar thane, Grumple Nagfar, filled the chair before the Hylar section. Shahar Bellowsmoke, thane of the Daergar, nervously sat with his back to the unpredictable Klar audience, while the Klar thane, Glint Ettinhammer, cleaned his nails with a dagger and studiously ignored the black glares of the eighty or so Daergar behind him. Thane of the magic-using Theiwar clan, Brecha Quickspring sat in a chair which was within an easy axestroke of the Daewar clan. The Daewar thane, Rughar Delvestone, sat half turned in his chair so that he could keep one eye on the Theiwar behind his back.

The chair of the king of Thorbardin sat at the bottom of the Hylar stair and faced the entrance of the Kingdom of the Dead, to remind him that all dwarves are mortal. The eighth chair, the empty chair reserved for the dead, sat at the bottom of the stair leading from their door and faced the Hylar entrance and the king. This unique arrangement of chairs, with each thane sitting with his or her back to their traditional clan enemy, was the only new part of the design of the Council Hall and had been imposed at Tarn's insistence, as a show of faith and brotherhood among all clans.

The ancient altar to Reorx—a great iron anvil on which a flame burned continually, remained at the center of the dais, not because the dwarves expected the temple to be used again one day (Reorx, like the other gods, had willingly departed Krynn in order to save it from Chaos), but because Tarn had never intended to make permanent use of the temple as the new Council Hall. For that reason, he had made no other alterations to the temple, and it stood much as it had since it was first built, uncounted centuries ago. And this was one of the few places that the forces of Chaos never defiled in their attack some forty years ago.

With regret swelling within his heart, Tarn passed through the Great Gallery and entered the Council Hall through the Hylar entrance. He paused at the top of the stairs for a moment. Five hundred silent dwarf countenances were intently turned upon him. He would rather have walked into the fire.

CHAPTER 13

Jungor Stonesinger looked up from his musing as the crowd in the Council Hall grew silent. For the first time since he began his rise to the thanedom of the Hylar clan, his spies and informants had failed him. No one had been able to tell him what news—dire or otherwise—Tarn brought home with him from Qualinost. There were rumors aplenty, but Jungor knew that rumors were about as useful as a third boot. His own analysis of the situation as he understood it offered no firm conclusions.

He knew only that Tarn had returned with a small force mostly made up of soldiers from Pax Tharkas; he knew that Tarn brought with him several dozen dead and injured dwarves, and that he himself had been injured in some way, though not severely. But one could draw two completely contradictory conclusions from this:

That Tarn and the elves had been utterly defeated and Tarn was returning with his tail between his legs, bringing the few survivors and the bodies of those survivors who had died along the way. Or:

That Tarn and the elves had been utterly victorious, as evidenced by the low number of returning casualties. So great had been the victory, perhaps, that Tarn had replaced much of the garrison at Pax Tharkas with soldiers from his expeditionary army, and returned to Thorbardin with the Pax Tharkas garrison, many of whom had not been home in many months.

If the first was true, then where were the other dwarves of Tarn's army? Jungor had a low opinion of Tarn Bellowgranite, considering him nothing but a vile half-breed. Daergar blood had never ruled Thorbardin until Tarn Bellowgranite sat on the throne. The Hylar blood that flowed in Tarn's veins did nothing to offset the Daergar taint, at least in Jungor's opinion. Tarn's own mother had been a leader in the revolt against the last true thane of Thorbardin, Baker Whitegranite, Tarn's own father, no less! Jungor's opinion of Tarn was deeply colored by his clan prejudices, but even he did not believe Tarn so incompetent that he could lose his entire army. He dared not believe it. Such a disaster had not happened since the Dwarfgate Wars.

But if they had won and Beryl was defeated, why did Tarn seem so strangely subdued, like a vanquished hero returning home in disgrace? Jungor had received word of the curious reception at the gate, or lack of one. Tarn had personally seen to the disposition of the wounded in the houses of healing, meanwhile keeping the Council of Thanes and thousands of anxious dwarves awaiting his tidings. Why? Truly, a king must love the soldiers who follow him into battle, or he is not a king. But a king must also send soldiers to their deaths, knowing they will die. He cannot unhinge his mind in mourning for those who fulfill their destiny on the field of battle.

If there was one thing Jungor abhorred, it was uncertainty. He liked to have everything neatly ordered and planned. His own plan was to take the throne and unseat Tarn Bellowgranite and that had been in place for years, all carefully ordered, all neatly scripted with a patience to rival the gods' own. Jungor was in no rush. He knew that, in time, he would be king.

Apparently, however, the first step had already gone awry, for Tarn had returned alive to Thorbardin. Thus Ferro Dunskull had failed him, and Jungor was deeply disappointed. Failure was not entirely unexpected, and he would not have been much of a thane if his entire scheme had hung on the competence of one Daergar, would it? Still, he was disappointed.

But even Jungor Stonesinger was not prepared for what he saw as Tarn entered the Council Hall, followed by Mog Bonecutter and Ilbars Bleakfell. Ilbars Bleakfell? The Daewar captain should have been the first to die in the ambush, according to the plan. So how had he survived? Had Ferro turned against him and informed Tarn of Jungor's plot? It would be just like a Daergar to stab him in the back. Was that why Tarn was so subdued, because he knew that he must confront Jungor before the Council of Thanes and accuse him of the ultimate crime—treason?

Jungor's eyes narrowed when he spotted Ferro enter behind the thane and his escort. The wretched Daergar traitor was purposefully not looking at him. Jungor almost sprang out of his chair in his anger, but he checked himself and covered his upset by crossing his legs, forgetting Thane Quickspring's staff leaning against his thigh. He had only recently taken to walking with it, after the battle in the arena and the loss of his right eye. It clattered noisily to the floor at his movement, breaking the pall of silence that had gripped the audience. Slowly, then, the people arose to greet the return of their king. Jungor looked up at Tarn and saw the king glance at him, a look almost of thanks on his worn and weary face. Jungor picked up his staff and rose as well, joining his fellow thanes, except for the Aghar thane, Grumple Nagfar, who was asleep, or drunk; it was hard to tell which.

Tarn reached the bottom of the stairs and paused a moment to bow to each of the gathered thanes. Mog remained at his side, but Ferro slipped past him and made his way to the Daergar section. As he did so, he met Jungor's eyes for a flicker of an instant. What Jungor saw there was not betrayal, but what was it? Something too brief to assess, but the Daergar thane was closely watching his subject. Meanwhile, Ilbars Bleakfell seemed at a momentary loss as to where to sit. Jungor thought this extremely odd, but few noticed it other than Ferro, the rest being absorbed by the actions of the king. Finally, someone in the front row of the Daewar section made room for Ilbars, and awkwardly he took his seat among them.

Tarn bowed first to the Hylar thane. Jungor was taken aback by this sly maneuver. It was clearly intended to catch him off guard, and it did—it was a moment before Jungor remembered to return the bow. He noticed that Tarn did not seem at all surprised or horrified to see that he had lost his right eye, and he wondered if the king's spies had kept him so well informed of everything going on in Thorbardin during his expedition to Qualinesti. Jungor had already gotten used to, and even begun to enjoy and make use of, the surprise and horror of those seeing him for the first time since his injury.

But more importantly, Jungor's hesitation had made him seem discourteous. He made up for his hesitation with the depth of his bow. He then made it a point to watch the other thanes as Tarn greeted them.

Next was Tarn's cousin, Shahar Bellowsmoke of the Daergar clan. Shahar returned the king's bow with a cool nod, which seemed to indicate that he was not, after all, in alliance with Tarn. Jungor's agents had yet to wring a confession from any of Vault Forgesmoke's accomplices, and Jungor had already begun to suspect that Shahar had acted alone in the attempt on his life in the arena. The frostiness of the Daergar's greeting only confirmed his suspicions, though he did not discount the possibility that Shahar was merely acting indifferently to throw Jungor off the scent.

Next, Tarn greeted the Daewar thane. The Daewar were the weakest of the six clans. Most had followed that visionary fool, Severus Stonehand, off into the blue, trying to reclaim the lost kingdom of Thoradin. The Daewar had long been the Hylar's greatest ally, but now there were so few of them that Jungor had been forced to recruit among the other clans in order to consolidate his power. Still, Rughar Delvestone maintained the traditional Daewar loyalty to the Hylar clan, and to their thane. Thane Delvestone was also a purist, and like most Daewar, suffered fanatical tendencies that clouded his judgment at times. Jungor had long ago learned to exploit those tendencies, and so the Daewar thane greeted Tarn with haughty reserve.

Next was the Klar thane, Glint Ettinhammer. Jungor didn't give the Klar a second thought. If the Daewar tended toward fanaticism, the Klar embraced it wholly and without reserve. After the Chaos War, Tarn had won the Klar's undying loyalty by unconditionally forgiving them for joining in the Daergar revolt, led by his mother and his uncle, Darkend Bellowsmoke. Their thane at the time, Tufa Bloodeye, had pledged undying loyalty to Tarn and Tarn alone, and his successor, Glint Ettinhammer, had renewed that pledge in the usual grisly Klar manner, by slicing open his hand and smearing his blood on Tarn's sword hand. Jungor had never even tried to woo the Klar to his side. They were a scattered, disorganized clan, anyway. More than half of them didn't even live in Norbardin. They still lived out in the ruined cities, preferring darkness and the constant danger to the light and safety of civilization. Jungor had plans for the Klar once he became king.

Tarn then greeted the other thanes by rank of seniority. Naturally, this offended the entire Theiwar clan, since he chose to bow to the suddenly resuscitated gully dwarf, Grumple Nagfar, before greeting Brecha Quickspring, thane of the Theiwar. Brecha was reckoned the youngest of the six thanes. Although no one could be entirely sure of the age of any gully dwarf, Grumple Nagfar certainly looked old enough to predate the mountain itself (as the saying goes).

Jungor knew that he could count on the support of Brecha Quickspring. The staff in his hand was hers; it had saved his life in the arena, and she had pledged the support of her clan soon after. Jungor suspected that the crazy dark dwarf sorceress might even be in love with him, and if that aided him in his efforts by assuring the support of the Theiwar, he wouldn't actively discourage her aspirations. Neither would he encourage her, as the thought of a Theiwar wife literally made his stomach churn. He had no time for wives or thoughts of marriage. When he was king, then he'd need a wife because he would need an heir to solidify Hylar supremacy on the Council of Thanes. But by then, he'd have his choice among the most powerful Hylar families. He could always deal with the Theiwar after he was king.

As for the gully dwarves, Jungor never even considered them. Few did.

Last of all, Tarn bowed to the empty chair of the Kingdom of the Dead. Jungor noticed that Tarn's gaze lingered perhaps a moment too long on that place, as though the king's thoughts were preoccupied with the dead. Glancing around at the crowd, Jungor noticed that many were now looking at him, and waiting for him to speak, or act.

A mystique had begun to surround him after he defeated Vault Forgesmoke in the arena. Without really knowing why, he had cursed his dead opponent's soul, speaking in the heat of his anger and his pain. Brecha Quickspring had built upon this incident by claiming to have seen the spirit of the dead dwarf bow in obedience. Dwarves who met him on the streets of Norbardin now shrunk from his scarred cyclopean visage, not out of fear, but from reverence. People whispered that he could speak to the dead and they obeyed his commands. Only a few days had passed, but already a cult had begun to grow around him. Its mistress was Brecha Quickspring.

After honoring the Kingdom of the Dead, Tarn sank into his chair. For a few moments, his chin rested on his bandaged chest. With a deep sigh, he then pulled himself erect and gripped the ornately carved arms of his chair. At his movement, Thane Rughar Delvestone rose from his own seat and spoke in tones rich with formality but empty of true feeling.

"The Council of Thanes welcomes King Tarn Bellowgranite home from his travels and adventures, and begs that he delight us with the tale of the honor and glory he won while abroad," Rughar said, then resumed his seat. Though the phrases were nothing more than mere formality, Tarn's face blanched when he heard the words "honor and glory." His will seemed to waver for a moment.

Sensing weakness, Jungor spoke. "I think the king is too ill from his war wounds to continue," he said, thumping his staff on the floor. "Perhaps we should reconvene when he has recovered his strength."

This stung Tarn back to his senses. "My injuries are of no concern," he said as he stood and walked to the center of the dais. "Indeed, I hardly feel them. I only wish that I could not feel the pain of what has occurred. I bring grave news before the Council of Thanes today."

Jungor's hand tightened around the arm of his chair as he leaned forward. The room grew deathly silent, so silent that even those in the Gallery outside could hear the depth of Tarn's sigh.

"I have failed," Tarn said. "My army is lost. Qualinost is destroyed, the home of the elves is gone." His last words were lost in the eruption of shocked cries. Tarn closed his eyes and allowed the thunder of voices to sweep over him and pummel him like hurled stones.

Jungor flew out of his chair and pounded the butt of his staff on the floor, demanding silence. Gradually the crowd noise died down to a low murmur, punctuated by faint roars as the crowds outside the Council Hall learned the news. "King Tarn, how did this happen?" Jungor demanded when he could be heard by most of the crowd. "Surely when you say that the army was lost, you do not mean that all were slain. Surely you only mean that you suffered a minor defeat in Qualinost."

Tarn shook his great blond mane. "All were lost, except for the dozen or so who were with me when the disaster befell us."

"And how did the king survive while thousands were lost?" Rughar Delvestone shouted, leaping to his feet.

Tarn tried to explain, speaking at some length, with frequent pauses to wait for the crowd noise to die down. He tried to explain how he and King Gilthas had plotted to destroy the green dragon Beryl and save the homeland of the elves. While the majority of the residents of Qaulinost had escaped through the tunnels Tarn and his dwarves burrowed beneath their city, several thousand elf warriors had remained behind, and, with the aid of some rebellious Dark Knights sympathetic to the elves, they prepared to lure Beryl into a deadly trap. Their plan was to draw Beryl in close and then launch strong strands of rope over her body, entangling and trapping her wings and forcing her to the ground. Tarn's army of dwarves waiting in the tunnels were expected to rise and up and slay the dragon once she was brought down.

Tarn explained that he had been with King Gilthas, leading the last refugees to safety, when the disaster struck. He told of what had happened to him and his guards in the tunnels, the collapses and the flooding that had nearly drowned them. "We found the elves' city drowned beneath a vast new lake. Our tunnels beneath the city must have been flooded, and the dwarves in them either crushed or drowned. To be perfectly honest, I do not yet know their fate. Some may have survived, but if they did, I could not find them."

Jungor turned to the other thanes, a horrified expression on his face. Many of the gathered dwarves tore their beards in anger and sorrow. Tarn's army had consisted largely of the newest generation of young warriors of Thorbardin. Among the youth he had found his readiest allies in his bold plan to aid the elves. Few families in the Council Hall had not given a son or daughter, nephew or niece, especially among the Hylar, Klar, and Daewar clans. Now the sight of their grief was terrible to behold, the sound of it like the roar of the wind in a tunnel. Jungor staggered, dropped his staff, and clutched at the hems of his fine silk robe—his own shock part genuine, part charade.

Tarn shouted over the crowd, "I cannot replace your lost children. I regret having gone against the wisdom of this esteemed Council of Thanes. I am not worthy to be your king. And therefore I must offer my resignation."

Jungor paused in the act of ceremoniously tearing his robes. His mouth fell open and he turned slowly to stare in surprise at Tarn. The other thanes, who had likewise been preparing to publicly demonstrate their grief and displeasure, were struck silent in amazement. The rest of the crowd was more slow to respond, as most of them had not been able to hear Tarn's declaration. But as word spread, a pall of silence spread over the dwarves.

"What did you say?" Jungor asked in disbelief.

Tarn cleared his throat and seemed to sway on his feet for a moment. "I am not worthy to be your king," he repeated after a moment.

Jungor's mouth snapped shut. He glared suspiciously at Tarn as the crowd erupted. Many began to cry, "Here! Here! It is time for a new king!" But this was quickly met by opposing voices shouting, "Never! Tarn is our king!"

"Tarn has failed us."

"He has led us well."

"My son is dead. My daughter is dead. He deluded his followers."

"Do not dishonor them with grief. Tarn is their king still."

"Let the Council vote."

"We demand a new high thane."

"Tarn Bellowgranite is our king!"

Tarn raised his hand, enjoining the crowd to silence. It took some time before they ceased their arguments long enough to hear what he had to say. Jungor had stalked back to his chair, his mind a confused wonder.

Finally the crowd grew quiet enough for Tarn to speak. Hundreds of grim faces looked down at him, standing alone in the center of the dais, surrounded by the six thanes. He cleared his throat, then spoke solemnly. "My mind is made up. I shall surrender my authority at the Council's convenience. When they have chosen a new king, I shall step aside. This is the least I can do to repay you for the disaster I have brought upon Thorbardin."

"Disaster?" Mog Bonecutter shouted angrily. Stepping up on the dais, he turned quickly to his clan's thane, Glint Ettinhammer, and asked, "May I address the Council?"

The Klar thane nodded his shaggy head.

Mog approached Tarn. He still carried the strange disk-shaped object wrapped in its blanket and resting on his back. "The king says that his plan to save the elves ended in disaster," Mog declared loudly. "But I say that a glorious victory was won. Most of the Qualinesti elves did escape, after all."

"As good as that is to hear, I hardly think the price we paid was worth it," Jungor interrupted. Not a few members of the crowd voiced their agreement.

"Very well. Then was it worth it to kill Beryl?" Mog angrily asked as he unslung his mysterious burden and flung it on the floor. Flicking back the tattered blanket, he revealed the huge olive-green dragon scale they had found.

This revelation struck the assembly like a lightning bolt. The cry "Beryl is dead!" rippled out into the Gallery and portico. Jungor was beside himself in his consternation. Why had news of this not yet reached him? He needed time to prepare for this news. Perhaps this was Tarn's game after all.

However, Tarn seemed to dismiss the claims of his own captain. "I am not yet convinced that Beryl is dead," he said in a low voice.

Mog grinned and shook his head, turning once more to the excited crowd. "We found this scale floating in the flotsam at the lake's edge. As you can see, there is still dragon flesh attached to it. No other green dragon on Krynn boasts scales so large, and Beryl does not drop them so casually, nor with her precious hide still attached."

Jungor rose from his chair and bent to examine the huge scale. He could not deny what Mog said. The scale was enormous and obviously came from a green dragon, and it had been ripped violently from the flesh of that creature. But . . .

"Did you see her carcass?" he asked the Klar captain.

"N-no, but—" Mog stammered.

"Never count a dragon dead until you have personally beheld her bleached white bones," Jungor said meaningfully. He then turned to address the crowd. "I think the king is correct in this matter," he said. "We cannot assume that Beryl is dead simply because we have found one scale."

Mog began to protest, but Jungor spoke over him, thumping his staff on the floor. "Indeed, such an assumption could well prove dangerous. Beryl might only be injured. She might even now be nursing her wounds and plotting the destruction of Thorbardin for the king's part in her injury."

"I agree!" a voice shouted from the Daewar entrance. All eyes turned to see General Otaxx Shortbeard descending the stairs. He was one of Thorbardin's oldest and most respected tacticians. Everyone knew that he was fiercely loyal to Tarn, so it came as a surprise to the king's supporters that the general should be arguing in favor of Jungor and against Mog.

Otaxx reached the dais. "I agree that we cannot assume that Beryl is dead. She may well be alive and planning our destruction. Which is all the more reason why it would be foolish, utterly foolish, to change leadership at this delicate and uncertain time!" A cry went up from the crowd upon hearing these words, and Otaxx stroked his beard in smug satisfaction. Jungor glared at him, but the old general only returned his stare with a smile.

He continued, "As general in command of Pax Tharkas, I know more of the outside world than anyone here. Let me tell you that there are rumors of huge armies marching in the north under the banner of a human girl, conquering in the name of the One God, whoever that might be. And even as our party drew near to Thorbardin, the king was ambushed by a large force of draconians. Draconians, very nearly on our own doorstep!"

Mog took over from there, striding about the dais with his wild hair flying and his bloodshot eyes starting out of his face. "Yes, we need a strong king to lead us now. This is no time to elect a new king, not when we face so uncertain a world outside our doors. When the armies of humans have finished fighting their battles, and when we know for sure that Beryl is dead and no longer a threat to us, then perhaps Tarn can rest, if he still wishes it. But not before!"

Suddenly, the crowd was turning in Tarn's favor. Several voices cried out, begging him not to abandon the dwarves of Thorbardin in their hour of greatest need. Jungor sank into his chair, shaking his head in wonder and disbelief. He almost felt compelled to applaud, though some might think him disrespectful, when actually he had nothing but the deepest admiration for Tarn's masterful performance. Yet he did not panic. He had never planned to win the throne at this time and place anyway. The hour of his victory was still in place, and nothing really had changed to upset his master plan.

CHAPTER 14

As the cries for Tarn to remain king grew louder, Tarn looked around the faces of his numerous supporters. Here he had come before the council in shame, begging their forgiveness and asking to be allowed to surrender his power to some more worthy dwarf. And in return for the disaster he had brought upon his people, they now begged him to remain as king. Their support humbled him, made him feel pity for himself—but also pride.

To think that forty years ago, few of the dwarves now gathered here would have given him an old pair of shoes if he had been barefoot and destitute. And to think that forty years ago he wouldn't have asked for a crumb from most of them, even if he were starving. Forty years, a war that nearly destroyed them all, the deaths of his father, mother, and promised wife, and a revolt among the Daewar that almost ripped all the clans apart, had changed him profoundly. The crown of Thorbardin had been thrust upon his reluctant brow by the death of his father, Baker Whitegranite, himself a reluctant king. He had learned, and learned grudgingly to love these, his own people—people who so often distressed him with their eternal clan strife, who brought him grief and expected him to bear it alone, who blamed him for everything that went wrong, and who claimed for themselves his victories and successes.

Now, seeing this upswelling of support despite his great failure, Tarn was nearly unstrung. He could have wept, if he had any tears left. Instead, he felt a cold thrill course the length of his body, making his hair stand on end and his beard bristle. The weariness seemed to fall away from him as the energy and love of the crowd flowed into his limbs. He grinned broadly.

Lifting his head he saw a face in the crowd looking back at him. She smiled lovingly and lifted her hand to him, and he was at once struck by how much he had missed her, and how he had not realized how much he needed her. He had been searching the crowd for her since the moment he entered the Council Hall, without even realizing it. Now that he had found her, it felt as though a burden was lifting from his bowed back. He felt whole again.

He returned her wave, kissing his fingertips in token of greeting. He noticed that she sat alone in the midst of the Hylar clan: Crystal Heathstone, his wife, daughter of the Neidar king, a princess of the hill dwarves. An empty circle surrounded her, not because she was the wife of the king but because the others were avoiding her—simply because she was a hill dwarf.

His smile fading, Tarn realized that there was still much for him to do as king.

Steeling himself, he shouted, "I relent. I will remain your king, so long as you will have me!" The roar that greeted his words shook the foundations of the old temple. Tarn paused, as Mog bowed before him and Otaxx Short-beard approached and vigorously clasped him by the shoulders. "I knew you wouldn't let us down," the old general joyfully said.

Jungor stood and lifted his hands in the air, begging the audience for quiet, crying, "Dwarves of Thorbardin! Listen to me! Listen to me once more!" Gradually the tumult died down while Mog retrieved his dragon scale and Otaxx found a seat among the Daewar.

Jungor had been quiet all this time, but now he gestured to indicate that he was ready to speak. His strange scarred visage was terrible to behold; his hand tightly clutched the weird staff, as though he were some sort of cursed Theiwar wizard and not the thane of the proud Hylar people. Though he wore a small bandage over the empty socket of his right eye, the horrible acid-burned flesh of his face was plain for all to see. Tarn had been initially surprised to see that Jungor had suffered such a horrible wound, but he had held his natural reaction in check. Now, looking at the Hylar thane, he could hardly suppress a shudder of revulsion.

"We are indeed glad that the king has chosen to lead us through these most difficult times," Jungor declared. "But because these times are so perilous, and we continue to be in danger, I must insist that we seal the North Gate without delay. It is the only way we can be safe."

The Hylar thane had led the Council's opposition to Tarn's plan to aid the elves, and he had been advocating for years to seal the mountain. Those who followed Jungor were of the same mind—they hated and distrusted the outside world. But those who had been born after the Chaos War were particularly open to his arguments, because they could see all around them how stone had failed to protect them during that terrible conflict. Also, they had no memories of the glory of Thorbardin to cause them to long for its return. They looked to their own future, not the past of the grandfathers and so they supported Tarn.

"No!" Tarn shouted furiously. "I forbid this. The gate must remain open."

"No?" Jungor asked, stepping closer to Tarn and peering at him with his remaining eye. His gaze was almost hypnotic. "You forbid it?" Jungor asked. "These are strong words from one who just moments ago was ready to abdicate his throne."

Tarn tore his gaze from Jungor's strange eye. He looked at the crowd, his eyes almost pleading with them. He knew that most of the dwarves felt as Jungor did. They preferred isolation and distrusted the outside world. Yet he had fought for years to build alliances, often against the wishes of his own people, because he believed the dwarves could no longer ignore the world.

"Too often have we turned our backs on the outside world," Tarn declared. "True, we live in perilous times, but there are too few of us to defend our homes against the forces of evil now loose in the world. The dragonarmies of old pale in comparison to the might of dragons like Beryl and Malys. We must have allies if we are to survive."

"Not the elves!" Jungor shrieked. "You haven't invited the elves here, have you?"

"No, certainly not the elves," Tarn replied, to the relief of nearly everyone in attendance. Jungor sighed, but Tarn couldn't tell if the Hylar thane was pleased or disappointed.

"There are other dwarves in the world," Tarn continued. "With the destruction of our army and the growing threats in the world, we need every axe and hammer we can muster."

The Daewar thane, Rughar Delvestone, rose from his chair, his round face flushing red. "I pray you aren't suggesting we invite the *hill dwarves* into our mountain," he hissed, nearly spitting the words "hill dwarves."

Jungor nodded and took a step closer to Tarn. "Long have we tolerated your infatuation with that tribe of rebels," he said as he lifted his hand and pointed at the king accusingly. His gaze strayed beyond the king to the female dwarf sitting alone on the front row of the Hylar section. Seeing the direction of Jungor's gaze, Tarn knew that the Hylar thane was looking at his Neidar wife, Crystal Heathstone. He felt his blood boil. Would Jungor dare to insult the wife of the king before the assembled council?

"We will not open the gates of Thorbardin to more hill dwarves," Thane Rughar said, stamping his boot for emphasis. "I'd rather share my bed with an elf."

This was going too far. Tarn was on the verge of demanding they speak their minds truly, so that he could have the honor of calling them out. But Glint Ettinhammer, thane of the Klar and Tarn's most loyal ally on the council, pushed his bulk up out of his seat, and said, "I must agree with my fellow thanes. We cannot hold the mountain passes against a determined invasion, especially if it is led by Beryl or any of her brood." He shrugged his great shoulders apologetically to Tarn, then resumed his seat. Tarn turned and saw Mog staring at his clan's thane with a look of disbelief. Tarn then looked to Otaxx, sitting in the Daewar section, who nodded sadly.

"Ten gully dwarves could hold our gates against an army of dragons," Jungor persisted, seeing Tarn's determination begin to dissolve.

"Two gully dwarves!" Thane Delvestone added, rousing a laugh from the crowd. Even the gully dwarves chuckled. Brecha Quickspring added her voice, readily agreeing that the North Gate should be closed. Last of all, the Daergar thane Shahar Bellowsmoke cast his vote with the majority. No one bothered to ask Grumple Nagfar what she thought.

With almost the entire Council of Thanes against him, Tarn could not follow his best instincts—not again, not after what had happened in Qualinost. With a deep sigh, he ordered guards away to close the North Gate at once. Then, with the business of the Council completed, the assembly began to break up. Crystal rose from her seat and rushed to Tarn's side, slipping an arm around him to help the weary dwarf king stand. He leaned against her gratefully, feeling old, sad, and defeated even at home.

As they left the Council Hall, they passed Jungor Stonesinger surrounded by a mob of freshly admiring dwarves. "Now that my will has prevailed and the North Gate is closed, we'll be safe," Jungor pronounced.

"It didn't stop the armies of Chaos," Tarn muttered under his breath.

CHAPTER
15

Tarn held on to his wife's arm while they were waiting for a column of wagons to pass in the street. The wagons were laden with ingots of raw iron newly smelted in the forges two levels below. They still smelled warm from the forge fire, the scent of hot metal lingering about them. The wagons, pulled by teams of shaggy, gray cave oxen and driven by Daergar teamsters, passed slowly with much shouting and cracking of whips and creaking of wheels. It did Tarn's heart good to see them. The cycle of life continued, and the dwarves of Thorbardin were still earning fair coin. He'd spent far too much time lately living with war, with fear constantly plucking at his sleeves, with the need to hurry and finish, with the sadness of the elven refugees fleeing their homes, with his grief over the dwarves he'd led to their doom.

He had almost forgotten what it was like to stand quietly with his wife, to nod to the people he met on the street, to not be in a hurry to go anywhere, or to do anything. He could not remember when he'd last had time to sit and enjoy a truly fine horn of ale, or to eat a home-cooked meal. He was sick to death of elf food. He wanted a good beefy ox steak, something that would bleed when he cut it, and a platter smoking with mushrooms swimming in butter. He wanted bread that he could tear with his teeth. He wanted to be able to sit at his own table and eat and slurp his beer and belch, and not have to worry about offending some elf's delicate sensibilities.

He clung to his wife's arm as though she were a rock in the stream that threatened to sweep him away. She bore him well and gladly, smiling to feel his hand gripping her elbow. Crystal was a good, stout dwarf woman, hardy, tough as horn, soft as butter, sweet as elf wine, regal as a queen of old, shrewd as a witch, with eyes like diamonds and a smile to melt the ice from the coldest greed-bitten dwarven heart. As the daughter of the hill dwarf king, she'd been trained to fulfill a variety of roles, from housewife to councilor to warrior to queen. Whether seeing to the domestic affairs of her husband's household, or advising the king in his war councils, she had long ago proven herself an invaluable companion. She hadn't replaced Belicia Slateshoulders in Tarn's heart, but then again she had never tried to. Tarn loved Crystal, and standing there at the roadside listening to the teamsters cursing at their recalcitrant beasts, and seeing her smile, he was reminded why.

Tarn leaned over and kissed his wife on her soft cheek, drinking in the smell of her hair. Crystal patted his cheek indulgently and let her fingertips linger in his beard for a moment. "There, the way is clear," she said. "We can cross the street now."

Tarn's residence was located on the third level of Norbardin within an area known as the Fortress, for it was, quite literally, a fortress built as the last line of defense against invaders of the North Gate. Tarn had chosen this location for his residence in the years before his marriage. There were finer homes elsewhere in the city, homes of greater beauty and luxury than his dark, windowless castle. He might have moved to one of these after his marriage and made a better home for his young bride. But Crystal had taken to the fortress almost from the start. Having grown up in a castle herself, she seemed to prefer cold stone walls, battlements, cavernous fireplaces, and paved courtyards that rang constantly with marching dwarfboots and the shouts of weapons instructors.

As the king and his wife made their way home along the streets of the third level of Norbardin, though, Tarn was taken aback by the signs of mourning already being displayed—doors glistening with fresh black paint, windows of houses and shops with dark curtains drawn, or the sight of a single candle gleaming in a black room. They encountered other reminders: dwarves with freshly shorn beards going about their daily business, and orphaned children being led to their new homes by aunts and cousins. Yet only a few of those they met on the streets cast dark glances their way. Most nodded respectfully and continued on their way; a few even stopped to greet their king and warmly welcome him home.

One young widow, her face streaked with tears, stopped to speak to him. "I know my husband died bravely," she said in a voice trembling with emotion. "I am glad he was with you, and that his sacrifice was not in vain." Tarn found himself without words to respond. He took the widow's head in his hands and pulled her close, kissing her on the forehead to still the trembling of his own lips. Relatives gathered her in their arms and led her away, fresh tears on her face, but now a smile shining through her grief. As Tarn turned to continue on his way, Crysal slipped her hand into his and gave it a squeeze.

"Who was she?" his wife asked.

"I . . . I don't know," Tarn answered, choking.

There were other such scenes before they reached the gates to their home. Though weary to the marrow of his bones, Tarn diligently stopped and paid his respects to everyone who approached, hearing their stories of grief, or answering their questions about how their husbands, sons, and daughters had died.

Mog Bonecutter and Tarn's other guards, ever near, watched the supplicants warily, but there were no incidents, no angry accusations. As they neared the castle, Crystal pressed close to Tarn and whispered, "Thee people seem genuinely happy to see you." Tarn nodded, his jaw muscles tightening, and she knew that he was exerting all his will just to hold himself together for public view. But he would not allow her to hurry him, nor to keep his people away, and the crowds at their gate were larger than any they had seen since leaving the Council Hall. It took nearly an hour for them to work their way through the throng of well-wishers and grieving families.

Finally inside the castle, they then had to run the gauntlet of the castle's guard. The soldiers, many of them too young or too old to have accompanied Tarn on his mission to Qualinost, had turned out in all their finery to welcome him home. With weapons polished and armor gleaming, they awaited his inspection in the courtyard. The king dutifully walked their lines, stopping occasionally to speak to an old friend, with Crystal remaining at his side, gently and inconspicuously supporting him by one arm. She was most pleased to find her apprentice, Haruk Mastersword, standing at the head of his squadron of young trainees, his beard brushed and gleaming like spun gold, his brilliant green eyes watching her intently through the slits in his helm. He looked the epitome of fierce dwarf warrior pride. Tarn clapped the young dwarf on the shoulder and asked him how his lessons were going.

"My master grants no quarter, nor expects any," the young Hylar warrior answered crisply.

"Good! Very good!" Tarn laughed before moving on. Haruk had missed being old enough to join the king's expedition by only a year, a mere puff of time for the long-lived dwarves but an eon for those who felt left behind. Tarn was now heartily glad for this quirk of fate. Crystal winked at her favorite student as she passed him, but Haruk maintained his formal warrior's countenance. It would not have been seemly to smile in the king's presence.

Next, they had to make their way past the welcoming servants. Here, too, Tarn saw signs of mourning in the form of black armbands and black ribbons tied in beards, for some of his servants had boasted sons and nephews in Tarn's army. Each symbol of grief that he saw plucked Tarn's own heartstrings all the more. But he was the king, and the king couldn't allow himself the luxury of showing weakness or vulnerability; he must appear strong for his people. So he greeted them heartily as they led him through the stately halls of his home to his family chapel.

Here, a family priest awaited them. As was his custom, Tarn lit candles to his father and mother, as he did whenever he returned from a journey away from Thorbardin. He also lit a candle to the spirit of Belicia Slateshoulders, his first love, the woman he had planned to marry before her untimely death more than thirty years ago. Crystal lit a candle to her grandfather, Connor Heathstone, while the priest chanted a hymn to the dead. It was one of the Hylar dwarves' oldest and most beloved songs, recalling those who had died in the long march from Thoradin to Thorbardin back during the Age of Light. Its refrains mourned anyone so unlucky to have died before setting eyes on their beloved mountain.

When the priest had done singing, Tarn and Crystal rose and left the chapel by way of their private entrance. A long candlelit hall led them to their living quarters. Though a warm fire and a delicious repast awaited them in the private dining room, Tarn entered their bedchamber. Crystal closed the door. When she turned, she found her husband had sunk to the floor, his head slumped against a bedpost, his back heaving with silent sobs. She knelt by his side and gathered him into her arms. He moaned garbled words, but she did not need to decipher them to know what was in his broken heart. She responded by rocking slowly, crooning a wordless tune and stroking his long golden hair.

They huddled together in this manner for what seemed hours. When Tarn's grief had poured itself out, they then spoke together in low voices for quite some time longer. He told her in detail what had happened and how he blamed himself for the deaths of so many noble young dwarves. She did her best to comfort him, but his heartache was still too fresh to be salved by mere words.

When, finally, Crystal saw that nothing she could say or do could make his pain any less, she rose and sat on the edge of the bed. Holding out her arms, she drew him to herself. He wrapped his arms around her and rested there, listening to the sound of her breathing. That is when he felt her grow suddenly tense, and the hand stroking his hair became awkward and heavy. He wondered what was bothering his wife, but he had little energy to inquire. She needed her own time to say what she was about to say.

Finally, Crystal sighed and said, "Even in times of great sorrow, great joy is born."

Tarn was silent for a moment, then asked, "What do you mean?"

She laughed nervously. He sat back and looked up into her cool gray eyes. They were moist, but not with tears. Her lips trembled with a smile. "What is wrong?" he asked. "What did you mean?"

"Just this," she said, her voice catching in her throat. She touched her fingers to her lips to calm herself, then continued, "By this time next year, you shall hold your son in your arms."

CHAPTER

16

Thane Jungor Stonesinger sat in his private study, his eyes roaming among the battle trophies he'd won over the years. Behind him, a broad window stood with its shutters thrown wide, while outside the window, twin gouts of water shot from the nostrils of a marble dragon's head, filling a deep granite bowl before spilling over into a stream. The stream flowed though the private gardens of Jungor's second level residence near the old temple of Reorx. A skylight cut through the living rock of the mountain let light in from the outside, filling his garden with sunlight and allowing his exotic collection of plants and trees to grow.

But at the moment, night ruled outside the mountain and moonlight was too wan to illuminate his garden. Instead, torches burned in golden sconces strapped to the trunks of the trees, flickering gaily in the pools formed by the stream and throwing their light in an ever-changing pattern against the white marble walls of his home.

Jungor sat facing the window, slowly removing the bandage from his empty eye socket, blind to the beauty of what lay before him. Behind him, his loyal guard captain, Astar Trueshield, and the Daewar thane, Rughar Delvestone, shared a couch near the fireplace. Thane Delvestone was sampling Jungor's brandy, while Astar contemplated the flames dancing in the grate, a dour look on his face.

Jungor tossed the used bandage onto his desk and turned to face his guests. They looked up at the movement, then recoiled in horror at what they saw. Jungor laughed. "Don't you like it?" he asked, pointing to the polished round agate resting in the bruised empty socket of his right eye. The gleaming black stone gave his already hellish visage an even more diabolical look.

"As you wish, my lord thane," Rughar said with obvious uncertainty. He sipped at his brandy nervously. But Astar had no such compunctions.

"Reorx's bones! Take it out, thane, before someone sees you," Captain Trueshield exclaimed.

Jungor laughed again, tilting his head forward until the stone rolled out of his face and dropped to the desk. It rolled slowly across the polished mahogany surface before dropping soundlessly to the soft carpet. "I am thinking of having a golden orb made," the Hylar thane stated with a jolliness that seemed incongruous with his recent defeat in the Council Hall. "Of course, I'd want it etched to look like a real eye, perhaps even with a blue enamel iris and a bit of black onyx set into the gold for a pupil. What do you think?"

"I think Tarn Bellowgranite should have died in those tunnels with his army," Rughar said grumpily, then tossed back the last of his brandy. His face flushed with the heat of the strong liquor.

"Naturally, my new eye shouldn't appear too real," Jungor said as he leaned back in his chair and laced his fingers behind his head. "I think gold is just the thing. It won't tarnish or rust or crack, and it can be polished to the smoothness of butter."

"I don't see how you can sit here and make jokes at a time like this, Thane Jungor!" Rughar exclaimed. "Tarn defied the Council and look what has happened—the loss of an entire army. What was gained by this sacrifice? A rumor of Beryl's death? A piece of loose dragon scale that may have fallen off as she razed the city of Qualinost down to its foundations?"

"It would take ten armies and more elves than there are in all Krynn to kill Beryl," Astar Trueshield scoffed. "What galls me is that Tarn was defeated and lost his entire army almost to the last dwarf, and yet we have practically begged him to remain as king!"

Jungor leaned forward in his chair and rested his elbows atop his desk. He pointed languidly at the Daewar thane. "You asked how I could make jokes at a time like this. How can you not? This has been a banner day in dwarven history. A spectacle, a well-written play, memorable theater if you like! I thought I'd continue the celebration with a little levity among conspirators."

"Thane Stonesinger, you go too far!" Rughar exclaimed.

"Oh, I haven't even begun, and you've no idea how far I'll go," Jungor said, his voice deadly calm. "I say this was a day of high theater. So masterful was the director that we all played our unwitting parts in Tarn's little play. It is as you say, Astar. Tarn returned in defeat and should have been stripped of his crown and tossed from the North Gate in disgrace, yet in the end we begged him to remain as our king! What inspired drama!"

He burst out in such a mad fit of laughter that it was some minutes before Jungor could catch his breath. His two companions looked at him as though he had gone completely insane. This only made him laugh the harder to see the foolish looks on their faces. "Oh, are your hearts so cold that you cannot admire him? Hate him, yes, for what he has done to us, for what we have become under his rule— a diminished people of diminished expectations. But still, you must admire his boldness. I could not have scripted a more sensational drama, and the people were mightily pleased by it. His confession and redemption before the Council were worthy of the Palanthian stage. Did you not want to applaud?"

"I must admit that I did not see it in that light before now," Thane Delvestone said skeptically.

"That is only because you are such a fool," Jungor laughed. "But I need such fools as you, Rughar. Please do not take offense."

"None taken, my lord," the Daewar thane conceded with a bow of his head.

"But what are we to do now?" Astar cried, slamming his fist down on the arm of the couch. "Have we lost everything? Has all this been for naught?"

"Have a care with the furniture, Captain Trueshield," Jungor chided. "Do not worry about the future. Nothing has changed, except perhaps that we are in a better position than we were before. Yes, even better!"

At his companions' dubious looks, Jungor shook his head in dismay. Could they be so blind? Like a teacher instructing children, he said, "The people needed comfort today. Any upheaval coming on the heels of their tremendous loss would only have made our jobs more difficult in the long run. But mark my words in stone, they will not always feel so kindly toward the king who led their sons and daughters, wives and husbands to their deaths. Give them time to mourn their dead, and to brood. In a few months, they will begin to wonder if the elves' rescue was worth the price we paid. And if they should not begin to wonder, then we shall remind them. We shall renew their grief, keep it fresh."

Rughar smiled as he began to understand where Jungor was leading them. The Hylar thane nodded. "Yes, you see now, don't you? I never expected Tarn to lose his entire army. Defeat seemed inevitable, but who could have imagined that so many should die so suddenly? We were going to have to create a crisis to exploit, but now a disaster has been dropped into our laps—and like a gift of the gods, greater than anything we could have arranged."

Jungor rose from his chair and stood looking out the window. His gaze was not on the beauty of his garden or the light of his torches. He was gazing into the future and its many possible paths. "And though I have lost my eye in the arena, this too has only added to our chances, enhanced my mystique. With all the things we have already arranged, plus with Thane Quickspring leading my cult, my power and influence will continue to grow while Tarn's erodes under our ceaseless campaign of propaganda. He will not even know that it is happening until it is too late."

A soft knock at the door ended Jungor's lecture. He motioned for Astar to open the door. With a scowl, the Hylar captain stood aside to allow Ferro Dunskull to enter. "Ah, Ferro, good of you to come. Thank you, Thane Delvestone, for stopping by. Everything will proceed as intended. Do not be frustrated or impatient. Remember that Thorbardin was carved one chip at a time. Captain Trueshield, will you show the thane to the door?"

Rughar bowed and took his leave, and Astar closed the door behind them as they left. Ferro dropped back to the corner farthest from Jungor, his dark eyes nervously darting around, taking in every object and item of furniture, every avenue of escape. Jungor eased around the desk and settled himself on the couch beside the fire. He pointed to a crystal decanter on a silver tray on a table by the wall. "That's very good brandy," he said. "Have some."

"No thank you, my lord. Brandy unsettles my bowels," the Daergar softly answered from his dark corner.

Jungor turned, his one eye twinkling in the firelight. "Then sit down and tell me how you . . . failed."

Ferro slunk around the wall until he reached a small chair standing beside the table with the decanter of brandy. He seated himself on the chair's edge, his hands nervously fidgeting at the edges of his studded leather vest.

"Don't be shy," Jungor said. "I know you have something to tell me, some tidbit of explanation. If I thought you had betrayed me, you would already be dead, dear Ferro."

Ferro started in his chair, nearly bolting for the door. With a supreme effort of will, aided by his stubborn Daergar pride, he was able to control his fear. "The draconians that I hired attacked Tarn's party before my agent could deliver the killing blow to the king. Stupid, stupid of them! Still, things might have gone as planned if General Otaxx had not appeared with a large force of the Pax Tharkas garrison. He was traveling behind the king, his soldiers being burdened with a large consignment of supplies for Thorbardin. When he heard the fighting, he quickly gathered his troops and rushed to the attack, turning the tide of the battle."

"So, what you are saying is, you failed to properly reconnoiter the situation and see what forces were arrayed against you," Jungor said with a pleasantness that belied the edge in his voice.

"I am afraid so," Ferro reluctantly admitted.

"I cannot abide a fool, especially if he is to be my master of scouts, Master Dunskull," Jungor said. "I assume all the draconians were killed to prevent them telling who hired them."

"We ourselves attacked the last group from the rear," Ferro said, "to cover our mistake."

"Commendable. And this agent, this assassin, what about him? He was eliminated as well?"

When Ferro did not immediately answer, Jungor sat up, glaring at him in the firelight. Finally, a small voice said from the shadows, "Not exactly."

"What do you mean? Where is he now?" Jungor demanded.

"You saw him today in the Council Hall," Ferro answered. "Ilbars Bleakfell."

Jungor's jaw dropped open. "You corrupted that pompous Daewar buffoon? By the gods, Ferro, I underestimated you."

"You do not understand, my lord," Ferro said nervously. "Captain Ilbars is not himself. The real Ilbars is waiting out eternity at the bottom of a bog, most likely. What you saw today in the Council Hall was a sivak draconian named Zen. He was the leader of the band I hired to kill Tarn. He indeed killed Ilbars and took his place, as was the plan." Jungor nodded, listening. He had heard of the sivaks' ability to assume the shape of anyone it kills. He was also keenly aware of how dangerous such a creature, loose in Thorbardin, could prove. If Tarn were to discover him . . .

Ferro continued, "The draconians sprang their ambush before Zen could get close enough to the king to kill him. But Zen survived the battle somehow and accompanied us back to Thorbardin, still in the guise of Ilbars Bleakfell. I have not had the opportunity to speak with him alone, therefore I am puzzled . . . that is, I am unclear as to his ultimate intentions."

"Unclear? Your euphemisms are tiresome," Jungor said, his patience worn thin. "So where is this failed assassin now?"

Again, it was some moments before Ferro was able to answer. Finally, his words came blurting out. "After the Council, he slipped into the crowd and disappeared. I don't know where he is. My agents are searching for him as we speak. All I know is that he's somewhere in the city."

Steeling his patience, Jungor rose from the couch with a deep sigh and slowly strode to the window. With his hands clasped behind his back, he stared out into the torch-lit darkness of the garden. "I trust that your agents will find him," he said at last

"Of course, my lord," Ferro said hurriedly. With Jungor's back turned, Ferro lifted the brandy decanter and poured a third of its contents down his throat. Coughing on the potent liquor, he said, "But with his shapechanging ability, Zen could be someone else by now. He could be . . . anyone."

Jungor nodded and hissed without turning. "Pray that you find him before he finds you. And may the gods who are no more help you if you fail this time."

A MOMENT

In a tiny room lit by fire, his haggard face starkly divided between light and shadow down the crooked line of his nose, the captain of the North Gate solemnly nodded his sweaty bald head. Released, the mechanism slowly commenced its turn. Driven by swift, icy water hidden behind stone, it propelled a gleaming steel screw thick as an Urkhan worm into the side of the mountain. The gate, a solid plug of stone, swung out of its cavern lair on hinged steel arms and slid into position over the coiling rod, silent as the first day of Creation. The floor shuddered with the leviathan waking of the machine.

In his bed deep inside his fortress home, in the dark with his wife breathing deep and slow beside him, Tarn Bellowgranite wondered if it would be enough. Enough to keep Beryl out, when she came, if she came. Enough to quiet the souls of those he'd led to their doom. Somewhere in the world above, the elves of Qualinost wandered alone. He wondered if they knew the price he'd paid for their freedom, sacrificing his own. He wondered if their young king deserved it. He wondered if he had the right to wonder or the wisdom to question. He fell asleep and clutched the sheets as he dreamed of drowning dwarves.

In the city beneath the stone, Norbardin, Jungor Stone-singer paused in his garden, submersed in sudden moonlight. By some unlikely chance, Krynn's pale moon had chosen that moment to peer down through the skylight and limn every line and shape in silver and forest green, startling him as though he had walked, unaware, onto a stage. In his fancy, the lights had come up and the crowd sat breathless in their seats, awaiting the chorus that would open the play. The blistered skin round his eyeless socket tightened as he recalled his lines and smiled. He had written this play himself.

In the darkness of the Anvil's Echo, Ferro Dunskull lost himself in a pale Daergar beauty, as rare and pure as a black dragon's tear, whose name he had already forgot. His fear and anger and loneliness he poured out like a bitter libation onto her floor, both needing and hating her, and she welcomed him into her small, well-apportioned room, hungry to share his power. Her limbs long and lithe, the flat round of her belly pallid as moonlight, she paused at the edge of the candle's light, a crystal decanter of black brandy hanging from the crook of her finger. He turned away to hide his sneer.

In the shadow beneath a barbican gate, Zen shucked off the mortal form of Ilbars Bleakfell, trading it for one less familiar, one less regarded. The pale gray corpse lay at his feet on the slick stones, blood pooling black behind its neck. Now Daergar in form, he set to work dismembering his victim and stuffing the sundry parts down a sewer grate, losing his patience when the head wouldn't fit between the rusty bars.

Into its uneven seat in the stone, silent as the dawning day, the North Gate twisted home, sealing the dwarves of Thorbardin inside their mountain once more. Through hidden windows high above, guards watched the northern horizon for dragon flame and the watch fires of camping armies. They watched the approaches to the gate, not to welcome visitors but to drive them away with arrows and bolts and falls of stone. As the gate sank into place, melding with the surrounding stone so perfectly that not even a dwarf could find it once shut, the air inside the mountain grew tight, and the guards at their posts smelled the hot metallic reek of melting lead. The plumber had come to seal the gate, humming a song and sucking the remains of his breakfast from his teeth while he stoked the fires of his portable forge. The captain of the North Gate waited with a signet stone to press into the warm lead seal, to finalize the Council's command to shut out the world.

He was glad no one had come to witness the sealing of the gate. He was glad for the heat of the forge fire and the sweat that hid his tears.

BOOK
II

CHAPTER
17

Tarn never tired of looking at him. He never tired of holding him in his arms or feeling his soft fat little fingers close around his own coarse one. "You will be strong, like your father," he whispered to the infant boy.

Tor Bellowgranite, son of Tarn Bellowgranite, smiled his blank, toothless smile up into his father's face. Crystal said he was too young to smile, but Tarn knew better. Tor was smiling because he knew his father. He shook his fists, like little balls of dough, at Tarn's face, and began to kick. Tarn laughed without really knowing why, feeling only a deep and abiding joy unlike anything he had ever known.

Dwarf babies were, to put it simply, quite ugly. Even dwarf mothers had no illusions about the beauty of their own infants. Though usually born with a full head of hair, dwarf babies did not come into the world already fully bearded, despite popular superstitions. Tor shared the Hylar trait of golden hair, just like his father. Crystal argued that Neidar babies were also born blonde-headed, but that they soon lost their fine golden baby hair and replaced it with a proper color. Tarn was pleased that his son, just six months old, still sported a magnificent shock of tawny locks.

Suddenly, the baby's fat little face scrunched up in a horrible grimace. Tarn stared at him in surprise, then recoiled as Tor sneezed. "He's caught something," he said in alarm. He turned to the open door and cried, "Auntie! Tor is ill. Fetch the healers at once."

"He's not sick. You've just tickled his nose with your beard again," a female voice answered from the next room.

Tarn felt a tug at his chin and looked down, chuckling as the baby pulled at the ends of his long beard hairs. "Where is your beard, Tor?" he murmured to the child. "Did your mommy shave it off to make you look like an elf child? Or maybe it was wicked old Aunt Needlebone."

"I heard that," the female voice said from the other room. A matronly old dwarf appeared in the doorway, a rag hanging from the fist planted firmly on her hip. With her other hand, she pointed a quivering finger at Tarn. "Stop filling that boy's head with your foolishness," she admonished.

"He doesn't understand what I am saying to him," Tarn said, gazing down at Tor. "He's just responding to the sound of my voice."

"Don't you count on it. This child is brilliant. I've never seen a more brilliant child in my three hundred and fifty years, not even his mother." Tor blinked at Tarn; he had his mother's gray eyes. "Sometimes he looks at you with that piercing gaze and you think he's about to whisper great secrets. You feel like you haven't got any clothes on, or that he is looking right through you. But the next minute, there he is a baby again. It passes like a cloud over the hill." Her voice trailed off in a sigh of longing. Tarn had heard the old dwarf woman sigh that way many a time since she came with Crystal to live inside the mountain. The old hill dwarf nursemaid missed her home in the hills west of Thorbardin. Only her love for Crystal, and now for the boy, kept her here.

Closing the nursery door behind her, Aunt Needlebone shuffled to Tarn's side and peered over his shoulder at infant Tor lying in his father's arms, quiet now, peering at their faces with his large gray eyes. "Sometimes I think he really can talk already. He just hasn't decided what he wants to say," she said.

Tarn smiled and shrugged. "I don't know about talking, but he'll certainly be walking before much longer."

Auntie laughed at the king. "Hill dwarf babies are already walking by Tor's age. Mountain dwarves are a bit slower, I hear."

Knowing that Auntie was only trying to provoke him, Tarn growled, "He's as stubborn as a hill dwarf, that's for certain. This morning, I tried to give him his wooden rattler, but he was having nothing of it. He wanted his gemstone shaker and nothing else would do. Such a voice!"

"He'll need that voice to be heard in this family," Auntie said.

The door to the nursery opened and Crystal entered. She was dressed formally, with golden hoops dangling from her ears and rings winking with gems on her fingers. Her face was rouged, her long auburn hair arranged with jeweled pins and combs into a tall coif atop her head. A wide belt of green felt circled her waist, into which was tucked a blouse of milky white silk. A skirt of tooled and gilded leather covered her legs, and over all she wore a robe of fine green wool lined with gray silk and trimmed in ermine.

She stopped just inside the door and looked at Tarn in alarm. "Aren't you ready yet?" she asked.

Tarn growled something unintelligible into his beard. Crystal sighed and adjusted one of her earrings. "The delegates will be here any moment, Tarn," she said.

"I'd rather stay here with Tor," Tarn responded sullenly.

"Well, you can't. You are the king. This is an important day, the celebration of the Festival of Lights, a time to honor the dead and to remember the destruction suffered during the Chaos War. You can't hide in the nursery, today of all days."

"Here, give me the child," Auntie said as she gently pried Tor from his father's arms. Tarn only reluctantly released his hold on the boy.

"I'm not hiding," he said angrily as he rose to his feet. "I enjoy spending time with my son. Is that so wrong?"

"You dote on him too much," Auntie said. "You'll spoil him."

Snarling, Tarn stalked from the nursery. Aunt Needlebone's fuzzy gray eyebrows rose in a silent question, but Crystal only shrugged and followed her husband.

As Tarn swept into the reception hall of his residence, guards along both walls snapped to attention, their boots thundering on the floor as one. Tarn wore his full ceremonial regalia—plate armor polished to a mirror sheen, kingsword at his hip, crown of Thorbardin encircling his golden mane of hair. A long cloak of wolf fur dragged on the ground behind him as he climbed the stairs to his throne. Crystal walked at his side and took her accustomed place to his left, standing a little behind the throne with her right hand resting on its high, dragon-carved back. Mog Bonecutter emerged from a door behind the throne and took his place to Tarn's right. Mog wore a full suit of golden-tinted chain mail, his unruly black beard poking fiercely from the circle of mail coif, a tabard of red silk emblazoned with the hammer and anvil symbol covering his chest and back.

The highest dignitaries of the Hylar clan bowed in greeting at the foot of the steps. Thane Jungor Stonesinger was foremost among them. Because the acid damage to his face had caused part of his facial hair to eventually fall out, Jungor had taken to braiding his remaining beard into three short plaits. Even today, when he and all the other dwarves of Thorbardin were dressing in their finest and combing out their beards to achieve the greatest fullness and luxuriance possible, Jungor chose to keep his severe style. With his ascetic's beard, long gray robes, wizard staff, and golden orb winking from the hollow of his right eye, he looked almost like a sorcerer.

Beside Jungor stood the wealthy merchant Hextor Ironhaft, gold fairly dripping from his fat fingers. Several dozen generals, former priests, nobles, and artisans made up the remainder of the delegation—the cream of Hylar society, both male and female. Most were dressed either in the most expensive silks imported from the north or the richest armor forged by dwarf or man. Several years ago, Tarn's engineers had opened several new ore veins in the stone near the North Gate. These mines had provided much of the reason for the dwarves' rising prosperity. Because of Tarn's policy of openness, dwarf traders from Thorbardin had begun to carry their goods all over the world. Wealth flowed through the North Gate, improving everyone's lives.

Flowed, that is, it until Jungor convinced the Council of Thanes to seal the mountain after the disaster at Qualinost. Now, the wealth of Thorbardin was being consolidated in higher and higher levels of its society, just as it was in the old days. Gold and iron still flowed from the mines and steel continued to be forged in its foundries, but these riches no longer flowed out with traders traveling to distant lands, bringing home the mundane goods and strange curiosities that once filled the markets of Norbardin. Now, money was hoarded rather than invested. The poor grew poorer, the rich richer. Some dwarves ate off plates of gold while other had nothing to eat at all. And as long as the mountain remained sealed and the economy of Norbardin forced to feed off itself, this situation would never change.

Tarn was well aware that Jungor wanted to keep it that way. The Hylar thane had made no secret of his ambitions in the last year, while Tarn had withdrawn ever deeper into family matters. As he had said, he'd rather spend time with his son. Instead, he was forced to participate in these endless ceremonies.

Crystal nudged him, bringing him out of his dark reverie. He coughed and cleared his throat. "Clansmen and clanswomen of the Hylar, I welcome you into the home of the son of Baker Whitegranite, son of Brom Whitegranite. In remembrance of those now gone to join the Kingdom of the Dead, I wish you a joyous Festival of Lights."

The Hylar nodded appreciatively. Although many of them had little enough love for their half-breed king, none disputed that Tarn had a remarkable talent for speaking on public occasions, especially rituals and formal ceremonies. There were many who said Tarn would have made a good priest, an observation that only made Tarn laugh when he heard it.

"Twelve boats await us at the old wharf," Jungor said. "The Hylar have begun to gather on the Isle of the Dead."

"Let us go then," Tarn said, rising from his throne. With Crystal resting her hand lightly on his proffered elbow, he descended the stairs. Mog walked behind them, his beard jutting out defiantly. But when they reached the floor, Jungor remained where he stood, blocking the king's path.

"Do you intend to bring *her?*" the Hylar thane asked, pointing at Crystal. Tarn stepped back in surprise. Crystal had joined him on the Isle of the Dead for the Festival of Lights every year since their marriage. No one had ever questioned her presence before, so why was Jungor making an issue of it now?

"Of course she is coming," Tarn said, clearly flabbergasted.

"She is a hill dwarf," Jungor said, stating the obvious.

"She is the mother of my son," Tarn countered, his temper growing dangerously short.

"Only Hylar may walk upon the rocky shore of our island," Hextor Ironhaft said.

"Impertinent swine! How dare you insult the king in the king's own house?" Mog snatched a halberd from one of the nearby guards and stepped toward the Hylar delegation. "Allow me to teach these dwarves some manners, my lord," he snarled.

Jungor took a step back, raising his staff defensively. "Call off your dog, Tarn Bellowgranite," he demanded.

"Mog!" Tarn shouted.

"The king can handle this," Crystal angrily admonished the Klar captain.

But Mog remained menacingly near. "And they say the Klar are barbarians," he growled, knuckles cracking around the haft of his halberd. Some of the delegation began to back away, and the guards along the walls grew nervous. Though valiant and loyal, Mog had a reputation for cracking heads first, begging forgiveness afterward.

Satisfied that Mog was properly restrained, Jungor resumed his position before Tarn. "The Isle of the Dead is sacred to the Hylar," he said. "It would be unseemly for your wife to come. Though nobleborn, she is Neidar."

"Dwarves of every clan died there that day," Tarn countered.

"Yes, attacking us. But it was our home that broke apart and fell into the waters of the Urkhan Sea. You, as much as anyone here, should understand how we feel. The body of Belicia Slateshoulders lies unburied in the ruins there, too," Jungor said.

These words stung Tarn to silence. He had long ago come to terms with the loss of his first true love, when a section of Hybardin that she was attempting to restore broke off and fell to the island below, carrying her and several hundred workers to their deaths. But Jungor's audacity to speak of her here, before his wife, robbed his voice of words to express his outrage.

Jungor turned to Crystal and said, "I pray you will understand this, Mistress," he said, bowing slightly from the hips. "But you cannot go. It is not I that must forbid it. The other members of my clan have spoken."

"Perhaps it would be better if I stayed behind," Crystal offered softly.

Incredulous, Tarn stared at her for a moment as though unable to believe his own ears. "You will not!" he shrieked, then turned back to the Hylar delegation, his face flushed a brilliant crimson that rose all the way up to the roots of his blond hair. "She is the mother of the future King of Thorbardin!" he raged, spittle flying from his lips.

Jungor calmly replied, "Primogeniture is our tradition, but it is not our law."

Again, for a few heartbeats, Tarn was speechless. Could this queer, misshapen, histrionic idiot of a Hylar thane really be so bold as to challenge him in this way, through his infant son? When he found his voice again, Tarn growled, "What is that supposed to mean?"

Emboldened by the king's frustration and Jungor's defiance, Hextor Ironhaft answered rudely, "The people of Thorbardin will never accept a half-breed as their king."

"They accepted me!" Tarn snapped.

"Indeed, but you are of Hylar and Daergar blood," Jungor said smoothly. "You became king when Thane Hornfel and your father, Thane Baker Whitegranite, died during the Chaos War. Your son, on the other hand, is a hill dwarf."

"Part hill dwarf," Tarn protested.

"The people of the mountain will never respect a king with any amount of hill dwarf blood," Jungor said. "They have borne many changes under your rule, Tarn Bellowgranite, but they will not bear that rupture of tradition. It is too great a thing to ask. Your son is a hill dwarf. He cannot be king. We only speak aloud what others whisper."

Before Tarn could answer with all the venom of his heart, Crystal stepped forward and placed a cool, restraining hand on his arm. "I'll stay here," she said, but not to

Tarn. Her icy gray eyes were upon the Hylar thane. "You go and honor your dead. I will remain behind with the living."

A terrified expression came over Jungor's twisted, misshapen face. Gripping the wizard staff in both hands, he hammered its butt end three times on the floor in rapid succession, chanting unintelligible words.

Tarn brushed his wife's hand from his arm, then gripped the hilt of his kingsword. Mog edged closer, his halberd held at the ready. "What are you doing? What evil are you trying to avert?" he demanded of Jungor. "What do you think, that my wife is trying to cast a spell on you?"

"She spoke words of ill omen!" Jungor cried defensively.

Tarn's sword nearly sprang out of its sheath. "*How dare you* accuse the queen of witchcraft!"

Jungor gripped his staff tighter and faced the furious king. What he said next surprised even the other Hylar. "She may be your consort, but she is not my queen."

"What! Get out of my house, you traitorous dog!" Tarn shrieked. "Get out! If you ever cross the threshold of this house again, I'll have your head."

Jungor made an obscene gesture with his hand as he turned and stalked from the reception chamber. Mog surged toward him, ready to split his head open with his halberd, but Crystal leaped between the two, stopping the Klar before he could revenge his king. The other Hylar quickly followed Jungor, angrily grumbling at the way Tarn had insulted their thane. Meanwhile, Tarn climbed the steps and flung himself down on his throne sullenly.

"You would only have made things worse," Crystal said to Mog when they had gone. She patted him on the cheek as she released him. He flung his halberd clattering to the floor and stormed out, the door banging against the wall as he left.

Crystal then addressed the guards. "Leave us. I would have private words with the king." Slowly the guards filed out, but not without many a backward, uncertain glance. Several of them were Hylar, and they felt torn in their loyalties.

When they were alone at last, Crystal stood at the base of the steps and glared up at Tarn. She said nothing, merely stood with one hand thrust against her hip, one foot impatiently tapping the polished marble floor. For a while, Tarn avoided her gaze. Finally, he looked up and shouted, "To the Abyss with them. To the Abyss with them all!"

"Tarn Bellowgranite, you know that you cannot afford to make an enemy of the Hylar thane," Crystal admonished.

"I did not make an enemy of him. It is he who has made an enemy of me," the king said, his fist slamming down on the arm of the chair. "How dare he insult you in our house, in my presence?"

"Jungor Stonesinger is the Hylar thane, and he has his own opinion about the way you rule Thorbardin," Crystal said as she slowly climbed the steps to Tarn's side. "He has the loyalty of most of the Hylar, whose support you need. And he is swiftly gaining followers among the other clans as well. You know as well as I do that he covets your throne. What will happen to us if you are driven from power? What will happen to our son?"

"I am thinking of our son. What would happen to him if his father were disgraced?" Tarn asked harshly. "This idiot thane pushes me and he pushes me, and I am expected to yield at every turn. Well, this time he has gone too far with his insults."

"You must not give Jungor Stonesinger any excuse to challenge you that the Council of Thanes would support," Crystal advised. She knelt beside Tarn's throne and laid her head in his lap. "And . . . I hate to admit it, but Jungor may be right. The dwarves of Thorbardin will never accept me, and they will never allow Tor to be king. The old hatreds run too deep."

Tarn reached out, stroking her hair. She had worked for hours preparing herself for this day, to look perfect for the Hylar delegation. Her hair was meticulously arranged, sparkling with jeweled pins. But all her work and consideration had been for naught. They didn't see the woman eager to please them for her husband's sake. They saw only a hated Neidar, a woman of the hill dwarves.

"I had hoped our marriage would heal the breach between our two peoples," Tarn said in a weary voice. "I overestimated my peoples' love for me. I thought they would come to love you for my sake and accept you as their queen. Instead, we've deepened the divide."

"I wouldn't go so far as that. We're but two people. There is still hope. Take my pupil Haruk, for instance. He is young but wise for his years. When he looks at me, he sees his weapons master, not a hill dwarf," Crystal said, smiling at the thought of the strong young Hylar warrior she had trained. After her marriage to Tarn, Haruk had joined their household and become her apprentice as part of an effort to ease the political tensions between Tarn and Jungor. Haruk was Jungor's nephew, the oldest son of Jungor's sister, a dwarf destined to be a powerful and influential leader among the Hylar. If his heart remained as pure as she knew it to be . . . "There is yet hope for the future," she concluded.

"I have never regretted marrying you, though," Tarn wistfully said. "No matter what happens, I shall always know that I did the right thing. Ours was a political marriage, but I would never have gone through with it had I not loved you, even then."

"You hardly knew me," Crystal laughed.

"I knew enough. I had spies in your father's court."

"Yes, I know," she said.

"See! That's why I knew that you would be a queen worthy of the title. Beautiful, wise, a formidable warrior, and your father's most trusted councilor; nothing got by

143

you, not even my most capable spies. I determined that I had to have you for my queen, and I always get my way," Tarn said, grinning fiercely.

But Crystal's face grew serious. "For once, then, listen. My advice was good enough for my father, so it is certainly good enough for you, Tarn Bellowgranite." She lifted her head from his lap and looked long and hard into his eyes. "Swallow your insufferable pride. Go to the ceremony on the Isle of the Dead and honor the souls of the Hylar who have laid their bones in the ground. I will stay here with our son, and we will await your return together."

Tarn closed his eyes, then nodded.

CHAPTER
18

"You wait here," the gully dwarf, Shnatz Ong, whispered around the corner.

"We follow you."

"You wait here," Shnatz repeated impatiently.

"You say follow you."

"That then. Now, you wait here!" Shnatz spun on his heel and began to creep along the narrow, dark passageway. He had gone several feet before he heard them coming up behind him again. He stopped, turned, and stamped his foot in anger, raising a cloud of dust. Someone sneezed.

"What you doing? I say you wait there," Shnatz hissed.

Twenty gully dwarves crept out of the shadows, cringing and mewling. One of them whined, "You not say how long we got to wait. We get scared. We not supposed to be here. This place forb . . . forb . . ."

"Forbidden," Shnatz finished for him. "That why you got to be quiet, stay where I put you bunch of knotheads." Someone dropped a pickaxe clanging to the floor, and everyone, including Shnatz, cringed. The noise seemed to echo forever through the maze of dark, rubble-strewn halls and passageways that made up this part of the ruins.

When the sound finally faded, Shnatz fairly shrieked, "Who did that? Come on, who did it?" There was a brief scuffle among the huddle of gully dwarves until one, a large, dull-faced lout, was booted to the front by the others. He slipped on the dusty floor as he skidded to a stop before Shnatz, catching himself on a section of fallen stone.

"What the matter with you?" Shnatz demanded.

"It slipped," the gully dwarf answered sheepishly.

"Oh, yeah? That okay. Accidents happen. Like now." Shnatz lashed out and cracked the clumsy gully dwarf on top of the head with the hilt of a small dagger he carried concealed in his grubby fist. The gully dwarf clapped his hands to his pate and sank to the floor, moaning like a felled ox.

"You dumb *puhungs* got to be quiet. Somebody catches you here, I hate to think what they do to you. This place forbidden, and that means you no go here. 'Cept now you got to go here 'cause that's what I tell you to do. You not do what I tell you to do, I hate to think what I do to you. You unnerstand?"

The cringing gully dwarves stared at him blankly, unresponding. Shnatz sighed and said, "You got that?" They nodded, twenty grimy, knot-bearded faces bobbing so vigorously that it nearly made Shnatz seasick—even though he had never been to sea, unless you counted the great underground Urkhan Sea lying somewhere below him at this very moment. Shnatz got seasick every time he crossed the Urkhan Sea, despite the fact that it had neither wind nor waves, tides nor currents.

"Dumb *puhungs* not even know what 'unnerstand' means," Shnatz grumbled as he turned and started up the passage once more. When he heard them surge into motion behind him, following at his heels, he stopped even trying to scout ahead. There was little purpose to scouting ahead, anyway. He'd been exploring this area for months, and he knew for a fact that no one had been to this part of the ruins in a dozen years or more. Dust lay thick among the crumbled walls and fallen pillars, and the only footprints he saw on the floor as he crept forward were his own from two weeks ago. Not even his fellow gully dwarves had taken up residence in the place, and that was saying something. Gully dwarves generally moved into any place where they would be left alone by the other clans.

But for some reason that not even Shnatz could name, gully dwarves had never invaded the ruins of Hybardin, the old home of the Hylar dwarves. There wasn't much left of it, for one thing. Weakened by the ravages of the Chaos dragons forty-one years ago, most of the great stalactite that had been the Hylar city had long since crumbled and fallen to the Urkhan Sea hundreds of feet below. This had led to the formation of a huge rocky island of jumbled ruins and broken stone that the Hylar called the Isle of the Dead. As with the ruins of Hybardin, the gully dwarves also avoided the Isle of the Dead. Only the Hylar went there anymore, and then only once a year, during the Festival of Lights.

Shnatz continued to follow his own old footprints through the dust. There were two sets of footprints—one going in and the other coming out. Shnatz was glad to have the footprints to guide him, because the map he had drawn had proven itself to be worse than useless. Jungor had forced him to draw a map, but Shnatz was a gully dwarf, not a kender. He wasn't much good with anything that had to do with paper or pens or desks or government clerks asking him what his mother's name was. His map had started in the wrong place and led in a big circle right back to it. After the third go-round, he had blown his nose into the map and tossed it aside.

Shnatz's footprints led through the dust of the cramped, broken passage, over piles of ruins and through narrow cracks into other halls and chambers filled with the charred bones of dead dwarves. Stripped of their flesh, one dwarf was as similar and as different as any other—Hylar,

Daewar, Daergar, Theiwar, and Klar. You could not pick up any one skull and say this was the braincase of a noble Hylar lord. It might just as well be the skull of a scheming Daergar assassin, or a blood-mad Klar berserker with his face caked with white clay. Even a gully dwarf's bones might be mistaken for those of a Hylar youth.

Shnatz didn't need to remind his band of twenty gully dwarves not to touch any of the skeletons. There was some power left in these old bones, power to chill the heart and fog the mind with terror. The gully dwarves wanted nothing more than to get beyond them. Finally, they left the scene of slaughter behind and entered a wide paved courtyard surrounded by darkly glaring windows and empty doorways. In the center of the courtyard, a fountain had once sent a stream of clear cold water jetting from the mouth of a cavorting wolf. But now the wolf's head lay in the bottom of the dust-filled basin; its tail and one of its legs were broken off and lost amid the ruin of shattered stone that had fallen from the porticos of the surrounding residences.

Shnatz's footprints crossed the courtyard in a meandering line, like a hound upon a scent. In places, the footprints bunched up and overran themselves. But Shnatz ignored the path now and made his way directly across the courtyard, to the place where the footsteps ended abruptly at a large paving stone completely free of any trace of dust. Fresh stone showed through in chips along its edges, and several lines of footprints led away from and back to it. Shnatz stopped here and pulled a small pry bar from some hidden fold of his second-hand tunic. He inserted it along the edge of the paving stone, and on the third try, the stone tilted. He caught it and slid it to the side before it could fall into the black hole beneath.

He turned to his companions and said in as firm a voice as he could muster, "Wait here. You got it?" They nodded in unison, a sea of bobbing heads that made his stomach roll over.

He stepped to the edge of the hole and dropped in, landing with a thump some twenty feet below and immediately splaying himself out on the stone to keep from sliding down the rather severe slope of the glassy floor. After a few moments to get his bearings, Shnatz slipped down the slope until he found the ladder. It wasn't much of a ladder. He had nailed it together from broken pieces of furniture that he scavenged from the ruins, and he certainly was no carpenter. Neither was he a stonemason, but he had managed to chip a pair of grooves out of the floor beneath the hole to set the ladder's feet in to keep them from slipping on the steep, glass-slick floor. Nevertheless, he was quite proud of his ladder and anxious to show it off, even if only to *puhungs*.

That's when he heard the first one hit the floor with a yelp and a clang of tools. He quickly stepped aside as the gully dwarf went shrieking by, sliding on his back with his pickaxe skittering and sparking behind him. Shnatz didn't even bother to try to catch him. Instead, he hefted the ladder and rushed upslope to try to stop the next one. The cries of the first one died away behind him even as the next one slammed into the ground in front of him. He threw his ladder down and grabbed her before the unfortunate creature could gather any momentum. She clung to his arm in terror, while at the same time instinctively catching her hammer as it streaked by, spitting sparks.

"Wait!" Shnatz hissed even as he saw the next one leaning over the edge of the hole. "Wait for ladder!"

He shook himself free of the gully dwarf he had rescued, after telling her to lie still. She obeyed without question. Feeling around on the floor, Shnatz found the grooves he had carved in the floor. He set the feet of the ladder into the grooves and pulled it up until its top rested just at the edge of the hole. "Come now!" he ordered.

"Is it safe?" one of the gully dwarves asked as he edged onto the ladder's first rung.

"Stupid *puhungs*," Shnatz muttered. "I not know why I bother with you stupid *puhungs*. Is it safe? It safer than jumping, stupid *puhung*."

Once they had safely navigated their descent, Shnatz ordered them to bunch together and hold on to one another. Standing alone, one might slip and fall, bowl into his companions, and send the entire throng sliding to their deaths. But close together, there was less chance that one false step would bring them all down. Plus, Shnatz was leading them and he didn't want to be swept up in the tide of their self-inflicted ruin.

Even so, it was a tricky and dangerous climb down the glass-smooth slope. No dwarf construction, this tunnel had been burned through the solid stone by one of the Chaos dragons that had attacked Thorbardin. After continuing downward for about a hundred feet, the passage made an abrupt right turn and leveled off. Here, they found the first gully dwarf who had dropped through the hole, the point of his pickax lodged firmly between his crossed eyes. Shnatz kicked him to make sure he was dead, then continued onward with a roll of his eyes. The other gully dwarves crept past their dead comrade, snickering nervously, death being one of their most familiar jokes, and the more absurd the death the better they liked it, unless they were the ones doing the dying.

The passage wound back and forth, as though the dragon that had burned it were chasing something that was trying its best to get away. At one point, they came to a place where a large section of the wall and a portion of the floor opened into empty blackness. "Where that go?" one of the gully dwarves asked.

Shnatz looked back over his shoulder and sneered. "Jump in and see."

The gully dwarf peered into the hole for a moment, a crisp, wet breeze weakly fingering the matted hairs of his beard. He turned to Shnatz and said, "You get ladder."

"Come on. We go this way. You follow me, don't fall in."
The nineteen remaining gully dwarves didn't need to be
told twice. They gave the hole a wide berth and hurried
after their leader, who had already ranged far ahead, his
torch winking in the darkness like a far-off star.

Eventually, Shnatz found the place he sought and
ordered them all to a halt. They thankfully dropped their
digging tools and sank to the ground, panting and weeping
of their weariness. "Get up! Get up!" Shnatz growled, kicking them. "We not done yet. We just get here. Now real
work begin." Moaning and snarling, the gully dwarves
crawled to their feet once more.

"We do job. We follow you just like you say. What we
gotta do now?" they complained

"See this floor?" Shnatz asked. In this section of the
tunnel, the slick, glassy floor and walls were covered in a
huge spiderweb of cracks. Some of the cracks were a
handspan or more wide. The gully dwarves examined the
floor for a moment, then nodded. Shnatz continued, "You
start digging here. Break open these cracks wider."

"What we dig for?" one of the gully dwarves asked.

"Treasure," Shnatz whispered, to get their full attention. He glanced around as though making sure no one
might overhear. The gully dwarves gathered near, their
grimy faces eager. "Ancient dwarf treasure of the Great
Hylar, left here when Hybardin abandoned."

"No fooling?" they sighed, all their greediest longings
kindled.

Shnatz winked and poked one of them in the ribs. "You
best diggers of all Aghar. That why I hire you. We all be
rich, rich as kings. But you gotta dig quick, before someone
find us and run us off, take all treasure for themselves."

The gully dwarves growled angrily that anyone would
dare steal their treasure after they had worked so hard to
find it. They set to work with gusto. Shnatz had them
spread out rather than all dig in one place. When asked

why, he said, "Treasure big. You gotta dig big hole!" which doubled their enthusiasm. Picks swung and rock chips flew, and only occasionally did they do each other serious harm. The injured crawled aside to cheer on their fellows, for all were promised an equal share. Shnatz stood well back, a grin slowly spreading across his filthy face.

It wasn't long before one of the gully dwarves shouted for their leader. Shnatz ordered them to stop digging and approached. "You find treasure?" he asked.

"No. But something wrong with this rock," the gully dwarf, named Hong, answered. To demonstrate, he struck the floor with his hammer. A section of the floor as large as a serving platter sank three inches under the blow.

Shnatz leaped back and began to edge away. "You do good work, better than I thought. Treasure almost ours. But you work hard, need break. Everybody take break. I be right back."

"Where you go?" Hong asked.

"I gonna go spit in that hole, see how deep it is. You stay here," Shnatz said, then hurried away.

Hong looked around at his companions and shrugged. Groaning, they sank to the shattered floor, stretched out their short, weary legs and began to discuss how they were going to spend their riches once they were all kings.

In previous years, the Festival of Lights had been Tarn's favorite time of the year. At no other time was his city of Norbardin more beautiful. Being exquisite metalworkers and skilled in the arts of stonecarving, the dwarves delighted in creating the most fantastic lanterns and lamps they could imagine. They made lanterns from the materials they loved most—gold and silver, copper and steel, as well as all kinds of beautiful stone. As he made his way through the city, accompanied only by the captain of his guard, Mog Bonecutter, Tarn delighted in the infinite variety of lights that lined the streets. Whether hung in windows or from lampposts or strung from wires from house to house, the streets of Norbardin glittered with a beauty and a brilliance to rival the stars in the night sky.

Tarn's favorite ornaments were the moon lamps that he saw sitting atop poles at the corners of many of the streets he passed. Carved into a hollow sphere inside which a single candle burned, the red lanterns were carved from red jade and glowed like the red moon Lunitari, the moon of neutrality. Far more popular were the white lanterns, which were carved from milky white crystal to represent Solinari, the silver moon of goodness. Though the moons of magic no longer brightened the night skies of Krynn (they, like the gods, had disappeared at the end of the Chaos War), the dwarves remembered them in their crafts and in their songs. Tarn loved to see the warmly glowing translucent globes hanging above his head once more. They reminded him of a simpler time.

At this time of the day, the celebrations of the festival were just beginning to start. Columns of dwarves paraded through the streets of each quarter of the city—Hylar, Daewar, Daergar, Theiwar, and Klar—playing harps and drums, and bearing lights to honor the dead and decorate the family shrines found in most residential districts. Each family had its own shrine, and the head of the family was its priest, presiding over a day of feasting. The dwarves celebrated their dead rather than mourning them, after the proper mourning period of six years had passed. So the Festival of Lights was a day in which a family might celebrate the lives of their grandfathers through riotous feasting and games, while at the same time wearing shorn beards and black armbands in mourning of someone who had recently passed away. It was not unusual to see a veiled widow kicking a ball in the streets with a gang of laughing children, or a grief-stricken father well into his cups singing songs with other customers at the neighborhood tavern.

Tarn made a point of touring the newer neighborhoods of the Anvil's Echo, though this took him far out of his way. On normal days, the Daergar and Theiwar never even bothered to light the streets of their home quarters; they were gifted with darkvision and had no need of lights. But on the day of the Festival of Lights, these two quarters were perhaps more brilliant than any other in the city. The Daergar made up in cleverness and dark humor for their lack of precious metals and rich stones with which to make their lamps. Instead, they had created an infinite variety of paper and wood constructions, and this material allowed them to achieve more fantastic shapes and a greater variety of colors. On one street, all the lamps were of fish, whales, and mythical beasts of the sea, shining with cool blues and soft greens that made the street look like some weird underwater grotto. Another street seemed to be on fire, with orange and yellow paper lamps shaped like open flames licking from every window and doorway. Such was the nature of the Daergar humor, which re-created the destruction of Chaos as part of their celebration.

In the Theiwar quarter, there were fewer lamps, but these were often magical in nature, burning without fire or heat, and with wildly varied colors. The Theiwar preferred to cast their magics into lamps of purest crystal and to decorate them with illusions, usually grotesque ones. Tarn's favorite was a new one set up before the house of Brecha Quickspring, the Theiwar thane. It was a towering piece of crystal carved to look like the mountain itself. Its light shone from the open North and South Gates, while illusionary dragons flew in slow circles around its snow-capped peak.

Tarn was surprised to see so many new magical lamps in the Theiwar section of the Anvil's Echo. Over the past three or four festivals, new lamps had been scarce, and some had even begun to whisper that the Theiwars' magic was failing. But now, the streets seemed to be filled with glowing lights and weird illusions to delight and terrify. Tarn had a natural distrust of magic, as did most dwarves, but he could appreciate the care that had gone into the Theiwars' decorations this year. Certainly, this proved that their magic had not waned one whit. While pleased, nevertheless he reminded himself that he needed to dig more deeply into this development and find out why.

Tarn's wandering journey through Norbardin was of course accompanied by Mog's constant wheedling. That street was much too dangerous; the people of this neighborhood dislike you; let me summon more guards, you shouldn't travel alone like this; I can't protect you from everything, I only have two eyes. . . . on and on. The Klar captain walked as though upon naked swollen nerves, always jumping at shadows, his hand flying to the axe at his belt at every slam of a door.

Tarn knew his job was to look as though he was comfortable enough to lie down on a bench in the seediest section of the Anvil's Echo and take a nice long nap. That didn't mean he wasn't wary. In the year since the disaster at Qualinost, the good will of the dwarves of Thorbardin had definitely soured toward their king. Not in obvious ways, of course. Few spoke openly against him, but in his public audiences Tarn had begun to detect a distinct undercurrent of disrespect. Nothing he could pin down with certainty, just the occasional sarcastic remark about his "leadership."

But more ominously, the dwarves he met on the streets no longer greeted him in their old familiar ways. They used polite formality to keep their distance from him now. In the weeks after the disaster, people had gone out of their way to greet him, to offer words of encouragement and support, seeking any excuse to shake his hand, or bend his ear. Now, people did little more than pause and bow coolly before continuing about their business. Some merely nodded, though everyone was meticulously polite.

Tarn tried not to let it bother him, but Mog, on top of all his safety concerns, was incensed by the change in public mood. He snarled and grumbled nearly constantly, promising a sound thrashing under his breath to nearly everyone they encountered. Tarn heard every word and feared the day Mog should ever be let loose on the innocent population. That was one reason why he had so thoroughly incorporated the Klar into his administration, assigning them duties at every level. With something positive to do and the honor of the king to protect and uphold, the Klar were less likely to cause themselves and others harm. Naturally, the other clans didn't understand this, and resented Tarn's apparent favoritism.

The Klar quarter was the one place in Norbardin where the people still greeted him warmly, sometimes too warmly. He lost count of how many times he had to free himself from being dragged into a tavern to join them in a round to toast the king's health. The Klar had lost more warriors in the disaster at Qualinost than any other clan, but they had never grown to blame Tarn. But not even among his own people did Mog relax his guard. If anything, he felt freer here to lay about with his fists in order to clear the way when the friendly crowd pressed uncomfortably close to the king.

Having finally cleared the Klar quarter, Tarn and Mog were able to make better time. They left Norbardin behind and followed a wide passage called the First Road to the West Warrens, where the mushroom fields that fed and clothed Norbardin were located. This huge agricultural area was many times larger than Norbardin, made up of a complex of interconnected caverns filled with a soft black loam, atop which their mushrooms grew. Even so, it was still quite a bit smaller than the North, South, and East Warrens, now inaccessible beyond the ruins of the dwarven cities.

The dwarves farmed several dozen varieties of mushrooms, some for food, some for fibers to make cloth, some for their medicinal properties, or for brewing into spirits. The largest variety were among the edible mushrooms, from the small spicy purple lumpkins to the big beefsteak mushrooms that had to be chopped down with an axe and butchered like a hog to separate the edible parts from the fibrous.

The Warrens were largely unpopulated this day. Except for a few retired overseers or independent mushroom farmers who had their residences right here in the mushroom caverns, most of the workers were away celebrating in Norbardin. Guards lingered near cavern intersections, for the Warrens needed constant guarding against raids by gully dwarves and other hungry creatures of the deep places. They saluted perfunctorily as Tarn passed by, most of them already half-sodden on dwarf spirits.

The Sixth Road led out of the south end of the Warrens to a wharf on the shore of the Urkhan Sea. Here, Tarn found a boat awaiting him, a half dozen Hylar rowers already sitting at the oarlocks with their hoods pulled up over their heads against the cold, moist air. Dark water lapped and spattered against the side of the boat and the piles of the dock as Tarn and Mog climbed down and took their places on a bench. Tarn apologized for being late. Someone muttered something unintelligible in response. Tarn placed a warning hand on Mog's arm, urging him back into his seat. The helmsman ordered the lines cast off. Oars rattled in their locks and dipped in smooth unison into the black water of the sea, as the boat turned and shot out over the glass-smooth water.

In the distance, a great bulk of darkness, dotted with lights at its near end, loomed up against the larger darkness of the enormous central cavern of Thorbardin. Few humans or elves had ever set foot inside the mountain, nor were they allowed the privilege of seeing one of the great wonders of Krynn.

The Urkhan Sea was a vast underground freshwater lake, one of the largest known freshwater lakes on the entire continent of Ansalon. Five miles across at its widest point, the lake once served as the primary conduit of transportation between the five dwarven cities of Thorbardin. Now the cities lay in ruins, uninhabited except by a few feral Klar and, of course, uncounted thousands of gully dwarves.

Travel across the sea was a rare event now, but the dwarves of Tarn's boat had not forgotten their skills. The helmsmen softly calling out the strokes, they plied the oars with practiced care, working in unison to pull the boat across the lake as smoothly as a shuttlecock sliding between the two weaves of a loom. The lights on the distant shore grew nearer by the minute.

The Isle of the Dead rose before them, hulking and black, jagged and fearful to behold, for this was the ruins of the fallen Life Tree of the Hylar, the wreck of Hybardin. Already somber and thinking ruefully of his wife and son, Tarn's mood darkened as they drew near. Somewhere on that island, buried under tons of rubble, lay the bones of his first love, Belicia Slateshoulders. Their marriage had been less than a month away when she died. Tarn reflected that, had they been married before the accident that took her life—when she, along with several hundred workers, plunged to their fates when the section of Hybardin they were attempting to restore broke free—his life would be very different today. Dwarves mated for life. If he had lost his wife rather than his betrothed, there wouldn't be a Crystal Heathstone or a Tor Bellowgranite in his life today.

In a way, he was glad they had waited to marry, but he meant no dishonor to her spirit, especially on this hallowed day. In his heart, he knew that Belicia never begrudged him his conflicted feelings. Nevertheless, he sometimes felt ugly inside, as though he had betrayed her somehow.

On the near side of the island, a low spur of land jutted out into the black Urkhan Sea. Down by the water's edge, tiny against the huge bulk of the island, the Hylar dwarves had built a small shrine to honor those doomed to lie in these ruins and thus denied a proper cairn burial. The shrine was carved out of purest white marble. Beside it stood a deep granite basin weighing several tons, resting atop a wide granite base into which was carved the names of those Hylar known to lie at rest on the island. A lesser shrine honored the Daewar who had died in defense of Hybardin during the war. Daergar and Theiwar had perished here as well, buried under tons of rubble during the first collapse, but they had died making war against the rightful rulers of Thorbardin and so received no memorial here.

Dozens of torches set atop tall poles surrounded the shrine and its small courtyard beside the lapping waters of the Urkhan Sea. Drawing nearer, Tarn saw that there were already many boats pulled up along the rocky shore or tied to the wharf. His was the last boat to arrive, and by the looks of it, the dwarves had already begun the Festival of Lights ceremony without him.

Atop the shrine burned hundreds of white and blue lamps, each made of wrought silver paned with sodalite or some other polished translucent mineral. Most were stamped or etched with some form of family crest or seal, symbolizing the ongoing dedication of the deceased's family to their fallen kin. More than any other ceremony on this day of ceremonies, this gathering of the Hylar was dedicated to those who had died in the Chaos War.

As Tarn's boat bumped into the wharf, he heard the deep mournful sound of dwarven voices lifted in song—a dirge for the lost dead. Tarn stood on the wharf while his rowers put away their oars. Mog remained sitting in the boat, a dour look on his face.

"I'm sorry, Mog," Tarn said when the rowers had climbed out of the boat and headed for the ceremony. "They won't allow you to join me on the island. Thane Stonesinger has convinced the others that this island is holy to the Hylar and the Hylar alone. There is nothing I can do to change their minds."

"You are the king. It's not proper for you to be without your bodyguards," Mog grumbled. "But I will follow your wishes."

"I am safe here, if nowhere else," Tarn said. Reluctantly, he turned away. Mog seemed so miserable sitting in the bottom of the boat, alone, the cold, moist air seeping through his clothes and into his bones, fighting an internal battle between his loyalty to the king and his burning desire to beat some Klar sense into the fools that seemed to surround him on all sides.

"I hope this won't take too long," Tarn muttered.

CHAPTER 20

As Tarn reached the edge of the crowd of Hylar dignitaries gathered around the shrine, their song was
just winding down to its long, dolorous ending. Only the
most important Hylar were allowed to be present at this
solemn ceremony, but at least one member of every Hylar
family, no matter how low in rank, were invited. Of all the
bloodlines represented here this day, only Tarn's was not of
pure Hylar lineage. But he was their king, and they opened
a way for him through the throng to the center of the
waterside plaza.

Thane Jungor Stonesinger stood beside the shrine, his
grotesque features twisted into an agony of grief. He
seemed not to even notice Tarn's arrival as he cried out,
"We commemorate this day those who met their end at the
hands of the shadow wights, foul creatures of Chaos,
whose touch not only destroyed flesh and spirit but also
memory. We know that they existed, even though we
cannot remember them, because of the effect they had on
all our lives."

Clutching a beautiful white lamp to his chest and glaring balefully at the heavens with his one eye, Jungor bellowed histrionically, "I live, yet I have no mother. No one

remembers my mother, not even my father, yet we know she lived. We feel her presence in every aspect of our lives. My sisters and I exist because she existed. Yet it is as though she never lived, never bore an honored name, and nowhere on Krynn will you find her tomb. It is to the lost dead of Thorbardin that I dedicate my lamp today."

Finding his place in the ceremony, Tarn stepped up beside the Hylar thane. Atop the shrine lay a tall gilded torch, nearly twice his height and unlit. He picked it up and held its flammable end to Jungor's lamp, lighting it from the lamp's tiny flame. The torch burst to life, its flame warm and yellow compared to the cold white light of Jungor's lamp. He lifted it so that all could see.

"Today we honor all our dead, those who died before Chaos, during Chaos, and after Chaos. Those whose tombs we know and those who lie in nameless tombs in the deep places of the world; those slain in battles far from home, and those who ended their lives surrounded by those who loved them. To all dwarves, to the Kingdom of the Dead, we dedicate these lights of remembrance."

As Tarn concluded his dedication, a death skald approached through the crowd. Dressed in black robes and wearing a death mask over his copper-bearded face, he was a fearful sight. This day, he represented death incarnate, the living representation of mortality, and he bore in his hand a book in which was written the names of those whose bodies lay unburied on the Isle of the Dead. This island was his place; no one knew his name, not even the king. His was a secret role assigned to his family in a time forgotten even by the dwarves—a true priest of the dead. Tarn suspected that the current death skald was none other than the merchant Hextor Ironhaft, but he couldn't be sure. If Jungor knew, he didn't say. In fact, it was forbidden even to ask, or to publicly speculate about the real identity of a death skald, and no one would even dare consider trying to discover his secret.

Stepping up between the king and the Hylar thane, the death skald opened a diptych and began to chant the long litany of names to be found on the pedestal under the granite basin. His voice, harsh and powerful, was nonetheless beautiful in its own way. Half song of mourning and half war cry, it spoke of the eternal grief of the dwarven peoples as well as their will to endure any hardship or loss. When he sang a name, those who had known the dead in life remembered their grief as well as their former happiness.

As he chanted, bearers appeared carrying large urns in harnesses strapped to their shoulders. Dressed like ancient priests of Reorx yet wearing none of his symbols, they approached the granite basin and bowed beside it, allowing the contents of their urns to pour into the wide stone bowl. The heady scent of fine dwarf spirits stung the nostrils of everyone gathered near the shrine.

As Tarn listened to the chanting of the names and the pouring out of libations for the dead, his mind began to drift back to thoughts of home, of his son. He wondered what Tor was doing, and not for the first time, he wished he were back home with the boy. The voice of the skald resonated with his thoughts, and when the name of his father, Baker Whitegranite, was pronounced, Tarn was overcome by a horrible vision—of himself, lighting a candle in memory of his son. Would Tor's name one day be added to the lists of the dead during his father's lifetime? All the nameless fears that had been tormenting him since the birth of his son were suddenly given life and form. He saw the myriad ways that a dwarf child could die abruptly— disease, violence, accident—and he knew, to his everlasting terror, that there was no way he could protect Tor from all of them. For the first time in his life, Tarn longed for a god to which to pray.

As the skald read the last name from his book, the last urn was emptied. A silence fell over the assembly. Shaken from his morose thoughts by the demand of his ceremonial duty, Tarn approached the basin, fluttering torch in hand. This was always a tricky undertaking, involving a certain degree of risk. Pure, unbridled dwarf spirits of the kind brewed in every local tavern were notoriously flammable, one might say explosively flammable. Battles had been won in the ancient past when walls were breached by dwarf spirit bombs being rolled against them and lit with flaming crossbow bolts. The king's spirits, being of a finer grade and brewed with better equipment and ingredients, were not so volatile, but still required careful handling. As was the custom, Tarn had donated from his private stores the urns of dwarf spirits to fill the drinking bowl of the dead. This was the way the king celebrated the Festival of Light, for this granite basin filled with dangerous spirits was his lamp, the only one he was allowed to light.

Standing well back, long torch in hand, Tarn touched the flame to the edge of the bowl. A blue-white column of fire shot up, roaring like a whirlwind, a plume of super-heated glowing smoke rising high into the darkness of the great subterranean chamber. Everyone scurried away from the intense heat. And, as usual, the ends of Tarns eye-brows and beard hairs were scorched and smoking as he turned his face away from the flames.

Shnatz Ong started in surprise. "That signal!" he whispered excitedly.

He sat at the edge of the collapsed section of the tunnel, gazing down into the blackness and carelessly dangling his feet over the ledge. Earlier, he had watched numerous small collections of lights cross the black Urkhan Sea and gather along the shore of the massive dark bulk of the Isle of the Dead, hundreds of feet below him. Now, he saw a jet of blue-white flame rise up from the midst of the lights. He didn't really care what kind of sentimental ceremonies the

Hylar conducted on the Isle of the Dead. Such was not his purpose in spying on them. Jungor had told him to watch for a pillar of blue-white fire, for that was the signal for him to complete his task. Leaping to his feet, he scurried off down the tunnel toward the light of the gully dwarves' torches.

His sudden return startled the lounging gully dwarves from their ruminations, waking the others from their naps. "Hurry, back to work. Dig! Dig!" he shouted.

"What wrong?" the gully dwarf named Hong cried as he clamored for his hammer and chisel.

"Somebody coming!" Shnatz said. "We got to get treasure before they get here."

"That just our luck," Hong muttered and he began to hack and bang at the stone. The other gully dwarves returned to their tasks with renewed fury. Stone chips flew under their pickaxes, and then the floor began to sink visibly, the walls to crack and moan.

"Must be some big treasure chamber!" one of the gully dwarves shouted excitedly as a large section of the floor beside him dropped away. He leaned over and looked into the hole it left behind. "I see twinkles, look like shiny rocks, whole bunches of shiny rocks, way far below!"

"Dig! Dig!" Hong cried. "How much deeper, you think?" That's when he noticed that Shnatz had disappeared again.

But of course, by that time, it was already too late.

CHAPTER

21

Tarn shook the ashes from his hair and stood back to admire the pure elemental ferocity of the fire he'd ignited. The pillar of blue-white flame rose forty or more feet into the air and burned with a steady magnificence that was startling to behold, even for a people much accustomed to the intense flames of the forge fire and the smelting pit. He felt the heat baking the flesh of his face, almost as though he had, for a moment, stood too close to the sun.

Then, as quickly and violently as it began, the flame winked out. A few gossamer whisps of bluish fire were all that remained, dancing like elf spirits along the edges of the smoking granite basin. Even so, the dwarves could still see a great mushroom of smoke rising up and up toward the place where their city once hung. Their prayers, their hopes, their regrets, and their collective grief rose up with that swirling cloud, leaving their hearts lightened and their spirits lifted. Someone began to sing an ode to joy—one of the rarest songs of the dwarven musical catalogue. Tarn felt his own fears and thoughts of death shredded by that rising cloud of smoke. He knew it was nothing more than smoke, yet it left him feeling strangely at peace with his past as well as hopeful for the future. It had been many years, more years than he could remember, since any sort of ceremony, religious or otherwise, had affected him so deeply. It had brought him from his accustomed apathy to the depths of fear and despair in the visions of his dead son, and left him, at last, as though upon a plateau of joy.

He noticed that others felt the same emotion, and he marveled to see dwarves from families long considered enemies standing side by side, their voices lifted in song. He searched the crowd for the death skald, but he had already either disappeared or shed his mask and cloak in order to blend in with the crowd. Shrugging, Tarn added his own voice to the song. He had a good singing voice, and some of the Hylar smiled to hear him use it.

But after only a couple of stanzas, the words died upon Tarn's lips, for the song tapered away as the crowd noticed a gathering commotion near the wharves. Suddenly, a bellow of agony stilled the voices of the last stalwart singers. Everyone turned to look what caused the interruption, including Tarn.

At first, he was relieved to see that Mog had not grown weary of waiting and had decided to join the festivities. But it comforted him little to note that Jungor Stonesinger lay at the center of the disturbance. "What now?" Tarn grumbled as he began to push his way through the crowd.

He found the one-eyed Hylar thane collapsed in the arms of none other than Hextor Ironhaft, the dwarf Tarn suspected of being the death skald. Jungor's body was shaking with paroxyms, foam flecking his bearded lips, and his hands clutching spasmodically skywards. His staff (as preposterous a theatrical prop as Tarn had ever seen) lay on the ground next to him. Hextor clutched the thane to his breast, crying out in despair.

Seeing the Hylar thane flopping about on the ground filled Tarn with disgust. It was obvious even to a blind gully dwarf that Jungor had been taking far too many theatrical liberties of late—his missing eye and acid-scarred face, the wizard staff, his beard and queer robes. But rather than seeing this charade for what it was, it sometimes seemed that the Hylar wished to be fooled by Jungor's theatrics. They preferred a lying charlatan promising all their dreams would come true, rather than a king who only wanted to improve the lives of all his subjects, from the lowest to the highest.

Jungor's performance only grew more exaggerated as Tarn watched. The Hylar thane's guard, Astar Trueshield, arrived on the scene with much bluster, bombastically ordering everyone to stand back and give the thane room to breathe. The gathered dwarves retreated respectfully, fear and concern written upon their faces. Tarn almost laughed, but held his tongue. Hextor and Astar worked over the fallen thane, loosening his robe, fearfully calling his name. Jungor continued to writhe on the ground, bawling like a wounded cave ox, heels drumming the stone.

"What's the matter with him anyway?" Tarn asked, his voice tinged with impatience. The other Hylar glared at him balefully, but he ignored them. He would have liked nothing better than to kick Jungor in the groin and see if that didn't set him right. In his eyes, the Hylar thane was nothing but a fundamentalist fraud, an advocate of an old way of life who was bent on dragging everyone else into the mazes of his delusion.

Soon, the thane's gyrations lessened. His eye assumed a faraway stare as he lay back on the cold stone ground, his closest advisors kneeling worriedly over him. Suddenly, he rose up and shouted, his voice like the blare of a trumpet. "Beware! Beware! The Kingdom of the Dead brings a warning. The dead are not pleased. Danger approaches, danger from above to send a warning and clear the way." Then he fell back, limp as a cloth doll, his good eye closed, empty eye glaring upward.

"What does he say?" Tarn demanded, leaning over Jungor's body. "What's this fool raving about?"

Astar stepped between the king and the thane, his hand resting on the hilt of his sword in warning, the features of his face set as though carved from stone. Tarn stepped back in alarm, but before he could challenge the Hylar captain, Hextor Ironhaft said, "The dead speak through Jungor Stonesigner. Just as the spirit of Vault Forgesmoke obeyed the thane's command in the arena, now the dead bring us a warning of danger. We must flee the island!"

Hearing this, many of the Hylar wasted no time in hurrying toward their boats lined up along the wharf or pulled up on the stony shoreline. Astar and Hextor lifted their thane between them and hustled him toward their own boat, a large craft of sixteen oars moored beside Tarn's boat. They didn't even bother to gather their lamps from the shrine.

Others shared Tarn's skepticism yet remained somewhat apprehensive, not sure whether to flee with the others or defiantly remain where they were. Tarn was of a mind to stand on the shore and shout words of ridicule to those who had fled the island so ignobly.

But then a rock the size of his fist struck the ground before him, shattering explosively and stinging his exposed flesh with tiny razor-sharp shards. Words of derision died upon his lips. Smaller stones began to fall about them like hail. Then a boulder smashed into the shrine, extinguishing the lamps in one concussive explosion. Choking dust boiled around them, casting them into sudden darkness. Tarn's eyes quickly adjusted to the dark, but the other Hylar were hopelessly blinded, while a sudden shower of pebbles pelted them. Screams of pain and terror echoed off the surrounding ruins.

Shouting for them to follow him, Tarn led the remainder to their boats. Luckily, it was only a short dash from the shrine to the water's edge. As Tarn rushed along the wharf toward his own boat, the stonefall slackened somewhat, though to look at the roiling surface of the Urkhan Sea, one would think it were raining inside the mountain. Mog held the boat to the wharf by threat of violence, else Tarn's rowers would have abandoned him already. Most of the boats had already left. He could see them cutting the water with their shining oars, fearful faces glaring back toward the Isle of the Dead.

"There's a light up there," Mog shouted as Tarn drew near. "I saw a light, high above, but just for a moment. I . . ."

That is when a concussive explosion of water flung Tarn onto his back, knocking the air from his lungs. Coughing and gasping, he climbed to his feet as a fine mist of rain began to fall about him. Mixed with the rain were bits of wood, metal fittings; a bronze oar lock clattered to the ground at his feet, then the frayed stump of an oar dropped beside it.

Tarn rushed to the wharf's edge and peered down into the water. His boat, and everyone in it, were gone. He stared in disbelief at the tattered bit of mooring line still tied to the cleat.

A shout from farther down the wharf brought him slowly around. Still stunned, he climbed down into a boat that had returned to retrieve him. He didn't even notice who the others were in the boat. He merely thanked them and sat down in the bow while the boat shot away from the island, stones raining down all around it.

A noise like a crack of thunder echoed through the vast cavern. The noise shook Tarn back to his senses. "Turn the boat around!" he shouted. "We have to go back for Mog."

"Listen!" someone in a nearby boat cried. The rowers paused in their strokes for a moment as everyone bent an ear to hear. Tarn heard it first—a distant chorus of shrieking voices, growing ever louder, somewhere high above.

"What new evil is this?" one of the rowers asked fearfully.

"Never you mind. Keep rowing. Bend your backs to it!" shouted the boat's helmsman.

"No! Turn the boat around! We have to go back," Tarn said as the shrieking quickly grew louder, like a dozen banshees dropping down upon them from the darkness.

"Row on!" the helmsman roared, ignoring the king, and his rowers obeyed him. Tarn's demands fell on ears deafened by terror. The banshee wails seemed almost atop them now. The dwarves in the boat ducked their heads even as they pulled frantically at their oars.

Then, the shrieks ended in a thunderous roar as a huge section of the mountain smashed into the island, utterly obliterating the shrine and the wharf. A concussion of hot air and blinding dust struck the boat broadside, nearly tipping it over. Tarn's fingers dug into the wood of the gunwale as he blinked the dust and stone splinters from his eyes and stared back at the island, desperately seeking any sign of the loyal, brave Mog.

"We must go back and look for him," he said in a voice utterly bereft of hope.

"It's too dangerous, my king," the helmsman said, not without sympathy. The rowers pulled their oars through the water, drawing the boat away from the Isle of the Dead. "He's probably dead by now. Even if he survived the stone that destroyed his boat, nothing could live through that last collapse."

They pulled in grim silence for a while, listening to the sounds of the other boats, the soft calls of the helmsmen counting out the strokes. No one spoke. All were still too numb with horror to appreciate the nearness of their escape.

Then, one of the rowers in Tarn's boat whispered to his benchmate, his voice pitched low so the king would not hear, "Jungor's warning saved our lives. He saved us all." But Tarn heard him, and as he heard the murmur of awe from the other dwarves in his boat, his heart grew cold with doubt. Such thoughts, such suspicions took root in his mind, so horrible that he dared not shine the light of reason upon them.

For Jungor Stonesinger had indeed saved their lives with his warning vision. And wasn't that marvelously fortunate?

CHAPTER

22

Mog had never been more comfortable in all his life. His bed was large enough that his entire family could have slept in it, its wooden frame exquisitely carved with elvish designs (probably an import from Qualinesti), its coverlets of an ancient weave, but sturdy and soft as the day they were made.

Across the oddly-shaped chamber where his bed stood, a merry fire burned beneath a bubbling iron pot, from which the most delicious smells occasionally wafted. Mog found that he had acquired a substantial appetite during his absence, and whatever it was that was cooking in the pot was winning a decisive battle against the delightful languid peace that had heretofore kept him in this bed.

Where had he been, he wondered absently, not really caring if he thought of the answer. Still, it was a pleasant diversion, to sit and think of his mortal life. For naturally, he was dead, and this must be the afterlife. Nothing else could explain it. He was certain that he was dead, because he could distinctly remember dying. His legs crushed, pinned beneath a boulder, he had at last succumbed to his fate after a valiant and vain struggle to free himself. And with only a passing regret for having failed his king, he had then taken his first and only breath of the bitter cold dark waters of the Urkhan Sea.

What a way for a dwarf to die, he remembered thinking.

But at least it didn't bar him from a pleasant afterlife, though he did wonder what had taken him so long to get here. He had the distinct impression that a substantial portion of time had passed since he first drank his death and when he awoke in this bed, only moments ago.

He stretched out his legs beneath the cool sheets, closed his eyes and watched the flames of the fire dance upon the underside of his eyelids. He was so wonderfully hungry, he didn't want to ruin it all by actually eating, not just yet. In the back of his mind, he wondered what heavenly spirit had built the fire and prepared the meal that awaited him. At the same time, he wondered if the afterlife would bring other pleasures as well, ones he had denied himself out of duty and loyalty to his king. Mog was certain that he must have earned a wife in the afterlife, preferably one of celestial origin. No ordinary dwarf woman would do for him. He had had high standards in life, and didn't intend to surrender them now that he was dead. Perhaps it would be better to just lie here until his wife returned, to pretend sleep so that he could observe her at his leisure. And if he fell asleep again while waiting, then so be it. He had nothing else to do, and he was fairly certain that one didn't burn one's dinner in heaven, no matter how lazy one was.

Perhaps he did doze off again. Mog couldn't be sure, nor did he care. His mind seemed to slip effortlessly between waking and dreaming, as though the two worlds were really one. But now he heard the sounds of someone moving about the chamber, stirring the pot, stoking the coals. Wood crackled with flame, and he heard the tinkle of crockery.

He opened his eyes a slit, then shot bolt upright in bed. A grizzled, copper-bearded male dwarf of indeterminate age glanced up from the cookfire and smiled. "Ah, awake at last, Lazy Bones?" he cackled.

Senses fully alert now, Mog took in his surroundings in one brief flashing glance. The "bedchamber," he realized, was really a cavern or cave scraped out of some huge jumble of ruins. One wall was covered in a brightly painted fresco of dwarves laboring at a forge, but the entire thing was upside down and half-buried in the uneven earthen floor. Statuary and broken pieces of columns and other architecture emerged like nightmares from the wall behind his bed. His bed, which he had imagined so luxurious, he now realized to be a creaking wreck, the headboard blackened by some ancient fire, one entire side of it propped up on unstable piles of stone. The cooking fire burned, not in a fireplace, but in an overturned marble privy, and the pot hanging above the flames bore the unmistakable silhouette of a chamber pot.

Perhaps he was not in heaven, but in hell. Still, the food cooking over the fire did smell wonderfully inviting, and he felt alive, his legs whole and strong. He was pretty sure they didn't serve such good-smelling meals in the Abyss.

"Now, I would stay in bed if I were you," the dwarf warned as Mog started to slide out from under the sheets. "You've only just begun to recover."

"Who are you?" Mog asked. "And where is this place?"

The dwarf strode up to the side of the bed and extended a paw-like hand, thick, rugged, and scarred. "Ogduan Bloodspike," he said with a broad, toothy grin that was just a bit more unsettling than friendly; the effect was a little like watching a lion yawn. "As for this place, I'm not sure what they call it nowadays. Used to be part of Hybardin." He waved a hand at the upside-down mural on the far wall.

"The Isle of the Dead?" Mog exclaimed.

"That's it," Ogduan said, snapping his big thorny fingers. He tapped the side of his head. "Memory's not so keen as it used to be."

"Then I'm still alive," the Klar warrior sighed.

"Looks that way, son," the older dwarf murmured.

"But how did I survive? The last thing I remember . . ."

"I pulled you out of the water," Ogduan said.

Mog closed his eyes, trying to remember. "I do recall something tugging at me, and a face . . . a face!" He slapped his knee and pointed at the old dwarf. "I thought you were death come to take me."

Smiling, Ogduan pulled a battered trunk from under the bed and flipped back its lid, revealing a carefully folded black robe, a leather-bound book, and a white skull mask. "Not death, just a death skald," he said.

Mog shrank back from the skald in horror. "But . . . no one is allowed to know the identity of a death skald. Why are you telling me?"

Ogduan shrugged, looking around innocently. "Who are you going to tell?"

Mog stared at the strange dwarf, pondering. "I can't place your name, stranger, and you look like you could be just about any of the five clans," he said. "So what clan are you from?"

"I'm not exactly of any clan," the dwarf said. "I'm a death skald, after all."

"But who are the Bloodspikes? I've never heard the name before."

The old dwarf shrugged as he returned to his place beside the cooking fire. "I'm not surprised," he said, lifting a battered pewter ladle from its hook and dipping it into the pot. He leaned closer, shielding his face from the heat of the fire as he stirred and stirred.

Resting his hands upon the coverlet, Mog waited for what the old dwarf would say next. "So you live here alone?" he finally asked.

"Mostly," came the gruff reply. "I expect you are hungry."

Mog nodded. "How long have I been here anyway?"

The old dwarf shrugged. In the corner beside the fire, an old cabinet leaned upon three legs, one of its doors hanging from one hinge. Ogduan opened it, and removed a pair of pottery bowls. "One day runs into another out here," he said as he carefully ladled each bowl full of steaming stew. He crossed back to the bedside and set one bowl in Mog's lap. He produced a pair of wooden spoons from a pocket of his somewhat tattered garments, then sat down on a low stool beside the bed.

Mog lifted his bowl and inhaled the aroma of the stew. He couldn't remember when he'd ever been so hungry, nor when he'd smelled anything so delicious. "I-I-I thought my legs were crushed by the stone," he managed to starmmer. "They seem fine now, so I must have been mistaken."

"Oh, they were badly crushed alright," Ogduan answered over a mouthful of stew.

"Surely I didn't sleep through the entire healing process," Mog said in surprise. "It would have taken months for me to heal." Ogduan merely shrugged and continued to blithely shovel spoonfuls of stew between his copper-bearded lips.

Mog tasted the stew and found it even more delicious than it smelled. Several different types of meat swam in a hearty thick brown broth. Some bits were so tender they fell apart in the mouth, while others had some bite to them, chewy but pleasant. "If I've been here for months, why didn't anyone come to look for me? Surely you told the people who bring your supplies to let someone in Norbardin know that I was here."

"No one brings me supplies," the old dwarf explained. "No one comes here at all."

Mog paused, the spoon lifted halfway to his lips. "Then where do you get your food?" he asked, somewhat alarmed.

"There's food to be found just about anywhere, if you know where to look," Ogduan answered.

Mog stared in horror at the bowl resting between his legs, at the strange little clumps of meat floating in it. Steeling himself, he asked, "What kind of meat is this, may I ask?"

"Gully dwarf."

Mog felt a solid column of gorge rise to the back of his mouth. A rank belch nearly gagged him. He set the bowl aside, biting back nausea.

Ogduan bellowed with laughter. "By my bones, you must think me truly depraved if you think I'd serve you gully dwarf just when you are beginning to heal."

Mog eyed the old dwarf suspiciously. "Well, what is it, then?" he asked.

"Urkhan eel and feral mushrooms. Didn't anyone ever cook Underdark Stew when you were a boy? By my beard, I shudder to think of the poor quality of practical survival education young dwarves receive these days," Ogduan said, his cheeks stuffed with stew and rich brown gravy dribbling into his beard.

"It's been a long time since I encountered Underdark Stew. I had forgotten," Mog chuckled as he resumed eating. Despite his hunger, he found that his appetite had been severely dampened by the old dwarf's joke. Though he knew well enough that he wasn't eating gully dwarf, a niggling doubt remained in the back of his mind.

"Besides, I finished off the last of the gully dwarf weeks ago," Ogduan added with a wink.

Mog set his bowl down. "I'd better take it easy," he said. "Too much rich food."

The old dwarf nodded in agreement as he continued to wolf down his meal. Between mouthfuls, he said, "Out here in the perimeter there are no markets, just stone and water and darkness and earth. There's the ruins and what you can scrounge for and dig for. When you're starving, you're not above boiling bones. Dwarves these days don't really know what hard times are like."

Mog snorted. "What about the Chaos War?" he asked.

"Chaos War? And how long did that last?" Ogduan replied, pointing at him with a dripping spoon. "It's been forty years now and what have you all learned? It was nigh on to three hundred years of misery after the Cataclysm before things started to improve. Forty years? A mere twinkle in the eye of Reorx! I piss in the milk of your miserable forty years."

"You talk like you've lived forever," Mog said, growing steadily irritated.

"And what if I have! Who are you to question me?" the old dwarf shouted, his own temper rising.

"You're crazy," Mog answered, dismissing him with a wave of his hand. "What are you, feral Klar? Bloodspike sounds like a Klar name."

"Klar? Klar?" Ogduan practically shrieked. "I piss in the milk of the Klar."

"Exile, then. A Hylar exile. Who exiled you?"

"No one exiled me. I was deceived. I was robbed and did not know it! Oh, wicked deceiver, evil temptress!" Ogduan was busy railing to the heavens. Mog sighed, realizing that he'd been rescued by some half-mad untamed Klar who had cast off dwarven civilization. Known as feral Klar, these pitiful creatures preferred to live as the ancient Klar had done, wild and free barbarians of the deep earth. Mog was only lucky that Ogduan hadn't murdered him in some pique of rage, after having bothered to rescue and heal him.

From now on, he'd have to be careful.

His dinner forgotten now, Ogduan raged up and down the room, raining down curses upon the heads of enemies both real and imagined. "Oh, foul vermin that should invade my home!" he screeched, pointing at a dark empty corner of the chamber. "I shall feast upon thy flesh and spit thy bones into my fire!"

Mog watched in growing curiosity as Ogduan crept to his makeshift fireplace and reached behind a pile of broken bits of wooden furniture (fuel for the fire). From some hiding place in the woodpile, he withdrew a gleaming silver warhammer. Hefting the massive weapon, he edged toward the dark empty corner in which he had spied his enemies.

Mog was both surprised and awed by the beauty of the weapon. At the same time, he felt some old memory niggling at his consciousness, a feeling that he had seen this weapon before. Surely so magnificent a weapon had once been the property of a dwarf of great power and influence. To see this mad dwarf stalking the ghosts of his dementia with such a noble weapon filled him with dismay. Flinging back the bedsheets, he tried to stand and grab it away. The floor tilted beneath his bare feet, dumping him back in the bed.

Meanwhile, Ogduan continued to silently stalk his unseen adversary. Lifting the hammer above his head, he brought it thundering down upon the shadows inhabiting the empty corner, bellowing a mighty war cry as he swung.

Mog heard a squeak cut short by a sickening thud. "Ha, that got you!" the insane old dwarf shouted. "What, another?" A small dark form shot out of the corner and scurried toward the bed. Ogduan leapt after the large rat, his giant hammer already streaking down. It smacked the floor just behind the rat, shattering the floorstone into a spiderweb of cracks. He raised it again, staggering toward Mog's bed, under which the rat had fled.

"Ai! Ai!" Mog shouted in alarm. "Do not crush me, fool. It's only a rat!"

"Only a rat?" Ogduan shrieked, the hammer still lifted above his head. "Why, that's our breakfast!"

"Give me the hammer, old one" Mog urged. "Please. Before you do me or yourself a harm." He held out his hands, palms upward, like a supplicant begging favor from a god.

"Aye, you're right, lad," the old dwarf sighed, the light of lucidity momentarily returning to his gray eyes. He pressed the massive weapon into Mog's eager grasp. "A hammer's no weapon to be a-hunting rats from under beds. One needs an ax, or tongs! Aye, that's it! The tongs the thing!"

Ogduan rushed out of the chamber, shouting for his tongs, his tongs, "My kingdom for a tongs!"

Mog gaped in bafflement at the mad dwarf's caperings. Then he turned his attention to the splendid old weapon in his hands. Of marvelous balance, the heavy warhammer was too large for any ordinary dwarf to ever hope to wield. It needed tremendous strength and skill, but ah! what havoc it could wreak in the hands of a skilled warrior. Mog gazed at it lovingly, for this indeed was a weapon worthy of a thane. A king, even. To think it had been so ill used, for hunting rats; it filled his soul with shame.

As he examined the warhammer, Mog noticed a fine etching in the silvered surface of its weighty head. Here were dwarf runes of an ancient style. Mog's formal education had been less than complete. He could read and write well enough to get along, but only common runes. These ancient letters took some time to puzzle out. He mouthed the sounds, fitting them together like a dwarf child in school, until he was certain he'd got it right.

He nearly dropped the weapon in his surprise. "Kharas!" he exclaimed.

Ogduan rushed into the room, a rusted old spear in his hands, and dove under the bed. "Rats!" he swore, rising up in disappointment. "He got away. Did you see him?"

"Where did you get this?" Mog demanded.

"They're everywhere. Lucky for you. What do you think you've been eating for the last week?"

"Not the rats, you old fool!" Mog shrieked. He grabbed the old dwarf by the tattered collar of his shirt. "The

Hammer of Kharas! Where did you get the Hammer of Kharas?"

Ogduan looked at the huge warhammer lying on the bed. "Oh, so that's what it is," he said, a smile bunching up the wrinkles around his eyes. "I found it lying around here somewhere."

"But it wasn't . . . it was with . . . it was lost!" Mog stammered in bewilderment. "How did it even get here?"

"That's a question I'm sure I can't answer," Ogduan said in sudden seriousness. "I'll thank you to let go of my shirt."

Mog released his hold on the old dwarf and sank back on the bed. "The Hammer of Kharas!" he sighed longingly. "Returned, and just when it is most needed by the king. I must get to Norbardin. I have to take it to Tarn."

"Come with me," Ogduan said, holding out one hand in assistance. As Mog slid from beneath the sheets, he felt a momentary dizziness, but the old dwarf's strong hand was sturdy as a rock. He leaned his weight upon him, still too weak in the legs to walk under his own power. Ogduan led him to the mouth of the chamber and outside onto a small landing high up the rubble-strewn slopes of the Isle of the Dead.

"That way lies Norbardin," Ogduan said, pointing north into the blackness. "It is a three mile journey through the icy waters of the Urkhan Sea. Can you swim?"

"No," Mog said hesitantly. "But surely boats must . . ."

Ogduan shook his head. "No one crosses the sea anymore, except to come here, and then only once a year. But I have a feeling even that tradition might finally have come to an end."

"But Tarn needs the Hammer of Kharas. It is the symbol of dwarven rulership. With it, all dwarves will acknowledge him as their king and he can end, once and for all, the challenges to his authority by Jungor Stonesinger," Mog said, the dismayed words spilling out in a rush.

Ogduan nodded his shaggy head. "Aye, he who bears the Hammer wears the Crown," he quoted. "And yet here it is. The gods are indeed capricious."

"The gods!" Mog snorted. "There are no gods."

CHAPTER
23

Orchag Bootheel minced past the watchful eyes of the Hylar merchant, his hands carefully tucked into the voluminous pockets of his tattered, baggy trousers, studiously ignoring the piles of doorknob mushrooms piled upon the merchant's cart. Only when Orchag was well past the cart did the merchant turn his attention to a pair of Hylar goodwives shopping for their family's supper. Orchag looked back over his shoulder at the merchant, a promise of murder flickering in his eyes.

Zen hated the way the other dwarves of Norbardin treated the gully dwarves. He hated having to take the form of a gully dwarf, but it was the only way to safely move about the city. With the other clans, it was too easy to be recognized. The magic that allowed him to take on the outward appearance of anyone he killed did not grant him their memories or insights into their personality. A relative or close friend might quickly identify him as an imposter. In the first month of his "captivity" in and around the environs of Norbardin, Zen had had three close calls while masquerading as various Daergar. Since then, he'd spent the better part of his time as one or another nearly nameless gully dwarf.

The problem was the same here as in any other large city that he had infiltrated during his long mercenary career. He had to kill his victim to take its place, which meant that sooner or later, the victim would be reported missing or its body discovered. And then, if he were spotted, he was sure to be questioned. Which meant he'd have to flee and find a new victim to mimic, sometimes without being able to take the time necessary to properly study and stalk his victim, which often led to mistakes or accidents that forced him to flee again, and find yet another victim.

With so many gully dwarves living in the city, he was relieved of this burden. No one ever reported a gully dwarf missing, for one thing. And if they found a dead gully dwarf, they didn't take the time to find out who he was. Gully dwarves died all the time from an infinite variety of maladies. Like the farmer said when he found a dead rat in his cupboard, "now there's one less rat to eat my cheese."

Also, to other dwarves, gully dwarves looked as alike as grains of corn. They simply didn't take the time to study them well enough to discern an imposter among them. The gully dwarves were the soft underbelly of the dwarven kingdom of Thorbardin. But Zen was not surprised that no one had ever tried to exploit this weakness. It was a singularly useless weakness, for the gully dwarves were a singularly useless race. One could not recruit spies among them, for they could not relay even the simplest of information. One could not bribe their leaders to fight on your side because they could not follow even the simplest orders. They were inherently cowardly, shy, and devious, utterly untrustworthy even as bribed allies. They had no cultural identity that could be exploited to motivate them, no enemies they hated enough to attack. In a word, useless.

Zen found no pleasure in killing them whenever he needed to assume a new form. It was like killing a cat—a hideous, ugly, noisy affair, that was best gotten over quickly. He even pitied the species a little, which did not ease his conscience whenever he was forced to murder them. He justified the murder by telling himself that he was putting the creature out of its misery. The saddest thing of all was that he was right—a gully dwarf probably was better off dead.

Zen had come to know the gully dwarf point of view all too well. He had felt the hatred and anger directed toward them because he had lived as them, walked among them, and shared their miseries. The other dwarf clans treated the gully dwarves little better than rats. They wouldn't go out of their way to kill a gully dwarf, but neither did they consider it a serious crime to kill one, either by accident or design. The only thing that kept the gully dwarves moderately safe among their larger, stronger, and smarter kin were Tarn's strict laws, coupled with the fact that there was so little point in killing a gully dwarf, no one bothered.

Exploring the city in the guise of a gully dwarf, then, Zen was forced to endure the injustices heaped upon all gully dwarves whenever in the company of their cousins. He couldn't buy food at a merchant stall, nor beer at a tavern, not even if he had the money, for no one would serve him. What he ate he begged or stole. He was allowed on some streets, but not all streets, and some buildings were strictly off limits. He dared not retaliate against those who slighted him, lest he be captured and his true identity revealed.

The sewers, on the other hand, were free to use as he wished. Combined with a vast network of dark alleys and cramped staircases, he was able to move pretty much anywhere within the city's three levels, but it had taken well over a year for him to learn them well enough to not get repeatedly lost. Once, he'd been hopelessly lost for three long days in the maze of sewers beneath the Anvil's Echo. Changing identities left one with a ravenous hunger, and he'd been forced to eat his victim to keep from starving. He still hadn't recovered from the taste of raw gully dwarf.

Zen/Orchag turned into an empty alley and quickened his stride. He knew this alley well, knew that no windows looked down upon it, and so he felt confident in shaking off the mincing, crouching posture of a gully dwarf and he deliberately loosed his stride. Slick with offal and rotting garbage, most dwarves avoided the alley. Yet it was the swiftest path to the edge of the Hylar residential area on the second level of Norbardin.

He was in a hurry. Jungor Stonesinger was holding audience from his rooftop, as he did most days at this time, and Zen was already late. He tried to come each day, not to hear Jungor preach, but because he was stalking his next victim. The same victim he'd been stalking for the past eighteen months, the dwarf who had betrayed him and murdered his lads that evening in The Bog.

They had made a deal. Ferro Dunskull had broken it.

Ferro was the most difficult mark that Zen had ever had the pleasure to stalk. The Daergar master of scouts (a euphemism for master of assassins) was wily and intelligent; an accomplished assassin himself, Ferro knew how to avoid assassination. And Ferro knew that Zen was stalking him, so he took extra care. He continually altered his habits, never traveled by the same road twice; there were numerous entrances to his house, all of them well guarded. Ferro had few discernible patterns to his life. He was surrounded by a tiny cabal of close confidants, and all others were kept at a safe distance. He and Zen had been playing a game of cat and mouse for eighteen months now with neither having made significant progress.

For his part, Ferro had been stalking Zen as well, but his early efforts were unorganized and crude. Ferro's agents had beaten the bushes, so to speak, many a time and always came away either empty handed or clutching the red herrings Zen had left in their path. In all likelihood, more innocent gully dwarves had died by Ferro's hand than by Zen's. But of late, the agent's methods had improved somewhat. Zen was forced to take greater precautions, to change forms more often, and to avoid other gully dwarves whenever he could. He had had to stop watching Ferro's house entirely; the guards were becoming too wary, questioning anyone who strayed near.

So Zen had switched tactics. He knew that every mark had a weakness. He had only to find it. It had taken him eighteen months, but he had found it at last.

The alley emerged in the Hylar quarter of the second level, between an armory and a warehouse belonging to Jungor Stonesinger. Zen found this entrance much to his liking, because there was always some activity around the warehouse—wagons arriving laden with crates and leaving empty, warriors drilling in the commons between the warehouse and Jungor's residence. A small crowd of dwarves was usually to be found outside the gates to Jungor's house as well—supplicants and worshippers in his rising cult of personality, as well as the curious and the skeptical. Once a day, Jungor appeared behind the rooftop battlements of his house to address the ever-growing crowds, to give them moral instruction. Dwarves brought their children to hear him speak of the glory of former days, for in his words those glorious times seemed reborn in the hearts of those who heard him.

As Zen left the alley, he once more assumed the crouching, obsequious mannerisms of a gully dwarf amid his larger and stronger cousins. Few gave him a second glance, and those who did quickly turned their noses away. A mixture of fresh dung and rotting meat, kept in his pockets and smeared on his clothes, was enough to convince most of his authenticity and send them lurching away, pinching their noses. A sizable crowd stood at the far side of the commons, gazing upward and listening in rapt awe to Jungor's speech. Zen was glad he hadn't arrived too late, but this was another of his precautions—a gully dwarf loitering about, waiting to hear Jungor speak, was sure to arouse suspicions. Especially if one were on the lookout for suspicious-looking gully dwarves.

Now Zen was able to sidle up to the rear of the crowd and surreptitiously observe his mark.

"But how long shall the clans be forced to remain here in this second-rate city?" Jungor asked. "Norbardin? That is too grand a name for the North Gate complex. For three thousand years it has been the North Gate. Why should the king wish to change that as well? Haven't we borne enough change? Haven't we suffered enough already?"

Zen barely even paid attention to Jungor's cries. Instead, he scanned the faces of those surrounding the Hylar thane, his inner circle of advisors and close confidants—captain of the guard Astar Trueshield, replete in silver armor and beard of spun gold; Hextor Ironhaft, fat and greasy eyed with money stains on his fingers; Thane Rughar Delvestone ever worshipful; Thane Brecha Quickspring, unofficial high priestess of Jungor's unofficial cult; and Ferro Dunskull, Jungor's master of scouts. There were also guards, and select citizens invited to join Jungor on the rooftop because of their wealth or familial connections. But Zen ignored everyone, focusing his attention solely upon Ferro Dunskull. He barely even heard Jungor's continued exhortations.

"When was the last time the king sent engineers and survey parties into our former cities? Too dangerous, he tells us. Dangerous for him, perhaps. Dangerous that we should resume our former lives in our former homes and thus move away from these cramped domains, away from his ability to control every aspect of our lives. We are not disloyal dwarves. We only wish to live free, as once we did. So I ask you again, how long has it been since the ruins were surveyed? How do we know that it is not now safe for you to return and begin rebuilding your lives?"

Zen smiled inwardly to see the dwarves around him nod emphatically, as though Jungor were but speaking aloud the secret desires of their hearts. "Yes, yes, what he says is true." Zen could have answered Jungor's question in two words, for he had been forced to retreat to those ruins many a time in these past eighteen months.

Death trap. That's what awaited anyone attempting to return to the ruins of Theibardin, Daerbardin, Daebardin or Klarbardin. Walls continually crumbled, floors collapsed without warning. He could not begin to count the number of gully dwarves and feral Klar he had seen buried alive over the past month alone. Whole sections of the cities were nothing more than jumbled mountains of ruin, their streets buried under tons of rubble and still endlessly collapsing down bottomless holes.

"You dwarves of the Theiwar, Daewar, Daergar, and Klar clans have homes you can return to," Jungor declared. "Only our home, Hybardin, is completely lost to us. The rest of you can rebuild. We must build anew. But build we shall, one day. One day you shall return to the homes of your grandfathers, and there you will find the mortar to fill that empty place in your hearts. We want to be dwarves again, dwarves of the mountain. Here, in Tarn's city, we live little better than hill dwarves, a people the king loves despite their history of treachery. I fear that one day we shall hear the tramp of hill dwarf boots in our streets."

"No! Never!" the crowd shouted, driven to a frenzy by the Hylar thane's meandering diatribe. The speech lasted for nearly an hour, but Zen had already slipped back to the alley before Jungor dismissed the crowds with a benediction that left them weak and warm. Zen marveled at the one-eyed dwarf's skill. The effect was complete—from the eyepatch to the tattered robes to the wizard staff, Jungor looked part prophet, part shaman, part ghost. Zen could appreciate Jungor's masterful manipulation of the crowd. Jungor would have made a good Dragon Highlord, Zen reckoned.

"He'll certainly be king someday, unless Tarn wises up," the draconian in gully dwarf disguise muttered under his breath. Zen knew that he was in a unique position to decide the fate of this miserable mountain and its miserable people. He held information that would ruin Jungor if revealed and assure Tarn's seat forever. But he wasn't particularly inclined to favor Tarn, either. In fact, he didn't care one way or the other who was king of all these filthy dwarves. All he wanted to do was to make Ferro Dunskull pay for his treachery. After that, he might see who was most willing to buy his information or his silence. He hadn't really planned that far ahead.

There was enough to occupy his mind in the present. He crouched in the shadows, watching the crowd break up. Opposite him across the commons, another alley passed between the home of Hextor Ironhaft and the east wall of Jungor's estate. This alley was much wider than the one in which Zen hid, and no one used it for their middens. Doors opened into it from both sides, and windows on the upper levels overlooked it. Six alert Daergar guards stood at the alley's entrance, crossbows held at the ready while they warily scrutinized anyone who wandered near. Zen dared not approach them, for he knew by their familiar faces and their livery that they were Ferro's personal guard. They had orders to shoot on sight any gully dwarf who came within thirty yards.

As Zen expected, Ferro emerged from a door letting into the alley from Jungor's estate. It would be indecorous for a Daergar to be seen exiting through the front door of the Hylar thane's house. Ferro was accompanied by a thin Daergar female wearing black leather breeches and a hardened leather breastplate. Her arms were bare, smooth and milky white, her black hair long and bound in a single loose braid that hung down the center of her back.

Ferro and the female Daergar consulted for a moment in the alley, then parted, Ferro heading toward his guards, the female strolling in the opposite direction, her hips lolling languidly from side to side. Her name, Zen knew, was Marith Darkforge, and she was one of Ferro's closest "advisors."

Zen pushed aside a pile of garbage and lifted a small iron grate from an opening into the sewer. As swiftly as any gully dwarf, he vanished down the hole, pulling the grate back into place above him. He landed with a splash inside a low, round sewer tunnel, quickly glanced both ways to make sure no other gully dwarves were around, then started off.

The sewer tunnel ran directly beneath the commons to the alley beside Jungor's estate, which it followed for some distance before splitting off into a larger sewer. Zen passed the place beneath which Ferro had stood only moments before, then continued down the sewer tunnel, where he followed the larger branch until it reached a wide collection pool. Here, the water and raw sewage surged and spumed down a drain to an even larger pipe some distance below. Pale brown rafts of foam raced each other in circles round and round the chamber. The sewage lay just below the level of a narrow access walk that led from the entrance pipe to a ladder cut into the stone wall and leading up. Zen crossed over and swiftly ascended the ladder, pushed aside a grate, and emerged in a carter's yard in the midst of a milling herd of yellow cave oxen. The sleepy beasts hardly even noticed his appearance, while their enormous bodies hid him from the sight of anyone who might happen by. He was lucky that none of oxen had been standing on the grate, and that the muckboy wasn't at this moment hosing down the stableyard.

Replacing the grate, Zen crawled between the legs of the cattle until he reached a low wall. He crouched behind it on his knees for a few moments, softly counting under his breath, "One-fifty one, one-fifty-two, one-fifty-three. When he reached one-sixty, he stood just in time to see Marith

Darkforge disappear around the corner of the building directly in front of him.

He leaped over the wall in one bound, crossed the crooked street crowded with laden wagons, and quickly ascended a narrow staircase cut into the side of the building. At the top of the staircase he found a small servant's door propped open by a lump of coal the size of a child's fist. He ducked through the door and entered a long, dark hall, removing the coal as he passed so that the door closed firmly behind him, its latch locking into place with a loud click. Pausing, he heard footsteps ascending a nearby staircase. He shrunk into a dark corner beside a closed door, ducked his head between his shoulders and began to make small retching noises.

As the footsteps reached the top of the stairs, they paused. He heard a sharp intake of breath, then a relaxed exhale. "Stinking gully dwarf," a female voice muttered as the footsteps continued, entering the hall and approaching him. "Is this what I pay good rent money to come home to?" Zen kept his head lowered, even as he felt a sharp kick to his shins.

"Gods! What a smell," she exclaimed. Zen rocked forward, clutching his bruised shins and mewling pitifully. This gave him the opportunity to shift his weight onto the balls of his feet. Another kick landed on his jaw, snapping his head back. "Get out of here, you filthy, stinking rat. How did you get in here?"

Zen heaved with dry retches, spittle flowing into the matted hairs of his beard. "Mercy," he moaned. "Me sick."

"Well get sick somewhere else," Marith yelled as she opened the door to her apartment. Zen heard the groan of the heavy door on its hinge and reacted immediately.

The swiftness of his attack caught Marith Darkforge by surprise. She had just turned to enter her apartment when Zen bowled into the backs of her legs, throwing her face first into the carpet. In an instant, she had rolled to her feet, two long, wickedly curved daggers in her fists.

Still in gully dwarf form, Zen closed the door and put his back to it. Marith gazed at him, her dark eyes sparkling with hate. "Why you miserable little gully dwarf!" she snarled. "What can you possibly hope to . . ."

Her sneering bravura died as she watched the gully dwarf swiftly transform into the gleaming, silver-gray body of a sivak draconian nearly seven feet tall. Zen towered over her, each of his fists nearly as large as her whole head, the muscles of his thighs thicker than her entire body.

His clawed feet dug into the black carpet covering the floor as he readied himself for her attack. He knew Marith Darkforge. He had studied her for weeks, had followed her through every routine of her life. He had watched her eat, watched her go about her daily duties, watched her train; he had followed her while she worked the gully dwarf warrens searching for him. He knew her reputation, her preference for two daggers, the way she always led with high right-handed feint while the left hand drove in low to the groin. She liked to spill the bowels of those she killed. Her martial skills were excellent if predictable. Surely she was one of the better opponents Zen had faced in his long and violent career; plus, he was weaponless and wore no armor, which meant this would be an interesting encounter.

She recognized her advantage, but she had not yet gotten over the shock of the draconian's sudden appearance. She had been hunting for this very one for the better part of a year. "You!" Marith hissed in surprise.

Zen smiled, parting his reptilian jaws to reveal long rows of back-curved fangs. This was one of the most alluring dwarf women he had seen in his eighteen months here. Adult female dwarves were mostly stocky and stout as though built out of bricks with too much mortar by a careless mason, neither handsome, nor ugly nor particularly well made. Utterly unremarkable. Human males lusted after female elves, but no one lusted after dwarf women. Not even dwarf men.

This one was different. There was something positively coltish about her legs. Her smooth, bare arms were muscular without being overwrought. Her black hair gleamed like the feather of a raven. Her chest, encased in its hardened busty torso of leather armor, heaved with excitement.

"My master has been searching for you," she said. Her lips, a moist dusky rose, parted in a nervous smile. "He urgently needs to talk to you."

Her right hand flicked up and forward, the blade winking in the dim light of the room. Zen ignored the feint and struck down with all his force, snapping the bones of her left wrist as she sought his belly with her blade. Her dagger clattered to the floor as Marith sank to one knee. Biting back her agony, she lashed out with her remaining weapon at the draconian's exposed knee. But her blow went astray as his claws sank into the back of her neck. He lifted her bodily from the floor, legs kicking, no longer silent, shrieking in agony and panic, dangling like a doll from his fist. Her small, wiry frame felt like a toy in his hands. He flung her across the small apartment, headfirst into the stone wall. She struck with a dull thud and slid between her bed and the wall, her screams cut short. She lay folded behind the bed, stunned and moaning.

Zen jerked the bed away from her, and she fell forward. She lifted one arm as though to ward off his next blow, but her hand hung limp and at an impossible angle from the jagged bones of her wrist. Blood tricked down her forearm to her elbow. He caught her around the throat and lifted her into the air again. Still dazed, she clawed weakly at the hard fingers tightening around her windpipe. Holding her aloft by the throat, he bent over and righted the bed, then flung her down on it. He stood over her a moment, admiring the awkward beauty of her limbs, even the shattered one with its bones sticking out of her flesh.

Glancing around the chamber, Zen spotted a bottle of dark brandy standing on a bookshelf. He jerked the cork loose with his teeth, poured half its contents down his own throat, then knelt beside her on the creaking bed. He pried open her jaws and slopped some of the brandy into her mouth. She gagged, coughed, then swallowed. Revived somewhat by the fiery Daergar brew, she glared up at her captor, all the pain and shame distilled to boiling hate in her dark eyes.

"Why don't you kill me?" she asked.

"In time," Zen said, his voice as cold as a wind off the Urkhan Sea. "But first, we shall have a talk. Look at your beautiful broken wrist, how delicately it hangs from the last tattered strands of your flesh. Your wrist and I will have a conversation. I shall ask it questions, and it will answer. If it doesn't answer, you must answer for it. Do you understand?"

With a snarl, she tried to rise, her lank legs kicking wildly. Frowning, he pressed her back into the bed and then gave her wrist a tweak that instantly stilled her protests. "That was not the correct answer," Zen said. "I shall ask it again."

"Brandy!" Marith gasped. A dribble of blood trickled down her chin; she had bitten through her lip. Zen obliged, pouring a gout of dark brandy into her open mouth, then emptied the remainder into his own. The empty bottle thumped on the floor.

"More," Marith said. "I need more. There's another bottle . . ." Zen retrieved it from the bookshelf, pulled the cork, and held the bottle to her bloodied lips. She drank its contents greedily, her throat rising and falling with each swallow, then flopped back on the bed, sated and exhausted.

"Now," Zen said, setting aside the half-empty bottle, "let us talk about you. Let us talk about Ferro Dunskull. But most of all, let us talk about you *and* Ferro Dunskull."

"You're going to kill him, aren't you?" she asked, writhing on the bed. The blood from her wrist soaked the sheet. Zen watched in undisguised admiration. This sweet morsel would wash the last vestiges of gully dwarf from his mouth.

"I am going to kill him, with your help," the sivak draconian corrected.

"I wish I could be there to see you spill his rotten guts," she moaned.

"You will be, my dear," Zen said, reaching for the bottle of brandy. He took a long pull, then wiped his reptilian mouth with a bloody corner of the bed sheet. "You will be."

CHAPTER 24

Tarn sat up in bed, hearing the last echoes of a cry. "Tor?" he wondered aloud. "Crystal, did you hear . . ." But Crystal was not beside him on her side of the bed. Maybe she was with the baby. He swung his legs out from the covers and stood, feeling the cold stone floor beneath this feet.

"Where's the carpet?"

"Where are my slippers?"

Tarn glared around the room, all his senses suddenly alert. He reached for the dagger beneath his pillow, but it, too, was not there. And this wasn't his pillow. It wasn't even his bed! And this wasn't his bedchamber either.

Or was it? It looked vaguely familiar, like something out of a dream. It was his bedchamber after all, for there in the corner hung a suit of chain mail that he had worn when he was a young lad of only twenty years. His old battle axe hung on the wall by the door, too. But the door was on the wrong side of the room, as was his bed. The bed was too small.

It suddenly dawned on him that he was in his old room, the bedchamber of his childhood, in his mother's house in Daerbardin. But that was impossible. His mother's house was a heap of slag and ruin, destroyed by the Chaos dragon. Yet everything here was exactly as he remembered it. He walked to the door and opened it, half expecting to see the old familiar servants bustling about their morning duties, or his mother come to scold him for sleeping late again.

Instead, the hall was empty. But not silent. He heard someone hammering, somewhere deep within the house. Somewhere else, he heard a childish voice humming a wordless song, a busy song without meaning or end, just a series of notes repeated to no purpose. Da da dee da dum da dee, la dum la dee, da lee da dum.

The hammering matched the rhythm of the song, as though the same person were producing both sounds. But the singing came from somewhere to the right, while the hammering was somewhere to the left. Tarn chose the singing. It sounded strangely familiar.

The hall outside his bedroom was barren and dusty, as though no one had ever lived here. Its clean rectangular lines stretched into infinity before him, but doors lined the hall to right and left. He stopped at each door to listen, then moved on, for the singing always seemed to be just ahead of him somehow. He wondered if it would lead him forever to nowhere.

But finally, he found the source. He opened the door to his old nursery. It was as barren as the hall, but in the middle of the square chamber sat a boy with his back to the door, dressed in pajamas, leaning over something with his long golden hair hanging down over his face, and humming the tuneless song. As Tarn entered, the boy stopped singing and looked over his shoulder. He looked familiar, like someone he had once seen in a crowd.

"Who are you?" Tarn asked him.

"Who are you?" the boy parroted.

"What are you doing here?"

"What are you doing here?"

"I'm looking for you," Tarn said.

The boy smiled a familiar smile, a familiar twinkle in his gray eyes. He turned away. "There is a crack in the floor here," the boy said.

"Really? Let me see." Tarn was interested in spite of himself. He approached and knelt beside the boy. Between his small, knobby knees was a small, black crack in the stone of the floor. The boy put his fingers over it and it began to whistle. As he moved his fingers, the whistling became the tuneless song. Da da dee da dum da dee, la dum la dee, da lee da dum.

"That's very good," Tarn laughed. "Where did you learn to do that?" The boy shrugged. Tarn placed his hand over the crack and felt a stiff, hot wind rising from it. In the deep earth, a hot wind is a sign of trouble. Cold wind you can expect. Hot wind means fire.

"We had better get out of here," Tarn said urgently. He stood and took the boy's hand. Together, they left the nursery and started back the way Tarn had come. The sound of hammering grew nearer, the closer they got to Tarn's old bedroom. It sounded like someone carving stone, like a hammer tapping a chisel. He had left his bedroom door open, and as he neared the door, it sounded like the hammerer was inside his room. He approached the door cautiously, keeping the boy well behind him, in case it was dangerous.

As he peered into the room, he saw that it wasn't his bedroom at all. It was the nursery again, and in the center of the nursery an old, red-bearded dwarf was busy widening the crack. The hot air rose up around him, blowing his beard into his eyes so that every few moments he stopped to brush it back down. But it was a pointless gesture, for as soon as he bent to his work again, the wind blew his beard up into his eyes again.

During one of his pauses, the old dwarf spotted Tarn standing at the door. "Ah, there you are, my lord. There is something wrong here. I have to get to the bottom of it."

"You fool! Who told you dig up this floor. Don't you feel that hot air coming?"

The old dwarf nodded as he removed a bright red handkerchief from the pocket of his coveralls and mopped his sweaty brow. "There's something wrong here, and I have to get to the bottom of it."

"Stop digging, I say. Wait . . ." Tarn turned and saw that the boy had slipped away. "Wait. Let me see where that boy went to. Don't widen that hole any more until I get back!" Tarn ordered.

The worker tucked his handkerchief into his pocket and said as Tarn hurried away, "There's something wrong here, and I have to get to the bottom of it."

Tarn moaned as he heard the tap-tap-taptap of the hammer resume behind him. There was nothing for it, however. He had to find the boy first. He couldn't let Tor get lost here.

He stopped. Tor? Was that his son, Tor? He hurried on, his panic growing. He began to call his name, "Tor! Tor! Answer me. Don't hide from me, boy. Tell me where you are!" But there was no sound, nothing, not even the sound of hammering this time. He hurried down the dark, empty, echoing hall, his footsteps stirring the dust but leaving no footprints. He stopped to open every door, but found all the rooms empty, barren, silent.

Ahead, he saw an open door, and he knew as he approached it, that it was the nursery again. He felt a cold dread come over him, but forced himself to the door. Inside, the worker was gone but the crack remained. It was wide enough for a child to fall into. His throat constricted in terror. What would he see lying at its bottom? His dead son? He forced his feet to keep moving, and when he was beside the crack, bent his quivering neck.

A long sigh escaped his lips. The hole was empty, and only a few feet deep. But a hot wind blew up in his face, tinged with the smell of sulfur. "Tor!" Tarn cried, turning on his heel and heading for the door again.

A tinkle of laughter brought him short. He heard it again, mocking, snickering, like a child pleased to have fooled his father. Tarn looked over his shoulder and saw there was a window in the wall opposite the door. He remembered that his nursery had had just such a window. Why hadn't he noticed it until now?

"Tor?" Tarn cried.

A titter of laughter answered him, and a small, golden-haired head passed beneath the window on the outside.

Tarn rushed to the window. Outside lay the streets of Daerbardin, thronging with Daergar dressed for battle. At the far end of the street was some commotion. Tarn saw halberds waving, the glint of steel. A banner, black with a golden ring upon it, wavered and fell.

The Daergar began to retreat. Retreat turned to panic, and then to rout. Dwarves flew wildly down the street, casting aside their weapons, horror etched into their faces. And behind them marched a mob of shadows, an army of fear. Tarn knew them. He'd fought them in the Chaos War forty years ago and in his nightmares ever since. They were shadow wights, beings of pure chaos whose touch ruptured the bonds of life and flesh and memory, obliterating not only the life but all memory of that life from those who knew it.

And then Tarn saw Tor, giggling and looking over his shoulder, dart from behind a pillar and rush into the street. The mob of terrified Daergar swept over him and the shadow wights descended upon his tiny broken body. Tarn screamed and threw himself against the window.

The floor beneath his feet lifted, then dropped away. The crack opened into a gaping black maw. At its bottom lay a swirling pool of fire. Tarn clutched the window ledge, his legs dangling over the pit, bellowing Tor's name so that he would not forget, so he would never ever forget.

CHAPTER

25

Tarn sat up in bed, hearing the last echoes of a cry. "Tor?" he wondered aloud.

Crystal grabbed his shoulder. "What was that?" she asked, her voice tight with fear. "Did we just have a groundquake?"

Without answering, Tarn leaped from the bed and threw back the door. Light spilled into the bedroom from the antechamber beyond. Mog's replacement, a young captain named Ghash Grisbane, stood in the doorway, his face wild with excitement. "My king, there's been a groundquake!" Ignoring him, Tarn thrust past, running naked out into the hall.

The servants were all awake and stumbling out of doors, half dressed, fuzzy-headed from bed. Tarn raced past them, his beard flying, naked feet slapping the floor. Around the corner, startled faces flashing by in his vision, he slid to a stop at the nursery door, his feet squeaking across the slick marble floor.

Aunt Needlebone awaited him, blocking the doorway with her body. "He's fine," she whispered. "He slept through the whole thing."

"Let me see him," Tarn demanded in a low voice.

"You'll wake him up, and then who will have to rock him back to sleep?" Auntie said. "Let him sleep."

Crystal trotted to a stop behind Tarn. Her long, auburn tresses hung almost to her waist, framing her face in molten bronze. She had thrown a robe around her shoulders, and carried one for Tarn. "Put this on," she scolded her husband.

That is when Auntie noticed Tarn was naked, turning her face away with a shriek. "Reorx's bones! I didn't need to see that!" she exclaimed. "Mountain dwarves have no shame."

Tarn thrust his arms through the sleeves of the robe and tied its belt in a quick knot around his waist, all while peering into the darkened nursery. His darkvision only slowly adjusted, hampered by the lights in the hall. Everything seemed to be fine, though, just as Aunt Needlebone had said. Tor slept soundly on his belly with his little bottom hiked up in the air and fists tucked at his sides. His toys, ranged along shelves on the wall, were only slightly disordered; one or two had fallen harmlessly to the floor.

Then, with a sharp intake of breath, Tarn shoved past Tor's nanny and entered anyway. Crystal angrily whispered after him, "Don't you wake him, Tarn Bellowgranite!" swiftly echoed by Aunt Needlebone, who was busy collecting her bruised dignity.

Tarn ran his hands along the wall behind Tor's crib until he felt what his eyes had seen—a small dark crack. He followed it to the floor, where it widened to a finger's width beneath the crib. "What's the matter?" Crystal whispered from the doorway. Like the Hylar and Daewar, their closest cousins, the hill dwarves did not have the gift of darkvision and could not see the danger. Tarn appeared suddenly before them, the sleeping baby in his arms.

"Now wait just a damned minute," Aunt Needlebone protested.

"Where are you going?" Crystal asked.

"I'm taking Tor to our bed," Tarn said, elbowing his way past them. "There's a crack in the wall and floor."

Alarmed, Aunt Needlebone stepped across the hall and snatched a candle from its wall sconce. She entered the nursery with Crystal at her heels. Together, they examined the crack. It seemed harmless enough, a weakness of the masonry, nothing that couldn't be repaired with a slap of mortar. Aunt Needlebone shrugged. "He's a mountain dwarf. Maybe those weird eyes of his saw something we cannot."

Crystal sat back on her heels and ran a hand wearily though her hair, pushing a loose strand out of her face. "Auntie," she said in a soft voice. "I don't know what's come over him of late. Ever since that accident during the Festival of Lights, when Mog was killed, he hasn't been the same. He's afraid of shadows, and all he seems to want to do is be with Tor."

"He's a new father, my dear," Auntie said in soothing tones, patting her on the shoulder.

"No, it's more than that. I can't put my finger on it. I don't know what to think anymore," Crystal sighed.

"You listen to old Galena, now, like you used to do," Auntie Needlebone said. "You know Tarn, but there is something about him that you have to realize. You know it in your heart, but you never really considered it. He's lost everything he's ever loved—his mother and his father, his first betrothed, his good friend Thane Bloodeye, all his fine young army that you and he trained, and most recently, his right arm, Mog Bonecutter. Why, those two were inseparable even before we came to the mountain."

"I know all that," Crystal said sullenly.

"So what's he looking at now? He's got you, Tor, and this place. Every day, that insufferable one-eyed prig steals just a little more of this city from him, turns the hearts of a few more of his subjects away from him. The dwarves he sacrificed everything to save now look at him with suspicion."

"Not all of them. Not even half of them. It's just that the few who hate him seem to be the only ones talking," Crystal said.

"And then there's the two of you. He knows you can take care of yourself, lass. You are better than he is with the spear and staff, if truth be told, and you can command in battle nearly as well as he. But how did that Belicia Slateshoulders die? Restoring Hybardin, that's how. They weren't married, yet she was actively involved in rebuilding the kingdom. Are you?"

"I do my part," Crystal said defensively.

"Were you with him at Qualinost?" Auntie snapped back. "She would have been. He keeps you here, inside the Fortress where it is safe."

"I train his guards," Crystal protested. "I fulfill a vital role."

"There's no one else in all of Norbardin who can train his guards, then?" Aunt Needlebone asked. When Crystal made no response, she continued, "You see what I mean. He wants to keep you safe. And now he has Tor to look after and worry over, too. Never has a father loved a child so dearly. I've never seen the like in all my years. Tor is so very young, and dwarf babies die every day of one malady or another. As king, he knows that better than any of us. He grieves along with the mothers and fathers."

Auntie stood and dusted the knees of her tattered woolen nightgown. "It's living shut up in this mountain!" she finished, swearing. "The clean air can't get in here to flush the place out. Pestilence breeds in the dark, and it is so very dark here sometimes. This place could use a good dose of sunshine. A bolt of lightning wouldn't do it any harm, neither."

"I'd better go see what Tarn is doing," Crystal said as she started for the door.

"You mind what I told you, girlie," Auntie called after her. "He's suffering inside, but he can't let it out or he won't be a leader of his people anymore, he thinks. But don't you coddle him. You'll ruin him for sure if you coddle him. He needs a swift kick more than a soft word."

The halls were still filled with milling, overwrought servants. Crystal did her best to calm their fears. It had only been a small trembler, not even enough to knock the tapestries off the walls. Yet a groundquake was such a rare occurrence in Thorbardin that no one could remember the last one. For a people whose lives were measured in centuries, this meant no such event had occurred here in a very long time. Despite her assurances, the servants remained edgy. "What does the king say about it?" many asked.

When she reached her bedchamber, she found the door closed and Ghash Grisbane waiting in the antechamber, nervously pacing the floor with an axe in his fist. "Put away your weapon, Captain," Crystal said in what she hoped was a friendly voice. She attempted a laugh. "What good is it against a groundquake?"

"I feel better with a weapon in my hand," the young Klar warrior responded sullenly. But he returned the battle axe to its place on the wall.

"Where is the king?" she asked.

"Inside." He nodded toward the door.

"Call the king's escort, then. Have them ready," she said. "Tarn will need to go to the Council Hall."

"He said he was returning to bed," Ghash said, a worried look passing over his face. "And he has the young prince with him."

"The king must go to the Council Hall," Crystal said firmly. "Summon the guard at once."

The young captain's features brightened at her assurance, and he hurried off to do her bidding. She waited until he had gone before opening the door. The light from the antechamber spilled into the darkened bedchamber, illuminating a large hump on the bed covered in blankets. Sighing, she took a candle from a sconce beside the door, entered the room, and began lighting candles on the walls and shelves.

Tarn looked up from the pillow, his brow furrowed. "What are you doing?" he asked. "Tor can go back to sleep between us. There's plenty of room." He gazed down at the boy peacefully sleeping beside him.

"He can go back to sleep, but you're not," she said brusquely, as she moved about the chamber, lighting still more candles. She wanted the room brilliantly lit. "You're going to hurry down to the Council Hall."

Tarn sat up carefully, so as not to wake Tor. He pushed back the hair from his face and watched his wife, a puzzled expression on his face. Crystal saw him out of the corner of her eye, and his bafflement only made her angrier. She plopped the candle down on a dressing table so violently that hot wax splashed on her hand. Hissing, she slapped the droplets from her skin, then sucked the back of her burned thumb.

"Tarn, we've just had a groundquake. The people need to be reassured by your presence. You have to go out and survey the damage. They need to see you in the street, unafraid, seeing to their needs and wants, and trying to solve their problems. You are their king. Even your own servants are frightened, and here I find you cowering in bed," Crystal said in disgust.

The injured look on Tarn's face nearly broke her heart, but she continued as Tarn reluctantly folded back the covers. "What's the matter with you, Tarn Bellowgranite? I shouldn't have to say these things to you. I've never had to tell you what to say or do before. Most of the time, darn it, you act without even seeking my advice. But lately . . ."

"I had the dream again," he said in a low voice. He remained seated on the edge of the bed. Tor stirred and sighed, and Tarn turned to look at his son, at his small round sleeping face. "I can't help it. Every time I leave this house, I wonder if it is the last time I will ever see him."

Crystal crossed the chamber and joined him on the edge of the bed. When she lightly touched her husband on his broad, muscular back, he jerked slightly as though startled. She realized that his whole body was alive with jangled nerves. His violet eyes darted nervously under drooping lids. A muscle along his jaw writhed, setting his beard into motion.

"Tor's a strong, healthy boy, like his father," she said gently. "There is nothing to fear."

"I never feared anything in my life," Tarn said angrily. "Until now. Until I became a father. Something terrible is going to happen. I can feel it in my bones, in the roots of my teeth. And it has to do with this boy, our boy, our only son." He rose from the bed and walked to the dressing table. He stood before the table a moment, looking at the cosmetic bottles and vials of perfume that had been upset by the groundquake. He raised his hand as though about to sweep them all to the floor, but he stopped himself at the last instant. His hand sank to his side. He turned.

"And now the groundquake and the crack in Tor's nursery. It's all straight out of my dream, but what does it mean?" he moaned in frustration.

"That's a question for the philosophers and the engineers," Crystal said. "The only thing you have to worry about now is making sure your people are safe, their fears dispelled. Now get dressed and prepare yourself to do your duty. You can't let your fears show." A bustle and rattle of armor outside the door announced the arrival of Ghash Grisbane and Tarn's escort of guards.

"Tor and I will be fine," she said. "I won't let anything happen to him."

Surrendering to her will with a nod and a sigh, Tarn began to dress.

CHAPTER
26

His escort of six Klar guards followed him to the gate. Ghash ordered it opened, and outside they found a crowd already gathering. The relief of seeing their king emerge spread visibly though the crowd, like a pebble thrown into a pond. Young and eager to prove himself, Ghash barged forward to prevent anyone from coming too close to Tarn.

Yet the crowd greeted him with friendliness that barely covered their nervousness. Tarn resented them only a little, because in his heart he knew the fear that they felt. Yesterday, most of the people at his gate wouldn't have wished him a good morning. Now they were gladly shouting his name. There was no getting through them easily. Tarn ordered Ghash to wait while he heard them out. The Klar captain sighed and nervously fingered his axe while standing close behind his king, his eyes scanning the crowd.

"First of all, is anyone injured?" Tarn asked in a booming voice.

A chorus of cries answered him.

"Grinder's mother cut her foot on a piece of broken crockery."

"I've bruised my hip from where I fell out of bed. I thought it was only my husband snoring!"

"There's a crack in my wall and now my door won't close."

Tarn raised his hands for silence. "We can deal with the damages later. The main thing now is to see to the injured and to make sure everyone is accounted for. Send Grinder's mother to the healers. Do you need someone to look at that hip?"

"It's nothing serious, my lord," the matronly dwarf woman answered with a smile and a curtsy. She gathered her children and turned away. "I'll go check on my neighbors."

"That's an excellent idea," Tarn shouted. "Everyone see to your neighbors. If no one is hurt, check your own homes for damage. I am going to the Council Hall now. If you have any problems or concerns, bring them to me there and I'll address them swiftly."

The crowd began to break up. Tarn and his guards slowly made their way through the people until they were into a clearer street. All along the way, in every neighborhood and market, they attracted a crowd. Again and again, he stopped and urged the citizens to see to the welfare of their neighbors, to take care of one another until some order and plan could be put into place. If they had serious and immediate concerns, they should follow him to the Council Hall. And though crowds gathered around them wherever they went, Tarn was relieved to see that only a few were following him to the Council Hall, and these seemed mostly to be the curious and the bored.

Tarn saw few signs of serious damage anywhere along the way; a toppled lamppost here, a jagged crack in the pavement there. One street near the Council Hall had flooded when the sewer pipe backed up, but engineers were already busy effecting repairs. At another place, the way was blocked by a herd of lowing cave oxen who had escaped their pen when its walls crumbled. Children stood in doorways, staring around sleepy-headed but excited by all the commotion; their mothers and fathers hovered near, reliving their experiences with their neighbors.

Tarn took the straightest route possible to the Council Hall, but all the interruptions and detours meant a considerable delay. By the time he arrived, he found Jungor Stonesinger there ahead of him, already holding audience on the Council steps outside, a throng of dwarves filling the plaza. Tarn heard Jungor's voice, deep and resonant, even before he saw him.

"There is nothing to fear," Jungor was saying. "All indications are that it was only a small groundquake. Such things are to be expected, every once in a while, even here in Thorbardin. Everyone should just go home and go back to bed. We'll take care of everything."

Growling a curse, Ghash Grisbane cupped his hands to his mouth and shouted, "The king is here! Make way for the king!"

The crowd split apart like the wave before the bow of a boat. Here at the Council Hall, the faces that greeted the king were not so friendly as those in his own neighborhood. Many stared at him as though he were an unwelcome intruder rather than the king. What was more, Tarn was the last of the Council Members to arrive. All the other thanes were already gathered on the steps—even Grumple Nagfar, the wayward thane of the Aghar.

As Tarn approached the steps, a wry smile twisted Jungor's acid-deformed face. "Ah, good! The king has come at last," he said in a voice dripping with sarcasm. "I just sent my master of scouts, Ferro Dunskull, to look for you."

"You needn't have bothered," Tarn answered coldly as he mounted the steps. Glint Ettinhammer greeted him with a smile and an apologetic shrug. Shahar Bellowsmoke ignored him, while Brecha Quickspring glanced at him briefly before haughtily turning away. Rughar Delvestone sat on a step at Jungor's feet, scribbling like a secretary in a large black logbook spread upon his lap. The Hylar thane stood above them all in his usual tattered robes and wizard staff and one-eyed hideousness. Unlike the other thanes, Tarn included, whose hair and beards were still rumpled from sleep, Jungor looked like he had never even gone to bed. Indeed, it made Tarn wonder, what had the Hylar thane been doing that he should still be up at this hour of the night?

Tarn climbed to a step higher than where Jungor stood, then swept his eyes round, casting a swift glance over the crowd before turning his attention to Jungor. Though he said nothing, his baleful gaze told Jungor to step aside. Jungor returned his stare with a cold eye, then bowed, moving aside for the king. But the smirk on his face promised that he would not always do so.

Satisfied, Tarn crossed his arms over his broad chest. "Now, what do we know? Were many folk injured? Anyone seriously?"

Thane Ettinhammer stepped up, elbowing past the Hylar thane. "So far, there have only been reports of minor injuries. The houses of healing are still taking a count, but to this point, we seem to have come through this relatively unscathed."

"We should begin taking an account of the damages to buildings," Tarn said.

"We had already begun to do so before you arrived," Jungor said briskly, turning to the Daewar thane sitting on the step below him. "Thane Delvestone, please continue to record the reports as they come in."

Tarn glowered at Jungor for a moment. "Then perhaps he could read to me what he has recorded so far," he said through gritted teeth.

The Daewar thane looked up at Jungor, who nodded his assent. This, more than anything else, infuriated Tarn—that Rughar should seek permission from Jungor to follow the king's order. Tarn's cheeks flushed scarlet to his beard, and the hot blood throbbed so loudly in his ears that he barely heard Rughar's voice.

"Engineers are still inspecting the transportation shafts. The entire Klar quarter of the Anvil's Echo has been flooded to a depth of several inches, we're not sure why. We've sent a team of engineers down to the first level to investigate a report of damage to the site of the new Council Hall, which is still under construction, as you know. Other than that, we seem to have suffered widespread but only minor damage to streets and buildings."

"Thank you, Thane Delvestone," Tarn growled. He stroked his beard for a moment, pondering his next move, then addressed the crowd. "I'm ordering that the engineers' office remain open throughout the night, to assess damage reports and begin to recommend repairs. Anyone in need of medical assistance should report to the houses of healing on their level. I will remain here to observe and assist as needed."

The crowd milled uncertainly, many of them staring up at Jungor, who silently leaned on his staff, his head bowed as though in thought. Tarn's blood began to pound in his ears again. "Everyone, I order you to return to your homes," he said a little too shrilly.

Jungor lifted his head and raised his hand, drawing everyone's attention. The crowd grew silent. "Anyone in need of any assistance whatsoever should come by my warehouses in the Hylar quarter of the second level. I have been storing food, water, medicine, bandages, bedding, tools, and other supplies in preparation for just such an emergency as this. Those in need may draw from my stores free of charge."

A cheer went up from the crowd. "I suggest that the other thanes return to their own quarters of the city to see to the needs of their people, especially Thane Ettinhammer, whose realm has been flooded. Everyone else should return home as the king suggests. What can be done is being done. We'll know more in the morning." Another cheer went up. The crowd began to disperse and the thanes hurried away to their homes.

Jungor turned and smiled up at the king. Tarn ground his teeth in frustration, but there was nothing he could say. Once again, Jungor had not directly challenged him, but had still somehow managed to wrest control from his grasp and leave him gaping like a landed fish. The people weren't in serious need of medical supplies, food, or water. It had been, after all, only a minor groundquake. But by offering them that which they didn't even need, Jungor had both managed to create a need in their minds and then satisfy it at the same time. Meanwhile, the king's thorough, efficient, and practical manner of resolving this crisis had been greeted with less favor.

Seeing the king's frustration, Jungor climbed to the step just below Tarn's. Still smiling innocently, he said, "Perhaps you should return home as well, my king. There is nothing more for you to do here."

Tarn clenched his fists, his beard quivering, but somewhere in the back of his mind, he could hear Crystal warning him—strike him and you give him the excuse he wants to act more boldly. Slowly, Tarn relaxed, and with a last baleful glare at the Hylar thane, he began to descend the steps, his thoughts already returning to his son. But a question niggled in his mind, like a worm on a hook. Why had Jungor been stockpiling supplies? What sort of disaster was he preparing for? Food, medicine, water, bandages, bedding—these were all things needed by refugees.

Or an army.

CHAPTER

27

Ghash met Tarn at the bottom of the stair, his face grim. "Where to, m'lord?" he asked.

"Home," Tarn answered shortly. Though most of the crowd had already left, a few remained behind in the temple courtyard, gathered in small groups talking about what had happened. Most fell silent as Tarn and his captain passed, and not a few shot disdainful glances their way. Ghash made a point of haughtily ignoring them, even when one group burst into laughter behind their backs. For once, Tarn wished his Klar captain would forget his manners and crack a few heads.

Having left the plaza surrounding the Council Hall, they turned north. Here, near one of the major transportation shafts that connected the various levels of the city, they found the houses of healing for the second level of Norbardin. Not far away stood Jungor's warehouses, and from the intersection of two streets, Tarn could see the crowd that had already gathered to receive the distribution of goods. Though obviously not in dire need as a result of the groundquake, the dwarves were not about to pass up free blankets and food. Tarn could not help but think that Jungor was buying the favor of the populace.

But this did not concern Tarn so much at the moment. What more readily attracted his attention was the large number of people waiting in the street outside the houses of healing. Most bore only minor bruises and scrapes, and he saw no one with truly serious injuries. But there were far too many of them, and Tarn noted that most were Daergar or Klar. Fifty or more stood on the curb outside the door and the line stretched around the far corner.

Tarn turned aside and entered, Ghash hurrying in his wake. They found the lobby more crowded than the street, with dozens of dwarves angrily demanding attention for their wounds from the undermanned staff. Tarn glanced around until he spotted a young female Hylar wearing the white robe and brown belt of a healer's apprentice. She was hurrying toward him with a tray of bandages balanced on one hand while she fended off the grasping hands of the patients who swarmed around her. Tarn pushed through until he reached her side, then took the tray from her hand and passed it to Ghash. "Distribute these," he ordered. The Klar captain stared at him in confusion for a moment before lowering the tray to within the reach of those clamoring around him.

"Wait just a moment. Those are for the doctor!" the apprentice healer shouted angrily. Tarn turned back to her, and it was only then that she realized who he was, so frazzled were her nerves. "Pardon my impertinence, thane. I did not see you enter. Are you injured?" She performed a quick curtsy.

"Not at all. Tell me, what has happened here? Why are there so many injured citizens on this level?" Tarn asked.

The girl pushed her hand through the mop of dirty brown hair hanging in her eyes. Her cheeks were flushed with exertion, her hair dank with sweat. "Oh, my king," she sighed. "The houses of healing on the first level have been flooded. We're getting patients from both levels now, and there aren't enough of us to handle them all."

"Where are all your healers, then?" Tarn asked, well aware of the precise number of staff assigned to each of the healing houses. "There should be more than enough healers here to handle this. And I was told that there aren't any serious injuries to speak of."

"That's true, my lord, or would be. There are only two doctors here. The rest of the staff is made up of apprentices and novices. Most of our doctors were ordered to the third level to deal with Hylar wounded," she said in annoyance. "That was before the first level houses of healing became flooded. Now we can't recall them."

"Ordered? Who ordered this?" Tarn asked, though he thought he already knew the answer.

"Thane Stonesinger," the girl said, confirming his suspicions. "Forgive me, my lord. The doctor is waiting for me." Curtsying again, she hurried away.

"Send the head doctor to me, when he has a moment!" Tarn shouted after her, and she waved to show that she had heard before vanishing through a doorway.

Tarn found Ghash standing by a window with an empty tray in his hands. Two other Klar stood nearby, and the three leaned together, speaking swiftly in their choppy, guttural dialect. Tarn noticed that the two newcomers were still wet up to their waists and dripping water onto the floor. One wore a blood-soaked bandage wound about his shaggy head, the other leaned upon a makeshift crutch. As Tarn approached, they ceased their whispered conference and turned to bow. Tarn immediately noticed a distinct aroma of sewage that surrounded them. They smelled like they had been wading in a latrine. The other patients had already identified the source of the odor and retreated to the other side of the chamber.

"My kinsmen," Ghash said, introducing them to the king. "Garn and Boros Bloodfist." The two bowed again. Tarn could not help but notice how much the one wearing the head bandage, Garn Bloodfist, looked like a younger version of his old friend Mog Bonecutter. Looking at him was like seeing a ghost from the early days of his rule.

"What passes on the lower level?" Tarn asked, trying not to stare at the young dwarf.

"The entire Anvil's Echo is flooded, my thane," the older of the two brothers answered. He shifted his position on his crutch, wincing when his foot touched the floor.

"It's the sewers," Ghash said. "They're backing up everywhere down below."

"I can't believe the sewers have failed this badly after such a small groundquake," Tarn said. "They're newly built and reinforced, after all."

"It wasn't the groundquake at all," Boros said. "The sewers didn't start backing up until the engineers began to inspect them for damage. My brother and I were assigned to these very duties. I can't speak for what happened to the others, but we discovered magical wards had been placed at the confluence of the sewage system beneath the first level houses of healing. One ward exploded while we were trying to remove it. That's how we were injured, and how the healing house came to be flooded with sewage. The entire pipe collapsed. We barely escaped with our lives."

"We've heard that there were other explosions, too," Garn added as he rubbed his bandaged forehead.

Tarn pondered their strange news in silence. Could it be? Magical wards had been set to collapse the sewers beneath the Anvil's Echo, thus flooding the most densely populated region of Norbardin with raw sewage. The place would be uninhabitable for months, until they could clean it up and repair the sewers. Who could have set those wards? There was no question as to who had the capability, much less the motive. Among all the dwarf clans, only the Theiwar had the skill to use magic, and the Theiwar were aligned, through their thane, Brecha Quickspring, with Jungor.

The question was, why? Why flood the Anvil's Echo? Who lived there? Daergar, Theiwar, and Klar, for the most part. A few Daewar had homes in the Anvil's Echo, but no Hylar would lower himself to live in that slum. Forcing the Daergar, Klar, and Theiwar out of their homes would only aggravate the clan rivalries in Norbardin, as they would all be forced to share an even smaller amount of inhabitable city. Tarn had only managed to keep the peace in Norbardin for these forty years by allowing the different clans to build their own enclaves within the city. Force them together now and it was sure to end in clan-on-clan violence. That must be the plan.

Did Jungor really desire the return of internecine war in the streets of Thorbardin? Should a civil war erupt, Tarn didn't have the manpower or the resources to stop it. He'd been holding the tiger by the tail for forty years now, living on borrowed time while he worked to break down clan hatreds. And prosperity, more than anything else, had helped to keep the peace. But in the eighteen months since the gates were closed, prosperity had faltered. Tarn knew that each day, the tinder beneath their society became a little drier, a little more ready for the spark that would light it into a conflagration.

All the while, Jungor had apparently been scheming, planning, preparing to take advantage of this disruption in the delicate social balance.

Tarn cursed himself for a blind fool. Now the dozens of reports and hints that had passed across his desk in the past year came flooding back to him. He only half read most of them, deeming them unimportant, and he had never connected the dots, until now. In the past months his son had been the only thing he really cared to attend to, and therefore he had neglected the duties of the king, while Jungor built up a sizable militia of Hylar and Theiwar warriors "in preparation for Beryl's attack, or any other emergency"; while he stockpiled food stores and blankets in his warehouses; while he comissioned dozens of new fountains to be built in the Hylar quarter that would provide plenty of water in case of a siege.

Perhaps it was not too late for Tarn to act. Maybe the groundquake had saved him from an even greater disaster. It had exposed the magical wards set to collapse the sewers beneath the Anvil's Echo, obviously before Jungor was ready to use them. Tarn felt a cold chill pass down his spine. Jungor must already be aware that his machinations had been laid bare. The Hylar thane couldn't afford to wait and see if Tarn would put the last pieces of the puzzle together and discover the extent of his treachery. He was probably already moving his forces into position to seize control of vital streets and transportation shafts, stairways and sources of water, prisons and centers of government. All he needed was an excuse to act, and Tarn had no doubt that Jungor could improvise such a contingency. A few acts of clan violence, a little rioting in the streets, some looting and arson to go with the flooding of the Anvil's Echo, and Jungor Stonesinger would be ready with his army of soldiers, ready to restore civil order and be proclaimed king of Thorbardin.

"We have to get back to the fortress," Tarn said in a low voice that Ghash knew was ominous. Instinctively, his hand flew to the axe at his belt.

"What's wrong?" Ghash hissed.

"There's no time to lose." Tarn started for the door, but a commotion in the street brought him up short. Ghash leaped in front of the king, axe in hand with a snarl peeling his lips back from his teeth.

A litter bearer stumbled through the doorway, tripping over the threshold in his hurry and nearly dumping the litter's occupant unceremoniously on the ground. The bearer at the other end of the litter fought to stabilize their burden while his companion regained his balance. Weaving a path through the other patients, they shouted frantically for the doctor.

Concerned, Tarn stepped nearer. Two apprentice healers appeared and swiftly knelt beside the dwarf on the litter. One peeled back the damp sheet covering him to reveal his naked body. His skin had turned a brilliant scarlet color and was covering with pustules from the middle of his chest to his knees. A few tatters of blackened clothing still clung to his flesh around his wrists and ankles.

"He's been burned," one of the apprentice healers said to his companion other. "Fetch a doctor at once." He then lifted one end of the litter, and with the help of one of the litter bearers hurried the patient from the room. The other patients, many of whom had been moaning pitifully about their cuts and bruises, grew silent at the sight of the horribly burned dwarf.

Tarn grabbed the other litter bearer and pulled him aside. Seeing who it was who had accosted him, the young Daewar dwarf swiftly knelt before the king. Tarn pulled him to his feet. "What happened?" he asked.

"A . . . a . . . an accident at the s-site of the N-new Council Hall, my king," the young dwarf stammered.

"Was it the groundquake?" Tarn asked impatiently.

"No, sire. I don't believe so. He was one of the engineers sent to investigate the crack in the foundation caused by the groundquake," the litter bearer answered.

Tarn's blood went cold in his veins—it was just like his recurring nightmare—the crack in the nursery floor, the hot breath welling from it, and the gaping chasm of fire. And each time, that dream had ended with Tor's mangled and broken body being torn to shreds by shadow wights.

"Crack? What crack?" he asked through lips suddenly gone numb.

"I can't say, my lord. Someone found him beside the crack, his skin scalded nearly from his bones but still alive. Of the other engineers, there was no sign."

"Wait, my lord!" Ghash shouted as Tarn bolted through the door.

CHAPTER
28

Though nearly complete, Tarn's new Council Hall
still had a good two years of work ahead before it
would be ready to hold its first meeting of the Council of
Thanes. Its architect, Gaul Quarrystone, had chosen the
location to take advantage of a natural bowl-shaped
cavern uncovered by silver miners a few years after the
Chaos War. The cavern lay a hundred feet beneath the
lowest level of Norbardin at the end of a broad sloping passage that wound snakelike into the heart of the mountain,
following a thin vein of silver that could still be seen
sparkling in the tunnel's walls. For the better part of ten
years, two hundred of Thorbardin's most skilled stonema-
sons had chiseled and chipped and cut and polished until
the cavern had become a thing of unmatched beauty. In
their diggings, they had uncovered deposits of golden-hued
quartz crystal, which they cut into panes to form the lamps
that would one day fill the Council Hall with warm golden
light. But for the most part, the dwarves sought to reshape
the caverns as little as possible, and what they did alter,
they used all their skill to make it look natural.

Were it not for the scaffolding rising to the ceiling a
hundred feet overhead, the piles of stone dust waiting to be

carted away, and the discarded tools of the workers litter-
ing the floor, one might have mistaken the chamber for a
natural amphitheater. Only the stairs were too regular, the
seats too evenly shaped, and the dais at its center was too
perfectly rounded to be an accident of nature. The dwarves
sought to improve upon the perfection of nature whenever
they could. This philosophy had been the inspiration
behind the wondrous Life Tree of the Hylar, their great city
built within a single huge stalactite hanging over the
Urkhan Sea. With Tarn's enthusiastic support, Gaul Quarrystone had envisioned re-creating just a little of that
former majesty here in the new Council Hall.

Tarn had no doubt that the brilliant young architect
would succeed in his aspirations. Though the Council Hall
followed the traditional design, this was a place unlike any
the dwarves of old had ever imagined. Natural rock
blended perfectly with shaped stone to form a fluid whole
of surpassing beauty.

But there was one flaw in Gaul Quarrystone's design—
apparently, the Council Hall rested over a significant fault
in the bedrock. The groundquake had opened it, neatly
splitting the central dais almost through its center. Tarn
and Ghash now stood at the edge of the gaping black hole,
peering down into a seemingly bottomless chasm from
which wisps of steam steadily rose.

Even more ominous, dried bloodstains and tatters of
burned clothing lay around the crack. Bloody palm prints
and streaks on the inside edge of the hole told of the surviving engineer's desperate attempt to escape. The fire from
below was intense, and dwarves feared fire more than any
other hazard of the deep earth. But whether the engineers
had accidentally stumbled upon a pocket of methane gas,
igniting it with their lamps, or whether they had encountered molten rock pushing up into the mountain, neither
Tarn nor Ghash could tell. Either way, this was a great
danger.

"Ghash, I want you to go and fetch more engineers. Bring Gaul Quarrystone here at once," Tarn said, adding when he saw the captain begin to protest, "Now, do as I say. Time is of the essence, and we must know what happened here."

"All the more reason that you should come with me, m'lord. It is too dangerous for you to remain here. If the Hylar thane's soldiers were to discover you . . ."

"They won't find me," Tarn snapped. "I'll be safer here than on the streets. Bring a squadron of my personal guard with you when you return. There is no telling when Jungor might . . . ." His voice trailed off as a faint sound rose from the crack in the floor. At first he thought it nothing more than the hissing of steam. But then a voice, distant yet clear, cried, "Someone help me! Please!"

"There's someone still alive!" Ghash exclaimed as he knelt at the side of the hole.

"Hello down there!" Tarn shouted. His voice was amplified by the empty chamber.

A faint, inarticulate cry answered. Without even considering the danger, Tarn sat at the edge of the hole and swung his legs over the side. The shattered rock provided plenty of handholds and ledges to place his feet, so that he had little difficulty negotiating his descent. Grumbling into his beard about the risk, Ghash followed even more nimbly than his king. The younger Klar was an accomplished mountaineer and soon was able to pass his king.

After about forty feet, the air became sweltering, the stone under their hands grew uncomfortably warm. "If it gets any worse, we'll have to turn back," Ghash said. Tarn said nothing, continuing his swift descent. But they had not gone much deeper before the rocks grew too hot to touch for very long. Both dwarves felt the pads of their fingers slowly being seared, their faces and chests baked by the heat. Even worse, the air scalded their lungs with each breath. Steam mixed with noxious vapors seeped from the stone around them, even as the crack narrowed and grew more steep.

"We have to go back," Ghash said in a strangled voice.

"There's someone alive down there," Tarn said. "If he can survive this long, we can stand it long enough to try to rescue him."

"And what if he is trapped? What is he can't escape? If we join him, we'll be trapped, too."

"Then we'll be trapped!" Tarn shouted angrily as he continued downward. After a dozen more feet, he felt the close air open around him and knew that they had entered a larger cavern. The smoke and mist prevented him from seeing much with his darkvision. He felt truly blind in the dark. The slope leveled off and soon he found himself standing at the bottom of the chasm. Ghash joined him, coughing and retching from the poisonous fumes.

By feeling their way along the wall, they discovered that they had entered a tunnel, roughly circular, with smooth walls that seared their fingers. Both knew immediately that no dwarf had delved this tunnel. Some more elemental force must have burned its way through the rock. Guessing that the tunnel was not very wide, Tarn pushed off from the wall and moved blindly ahead. Almost immediately, he stumbled over something on the floor. The sickly sweet odor of cooked flesh assaulted his nostrils.

He and Ghash found six more dwarf bodies lying in the immediate area. They didn't need to see to know that all of them were horribly burned. But the last body that they found stirred when Tarn touched it. "Here he is!" Tarn cried to Ghash.

"I can't see!" the injured dwarf moaned. "My eyes! My eyes are gone!"

"Lie still and quiet," Tarn said as soothingly as he could. "We've come to rescue you."

He and Ghash each took the injured dwarf by one arm and tried to lift the poor fellow to his feet, but as they stood, his skin slipped loose from the flesh of his arms and he toppled to the floor again, groaning pitifully.

"This is hopeless!" Ghash cried in horror as he shook the loose folds of skin from his fingers. "He's as good as dead already. We must leave, my king."

"King!" the dying dwarf shouted deliriously. "Must warn . . . !"

"Warn of what?" Tarn demanded. "What happened to you down here?"

A gurgling sigh was his only answer.

"He's dead, m'lord. We must go now," Ghash insisted. He began to pull at Tarn's arm, dragging him away from the bodies.

Tarn lashed out and struck the Klar's hands aside. "We'll go when I say," he shouted angrily. But almost as soon as he said it, Tarn regretted having not listened to his captain.

For behind them, a great red glow began to swell. A hot rising wind scorched their faces and started their beards to smoking as they turned toward the light. Now they saw this was no tunnel. It was a vast subterranean chamber, many times larger than the new Council Hall, but of similar proportions. It was like a great bowl that had somehow been burned out of the rock. The walls and floors were smooth as glass, except where the crack above their heads broke through, forming this tiny ledge high up the wall of the chamber. Had they not tripped over the bodies of the dwarves, they might have walked blindly over the edge and fallen hundreds of feet to their certain deaths.

But even this was preferable to the horror filling the bowl of the chamber below them. A vast winged serpentine form, seemingly composed of molten rock yet somehow alive and stirring, came into view. Its sinuous, catlike movements appeared to stoke the fires of its flesh, for it began to glow even hotter and brighter as they watched, abruptly heedless of the smelting furnace heat that assaulted their flesh. The two dwarves felt suddenly very naked and small. A deep, rumbling purr trembled through the stone beneath their feet as the dragon settled back to its slumber. And its fire began to dim.

By their dying flames, Tarn saw ropes dangling over the ledge, still tied to several pitons hammered into the stone. As he backed away from the ledge, he began to understand what must have happened to the engineers. They must have discovered the ledge and tried to descend into the chamber beyond, only to be overcome by the heat of the slumbering dragon's body.

For this was no ordinary dragon, nor one of the feared dragon overloads, like Beryl and Malys, who had appeared after the Chaos War. This was a chaos dragon, a creature of living fire, maybe even one of the very chaos dragons that had attacked Thorbardin during the Chaos War. Tarn had thought them all banished or destroyed when the gods defeated Chaos. But apparently, one had survived, spending the past decades slumbering away unsuspected in the heart of their mountain. Or had Chaos returned, and with him his minions? Either way, Thorbardin was in grave danger. The gods were no longer here to save them from Chaos, and all the dwarves in Thorbardin couldn't hope to defeat one of his fire dragons.

————◆◆◆————

A terrified-looking Tarn, battered, scorched, and pale with fear, burst into the nursery, nearly frightening Aunt Needlebone half out of her frowsy, moth-eaten nightgown. "Where is Crystal?" he demanded.

"In the next room with your son. He just finished his breakfast. You're lucky Tor wasn't asleep. You come storming in here with your beard all in a knot, looking half crazy and dead, demanding this and ordering that at the top of your voice," Tor's nanny scolded the king.

"Shut up, old woman! Start packing Tor's things. Take only the essentials," Tarn ordered as he crossed the floor toward the door Auntie had indicated.

The humor vanished from the old hill dwarf's face. "So it has begun, has it? The beginning of the end? We're under attack?"

"No. Worse than that," Tarn said as he jerked the door open.

"What could be worse?" she asked after him. "And what happened to your face? You look all sunburned."

Tarn found Crystal in the sewing room bending over a piece of needlework, Tor playing at her feet. She looked up, smiling to see him, but the smile quickly faded from her face. "What's wrong?" she asked.

"We have to leave. We have to go, now. Pack only what we cannot live without," he said.

"Where are we going?" Crystal asked as she tossed aside her needlework and picked up the baby. She clutched Tor fearfully to her breast, afraid because she saw the same emotion clearly writ in her husband's face. "You always said we'd be safe here."

"Nowhere is safe now," he barked. "Be ready for when I come back. Be ready to leave immediately."

"But where are we . . . are you going?"

"To see Jungor," he answered grimly as he stared at his infant son in her arms. For a moment, she saw his resolve waver. She clutched her baby tighter and hardened her heart.

"Tarn, tell me what has happened so that I can know how to advise you," Crystal demanded. "What is happening? Where are you taking us?"

Quickly but without sparing details, Tarn recounted his discovery of the chaos dragon in the crack beneath the Council Hall. "Reorx help us!" Aunt Needlebone, standing behind him, exclaimed.

"Reorx is gone, old woman," Tarn snapped. "We have to help ourselves now. We're leaving the mountain before the dragon awakes. There's no time to spare, but I must warn the other thanes, beginning with Jungor."

"How can we leave a mountain sealed from the outside world?" asked Auntie Needlebone.

"Not by standing here flapping our gums, but first Jungor must hear this news from me and listen to reason."

"He won't, and you know it. But I'm going with you," Crystal said as she handed her son to his nanny. "We have servants to do the packing."

CHAPTER
29

Jungor pushed back his empty plate, sighing content-edly. That was the first decent meal he'd eaten in weeks, and he couldn't remember the last time he slept. He missed his meals sorely, but the lack of sleep was a mere nuisance. All he had to do was imagine himself wearing the crown of Thorbardin and the weariness slid from his shoulders like oil from a hot anvil. The crown seemed almost within his grasp now. His preparations were complete, his forces hovering.

Certainly, the groundquake had forced him to act more quickly than he had originally planned. The discovery of explosive mines in the sewers beneath the Anvil's Echo was unfortunate, but perhaps inevitable—not really so huge a disaster that it couldn't be overcome. Everything was already in place. All he lacked was the catalyst to set things in motion. And that would come soon enough. Whether Tarn challenged him of his own initiative, or events allowed Jungor to assert his right to rule in Tarn's place, the crown of Thorbardin would be his.

Having finished his repast, Jungor nodded to a servant waiting beside the dining room door. "Let them in now," he said. The servant bowed and opened the door, allowing those waiting in the antechamber beyond to enter.

The first to enter was Rughar Delvestone, thane of the Daewar. In preparation for this day, he had changed to battle gear and wore a warhammer at his side. Next came Brecha Quickspring, her dark eyes burning with fervor even as her skin seemed to have only grown more pallid. Behind her, Hextor Ironhaft entered, wearing the robes of a Hylar thane. Jungor raised his eyebrows in alarm at the portly merchant's premature assumption of the seat promised to him, but decided to let the fat old dwarf enjoy himself. He was in too good a mood to reprimand anyone, not even Ferro Dunskull, who entered next, followed closely by one of his trusted assassins, a female Daergar who interested him not only for her mastery of the deadly arts.

Jungor usually didn't show much interest in the opposite sex. To his mind, women were for marrying and improving oneself politically and financially. But this Daergar minx had long ago caught the Hylar thane's eye. Not that he would ever disgrace himself by dallying with a dark dwarf, but even he had to admit that she was a singular creature upon which to rest his gaze. As she entered, he stared at her, and she caught Jungor's eye, returning his frank appraisal with a haughty coldness that he found particularly appealing. He pummeled his brain to remember her name—Marith something.

Astar Trueshield entered last and closed the door, dismissing the servants after they had cleared the table of the breakfast dishes. Jungor remained seated at the table, contentedly picking the last bits of his breakfast from between his teeth with the nail of his pinky finger, making the others wait. The conspirators settled into chairs along either side of the long dining table, only casually pausing to admire the fineness of the wood paneling covering the walls or the tapestries hanging between marble busts of Jungor's grandfathers.

When all were seated, Jungor at last stood and pushed back his chair. "Please, remain seated my friends," he said patronizingly, when they started to rise as though to follow him. "Do not trouble yourselves." He strode slowly around the corner of the table and thoughtfully placed his hand on the first marble bust standing on its granite pedestal beside the wall. Rughar was the first to notice that this was Jungor's own, almost-forgotten image, carved before the vitriol attack in the arena that had destroyed his right eye.

"I am glad you have come," Jungor said, somewhat distracted in contemplation of his own bust. Sighing with perhaps a tinge of regret, he turned toward the others. "Because the time has come to make our move. Last night's groundquake is a clear sign of the revolution sure to shake the mountain to its foundations." The Hylar thane returned to the end of the table and stood, leaning forward on his fists, his one eye glittering excitedly. "Thane Quickspring's mines beneath the Anvil's Echo have been discovered, unfortunately, but the groundquake has given us the opportunity to display the quality of our leadership while showing everyone how weak and ineffectual is the king. We have won many friends today. The people will support us, especially after Tarn is dead . . . at the hands of his cousin, the Daergar thane."

"What!" Hextor exclaimed. "Do you mean to say Shahar Bellowsmoke has chosen to join us?"

"Quite so," Jungor said with a predatory smile. "Only he doesn't know it yet."

Ferro Dunskull made a show of tossing a small, ornate dagger on the table. The others stared at the dagger, little more than a handspan in length, its narrow blade tapered to a needle point. Its hilts were decorated with skull and rose motifs, for Shahar Bellowsmoke had taken it from the body of an emissary of the Dark Knights of Neraka who had come some years ago to try to recruit the Daergar to their side. "I have borrowed this dagger from my thane's personal treasury. You are all familiar, I am sure, with the story of how Shahar Bellowsmoke killed the ambassador from Neraka. When Tarn Bellowgranite is found with this dagger in his throat and its poison in his veins, no one can but doubt that it was the Daergar thane who executed the deed. Nor will very many care to investigate the king's fate, for we feel confident the populace has turned against Tarn, thanks to our careful work."

"Good! Very good!" Hextor chuckled to himself. "I compliment you on a master stroke, Master Dunskull." Ferro returned the praise with an appreciative nod.

"Are you prepared, then?" Jungor asked.

"We are," Ferro answered, rising from his chair. He picked up the dagger from the table and returned it to his belt. His comely companion joined him as he strode from the dining hall, only pausing once to cast a curious gaze at the others before quietly closing the door behind her.

When they had gone, Jungor turned to Brecha. "And are the Theiwar prepared?"

"We are, my king," she answered fervently. "A nursery has been prepared for the young prince. When Tarn and his witch wife are dead, I will take Tor and raise him as my own child, with you acting as regent until he reaches the age of majority. That should pacify any skeptics until, of course, the child succumbs to a mystery illness or tragic accident."

"Excellent. Well then, we have only to wait for news from Ferro . . ." Jungor's voice trailed off as he caught sight of the dour expression on Captain Trueshield's face. The Hylar warrior seemed to have swallowed something that disagreed with him.

"Whatever is the matter with you Astar?" Jungor asked.

"Forgive me, my lord," the captain answered without meeting Jungor's eye.

"Are you sick?"

"Only of dark dwarves, my lord." Brecha shot the Hylar captain a murderous glance, which he returned with the frigid glare that was the birthright of his clan.

"Well, that cannot be helped for now," Jungor said, a trifle disconcerrted.

"But my lord—" Astar started to say. A knock at the door cut off his words. Rising from his chair, he crossed to the door and opened it.

Jungor waited impatiently while the captain conferred in low voices with one of Jungor's servants. After a few moments, the captain returned. "Glint Ettinhammer is in the street outside, demanding to see you, my thane," he announced.

Jungor's remaining eyebrow rose in surprise.

As Tarn and his wife neared Jungor's residence, they could hear the voice of Thane Ettinhammer bellowing about something. Crystal glanced at Tarn in surprise, and they quickened their steps, forcing their company of bodyguards to hurry after them. Crystal had insisted upon the escort despite Tarn's protests, and it was well that they had brought along the twenty wild-eyed Klar warriors. This was, after all, the center of Jungor's realm of influence, and the dwarves they met on the streets here looked upon the king practically with murder in their eyes. Without their bodyguards, they probably would not have made it this far.

Rounding the corner, they entered the plaza that lay between Jungor's splendid mansion and his warehouses. At the far side, Glint Ettinhammer stood upon the steps leading up to Jungor's door. Two steps above him, the Daewar thane, Rughar Delvestone, held his ground, backed by three of his personal guard. Glint was alone, but one look at his massive arms and the double-bladed axe in his hands was enough to keep the others at a safe distance.

Tarn arrived in time to hear Rughar angrily shout, "He doesn't have time to see you now! Come back tomorrow when you are sober, Thane Ettinhammer."

"By the gods, I wish I were drunk. You won't see tomorrow if you don't let me in!" Glint roared as he surged up the steps. The Daewar retreated in alarm.

Leaping up the steps, Tarn caught the Klar thane by the arm before he could swing his axe. Wild-eyed, Glint turned on him and nearly struck him before he realized that it was the king.

"Ah, forgive me, my lord!" he shouted, half laughing as Tarn ducked the blow that probably would have broken his jaw.

"King Tarn!" Rughar angrily cried. "Take this drunken fool away before he gets himself killed. The Hylar thane has no patience for Klar antics today."

Glint spun, spittle flying from his bearded lips as he shouted, "The only fool likely to die today is this pathetic toady."

"Be quiet, Glint!" Tarn ordered. "We've no time for this."

"Bah!" Glint spat in frustration. "That fool wouldn't know when to wipe his own arse if Jungor Stonesinger wasn't there to tell him."

Crystal climbed the steps and quietly slipped a hand under the Klar thane's arm. The effect was remarkable. At her touch he gave a start, but then he looked down at her and smiled. His berserk fever seemed to cool.

"Where is Captain Grisbane?" she asked the Klar thane in a low voice as Tarn climbed the steps to the door.

"Looking for you. He brought me the news and I came here at once, but he insisted on going back to the Fortress to find Tarn," Glint answered.

Tarn had reached the door to find it still blocked by Rughar Delvestone and his cadre. "Out of my way, Rughar," he growled. "I must speak with Jungor."

"Thane Stonesinger is indisposed," Rughar stubbornly maintained. "Come back tomorrow."

"Listen, you miserable dog—" Tarn began, his blood rising into his cheeks, but a voice from behind the door cut him off.

"It's all right, Thane Delvestone. The king has honored us with his presence. We mustn't refuse to see the king." With these words, Jungor appeared in the doorway, leaning upon his staff as though the weight of the mountain rested upon his shoulders. Rughar bowed and slipped to the side, pulling his guards with him. Crystal glanced around and saw that a crowd was gathering behind them. She noticed that a fair number were warriors armed for battle. Clutching the Klar thane, she pulled him up the steps to stand with their king. Meanwhile, Glint eyed the Daewar thane and fingered his axe.

Jungor stepped over the threshold and greeted Tarn with a bow that was all but an obvious mockery of respect. Tarn ignored the insult. "I must speak with you," he said in a low voice, even as Brecha Quickspring appeared in the doorway behind Jungor. "Alone," he added.

"Come now, we can speak freely here, can we not?" Jungor asked solicitously as he stepped past Tarn and spoke so that his voice would carry to the crowd below. "We have nothing to hide from the people of Thorbardin. And unless my eye betrays me, we have a majority of the Council of Thanes in attendance as well. How very convenient."

Glowering, Tarn said, "Very well then. I have come to say that we must put aside our petty differences because—"

"I couldn't agree more!" Jungor loudly interrupted.

Tarn raised his voice and continued, ". . . because we are all in grave danger!"

Jungor looked at him in genuine surprise. "Grave danger? What kind of danger? Is the king having more bad dreams?" he asked.

"That was no groundquake that shook the mountain last night!" Tarn said angrily. "It was a fire dragon slumbering in the depths of Thorbardin."

Silence descended on the plaza as everyone stared up at the king in shock. It was as though a spell of fear had been cast over everyone, fear born of their memories of the

JEFF CROOK

Chaos War. Even Jungor seemed momentarily taken aback, until he shattered the silence with a hideous peel of laughter. "A fire dragon!" he shrieked. "By Reorx's bones and boots, that must be some fire dragon if it can shake the whole mountain!"

Slowly, others began to chuckle, none with more smug glee than Rughar Delvestone. Growling deep in his throat, Glint's fingers tightened around the haft of his axe. Crystal slipped her hand from his arm to the dagger secreted in her sleeve. The Klar thane glanced down at her, and she returned his gaze with a grim expression.

Jungor continued, "Are you sure it isn't Beryl?" he asked the crowd. "No, we've heard not a peep from the great green bitch, despite the king's most dire prophecies. Maybe it was Malystryx, then." The crowd began to roar with laughter.

"It was a chaos dragon I tell you!" Tarn shouted, his voice cutting through the levity like an axe stroke. "My captain and I discovered its lair beneath the new Council Hall. You can go and see for yourselves, if you don't believe me. It is asleep now, but stirring. It may awaken at any moment. We must evacuate the mountain."

Jungor glared at Tarn for a few moments, his misshapen face writhing. "A chaos dragon? But the chaos dragons were all destroyed. As you yourself have attested, all the minions of Chaos were destroyed, and by your own father when he released the power of the Platinum Egg. May the name of Baker Whitegranite," he added quickly, "be forever praised!"

"Go and see for yourself, I tell you!" Tarn responded. "But I warn you, when that beast awakens, it will be the horrors of Chaos all over again."

Jungor ignored the king. "So now you would have us abandon our homes once more, to make your father's sacrifice a vain and empty one!"

"Are you the only one who has seen this supposed dragon?" Rughar Delvestone asked accusingly.

240

"No, Ghash Grisbane, Captain of the King's Guard, also saw the dragon," Glint said as he stepped nearer the Daewar thane.

"And where is *he*, pray tell? Not here to confirm the king's words, I notice," Rughar sneered. "There is only you, Tarn's ever-loyal lackey."

"I'll only warn you once to keep a civil tongue between your teeth, Thane Delvestone," Glint growled.

"Don't speak to me of civilities Thane Ettinhammer. How many innocent Hylar and Daewar did you slaughter during the Chaos War? Their blood still cries for vengeance!" Rughar shrieked.

"Very well then," Glint said as he calmly hefted his axe.

"You wouldn't dare," Rughar hissed as he fumbled at his own sword.

"I told you I would only warn you once," Glint said.

"Glint! Wait!" Tarn cried as he leaped for the Klar thane, but too late. Glint's huge, double-bladed axe swept up, cleaving through armor, bone, and flesh. Rughar's head leapt from his neck in a spray of blood that doused both Jungor and the Theiwar thane.

Tarn swore furiously as madness seemed to erupt. His guards retreated to within a few steps below him, forming a defensive barrier of steel to protect their king. Jungor's forces poured in from every side of the plaza and fought their way through the frenzied crowd. Glint swung again and cut down one of Rughar's bodyguards even as Crystal drew her dagger and slammed it into the throat of another. As the dwarf fell, blood spurting around the blade in his windpipe, she snatched the spear from his fist.

The third bodyguard drew his sword and attacked Tarn. His own sword still in its sheath, Tarn managed to dive beneath the blade and slam his shoulder into the dwarf's belly. Standing up suddenly, he lifted the Daewar warrior and flung him down the stairs, ripping his sword from its scabbard at the same time.

He turned as a sibilant whisper of magic froze his blood. Jungor now filled the doorway behind Brecha Quickspring, his face contorted with hatred. Lost in the ecstasy of her magic, Brecha seemed not to hear Jungor's warning shout. Her words shivered the air, drawing power as the spell found shape and substance around the amber rod in her hand. But the spell died on her lips as Jungor grabbed her by the belt and pulled her through the doorway an instant before Crystal's spear would have skewered her dark Theiwar heart. Instead, the missile thudded into the doorframe and stuck quivering in the wood, just as Jungor unceremoniously slammed the door.

Tarn leaped after him, but as his hand closed around the ornate bronze knob, a bolt of electricity arced from the metal to his fingertips. He jerked his hand away and wrung his numb fingers.

"That witch has magicked the door," Glint shouted over the din of battle. "We have to get out of here before she has time to do worse."

Tarn nodded as he switched his weapon to his left hand. Crystal jerked her spear free and dropped in behind Glint as he strode down the stairs, bellowing orders to Tarn's guards. They quickly formed up in a defensive wedge, with the Klar thane at the point, and drove into the first of Jungor's soldiers to reach the stairs. So ferocious was the assault of the battle-mad Klar warriors that they easily clove through the disorganized resistance they met.

Fleeing the shrieking Klar charge, the crowd was met on the other side of the plaza by Astar Trueshield, leading a large force of Hylar and Theiwar warriors—the best of Jungor's troops. Swirling in confusion, the crowd coiled upon itself for a moment, then turned and fled back the other way, quickly colliding with Tarn's small group of warriors. In seconds, he and Crystal found themselves separated from their bodyguards. Glint's voice roared about the din of the mob as he was carried away, axe flailing.

Crystal clung desperately to Tarn's arm to keep them from being pulled apart, even as he laid about with the flat of his blade, to little avail. Soon, they found themselves swept into a close, cramped alley stinking of garbage, pressed murderously on all sides by the panicked mob and Jungor's troops. While clinging to one another and fighting to keep their feet beneath them, the tide swept them along, but to where, they did not know.

CHAPTER
31

Having at last escaped the mob as it dissipated into the maze of streets and alleys of Norbardin, Tarn and Crystal hurried along a darkened street, hand in hand, each encouraging the other to greater speed.

Their fortress home was near enough now that they no longer kept to the shadows. The section of the third level nearest the fortress had remained loyal to Tarn through all the difficulties of the past year. Perhaps it was the inherent nature of neighbors to support their own. Dwarves were fiercely loyal to clan and family, but in Norbardin, many of the families had been forced to live in different sections of the city due to space limitations. There were, for instance, four Klar quarters of Norbardin and seven small enclaves of the Daergar clans. In some places, especially around Tarn's fortress, Klar and Daergar, Hylar and Theiwar lived side by side, shopped at the same markets, drank in the same taverns. Over the course of nearly forty years, they had begun to feel the same fierce loyalty for their neighbors that they had formerly reserved only for clan and family.

This had been Tarn's dream for his people all along, but it had only been manifested thus far in a few scattered portions of the city. Now the dream seemed lost. Jungor had succeeded in polarizing dwarven society into its ancient castes. But more important, he had brought together the disparate clans in a way Tarn could only dream of doing, though not for the mutual good of all. Though Jungor longed to return the Hylar to their place at the top of dwarven society, his followers were united by their mutual hatred. Tarn wondered if the whole world hadn't gone completely mad.

Here in his neighborhood, at least, things still seemed sane. Jungor's revolt had not spread, and the people, worn out with worry over the groundquake, had finally returned to their beds to catch an hour of sleep before the morning watch announced the new day. The street leading to the fortress's main gate was empty, but not completely silent. A child wept behind some door, its mother's soft voice crooning a lullaby. An alley behind a bakery grumbled with the snoring of contented gully dwarves.

Across the way, in the shadow of a tannery wall, something crouched on the ground, mewling pitifully. Tarn and Crystal skirted it warily, hands on their weapons. Probably it was only some drunken gully dwarf crawling home from his beer-mopping job. At the far end of the street they could see the torches burning beside the entrance to the fortress, and the guards in their hauberks and iron helms walking their watches.

A soft cry from the miserable creature stopped them. Tarn peered into the shadows for a moment. "That's no gully dwarf," he hissed. "It's too big. Stay here."

"Call the guards first," Crystal hissed after him.

But Tarn had already approached the creature, sword drawn. He nudged it with the toe of his boot, causing it to writhe like a snake. "What's the matter with you, old one? Too much dwarf spirits?" Suddenly, Tarn dropped his sword and fell to his knees with a cry. Crystal rushed to his side.

Tarn knelt on the walk, hugging Ghash Grisbane to his breast. The Klar warrior's body shuddered with spasms, bloody foam poured from his mouth. He clutched at Tarn's shoulder, finger's digging into the king's flesh. His distended, bloodshot eyes rolled in their sockets. Horrible purple veins streaked the flesh of his throat from beard to breast.

He tried to speak, his words a long tortured groan. "I came back for you, but you had already gone. Someone—"

"What happened, son?" Tarn cried. But Ghash was already gone. His wracked body slowly relaxed, his head sank back, the mouth open in a horrible, silent scream. "Ghash!" the king wailed, rocking back and forth with the corpse in his hands.

"Come, my love. It's too dangerous here," Crystal said softly, gently trying to pry Tarn's hands from the dead Klar's body. "We have to leave. We can come back in force to recover his body. But whoever killed him is probably still around."

A low, murderous chuckle seemed to answer her suspicions. Two figures slunk out of the alley opposite, one short and powerfully built, the other taller, leaner, and obviously female. "Indeed, we are still around," the shorter figure laughed as he advanced toward Tarn and Crystal. His female companion followed just behind and to his right, sword drawn.

Tarn rose to his feet with a roar. He snatched his sword from the pavement and lunged toward the two. Crystal spun her spear around into an attack stance. "So the two of you murdered him," she shouted angrily. "Let's see how you fare against the king and his woman."

The tall female dwarf lifted her sword and charged. The shorter figure only laughed and raised a hollow tube to his lips to shoot a poisonous dart. His cheeks puffed out and he expelled a breath of air in a sharp cry, however, as his companion's sword unexpectedly cleaved through his shoulder, ribs, and heart to wedge itself in his spine. His dart, weakly blown and knocked askew, bounced off Tarn's hauberk and fell with a ping to the paving stones.

Already dead, the shorter dwarf fell between the strange female and the king. Crystal circled to her right, spear ready for throwing or thrusting at this turncoat. Dumbfounded by this turn of events, Tarn waited. He knew that Daergar were treacherous, but he sometimes forgot how treacherous they could truly be, and this could be a trick. The dead dwarf had fallen, face up, and Tarn recognized him as one of Jungor's most trusted advisors—Ferro Dunskull. But the female dwarf was a stranger to him.

"Why did you kill him?" Tarn asked.

"He betrayed me," the female dwarf answered simply. "I've waited a long time to avenge my companions. Now was a good time."

"If he betrayed you so, I am surprised he allowed you behind his back," Tarn said. "Ferro Dunskull was never one to make a mistake about his friends."

"He thought I was someone he could trust," she answered. She folded her arms across her breasts. "The price I paid for that trust has only fanned the flames of my revenge."

"I thank you for saving us." He stamped his boot over the tiny silver needle, shattering it and driving its point between the paving stones.

"My only thought was vengeance. I am sorry your friend had to die, for he was not part of my designs," she said, nodding toward the body of the Klar captain.

Tarn's face darkened. "Yes, my friend. And what are those designs?" he asked suspiciously.

"Our fates are intertwined, Tarn Bellowgranite. I was hired to kill you by this dwarf, but he betrayed me before I could finish the job," she said.

"I knew it—Ferro was working for Jungor!" Tarn cried excitedly. "If you will tell your story before the Council, Jungor'll be exiled for the traitor that he is!"

But the female dwarf only shook her head and laughed. "They will not believe me," she said.

"Why not?" Crystal demanded. She stepped closer, threatening the Daergar with her spear.

"Because I am not a dwarf," Zen answered. Both Tarn and Crystal stepped back in alarm as the female dwarf transformed into a gleaming, seven-foot-tall sivak draconian.

"I killed the woman Marith Darkforge so that I could take her form and get close to Ferro. My revenge is now complete. What happens next is no concern of mine. I only want to get out of this madhouse," Zen said, his voice a reptilian growl.

"No, you killed Ferro in my presence for a reason," Tarn said, sheathing his weapon. "You wanted me to see you do it. You could have murdered him a dozen times before now, I imagine."

"Yes, it served my purpose to gain a powerful ally, should I need one," Zen acknowledged. "Only a king or a thane can order the gates of Thorbardin opened, and I'm sure that Thane Stonesinger won't oblige me once he learns I have killed his assassin and exposed his plots to the king."

"Tarn, you can't let this monster go free," Crystal urged in a low voice.

"Be quiet, woman!" Tarn snapped, then immediately regretted his words.

Crystal grew livid. "How dare you! I am not some scullery maid to be ordered about." Glaring at him, she cupped her hands to her mouth and shouted for the guards. Her voice carried down the length of the street. Several gate guards paused in their patrols and stared, pointing.

Hurriedly, Tarn said to the draconian, "I will order the gates opened, but there is a price."

"Tarn!" Crystal said in surprise.

Tarn ignored her. "You can take Ferro's form and get close to Jungor, am I right?" In answer, the draconian swiftly shrank, his silvery skin taking on the pale hue of the Daergar's flesh. In moments, his appearance exactly mimicked that of his victim.

Tarn nodded appreciatively, but Crystal gasped in horror. "Tarn, you can't mean to do this," she said, catching him by the arm. "You can't mean to hire this monster to stalk your rival."

"As long as Jungor is around, the people will never leave the mountain."

"This is wrong, Tarn. Jungor tried to have you murdered, and so you have decided to return the favor? What of your precious laws, Tarn's celebrated Laws of Redress? Will you now cast them aside?"

While they argued, Zen conducted a swift operation on Ferro's corpse with the heel of his boot. Soon, the dead Daergar's face was an unrecognizable, bloody pulp. He removed the dagger that Ferro had intended to plant on Tarn's murdered body in order to implicate the Daergar thane. It was only a small blade, but deadly. He slipped it into a hidden pouch in his cloak.

"This is our way," Tarn said, his anger rising. "So it has been for thousands of years in Thorbardin."

"It's not my way," Crystal returned cooly. "And it won't be the way of our son. The Law is the same for both king and commoner, or it is no law at all."

A company of twenty guards arrived at that moment. Their captain stared in wonder at the two bodies lying at the edges of the street, then at the king. Tarn glared at Crystal, but said nothing. She stepped close to him and fiercely pleaded, "You mustn't sink to Jungor's level. I beg you. For Tor's sake! Let's just gather what we can, take those loyal to us, and leave this place."

Finally, Tarn relented. "But I do not care to expose the draconian yet," he whispered back. "I may yet need his assistance." Crystal sighed but nodded in agreement. She turned to the guards.

"Ferro Dunskull and his accomplice have attempted to murder the king. Arrest him," she said. The guards surged forward and swiftly pinned Zen's arms behind his back. He didn't resist them. Instead, he focused all the hate of his draconian being onto the one who had betrayed him. Not Tarn—who turned his head away, but Crystal. She shuddered to look into his black, soulless eyes as the guards wrapped his arms in tough cords of mushroom fiber. She knew at that moment that this creature would stop at nothing to kill her.

"Do not take him to the fortress," she declared, as they started to drag him away. The thought of the draconian locked up within the same walls as her family filled her with terror. "Imprison him in one of the first level dungeons." Nodding, the guards started in the other direction. Half the guards remained behind to escort the king the remaining distance home and to see to the bodies of the dead.

CHAPTER

32

Jungor's fist struck the table, splitting it down its length. Glassware and crockery leaped into the air and crashed down, spilling their contents.

"It all comes of trusting a Daergar," Hextor Ironhaft yawned. He righted his glass, then motioned for a servant to refill it and clean up the mess.

The news had interrupted their breakfast. Jungor hardly looked at his food. Not that he ever ate much; he drank copious amounts of mushroom brandy, and took little else for nourishment. Since his disfiguration in the arena, the Hylar thane had lost weight, his already predatory features gone thin and gaunt. The flesh of the right side of his face looked as lifeless as wax that had melted and then hardened into a hideous mockery of flesh.

But at times of extreme emotion, the curdled flesh flushed with blood and seemed almost to pulse. As the servants hurried forward to clean up the mess, Jungor grabbed the edges of the table and flipped it onto its side. Hextor sighed and stood, crossed the chamber to the fireplace, and took a crystal decanter from the mantle.

"That fool of a Daergar has failed me for the last time," Jungor swore. He sank into his chair while servants scuttled all around him, collecting broken crockery and mopping up the mess. He watched them for a few moments, a sneer curling the left side of his face. Most took care not to come within his reach, but one young maid made the mistake of forgetting where she was. Jungor's boot lashed out, smashing into her hip and sending her flying across the room.

Hextor stepped over her prostrate body on his way to the couch. A servant quickly dragged the weeping maid from the room so as not to disturb the thane any further. The others finished cleaning up and hurried away. As the last one exited the dining chamber, Astar Trueshield entered, a sheaf of papers tucked under one arm.

"Bad news. I hear that Ferro Dunskull was captured," he blurted out.

Hextor winced and placed a finger to his lips. Astar paused, then bowed in gratitude for the warning. "Our troops are nearly all in their positions," he said, swiftly changing the subject to more positive matters. "Once word of Tarn's demise . . . oh!" His face flushed red. "I mean . . ."

"Oh, he says," Jungor snarled. "Yes, it finally dawns on him that we can hardly move to take control of the city if the king is still alive and in command. And Ferro *might* betray us after all. He is Daergar."

"I warned you not to take any dark dwarves into your confidence," Hextor said as he sipped his brandy.

"Your tongue will cost you your head one day, Hextor Ironhaft," Thane Brecha Quickspring cautioned from the dark corner where she had been sitting the entire time, a spellbook open upon her lap. "Just as Thane Delvestone's cost him his."

"My lord, are you going to allow this Theiwar witch to threaten me, a Hylar of your own clan?" Hextor protested.

"This Theiwar witch is a thane of the Council," Brecha haughtily responded. "For forty years, we Theiwar have scraped and scratched for our rightful place here. We will not be ignored."

"Fine words," Hextor snapped back. "How much did Tarn Bellowgranite pay you to say them?"

"Do you dare accuse me of double-dealing?" the Theiwar thane cried as she leaped to her feet. She turned to Jungor. "My lord, I demand—!"

"You will demand nothing!" Jungor roared, leaping to his feet. With one swipe of his long arm, he sent her crashing back into her dark corner, her spellbook flying from her grasp to land in a disordered heap. Two long strides brought him to the couch. Hextor Ironhaft cowered before him.

Jungor bent over him and shrieked into his face, "Shut up! Shut up! The both of you must end your bickering, or I will end it for you! I cannot think clearly for all your endless prattle!" He spun and stalked away. Nursing a bruised jaw, Brecha climbed to her feet and righted her chair. Neither she nor Hextor dared to speak, much less apologize.

"None of you seem to realize our imminent danger," Jungor said as he walked to the window and looked out over his garden. As swiftly as it had flared, his anger disappeared. He realized what he must do, and now spoke calmly, rationally.

"Shahar Bellowsmoke will demand the right to question Ferro, once he is informed of the attempt on Tarn's life. If he is allowed to exercise the full talents of his interrogators, Ferro will confess everything that he knows and probably much that he doesn't know. We cannot let that happen. The problem of Ferro must be solved."

"Of course," Hextor Ironhaft said.

"We cannot rescue him," Brecha said cautiously. "That would only incriminate us in the assassination attempt."

"Who said anything about a rescue?" Jungor asked with a shrug.

"What, then? We can't kill him, for the same reasons. And if he has already confessed, it won't matter what we do," Astar said.

"Exactly!" Jungor exclaimed. "We must assume that he has already told everything. I want you to concentrate your efforts on securing the dungeon where they are keeping him. We'll need those cells. But do not touch him yet. He has disappointed me for the last time. I want that miserable Daergar for myself."

Astar's face grew pale and he dropped the sheaf of reports he'd been holding. "Take the dungeons? Now? But that means . . ."

"War," Jungor said, his scars flushing red. "The time of Daergar plots is ended. We fight now for control of Thorbardin. Our soldiers were trained to quell a civil war, not start one. But they are ready and willing, and the populace supports us. After Tarn is defeated and dead, or driven from our sacred home, the people will embrace my rule. Those who do not love us will learn to fear us. But they will embrace our rule."

CHAPTER

33

The third watch of the morning had just been called when Tarn strode into the courtyard. Fully armored now, his sword at his hip, long golden beard brushed and braided for battle, he looked every bit a king. A roaring cheer went up from his soldiers gathered along the walls and mustered in the courtyard.

Tarn greeted them with a joyfulness that he did not feel in his heart. Word had come within the hour of fighting in the Daergar quarter of the Anvil's Echo, in the Hylar and Daewar markets of the first and second levels, in the Klar quarter of the second level, around the Council Hall, and at all forges and dungeons on the first and second levels. Jungor's followers had struck everywhere at once, it seemed, in a marvelously coordinated assault that achieved many of their objectives with little or no loss of life.

Tarn reviewed his maps as the reports came in. Jungor had moved to cut off the third level at all the transportation shafts, isolating Tarn from his food supplies and his armories. The Council Hall had fallen without a fight, the majority of its guards being loyal solely to the Council of Thanes. Since the majority of the Council were allied with Jungor, the guards had merely turned over control of the

Hall to Astar Trueshield. Now, Jungor's captain was using it as a base of operations and communications center to coordinate the takeover on the southern half of the second level. The northern half—containing the largest concentration of Hylar and Daewar in Norbardin—was already under control. Those council guards still loyal to Tarn had slipped away before Astar's appearance on the scene and now had joined their king at the fortress. Among them was General Otaxx Shortbeard.

Tarn was heartily glad to see his old friend, even under such difficult circumstances. They greeted one another with a boisterous embrace before Tarn pulled him aside for a brief exchange beneath an arch. "Old friend, I honor your loyalty, but you risk much in defying your own clan in this."

The old general burst out laughing, shaking his gray beard. "You should know that the Daewar are divided now that Rughar Delvestone is dead," he said. "Some remain loyal to Jungor and would have him *select* the next Daewar thane. How that can be considered loyalty, I'll never know. Others have sided with you, but they are scattered and confused. It will take some time for them to gather their wits and come along here. Some fool has even suggested that I would make a good thane! Hah! So now my fortunes rise or fall with you, my king. If you fail, then so do I."

Tarn greeted this news with a fierce smile. "Good! I knew I could count on you," he said. "Ever have you come to my aid in time of need, Otaxx Shortbeard."

"And may it ever remain so," the old general responded.

Clasping hands, they returned to the courtyard. There they found Crystal Heathstone and Thane Glint Ettinhammer surrounded by a band of the thane's handpicked Klar guard. Tarn shouted to them in greeting. Tarn and Crystal embraced briefly. She had changed into a shining mail hauberk and leather greaves, with a mail coif. She carried a stout spear in her fist. Glint wore his usual battle-scarred plate armor and carried a black mace resting on his massive shoulder. Rather than a helm, he wore a gleaming ivory-colored bear skull on his head, with a bearskin cape dangling at his heels. Like all the Klar gathered around him, Glint's face was coated in dull white clay, but the circles of his eyes and his lips were stained deep purple, almost black, giving him a terrifying, death-like visage.

After clasping hands with his loyal thane in greeting, Tarn surveyed the courtyard, taking a swift mental count of their forces.

"So few?" he asked with dismay, under his breath.

"We were caught unprepared," Glint answered frankly. "We have this many ten times over, but they range throughout the three levels, many of them bottled up in their neighborhoods. Thane Stonesinger knew what he was doing, that's for sure, when he cut them off from us here."

Tarn smiled grimly, slapping the hilt of his sword. "We'll have to make do with what we have for now. But we need reinforcements to help us break out and relieve our allies. Shahar Bellowsmoke has sent word pledging the support of the Daergar if we can reach him. Jungor has him cornered in a tight place in the Anvil's Echo, and he can't break out. If we can join up with the Daergar, we can march through the city and take on Jungor's forces in small groups before he has a chance to consolidate them."

"There are Klar aplenty in the ruins," Thane Ettinhammer suggested.

"No one is supposed to be in the ruins," Tarn admonished him. "Are they under your command?"

"Strictly speaking, they aren't under anyone's command," Glint said. "They're feral Klar, beyond any law or loyalty. But if we can get word to them that there is fighting to be had in the city, they'll come out of kinship, and they'll come for the sheer love of violence."

"Hmm. But how will you control them once they are here?" Crystal asked. "They could prove a double-edged sword."

"Oh, they'd better follow me," Glint bellowed, eyes glittering dangerously from his death mask face. "But I'll have to be there to meet them when they arrive, else they'll join up with the first force they meet."

"That means we have to get control of the south transportation shafts on the second and third levels. And at the same time, we'll have to try to retake the Council Hall," Tarn said. "Who can you send to rally these feral Klar?"

"I have just the fellow," Glint said with a fierce grin. Reaching out, he grabbed one of his guards and pulled him toward the king. His painted face and beard could not hide his youthful features. "Captain Garn Bloodfist, one of my very best. Bow to the king, boy!" The young captain managed a clumsy bow without dropping his axe.

"The Captain and I have met already," Tarn said with a ferocious grin. "How is your head?"

"Better, my king. It was only a scratch," the young captain answered quickly.

"You know what we need of you?" Tarn asked, more than ever keenly aware of how much the young Klar looked like his old friend, Mog Bonecutter. "Gather as many as you can, spread the word, and return before the day is out. Delay is death for us. We must strike a blow today or strike none at all."

"I will not fail you," the captain said, bowing again to both the king and his thane. He hurried away, already wiping the paint from his face and stripping off his heavier armor.

A cry from the gate brought them round. The gate opened a crack to allow a party of scouts through. Several bore strange wounds, burns and scores that were caused by no sword or steel arrowhead forged by dwarves. One was shown straight through to the king to give his report. He bowed, clutching his side to ease a cramp. His chest heaved like a bellows.

"Theiwar battle mages have seized the transportation shaft south of the fortress," he said. "Their magic is taking a terrible toll. We can't get near them."

The four experienced leaders glanced at one another, all sharing the same thought. Jungor had anticipated that they might seek help from the feral Klar and thus had moved to block their path. Tarn and Crystal shared a grim glance. Otaxx nodded solemnly while stroking his beard. Glint growled in frustration. "Everything we think of, he's a step ahead of us."

"Jungor began this game months ago, I now see," Tarn said. "I underestimated his ambition. The groundquake was a coincidence, but he has used the confusion and chaos it caused to his advantage. If only I had been paying closer attention instead of lollygagging!" Once more, his violet eyes met the cool gray eyes of his wife. Silent words passed between them.

"I need to stay here," Crystal suddenly said. Tarn sighed in relief. He could think of no safer guardian for his son, and felt grateful that his wife, a formidable warrior who wanted to fight the coming battle as badly as any of them, had read his mind; she would stay behind and protect their child.

"I hadn't considered the Theiwar," Tarn continued grimly. "After forty years, I had grown accustomed to discounting their weakened magic. I should have remembered our lessons from the Chaos War, when Theiwar battle mages decimated our ranks with their fireballs."

"When wizard practices his art, archer loose thy feathered dart!" Glint quoted from ancient dwarven wisdom. "What we need are dozens of archers to go against wizards. But you have too few here, I fear, my king." The courtyard was filled with foot soldiers. The only archers in the fortress were posted on the walls, and these could not be spared from the defense.

"There's a Daergar enclave on the second level near the transportation shaft," Tarn said. "If we could break them out of their siege, they could join us in an attack against the Theiwar. The Daergar have plenty of archers. They do not consider it a cowardly weapon, unlike some."

Tarn turned to the general. "Otaxx, you take a third of our forces and move to within sight of the transportation shaft on this level," he said. "But approach no closer and do not threaten them immediately. Fortify your position. They will think you plan to hold them there. Meanwhile, Thane Ettinhammer and I will take another third of our dwarves and descend to the second level by way of the stairs. When you see the Theiwar dissolve in disorder, you'll know we are threatening their rear. Launch your assault then. The last third will remain here under command of Crystal Heathstone.

Otaxx nodded, beginning to order his troops. Tarn addressed the company. "Kill only those you must, take captives when you can," he implored, his voice rising above the din. "These are your neighbors, your own kin that you are fighting, and when this is over, you will have to live with them again." But even as he said it, he knew his words were pebbles tossed down a well.

CHAPTER
34

Tarn and Glint waited in the dark alley, soldiers crowding around them. Orin Bellowsmoke, younger brother of Thane Shahar Bellowsmoke, knelt at Tarn's side, repeatedly stabbing a dagger into the dirt between the cobblestones at his feet. The two limbs of his crossbow jutted up behind his back, and a battered quarrel box hung by a thin leather cord from his shoulder.

All the alleys on either side of the street were similarly packed with anxious soldiers. Nearly a third of their number was made up of newly liberated Daergar, eager for a chance to strike a blow against the forces of Jungor Stonesinger, who had bottled them up in their small enclave and besieged their thane in the Anvil's Echo. Tarn had promised to help them lift that siege, and so they eagerly followed him.

Orin Bellowsmoke was about as untrustworthy a Daergar as had ever lived, but Tarn needed all the allies he could muster. This Daergar was a creature of Norbardin's dungeons, having spent a good part of the past thirty years occupying them for one crime or another. The "enclave" that Tarn and his forces had rescued was really nothing more than a band of cutthroats, murderers, and thieves loyal to Orin Bellowsmoke because his brother, the thane, could offer them some protection from Tarn's law. But every one of them could pin a cockroach to a wall from a hundred paces. Some of them poisoned their arrows. Tarn pushed this knowledge to the back of his mind along with a hundred other issues he had neither the time nor the luxury to ponder.

Word had reached him that Jungor's forces had secured the first level dungeons. That meant the draconian assassin was now in Jungor's hands. Tarn couldn't be sure if Jungor had taken the dungeons for this purpose, but he had come to learn that nothing the Hylar thane did was by accident. Tarn's last resort for dealing with Jungor was now no longer even an option. Feeling desperate, he wished now he had not thrown it away so carelessly.

But Jungor had foolishly divided his forces into numerous small sieges scattered throughout the three levels of Norbardin. If he could attack these one at a time but in rapid succession, he could defeat them all with a smaller force than Jungor's combined army. But success depended on three things—speed, access to at least one transportation shaft, and the arrival of the feral Klar. Without the feral Klar, he wouldn't have enough reinforcements. Without the transportation shaft, he couldn't move large forces rapidly from level to level. He'd be forced to send his forces down the numerous small stairs that led from level to level. And the stairs, being narrow and steep, were marvelous places for ambush and disaster.

With each delay, Jungor had the opportunity to intuit his strategy and respond by massing his force for a single decisive onslaught. Tarn couldn't allow that to happen. Speed was imperative, too much delay spelled doom. And now the street leading to the transportation shaft was blocked by some kind of invisible wall of force. The Theiwar had indeed grown powerful in their magical abilities in the past months. Tarn sent scouts into all the alleys ahead to see if they could find a way around the invisible wall.

Glint Ettinhammer ground his teeth in frustration. He knew the futility of assaulting the Theiwar's magical defenses, but at the same time he hated all this slinking about. He preferred a straight battle, nose-to-nose with his enemy, and longed to crush some skulls. He didn't share Tarn's desire for minimal bloodshed, nor did he have the patience to take captives. The king probably planned to pardon their captives when all this was over, anyway. It was simpler and easier to come to grips with your enemy as quickly and directly as possible, then kill him. That way you didn't have to fight him twice.

The Klar thane's warriors were as restless as he was, and they did not enjoy sharing the cramped alley with a bunch of Daergar brigands, either. Old feuds between their clans threatened to boil over at any moment. Only their shared danger kept them from slitting each other's throats.

Glint cracked his knuckles impatiently. Tarn smiled and shook his head, putting a finger to his lips even as he leaned around the corner of the building to make sure their force had not been spotted by the Theiwar garrison less than a hundred years away. A low murmur erupted at the other end of the alley. Glint stood and glowered over the heads of the soldiers packed like gully dwarves into the cramped passage. The soldiers grumbled as they were forced to make way for a returning scout. Tarn eagerly awaited his arrival. Glint tested his mace's weight for perhaps the hundredth time.

The short, pasty Daergar crouched at his master's side, quickly delivering his report. Orin nodded, then turned to Tarn. "All the alleys are blocked or guarded, but he has found another way," he said.

"It's about time!" Glint growled.

The Daergar scout led them via twisting alleys and through empty courtyards about a hundred yards farther north of the transportation shaft, out of sight of the Theiwar guards. Next, he took them by a cross street to a road that ran parallel to the one they had just left. Then, he started south again. Glint jerked him to a stop.

Orin Bellowsmoke snarled, "What's the matter with you?"

"This road doesn't lead to the transportation shaft," the Klar thane said.

"Of course it doesn't, stupid Klar!" the Daergar scout spat. "If it did, it would be guarded. But they are only watching the streets and alleys, while their back door stands open."

"Stop speaking in riddles and tell us what you mean," Tarn demanded.

"What lies to the west of the transportation shaft?"

"Nothing. A few warehouses." Glint said.

"Three warehouses with back doors facing this road and front doors facing the transportation shaft," the scout said.

"Surely the doors will be locked," Tarn said.

"Locks!" the Daergar snorted, shaking his head.

"If memory serves, those warehouses have three floors, and each floor has several windows," Glint ventured, a smile growing on his painted white face. "Windows from which archers could provide covering fire while we rush the Theiwar position."

The Daergar scout nodded.

"I'm beginning to see the value of your plan," Tarn said. "But we must move swiftly and silently. When we arrive, I will lead the way through the middle warehouse. Thane Ettinhammer will take the right-hand warehouse and Orin Bellowsmoke the left. Archers should fill the windows and be ready to fire upon my command."

His orders were swiftly relayed to the warriors and their officers. Daergar archers divided themselves among the three columns. When everything was ready, they set off at a quick march. Within minutes, they had reached their objective without being noticed. Orin Bellowsmoke and several of his companions made quick work of the locks. Huge double-valved doors swung wide to admit the three columns of dwarf warriors.

Stacks of crates rose from floor to ceiling, forming a narrow passage down which Tarn and his warriors cautiously advanced. An identical set of double doors stood at the opposite side of the warehouse, leading out into the transportation shaft courtyard. Near the entrance, stairs led up to catwalks that crisscrossed above them. The Daergar archers swiftly ascended and made their way to the second- and third-story windows, their hobnailed boots ringing on the metal walks. At the lowest level, all the windows were blocked by crates, but the higher windows provided a clear field of fire for the Daergar archers.

The Daergar archers lining the catwalk above Tarn's head watched for danger. Crouching behind the door, the king waited until he felt his two other commanders had had enough time to move into their positions in the other warehouses. Then he looked up, checking with the Daergar at the windows. The scout who had led them to this point rose up on his knees and peered out of the window for a moment, scanning the courtyard beyond. Then he looked down at the king and nodded. All was ready.

As Tarn reached for the door, it opened of its own accord, pulled wide by a Theiwar warrior among the force waiting beyond it to surprise them. Above him, the Daergar turned their crossbows against their allies, two score deadly shafts poised to wreak havoc among the warriors packed in the narrow lane between impassible stacks of crates. At the same time, the rear doors swung wide. Hylar and Theiwar soldiers poured in, sealing the trap.

Snarling a curse, Tarn spun, ready to hack a way through to the transportation shaft. The sounds of battle would bring Otaxx's attack on the third level, and that might be enough to draw off the Theiwar sorcerers and allow his dwarves to escape. "It's a trap!" the king roared and lifted his sword. But as he led the charge into the courtyard, his battlecry died in his throat, his muscles froze. Eerie words of magic seemed to surround him, binding him in invisible cords until he was no longer able to move. Around him, his soldiers were cut down by arrows or struck senseless by Theiwar spells. A strangled cry of frustration and rage burst from his lips as his sword fell from his fingers.

Meanwhile, the warehouse in which Glint Ettinhammer and his Klar warriors awaited the signal to attack was largely empty except for a row of crates stacked against the windows of the first level. This arrangement prevented him from seeing into the courtyard, an inconvenience that he could not help but notice. Above him, two dozen Daergar archers crouched along the metal catwalk beneath the open windows of the second level. He didn't like having those untrustworthy brigands above him, but there was little he could do. They dared not try to move the crates from the first floor windows lest they be spotted by the Theiwar guarding the transportation shaft.

Glint was suspicious; worse, he was worried. Their entry into this place had been far too easy. He had trouble believing that Theiwar careful enough to block every alley with a spell would overlook such an obvious hole in their defenses. Tarn had divided his own forces for the plan, and was now blind to the movements of his enemy; plus he was separated from his friends. Glint was heartily sorry that he had not advised a more careful reconnaissance of the terrain. Impatience had clouded his thinking.

The Klar thane's nerves were on edge. After he had waited what he thought was plenty of time for the others to get into attack position, Glint couldn't sit still any longer. "I'm going up to have a look," he said to the Klar captain at his side. "If the signal comes while I am upstairs, you lead the charge. I'll be right behind you."

"Yes, my thane!" the captain said, excited to be given such an honor.

Slipping swiftly and relatively silently along the wall, Glint had just reached the stair leading up to the catwalk when he heard Tarn's shouted cry. The words were faint, muffled by distance and by the walls that stood between them, but the old Klar warrior knew what it meant. Out of the corner of his eye, he saw the Daergar stand and point their weapons down on those beneath them. Both sets of doors banged open. Theiwar and Hylar warriors poured through.

Glint crouched in the shadows for a moment. His warriors clustered together on the floor, shields raised against Daergar crossbow bolts that fell like winged hail among them. Theiwar sorcerers stood in the courtyard, casting their spells through the doors, felling warrior after warrior with bolts of energy and magical sleep. After that one strangled cry, no further sound or sign of his king had reached his ears. The door to the street stood open only a few yards away. His soldiers were being cut down before his eyes, the Daergar traitors were howling with laughter as they ceased their fire to allow the Hylar and Theiwar warriors the pleasure of mopping up the survivors.

That is when Glint leaped into the open doorway and with one blow of his huge mace felled both Hylar warriors standing guard outside. He turned back, laughing into the surprised faces of those within the warehouse. "Klar! To me!" he roared.

Roused by their thane, the Klar came alive. Glint held the door open against a dozen foes until his soldiers hacked a way through to him. Together they poured into the empty street, where they immediately fled like gully dwarves in a dozen different directions to baffle pursuit. In the twinkling of an eye, the street was once again empty save for a few confused and stunned Hylar who had stumbled out too late to give chase.

CHAPTER
35

Mog Bonecutter awoke with flames leaping around him, his bed afire. Ogduan Bloodspike stood at the foot of the burning bed, the torch still in his hands, his mouth stretched open in a peal of hideous laughter. Mog yanked the flaming sheets off the bed and flung them aside, but to his horror saw that the remainder of their small chamber, dug from the ruins of Hybardin, was already engulfed in flames. The exquisite upside-down fresco sputtered and popped, the ancient faces of the dwarves at their forges melting into madhouse smiles. Thick black smoke hung halfway to the floor and poured through the uneven entrance to the chamber.

Mog snatched the Hammer of Kharas from the wall above the bed, then leaped over a rising column of flames, landing on his bare feet already running. "You crazy old fool!" he screamed. But Ogduan had already fled shrieking and giggling from the chamber. Mog had been waiting for weeks for the insane old Klar to try to kill him, but he never imagined he'd burn down his own house at the same time!

Mog escaped the burning ruins wearing only a loincloth, the Hammer of Kharas swinging in his fist. The jagged ruins cut and bruised his feet as he leaped and bounded down the hillside in pursuit of his marooned comrade on the Isle of the Dead. Behind him, flames belched out of the cavern like fire from a dragon's mouth, illuminating the shattered ruins of Hybardin down to the water's edge.

For a moment, Mog lost sight of his quarry, then spotted the old dwarf crawling down a wrecked staircase only twenty yards below, a battered box clutched to his chest. He set off again, down a slope of scree that reached down to the shoreline. Slipping and sliding in the loose stones, Mog reached the narrow, pebbly beach just as Ogduan rolled down the last few steps, still laughing hysterically, his box flying from his hands to land in the black water of the Urkhan Sea.

Mog caught up to him before the old Klar could regain his footing. Stepping on Ogduan's leg to hold him still, he lifted the Hammer of Kharas over his head and swung. But the ancient weapon, glistening with moisture, slipped from his grasp and went sailing off into the rocks beyond.

Heedless of its loss, Mog knelt on Ogduan's chest and began to throttle him, his fingers squeezing around his windpipe to choke off the life of the one who had rescued him from drowning only to attempt to murder him with fire. Ogduan continued to laugh as long as he could draw breath, even as his face turned purple and his lips swelled with blood.

"Hello on shore!" someone cried. "Is there anyone there?"

Releasing his grip, a startled Mog spun and raced to the water's edge, flailing out until the cold, black Urkhan Sea was up to his waist. "Here! Here!" he cried joyfully. "Is someone there?"

"There!" he heard someone shout. "Row for that point beneath the flames."

A long sea boat hove into view, one of the old merchant craft that had once plied the waters of the Urkhan Sea. Towed by miles-long cables, these vessels had carried supplies and passengers between the five cities of Thorbardin. Oarlocks had been fitted to the boat, since the cables had long ago broken and sunk to the bottom of the sea. Now, a dozen Klar warriors guided the boat into shore, while a score more scowled at one another in the hold.

Mog gripped the edge of the boat and walked along with it the last few feet to shore, his joy as boundless as his surprise, a thousand questions getting in the way of one another and momentarily leaving him unable to voice even a single word. A young Klar captain commanded the craft from the bow. With his boat safely beached, he stepped forward.

Now it was his turn to be rendered speechless. After a few moments of stammering, he managed to cry, "Captain Mog? Mog Bonecutter?"

"Bloodfist? By the gods! What are you doing sailing out here on the Urkhan Sea?" Mog asked in turn. "Surely not looking for me?"

"No, we thought you dead these two months."

"Two months? Has it only been two months?" Mog asked in bewilderment. How could he have healed of his injuries in only two months? Nay, one month! He'd woken fully healed a month ago. But these questions were immediately driven from his mind by Captain Bloodfist's next words.

"I was out recruiting among the feral Klar and headed for home when we spotted your fire," he said.

"Not my fire!" Mog said, turning and looking at Ogduan. The old Klar had struggled to his feet and stood at the edge of the ruins rubbing his neck. "Why, that old fool tried to burn down his own house with me in it!"

"We'd never have stopped here if we hadn't seen it. Not even feral Klar are known to live on the Isle of the Dead."

"But what sends you out among the feral Klar anyway?" Mog asked.

"The king desperately needs their help. Jungor Stonesinger has risen in revolt. By the gods who are no more, the king will be glad to see you!"

"Whether by fortune or design, I'm glad you're here," Mog shouted. He climbed up into the ruins, searching for the Hammer. After a few frantic moments, he found it wedged between the broken curb of a pool and a shattered pillar.

By the time he returned to the boat, Ogduan had already climbed aboard and seated himself among the feral Klar as though nothing at all had happened. He gripped his dripping-wet box to his chest and watched as the flames and smoke rose from the mouth of the cave that had been their home this past month, a merry smile on his demented old face.

"What's he doing coming with us?" Mog asked, angrily pointing at Ogduan with the Hammer of Kharas. The other Klar oggled the magnificent weapon, their beards dropping open in astonishment.

"He begged leave to join us," Captain Bloodfist answered distractedly. "The king needs every possible ally. By the gods who are no more, where did you get that hammer? I've never seen its like in all my days."

"That old fool found it in the ruins and was using it to kill rats," Mog explained as he clambered into the boat. He stood in the prow and held the hammer aloft for all the dwarves to see. "This, my cousins, I believe to be the Hammer of Kharas. Lost in the Chaos War and presumed forever buried at the bottom of the sea, the Hammer of the heroes of old has returned to a fresh war. To Tarn Bellowgranite it shall go. Let us take it to him."

"Aye, this is a great day!" Captain Bloodfist exclaimed. At this command, the dwarves backed water and swung their boat around. Shouting out the strokes, they steered north rather than west, toward the ruined docks of Theibardin, where the feral Klar, hungry for war, had begun to gather.

Mog sat in the stern, the Hammer resting on his knees as he stared at the backs of the rowers. Beside him, Ogduan Bloodspike stirred restlessly and opened his box a crack to peer inside. He glanced at Mog under the hanging locks of his unkempt hair as though about to speak.

"Do not talk to me, old fool," Mog growled before he had the chance to utter a word. "I still plan to kill you when this is over."

Ogduan sighed. Reaching inside his box, he removed a flat oval of pure white ivory, from which clung two ribbons of black silk. "I wanted to give this to you. I think it would serve you well for the work ahead you," Ogduan said in low voice.

Mog glanced down at the death skald's mask resting in the old Klar's hands. A flicker of a smile played across his face as he took it. "Indeed it will," he said.

CHAPTER
36

Someone had dragged an old chair into the chamber in preparation for Tarn's arrival, obviously intending it to serve as a mockery of a throne. But by the time Brecha Quickspring and her minions had grown weary of taunting the king and had dragged him to the dungeon, the jailer was too drunk to do his job properly. He chained Tarn to the battered old throne too loosely before stepping back to admire his handiwork, swaying and squinting in the dim light of his torch. In the hall outside, a half-dozen Theiwar guards waited to see that the door was closed and locked before departing, else Tarn would have slipped his bonds immediately and relieved the jailer of his keys.

Instead, he was forced to silently endure the jailer's drunken gibes. Frustrated by not getting a rise out of the king, the jailer coughed up a mouthful of cloudy phlegm and spat it into Tarn's face. Tarn turned away, his fingers digging into the wooden arms of the throne to keep from casting aside all reason and murdering this disgusting beast on the spot.

The jailer laughed uncertainly. He had hoped for better sport from the high and mighty Tarn Bellowgranite, King of Thorbardin. Turning, he ducked through the low portal and pushed the swollen door shut with his shoulder. Pausing at the grate to take a final look at the king, he spat again. "You were never my king," he snarled.

With the torchlight gone, Tarn waited for his eyes to adjust to the darkness. Soon, he could see the general outline of his cell, the door and its grate, and the chains hanging loosely about his limbs. Grasping them in his hands, he twisted and pushed until he was able to slip his upper body through its strictures, then went to work on the chains wrapped around his legs. In scant moments, he was free. Weaponless, locked inside a chamber somewhere in Norbardin, bruised and battered, but free. All he needed now was to escape. Somehow. He sank heavily onto the throne, chin resting on his fists, while the silence of emptiness echoed around him.

It took some time before Tarn recognized this was no ordinary dungeon cell, cramped and rank with sewage, dead bodies, and rotten straw. The ceilings here were high and vaulted, upheld by crafted pillars. His throne sat atop a sort of dais, with steps leading up from the dusty floor. They had carried him here blindfolded, but he now knew exactly where he was—an old training hall for the guardians of the North Gate. There were still holes in the walls where racks of weapons once hung. The floor was worn into deep tracks where centuries of feet had pounded the tiles.

Why had they put him here? Tarn wondered. Why not a more secure dungeon cell? The answer was immediately obvious. Jungor wanted a large audience when he came to taunt the king. He very well couldn't lord it over Tarn Bellowgranite in a tiny cell which forced him to limit his witnesses.

Tarn wondered how long it would be before the Hylar thane arrived with his fellow traitors and lackeys. A chamber this large could easily hold fifty or more Hylar dignitaries and their retinues.

Tarn had no intention of waiting around to count them. One thought was uppermost in his mind—the dragon. Even now, it might be stirring in its sleep, roused by all the commotion. The dwarven nation couldn't hope to fight such a creature, neither could they seal off its lair, for chaos dragons could pass through stone as easily as air. All those innocent fools, he thought ruefully, they had laughed when he warned them of the dragon.

At least Tor was safe. Crystal would not long remain in Thorbardin once she learned of Tarn's fate. But what would happen to Tor once he was gone? Would Tor, years hence, even remember his father? Would Jungor be satisfied with exile for the son of the king of Thorbardin, or would he have the child murdered to prevent any future claims to the throne? The thought of that innocent child lying dead, hacked apart by cowards, brought Tarn to his feet. His heart pounded in his chest, gripped in sudden panic.

He knelt down. "Oh Reorx, save my son," the dwarf king prayed, perhaps for the first time since the Chaos War. Though he knew that the gods had left Krynn at the end of the war and could not answer his prayers, still he prayed. "Oh, gods, please save my poor dear innocent boy!"

But after he prayed, he jumped up and considered his options. The ancient wood door was not only locked, but swollen so that the jailer had had to force it shut with his shoulder and kick it several times just to get the key to turn in the rusty lock. The chamber had long ago been stripped of its contents, but he eventually found an old stone baton lying in a corner under heaps of dust. Once used in drills for strengthening arm muscles, it would make an effective if crude weapon. He thought about using it to batter down the door, then gave up that idea as too noisy. The guards would only return, and the next time they wouldn't be so careless with their chains.

Tarn resumed his seat and rested the stone club on his knees. What he really needed was rest, but he couldn't risk closing his eyes for a moment; he might fall into a deep sleep. He had to get ready. If nothing else, he would spend his life to see Jungor Stonesinger's brains splattered all over the floor.

He jerked awake and caught the stone baton as it rolled off his knees. He wasn't sure how long he had been asleep. But he heard footsteps coming, and then the key rattling in the lock. Thinking quickly, Tarn rested the baton next to his thigh while he slipped the chains back around his legs.

The door groaned on its rusted hinges to admit the jailer. He was soberer now than he had been, though in much worse temper. He carried an old bucket and a large sponge in one hand, a smoking torch in the other. As he entered, slopping water onto the floor and cursing, Tarn noticed that the jailer was alone. The hall outside appeared to be empty.

The jailer crossed the chamber and stopped at the bottom of the steps, setting his bucket down. Soapy gray water slopped over the sides. He dropped the sponge into the bucket, then started up the short flight of steps to Tarn's throne.

"Jungor has sent word to make you presentable. He wants you pretty, it seems, so you don't offend the Hylar sensibilities. I have to rinse the piss stains from your trousers," he growled. "But first let me see to your chains. I . . ."

The jailer gaped as Tarn rose up before him, his chains sliding from his limbs. Before he could shout or scream, the stone baton had crushed the dwarf's skull to the earholes. Tarn stepped over him, stooped to the bucket, and washed the dried phlegm from his beard. Then he took the jailer's keys and ghosted from the chamber.

Slipping into the hall, Tarn paused. To his right, the passage descended sharply downward for about forty feet before entering a wider room lit by flickering torches. Twenty yards to his left, the passage ended at an ironbound door, which stood partially open, revealing a dark staircase heading up. He knew that the downward passage led to an old dungeon level, little used these days. But the stairs led to a tower of the North Gate fortifications. He didn't relish the idea of trying to fight his way through a garrison of troops loyal to Jungor Stonesinger. Just as well to sit in his cell and wait, than to try to run that gauntlet. But the dungeons didn't offer any better prospect.

He started for the stairs. At least that was a way out, even if not a very certain one. But the quick thunder of boots on the stairs sent him scurrying back in the other direction. He hurried down the sloping passage and into the room at the bottom just as dozens of dwarves tumbled down the stairs and slammed the door behind them. Tarn heard shouts and curses, and something heavy began to pound on the door. "Kill the king before they break through!" one of the guards shouted.

Tarn cast a quick glance around the small subterranean room. Chains and manacles hung from pegs on the walls, while a large, battered table surrounded by benches occupied the center of the chamber. This was another guardroom, luckily unoccupied at the moment. Opposite the entrance, a rusted metal gate blocked the entrance to a narrow passageway lined with doors—more prison cells. The door to his right was, in all likelihood, the jailer's quarters.

Tarn raced to the metal gate and tried the largest and most ornate of the keys he had taken from the jailer. It twisted in the lock with surprising ease; apparently someone had recently oiled the mechanism. But in his haste, Tarn dropped his weapon. The stone baton, bloody and slippery with the jailer's brains, broke cleanly in half on the hard stone floor. Swearing, he glanced around the room for another weapon. A bench or a length of chain would prove singularly useless against the swords and axes of trained warriors, but the jailer's room held the promise of something more suitable.

He found the door unlocked and quickly entered, silently closing it behind him. The room was tiny and unlit, and it stank to the heights of heaven with the odor of unwashed dwarf. A bent dagger lay on a dressing table beside the sagging wooden bed. Several whips and a cat-o-nine-tails hung inside a wardrobe beside the door. But on the opposite wall, a shield and a pair of goblin swords were displayed atop a cabinet which housed a dinted horsehair-crested helm—testimony of better and more honorable days perhaps, when the jailer had served in the king's army. Tarn ripped the shield and one of the swords from the wall. The shield's leather fittings, old and dry rotted, crumbled as he thrust his arm through the strap, but the sword seemed serviceable enough, if ill-balanced and poorly forged. Thus armed, he crept to the door and leaned against it, straining his ears to hear.

The guards had poured into the small chamber outside the jailer's door. Seeing the open gate, several raced through, the shouts of their fellows encouraging them. "Find the king! Don't let him escape!" Tarn smiled grimly and tightened his grip on his sword.

Just then, in the passage above, there was an explosive noise—the wooden door guarding the stairs bursting from its hinges. Footsteps pounded, and dwarven voices roared battle cries that shook the stone. Tarn opened the door a crack. The guards—a dozen hard-bitten Hylar warriors— had thrown up the table and benches to form a sort of breastwork across the entrance. They crouched behind it now, gripping crossbows and spears. Six Theiwar hung back with loaded crossbows, anxiously watching the gate. By his black robes and belt of pouches, one of them appeared to be a sorcerer. Tarn eyed this one narrowly, knowing him to be the most dangerous.

"Come out, you dogs, and submit to the king's justice!" a voice roared from the passage above. Tarn smiled to hear his old friend Glint Ettinhammer, thane of the Klar, who had somehow rushed to his rescue.

"The king is dead," one of the Hylar guards shouted back. Just then, the four dwarf warriors sent down the prison hall to search for Tarn returned, sliding into the chamber with baffled expressions on their bearded faces.

"Nothing but prisoners. He's not among them," one said to the Theiwar sorcerer. The magician gaped in surprise for a moment before his dark eyes narrowed. He turned his pale visage toward the door to the jailer's room. Tarn stepped back from the door. He picked up the shield, useless for defense to be sure, but an effective distraction if flung into someone's face.

Outside, the Hylar guard's words were met with cries of dismay from above. One in particular rose above the rest. "Kill them all then! Traitorous dogs, assassins! No mercy for anyone with the king's blood on his hands." Tarn started, wondering whether his ears were deceiving him, or if the dead had joined the living to revenge their king. For surely that was the voice of his old friend Mog Bonecutter, leading the charge.

Tarn jerked open the door, surprising the Theiwar warriors slinking toward it, crossbows at the ready. At his sudden appearance, the sorcerer lifted his hands and began to chant a spell. Tarn flung the shield. The closest warrior ducked the goblin shield, discharging his crossbow into the ceiling in his excitement. The shield careened off the sorcerer's shoulder, staggering him momentarily, and breaking the intense mental focus so vital to spellcasting. He was forced to begin his spellcasting anew.

Tarn slammed the door shut just as a half-dozen crossbow bolts shuddered and splintered into the wood, then nearly snatched it from its hinges as he swiftly charged out, bellowing, "Thorbardin!" His goblin sword cleaved the closest Theiwar warrior to the spine. His next blow shivered the brittle goblin-forged blade to splinters over the iron helm of one of the Hylar warriors. Momentarily stunned by the impact, the dwarf was powerless to prevent Tarn from yanking the war axe from his belt. Before the other Theiwar could reload their crossbows, Tarn was among them, laying about with the flat of the axe blade, cutting down Hylar and Theiwar alike.

Despite surprise and a valiant effort, the king would quickly have been overcome where it not for the simultaneous assault led by Mog Bonecutter and Glint Ettinhammer. As Tarn slashed a path toward the Theiwar spellcaster, the contingent of Klar rescuers slammed into the hastily erected barrier and cast it aside. For a few brief moments, seasoned Hylar veterans grappled beard to beard with half-mad Klar shock troops, before the rescuer's momentum and superior numbers overwhelmed the Hylar guards. Those who could broke and ran, sweeping past the remaining Theiwar, who quickly followed them into the dead end of the prison section. Their passage jostled the sorcerer just as he was about to cast another spell. Before he could recover, Tarn felled him with a blow to the jaw; as the sorcerer dropped to the floor, a handful of glistening black powder spilled from his fingers.

A dozen Klar warriors pelted after the guards, Glint Ettinhammer in their lead. Half mad with battle lust, Tarn cast about for another foe. What confronted him chilled his blood—a dwarf wearing the mask of the death skald and bearing a gleaming warhammer in his scarred fists. Feeling the ancient dread of the skald, Tarn backed away from this new enemy, war axe warily lowered. But then the dwarf dropped to one knee and tore aside the mask, revealing the tear-streaked face of his old captain of the guard, dead these two months and thought buried under the ruins of the Isle of the Dead.

"Mog?" Tarn asked, his hackles bristling in horror. "Have you returned to haunt me?"

"I am sorry flesh, my king," Mog wept with joy. "I live. So long as you have need of my sword, I will smite your enemies, even unto my own death." These were words from the ritual that Tarn used to induct new members into his personal guard. Hearing them now struck him to the soul.

"My old friend, I did not believe miracles possible anymore," Tarn said, his voice cracking with emotion.

"There's still one or two miracles left to this old world," one of the Klar warriors said with a laugh. He was older than any of the others by more than a century, and Tarn wondered why they had even bothered to bring him along.

At his look of bafflement, Mog answered the king's unspoken question. "My lord, this is Ogduan Bloodspike, the true death skald of the Isle of the Dead. He saved my life," he said with a barely suppressed sneer. "How he came to follow us here, I don't know."

CHAPTER

37

G lint strode down the narrow prison hall toward the sound of fighting. As he passed each cell door, he stopped and peered through the narrow grate. So far, all the cells were empty. But as he turned a corner and saw his warriors cutting down the last of the resisting Hylar guards, he found one cell that still contained an occupant. He stared through the tiny metal grate into the lightless cell. A small, weak voice spoke from the far corner.

"Help me. I am a loyal dwarf wrongfully imprisoned."

"Loyal to who?" Glint asked as he stepped back. With a single swipe of his war axe, he shattered the rusty lock. He shot back the bolt and pulled the door open on its ancient creaking hinges, then stepped inside.

Flickering light from torches in the hall illuminated the interior of the tiny cell and its miserable occupant. Beaten and battered, his pale skin bruised purple around his lips and eyes, Ferro Dunskull blinked painfully.

"Ah, here's the traitor now!" Glint said with glee. "How I've longed to cleave your scrawny neck." He strode across the floor of the cell in two steps and jerked the cringing Daergar to his feet.

Ferro slumped against him, mewling in terror and clinging to the Klar thane's arms. "Please, have mercy on me," he whined.

Furious, Glint tried to untangle himself. "Stand up, you coward! Stand up and take it like a dwarf. I want to get a clear swing at your neck. Ah!" Glint leaped back in surprise, his eyes nearly popping from their sockets as he stared at the hilt of a small dagger protruding from between the overlapping plates of his chest armor. "Ah, you dog! You stabbed me!"

Lifting his axe, the Klar thane intended to end the life of this miserable traitor at once, but his weapon felt strangely heavy in his hand. His fingers grew numb and his vision began to narrow and darken. His knees buckled and he sank to the floor, his axe clattering on the stones. "Damn it all to hell!" he swore thickly. "And such a pitifully small dagger." He toppled back, his great shaggy head smacking the hard stone floor.

Zen picked up the dead thane's war axe even as his arms lengthened and grew more muscular, his pale skin flushed with a healthy glow. His lank black hair became bushy and red, his beard full and bristling. Prison rags changed to gleaming plate armor. Hefting the axe, he stepped into the hall and closed the cell door just as the Klar warriors were returning from the slaughter. A few bore evidence of the valor of Hylar arms.

"Did you get them all?" Zen asked in Glint's jovial booming voice.

"Aye, Thane Ettinhammer. Not a one escaped!" one of the Klar soldiers answered.

"Good. There's nothing in there but a Theiwar, dead more than a week," Zen said, pointing with his thumb. "Gods, what a smell! Let's find the king."

Striding ahead, the draconian led them back along the prison hall and into the small chamber. The Klar loosed a thundering cheer when they saw Tarn alive. The king smiled to hear them and welcomed them with open arms. They surged around him and tried to lift him onto their shoulders, despite his protests. Angrily, Mog began to lay about with his fists, driving them back. Half the group were feral Klar, and he barely trusted them more than their enemies. The Theiwar sorcerer glowered from a chair in the corner, his hands tightly bound behind his back with mushroom-fiber cords, a rag stuffed in his mouth. A large purple knot rose from the side of his face. Zen stepped past him quickly, in case the wizard still had some spell in effect that might reveal that the draconian was now disguised as Glint.

"Thane Ettinhammer!" Tarn shouted. "Where are you going?"

Zen stopped short, just within the exit. Remembering Glint's excitement at finding him in his cell, he quickly responded, "Ferro Dunskull is not here. I hasten to search the other dungeons for that miserable traitor."

"Leave off. We have larger concerns than him," Tarn answered. But the Klar thane had already gone.

———✦◆✦———

Brecha Quickspring, thane of the Theiwar dwarves, stood on a rooftop overlooking the North Gate plaza. This high vantage point gave her an excellent view of the situation, which was deteriorating. Below her, a hundred or so Hylar and Theiwar warriors faced a mob of two thousand dwarf citizens of every clan. Most of those in the crowd were well armed. Here and there a spear or halberd pricked angrily above the sea of bearded faces. The dwarves of Thorbardin had a long history of maintaining a well-armed populace. It was a dangerous world and each dwarf was expected to be ready to defend his home and homeland at a moment's notice.

Brecha made a mental note to speak to Jungor about changing the law, once his position as king was firmly established. An armed populace was a dangerous populace, independent and difficult to govern, as amply demonstrated by the scene unfolding below her. Word had spread that Tarn Bellowgranite had been captured and taken to the guard tower on the north side of the plaza. The tower lay conveniently near the Hylar district on the first level of Norbardin. It seemed that the crowd had formed largely without any express purpose—curiosity more than anything else. And no one knew yet how to react to the sudden seizure of power by Jungor Stonesinger and his allies. But in some quarters of the city, Jungor's forces had not yet gained control, especially in the fortress area of the king's residence. There were also pockets of resistance in Klar and Daergar neighborhoods.

This large mob filled Brecha with misgivings. Normally content to allow their leaders to lead them, they could turn dangerous if sufficiently provoked. Brecha didn't think it was word of Tarn's capture that had stirred them up. The king was too unpopular. Some other power was at work here, and she had quickly sent word to Jungor of the crowd gathering. She stood on the roof, her hands folded into the sleeves of her black robes, while she waited for her agents to return with their reports. Jungor was still in his home on the second level, where he and a dozen loyal Hylar leaders had gathered before coming to pay their "respects" to the captured king.

A movement of the crowd below brought Brecha to the roof's edge. A party of armed dwarves had suddenly poured out of the guard tower, joining the Hylar and Theiwar guards ringing the tower's base. As the crowd drew back, Brecha swore bitterly and slammed her fist against the stone ledge. "Fools! What idiot ordered a sortie? Surely they don't mean to force . . ."

Her voice dwindled away as the noise swelled up from the plaza below. The dwarves from the tower weren't joining the guards; they were attacking them! Brecha quickly spotted in their midst the unmistakable golden mane and towering frame of Tarn Bellowgranite. A massive silver warhammer gleamed in his fist as he struck right and left. Now the crowd had reversed its direction and was sweeping toward the guards battling for their lives. In moments, the Hylar and Theiwar were overwhelmed.

Brecha clutched the roof battlements to steady herself. The words to a teleportation spell came unbidden to her mind, but she hesitated. The news of Tarn's escape needed to be delivered to Jungor without delay. Yet at the same time, she was in a perfect position to strike him down from above. She knew several spells that could kill the king from this distance. But would Jungor mind if Tarn died thusly? Was it the wise thing to do?

While she hesitated, she saw that the battle was already over. Surrounded by the cheering mob, Tarn crossed the plaza and climbed the steps to the building whose roof Brecha occupied. The Theiwar thane peered between the battlements, unseen by the fickle crowd, now celebrating wildly. Brecha spotted numerous Hylar and Daewar in the crowd, even a few of her own Theiwar. Had how Tarn pulled off this unlikely resurgence?

A fireball would kill him, the Theiwar thane decided. By the time the people in the crowd recovered from the explosion, she would be long gone, lofted away on the wings of a teleport spell, and safely at Jungor's side, explaining everything. Digging a ball of bat guano from her pouch of spell components, she mouthed the words to the spell, silently rehearsing to make sure she recalled the proper cadences and pronunciations. She leaned out over the battlements, holding the ball of dung mixed with sulfur aloft, looking down contemputously as Tarn lifted his silver warhammer above his head, drawing yet another thunderous cheer.

With her mind now focused on the magic, Brecha almost didn't hear the surprising words shouted by those below her. "The Hammer! The Hammer of Kharas!" Tarn thrust the mighty weapon over his head, holding it to its full height so that everyone in the mob could see it in his hand.

The ball of dung fell from Brecha's fingertips, the words of the spell slipped from her mind. She staggered back from the battlements, silently thanking every god that she could name that she hadn't cast that spell. The Hammer of Kharas! He who wielded that famed dwarven relic was the true king, and no dwarf would dare challenge his rule. Its powers were many and little understood. In all likelihood, her fireball would have slain everyone around Tarn but left the one holding the Hammer unharmed. She had no way of knowing, and the main thing now was that Jungor must know this news.

Whispering a quick word of magic, she brought to mind an image of Jungor Stonesinger and vanished, just as another thunderous roar swept over the battlements.

"To the Hall of Thanes!"

CHAPTER 38

Crystal paced the wall that ran along the north entrances of her fortress home. A cap of steel on her head and a spear in her fist, she looked no different than the hundreds of other dwarves lining the battlements or filling the courtyards. Yet the silent dwarves defending the fortress snapped to attention as she passed, returning to their vigilant watch when she moved on.

Tarn had been gone what seemed an eternity when Glint Ettinhammer returned with a handful of Klar and the news of her husband's capture. Despite their failure to capture the transportation shaft on the second level, Otaxx Shortbeard had managed to take the third-level shaft, and to hold it against the Theiwar sent to dislodge him. The general was a veteran warrior and had fought the Theiwar during the Chaos War. He knew how to battle magic, and his foothold was enough to secure the southern half of the third level. Right now, though, she had no reserves to relieve him. And she must hold the north gate of the king's fortress, as this was the other major entry to this district. As yet, they had not been attacked. But with Tarn captured, Crystal knew it was only a matter of time before Jungor challenged her.

She was still numb to the dire reality of her pedicament. Whenever she thought of Tarn being held prisoner in a cell somewhere, she could barely stand to bring that image of him to her mind. Her heart refused to accept such a defeat. She felt as though he were merely away on an errand, and more than once caught herself thinking, "When Tarn returns, I need to speak to him about . . ."

The idea that Tarn might never return lurked at the edge of her thoughts. She knew that if she seriously entertained that notion, she would break down utterly and be unable to continue. And she couldn't allow herself that luxury. Tor needed her, and so did the forces watching her as she paced nervously amidst them. She was the last thing standing between her baby and Jungor Stonesinger's fanatic minions. What they would do to the son of the king, she didn't dare to guess. She only knew that they would reach him only over her own dead body. Perhaps, if she held out long enough, she could strike a bargain that would allow their escape into exile. . . .

She went cold at that desperate thought, her heart hammering in her chest. Sooner or later, she knew, she would have to accept that Tarn was doomed if he was in Jungor's hands. He was probably already dead. She had no hope that Glint Ettinhammer and Mog Bonecutter would succeed in their mad scheme to rescue the king, but she hadn't dared to try to stop them.

The appearance of their old captain of the guard, believed dead since the Festival of Lights celebration, had surprised her when she thought she could no longer feel any emotion. And for a few brief moments, she had felt hope rekindled. True to his character, the Klar thane had tried to encourage her by pointing out that Jungor's forces had merely captured Tarn, while they had slaughtered everyone else. They must therefore want Tarn alive for a reason.

But ever since Mog, Glint, and their company had departed, the bleak reality had returned to shadow her.

The Hammer of Kharas already seemed a figment of her imagination. The Hammer was not a relic as much revered by the hill dwarves and so she placed little faith in its powers anyway. Nor was she particularly comforted by the assurances of the strange old Klar who had gone off with the rescue party. Before leaving, he had patted her hand and said in a gentle voice, "Don't you worry, lass. He won't go and get himself killed just yet." She wasn't sure if the old dwarf had been talking about Tarn or someone else, and he had slipped away before she could reproach him.

At least Tor was safe. Right now, he was deep inside the fortress with hundreds of feet of stone between his room and their enemies. And he could have no more formidable bodyguard than Aunt Needlebone, though Crystal had been sure also to place her most trusted guards outside the door to the nursery—dwarves she had trained herself in the years since her marriage to Tarn.

It was the darn waiting that really grated on her nerves. Though she had little hope that Glint and the others would succeed, still that tiny spark of hope tormented her. She restlessly walked the battlements, her boots stamping on the stone, cursing the darkness of this underground city and its walls that prevented her from seeing very far in any direction. She missed the wide open spaces of her homeland, the wild hills and the wind rippling through fields of grain. For perhaps the thousandth time, she peered down the dark street leading away from the gate, looking for any sign of dwarves massing for an attack. But for the thousandth time, she saw only an empty street that disappeared into darkness beyond the light of their torches. A dwarf operating a large bull's-eye lantern from atop the postern gate swept the nearer shadows, but no, she couldn't even detect a gully dwarf in its light.

A clatter of dwarf boots in the courtyard below distracted Crystal from her thoughts. She turned to look and saw a pair of Klar talking animatedly with one of the Daewar guards assigned to this entrance. The Daewar turned and pointed up at her, and she felt her heart stop.

"What is it?" she cried, running for the nearest tower without even waiting for an answer. In moments, she had descended the stairs and had joined the two Klar. The dwarves lining the battlements watched, their faces also dark with worry. "What has happened?" Crystal asked breathlessly.

"Thane Ettinhammer is at the south entrances," one of the Klar guards said.

She felt her hands go cold and numb. "Alone?" she asked.

The guard nodded.

Her passage through the fortress was a blur. Her feet hardly seemed to touch the ground. Word spread quickly through the residence that Glint had returned alone, and others followed behind her as discreetly as possible. It seemed to take an age to reach the south entrances, and then even longer to go from entrance to entrance until she found the Klar thane.

As soon as she saw Glint's pale, drawn face and slumped shoulders, she knew the worst. She hardly recognized him. The Klar thane had been a figure of brash confidence since the day she had first met him. Now, she found him slumped on a curb near the southwest entrance. A dozen guards stood nearby, trying not to stare at him. When Crystal appeared, they looked away from her as well. She stood for a moment beneath a stone arch, too frightened to move, wondering if she would ever be able to draw breath again. It was some time before Glint looked up and noticed her. A strange expression passed across his face, a strange rictus grin that she didn't fathom. His pallor was bloodless. He rose wearily to his feet to meet her.

Crystal greeted him silently, taking his old scarred hand in hers and pressing it. She could tell by the way he avoided looking her in the eye that this was perhaps the most difficult thing he had ever done. "Is there . . . someplace we could . . . go?" he asked in a voice strained with emotion.

Nodding, she led him into a passage between the entrance courtyard and an inner court. There, they found a stout, ironbound door, which opened into a small armory. Little remained of its contents; the shields, armor, and weapons had been almost entirely distributed among the troops loyal to Tarn Bellowgranite. Only a few spears and an old battle axe remained.

Crystal swung the door shut on its silent hinges and then leaned her back against it. She drew a deep breath, as her mind reeled. Was there even a need to ask? The story was writ plain enough on the Klar thane's face.

He turned to her, eyes downcast, his great shaggy head sunk almost between his shoulders. "I'm sorry," he blurted, choking back a sob. Crystal flew into his arms, a wordless moan wrenched from her breast. She clung to his thick neck, her face buried in his chest. He wrapped his huge, burly arms around her and pressed her tight, endlessly repeating, "I'm sorry. I'm sorry." It was as though he had been robbed of the ability to speak any other words.

She didn't know how long she clung to him. He bore her weight patiently, even though he seemed on the verge of collapsing with weariness. He shifted, gathering her with one arm while the other hung limply at his side. Perhaps he had been injured, though the thought barely penetrated Crystal's consciousness. Gradually, her sobs lessened, though she doubted her grief would ever be dulled. Every time she would look at their son from now until death claimed her, she would be reminded of his father.

She needed to hear the words spoken, no matter how painful.

"So Tarn is dead then," Crystal asked, her face still pressed to the Klar thane's chest.

"He will be soon enough," Zen disguised as Glint answered. "As will you."

Crystal looked up to see the rictus grin had returned. Glint's pale eyes hardened to dark pinpricks; his face took on an explicable reptilian pallor.

The door creaked open. It was enough distraction to give the draconian assassin pause. The dagger in his fist hesitated just inches from Crystal's throat.

It was Haruk Mastersword standing in the doorway. "Mistress, here you are. Graps said you had . . . Mistress!" Crystal saw light flicker off the dagger in the Klar thane's hand. With warrior's reflexes, she reacted instantly, striking the blade up and aside even as the hand that wielded it plunged toward her throat. The point of the blade gouged a furrow beneath her chin but otherwise passed harmlessly aside. Zen swore a dwarven oath.

Crystal twisted out of his grasp as he reversed the blow with a backhanded slash. She ducked beneath the attack so that it merely scraped shrilly across her metal armor, throwing a spray of sparks into the air. She had left her spear back at the north entrance. But before Glint could renew his attack, Haruk stepped between her and the thane, his sword drawn.

Shrugging off the form of the Klar thane, Zen once more assumed his natural shape—that of a sivak draconian—astonishing the two dwarves now confronted with his seven-feet-tall form. Taking advantage of their surprise, Zen snatched a battle axe from the weapon rack on the wall behind him and struck.

Haruk barely managed to fend off the attack at the last instant. The power of the huge draconian's blow numbed his arm, but he maintained his grip on his weapon and parried another devastating slash. Sparks exploded in the air as the two weapons collided like a thunderclap. Haruk staggered, trying to maintain his position between the draconian and his mentor.

Meanwhile, Crystal dragged a spear from a barrel. It was ill-made and too lengthy for her, but she had to help Haruk somehow.

Zen swung his axe in a low arc. Once more, Haruk parried it, but this time his numb fingers could no longer maintain their grip. His sword torn from his grasp, the force of the slash sent him staggering back. Crystal stepped to her left and slipped past him. A quick thrust of her spear distracted the draconian long enough to allow Haruk to move out of the creature's reach. Haruk shook his hands to try to regain some feeling, while Crystal's drove the draconian back a step with a series of lightning feints.

But the draconian was fast. Crystal feinted once too often. Timing his attack perfectly, he slashed out with the axe, lopping off her spear just below the steel head. His next blow was aimed to do the same to her head.

Picking up his sword, Haruk shrieked his battle cry and leaped at the draconian. Crystal instantly recognized Haruk's habitually futile reaction to an opponent he could not defeat, knowing that he intended to sacrifice himself in order to strike a major blow. The young dwarf's attack was slow, clumsy, and easily thwarted, yet it was intended to distract the creature. Crystal seized the moment and struck with the staff portion of her spear, shattering the draconian's knee. Zen cried out and stumbled, his axe dropped, and Haruk, off balance and swinging wildly, tumbled over him.

Before Zen could recover, Crystal tossed aside her by now useless weapon and grabbed another spear from the barrel. Zen struggled to rise, but Haruk had become entangled with his legs. Crystal thrust with all her might, not knowing how thick the draconian's scaly hide might be. The sharp spear head sheared through scale and muscle to emerge an arm's length from the creature's back.

Black draconian blood erupted from Zen's mouth. Feeling the imminence of death, he spoke now in the language of dragons, which few mortals knew or understood. But the import of his words and the hatred with which he spoke, spitting blood and phlegm with each phrase, was all Crystal needed to hear to know that the creature was calling down its blackest curse upon her head. An involuntary shudder passed down her spine.

With his last, dying words, Zen laid his great reptilian head down on the cold stone floor stained black with his own blood. For eighteen months he had lived by his wits undetected in the halls of Thorbardin, slaying at will until his revenge was completed. And now he had been killed by a woman and a mere child. His shame knew no bounds, and he prayed to whatever god would listen that his curse be granted. His prayer ended unfinished.

Crystal dragged Haruk away from the filthy creature. Though it no longer seemed to breathe, neither did it seem to be entirely dead. Its muscles continued to twitch, its mouth to champ. Even as they watched in horror, the creature began to transform once more. But this time, it took on the appearance of Crystal herself. After a few moments, they found themselves looking at her own dead body stretched out on the floor with a spear wound in her chest. Crystal stared at it a moment longer until she was nearly overcome with revulsion.

She turned to Haruk and quickly looked him over. "Are you badly injured?" she asked.

"What is that thing?" the young dwarf answered absently as he continued to stare at her corpse.

"Haruk, listen to me," Crystal demanded. The tone of command in her voice broke through his shock. He jerked to attention, just as he had done from the first days he was a lowly student in her spear class.

"N-no, I am uninjured," he stammered.

She breathed a quick sigh of relief. Multitudinous questions boiled in her mind, but she asked the most obvious one first. "Haruk, what are you doing here? I thought you were with your uncle."

"I am, or, I was," he said. "Uncle Jungor sent me here with a message, knowing that you would be obliged to see me."

Crystal frowned in disappointment but nodded that she understood. Perhaps this was the bargain she had hoped for, the trade that would allow her to escape into exile with their son. "What does the Hylar thane have to say?" she asked.

"He offers a trade," Haruk answered ashamedly, and sheepishly too, the words leaving a bad taste in his mouth.

"Very well. What does he want for Tarn's freedom? Whatever it is, we'll pay it. I hope you understand, Haruk, that I bear you no grudge. But I am sick to my soul of mountain dwarves and their wars and intrigues."

"Tarn's freedom?" Haruk asked in confusion.

"Yes, what does he want in exchange for the king?"

"But Tarn . . . that is, the king is already free. He escaped. I . . . I thought you knew," Haruk stammered.

With a shriek of joy, Crystal wrapped her arms around the young Hylar warrior and lifted him off the ground. "Escaped, you say?" she cried as she set him on his feet. "Escaped? Then what could Jungor possibly want to trade for?"

"The Hammer of Kharas," Haruk answered solemnly, gathering his dignity. Hearing the sounds of battle, several dwarves had gathered at the door. They gaped to see the two Crystal Heathstones—one dead and sprawled on the floor, the other quite alive. Not a few wondered which was the real one.

"The Hammer? And what does the *Hylar thane* offer for it?" Crystal said.

Haruk's face blanched, and he seemed to struggle to produce the answer. Finally, he said in a cracking voice, "My uncle offers . . . the life of your son, Tor Bellowgranite, in exchange for the Hammer of Kharas."

CHAPTER
39

Tarn hurried north toward the fortress. With the Hammer of Kharas in his hands, he had marched through district after district, rallying the people of Norbardin to his banner, quickly relieving the besieged Klar and Daergar quarters in the Anvil's Echo with hardly a fight, so great was the mob that swarmed to follow him. Arriving in the Council Hall, he and his force were met by Shahar Bellowsmoke, standing amidst a scene of bloody slaughter. The Daergar in his command had killed hundreds of dwarves loyal to Jungor Stonesinger, many after their surrender. Among the dead were Shahar's own brother and Astar Trueshield, captain of Jungor's personal guard, slain by Shahar's own hand in single combat on the council steps. Shahar, still drunk on revenge and murder, greeted the thane with a soot-stained face and gore-soaked hands, grinning fiercely.

Not a few recalled that the Council Hall was once a temple dedicated to the god Reorx, father of the dwarven race. No one dared to guess how Reorx might have viewed the fratricide in his own hallowed halls. Tarn walked among the carnage for nearly an hour, horrorstruck by the depth and ferocity of the Daergar vengeance; the sweetness of his rescue and victory was forever tainted. The death skald, Ogduan Bloodspike, sat on the temple steps and wept so pitifully that even Mog had tried to comfort him.

Little now remained of Jungor's resistance, however. The last remaining Theiwar had fled their defenses at the transportation shaft. Here, Tarn found more bodies piled up—the bodies of those who had followed him into the trap. And here also he met Otaxx Shortbeard. The old general looked worn with care and grief, for he bore ill news. Something had happened at the fortress—an attack of some sort. He wasn't sure, and he dared not speculate before the king, for the reports he had were merely rumors. Some said that Crystal was dead, others that Tor had been killed.

The Hammer of Kharas swung forgotten in Tarn's fist as he strode up the short street from the transportation shaft to the southeast entrance of the fortress. Crowds thronged both sides of the street, though they were silent for the most part. A few tried to rouse a cheer for the king's return, but these were met with frowns. This, more than anything else, confirmed Tarn's deepest misgivings. The gates swung wide in greeting, the way lined with his warriors. Otaxx Shortbeard trudged along behind Tarn, his chin nearly on his chest, while Mog Bonecutter and his Klar silently brought up the rear. They passed though the tall entrance, through a wood gate and beneath a massive iron grate into a courtyard flanked by towers. An archway led a short distance into another court beyond. Here, they found dwarves carrying something on a litter from the gate's armory.

Stumbling forward, Tarn ordered the litter bearers to a halt. They set their burden on the ground and stood back. Tarn glanced at them without recognition as he knelt beside the litter and flipped back its covering sheet.

The powers that had set themselves against him were indeed cruel, he now knew. There was no reckoning with them. He rose to his feet and noticed that the Hammer of

Kharas was still in his hand. The Hammer created in recognition of the gallantry of the heroic dwarf Kharas had come to represent all that was good and noble about the dwarves. It was the symbol of his right to rule Thorbardin. Only the Hammer could forge a true dragonlance, a blessed weapon of the gods. It had never been used for evil purposes.

But now, Tarn felt the blood well in his heart and burn like the fires of the molten earth bursting up through rents in the stone, searing through reason and sanity. Even his fears of the chaos dragon sleeping in its chamber beneath the city vanished in his lust for revenge. One thought remained to him. He would see Jungor Stonesinger dead for the murder of his wife. He would crush the Hylar thane's skull with the Hammer of Kharas, even if the blood of a fellow mountain dwarf defiled the holy weapon beyond any atonement.

"Death to Jungor Stonesinger!" he roared. "Death to all traitors!" He started toward the gate, outside of which a huge mob of dwarves waited for him to lead them on a rampage of revenge through Norbardin. Forty years of unresolved feuds boiled just beneath the surface, awaiting any excuse to explode.

But Ogduan Bloodspike stepped into his path. The old dwarf laid a restraining hand on the king's arm. And at his touch the red haze of battle evaporated from his vision, as though icy water had been dashed into his face. Tarn stepped back, fear and wonder in his eyes.

"That's not your wife," the old dwarf said. "I've been trying to tell you, but you are possessed."

"Wha . . . ?" Tarn glanced at the faces of the dwarves around him, noticing that one of the litter bearers was Haruk Mastersword.

"Haruk? What are you doing here?"

"This is not your wife," the young dwarf said. "This is a draconian that she and I killed. It was trying to murder her, and took her form in death."

"Draconian?" Tarn exclaimed. "Then Crystal is still alive?"

Haruk nodded, but his face was etched with lines of grief too deep for someone so young. His eyes, once so youthful, had the look of someone betrayed.

"Where is she?" Tarn demanded.

"Inside the residence."

"With Tor?"

No one answered. Haruk hung his head, his face flushed scarlet with shame. Tarn grabbed him by the shoulders and shook the young dwarf violently. "Tell me. What has happened to my son?" he cried.

CHAPTER
40

The Hall of Thanes stood empty, its great echoing dome rising into the shadows high above. Tarn paused at the entrance and gazed around the rows of benches. In all his years, he had never seen this place not filled to capacity, the air thick with torch smoke and the reek of unwashed bodies. Now, the halls and balconies outside were vacant and dark.

A pall of fear hung over Norbardin. Its streets were silent save for the tramp of Jungor's soldiers. Patrols of Hylar and Theiwar warriors were scouring the streets and alleys, enforcing martial law with brutal efficiency. His people cowered in darkened rooms with their families gathered about them, behind bolted doors and shuttered windows, fearful of looking out and violating the laws of the new king of Thorbardin.

Tarn had doomed his people to this fate by agreeing to Jungor's terms. The Hylar thane had wasted no time seizing power, even before the Hammer of Kharas was delivered into his greedy hands. Martial law was ordered, dissenters and troublemakers imprisoned "for their own safety." From the ranks of dwarves still loyal to him, Jungor chose new thanes for the Hylar, Klar, Daergar, and

Daewar clans. Dwarves who had always enjoyed the privilege of voting for their thanes or seeing them chosen in trials of combat learned of their new leaders by way of official proclamation.

Tomorrow, Jungor had promised, martial law would be rescinded and the normal daily activities of Thorbardin would resume, but Tarn didn't deceive himself that the new king would be a just ruler, nor that those already imprisoned would ever be released. The Council was filled with his puppets, the streets crowded with his soldiers.

Many of Tarn's own house guards had been "recruited" into Jungor's service. Less than a score of dwarves had volunteered to accompany Tarn to the empty Council Hall to complete the act that would hand over final power to the new king of Thorbardin.

His wife, Crystal Heathstone, was at his side, of course. Her face was stricken with grief and worry, so that he hardly recognized the beautiful young Neidar princess whom he had married not that many years ago. Though Jungor promised that Tor would not be harmed and would be handed over in exchange for the Hammer, she no longer trusted the decency or honor of any mountain dwarf, not after the brutal way they murdered Aunt Needlebone while kidnapping her son.

Mog Bonecutter carried the Hammer of Kharas before him, wrapped in a cloth of gold that had been stained black with the blood of Tor's nanny. Also in Tarn's small party was the ever-loyal Daewar general, Otaxx Shortbeard, whose own fortunes had risen and fallen with his king's. Haruk Mastersword escorted them as the representative of Jungor's new government. The others in their party consisted of a mixed dozen of Klar, Daergar, and Daewar warriors. Shahar Bellowsmoke, former thane of the Daergar and cousin of the king, walked at their rear beside the death skald, Ogduan Bloodspike.

This was all that was left of the thousands who had marched just two days ago through Norbardin, following the Hammer of Kharas to victory over Jungor Stonesinger's fanatic rebels. Tarn believed that, with the Hammer in his hands, he could have swept into Jungor's palace and killed the rebellious Hylar thane, and his people would have cheered him for it. But Tor would have been killed. Without the Hammer, he could never again be king, but without his son he didn't know that he could continue living. The choice was easy for him. He only delayed in order to try to win concessions for his followers and for the people he would leave behind. But he had failed in this as well. Jungor considered it an even bargain—the Hammer of Kharas for the life of his son, and in the end, Tarn was forced to accept.

Now, as Tarn began to descend the stairs toward the center of the empty Council Hall, a light flared to life on the floor below, a brilliant white glow that emanated from the stone atop Jungor's staff.

The new king of Thorbardin sat upon the throne of the dead, a seemly chair, Tarn deemed. The golden crown of the king looked small and preposterous on his skull-like head. Beside his throne stood the Theiwar thane, Brecha Quickspring, a large basket resting at her feet. To their right and left sat the new thanes chosen by Jungor to lend an illusion of legitimacy to his dictates. Tarn didn't even recognize most of them—petty functionaries or merchants of minor wealth who had somehow wormed their way into Jungor's graces. However, he was not surprised to see Hextor Ironhaft occupying the seat of the Hylar thane. Tarn silently hoped he enjoyed his new position, for he had probably paid enough for it. Of the thane of the gully dwarves, there was no sign. Even her chair had been removed.

Haruk Mastersword paused at the door to allow the others to enter, for Jungor had ordered that no one be allowed to witness what transpired in the Council Hall this day. As Crystal passed him, the look of shame on his face nearly tore her heart from her chest. But she said nothing, knowing all too well that Jungor Stonesinger was keenly watching his nephew and would punish any sign of weakness. She touched his arm for a moment before moving on. The young dwarf turned away and fled to hide his tears.

As they neared the floor of the Council Hall, Tarn kept a keen eye on his captain. Mog was the only armed member of their group, and this only because he had been chosen to carry the Hammer of Kharas. Tarn feared that Mog might be planning some final act of defiance. Yet he could not deny his captain the honor of carrying the weapon he had brought back from oblivion, even if his job today was to hand it over to their worst enemy.

He breathed a heavy sigh of relief when, as they reached the floor, the Klar captain stepped to his right, unwrapped the Hammer of Kharas from its gruesome shroud, and presented it to Tarn. Tarn took it in his grasp and stepped up onto the dais.

A greedy hiss escaped Jungor's lips when he saw the fabled weapon in Tarn's hands. No dwarf of the mountain could look upon the Hammer of Kharas and not feel his soul stirring. They drank its legend with their mother's milk and dreamed of its power into their last doddering years. No other icon so perfectly symbolized their ties to their mountain home, to their history, to their god, and to everything that made them dwarves. The Hammer represented honor, might, righteousness, and the covenant of the dwarves as the chosen people of Reorx.

Jungor rose to his feet and pushed the glowing staff into Brecha's hands, while his own hands curled into claws that began to twitch in anticipation. Biting back the column of bile that rose in his throat, Tarn started toward him.

"Stop!" Jungor shrieked, holding up one claw-like finger. "Come no closer, Tarn Bellowgranite. I do not trust you." Tarn grabbed Mog, who had started forward, too.

Crystal stepped onto the dais, fiercely whispering Tarn's name.

"Be quiet!" Tarn hissed over his shoulder. "No one move."

"Lay the Hammer on the ground," Jungor ordered.

"First, where is my son?" Tarn demanded in return.

"He is here, and unharmed," Brecha Quickspring answered with an evil smile. Holding one hand above the basket, she closed her eyes and chanted a brief spell. A disk of greenish light formed beneath the basket, then rose, lifting it into the air.

"Such a noisy boy, like his disagreeable nanny," she sighed. "I am glad to give him back."

"Now put the Hammer on the ground," Jungor said. Tarn laid the weapon on the ground at his feet, then rose up and glared at Jungor across the dais.

"Step away from it," Jungor ordered.

"My son," Tarn said firmly, refusing to move. Jungor nodded to Brecha, who sent the glowing disk of green light floating toward Tarn. He stepped away from the Hammer and grabbed the basket as it passed near to him. Setting it quickly on the ground, he threw back the blankets to reveal his infant son, soundly asleep in a deep nest of rich blankets. A shudder of relief passed through his frame. He moved aside as Crystal plunged her hands into the basket and swept her son to her breast, sobbing hysterically.

When Tarn turned back to the council, he saw that Hextor Ironhaft had already grabbed the Hammer. The new Hylar thane knelt and ceremoniously presented the holy weapon to his new king. As Jungor's fingers closed around its haft, he seemed to stagger under its weight. But he quickly regained his composure, glaring triumphantly at the other thanes. Last of all, his hawklike visage turned to the king he had finally replaced.

"Before I go," Tarn said. "I want to warn you one more time. I want to warn all of you that you are in great danger." Several of the new thanes rolled their eyes and shook their beards in disbelief. Even defeated, the half-breed would not give up.

Infuriated, Tarn continued. "No! You will listen to me this one last time. There is a chaos dragon asleep beneath the new Council Hall being built. Captain Grisbane and I saw it with our own eyes. I beg you to take the architect and make an investigation. The creature is a monstrous—"

"Gaul Quarrystone is dead," Jungor interrupted, laughing as he spoke. "As is Captain Grisbane. Conveniently, no one other than you has seen this creature."

"The creature is there. Go and look for yourself, if you have the courage," Tarn angrily fired back.

"I have looked," Jungor responded patronizingly. "There is nothing there but an old lava tube, which will, unfortunately, force us to abandon the construction of the new Council Hall. Like all your other machinations, Tarn Bellowgranite, the new Council Hall was ill-planned and poorly executed. Its empty shell will serve as a monument to your rule."

"Nothing there?" Tarn asked disbelievingly. "You saw no dragon?"

"The lava tube was empty and quite cool," Jungor said.

"Don't you see what this means?" Tarn cried. "The dragon is awake and on the move! You must abandon the city at once, before it attacks!"

"Begone from this city, you babbling fool!" Jungor shouted, pointing with the Hammer of Kharas toward the north. "No longer will we listen to your gibbering cries of danger. The dwarves of Thorbardin shall return to their former homes and rebuild our kingdom under my rule. As king of Thorbardin, I banish you from the mountain and the realm of the dwarves forever. You and all your ilk! If ever I see your beard again, I shall order it, and the head that grows it, spitted on a pike atop the Isle of the Dead!"

CHAPTER

41

Carrying his son on one arm, Tarn led his group through the silent streets of Norbardin. No soldiers accompanied them, no curious onlookers hung out their windows to watch him pass. If not for the occasional thump or muffled cry that they heard behind doors, they might have thought they were passing through a realm long abandoned by its dwarven occupants.

Tor was awake now and clung to his father's beard and shoulder. He peered about curiously with his wide gray eyes. As he was still only an infant, the little boy scarcely understood what was happening to him. For a few moments, Tarn felt a sudden pang of grief that Tor would never know this place except in the stories of his father and mother. Thorbardin was the birthright of all dwarves, he truly believed, and as much pain and grief as this place had brought him, it only caused him to love it the more.

When they reached the North Gate, Tarn was surprised to find more than three hundred dwarves had gathered. There were whole families from every different clan, except the gully dwarves. They had gathered their belongings and stood in the North Gate plaza with their carts pulled by lowing cave oxen, loaded with such boxes and bundles that they could gather on short notice. These were all the dwarves of Thorbardin who had chosen to follow Tarn into exile. But he knew that for every dwarf here, there were several hundred more who might have followed him, but were more afraid of leaving Thorbardin than of dying in their mountain home.

Several hundred of Jungor's most fanatical Hylar warriors stood nearby in close ranks, weapons at the ready, watching the crowd of exiles with wary disgust. At Tarn's arrival, their captain ordered the North Gate opened. The huge mechanism began to turn and the door, a great plug of stone shaped to be undetectable from the outside, slowly revolved backward on its great steel screw. Finally, it tilted and rolled into an alcove, opening the way to the outside. Sunlight streamed into the mountain for the first time in nearly two years.

Slowly, the exiles began to file out under the close watch of Jungor's troops. As he waited his turn in line, Tarn glanced around one last time at the city he had rebuilt out of the ruins of the Chaos War. Somewhere among the many blank windows that looked down upon the plaza, he knew Jungor Stonesinger was probably watching, gloating, hunched over the Hammer of Kharas as though it were a prize he had won in the Arena.

Now, he truly felt sorrow for those he was leaving behind to suffer under Jungor's rule, however long it might last. The chaos dragon would bring all that to an end, probably more quickly than any of them dared imagine. He deeply regretted his many failures, but none more so than to have disappointed his people and allowed Jungor Stonesinger to wrest the throne from him. That Hylar fool would lead the dwarves of Thorbardin to no good end.

His followers went first. Tarn and his close companions were the last to exit through the gate. They stopped to watch the door slowly screw back into place. Then Tarn turned and looked north toward the wide sodden plains that stretched between Thorbardin and the former elven realm of Qualinost. The other exiles continued to file down the narrow path away from their homeland. Reaching up, Crystal tickled Tor under the chin and said, "Look! The sun is setting. Tor has never seen the sun before."

Tarn smiled to see the look of wonder and delight on his son's face as he gazed at the brilliant reds and golds painting the western sky. He himself had not seen the sun for two years, had scarely given a thought, he was ashamed to admit, to the world outside Thorbardin. What had happened to the elven nation, and to all the troubles of the realms above ground?

He was filled with a sadness and loss that knew no bound. He knew that his duty lay with his people still inside the mountain. Yet there was no time for regrets. He must begin at once to plan a refuge for his followers.

"I know what you are thinking," someone said behind him. Tarn looked over his shoulder to see Ogduan Bloodspike leaning his back against a boulder.

"What's that you say, old one?" Tarn asked.

"I said I know what you are thinking," the death skald answered.

"Tell me then. Because I don't know what I am thinking, myself."

"You should probably go to Pax Tharkas," Ogduan said.

"And why is that?" Crystal asked.

But Tarn's thoughts were already elsewhere. He walked to the edge of the path and looked down toward the exiles. "Where is Mog?" he asked. "Has anyone seen Mog?"

Otaxx shrugged, then turned back to the old dwarf. "I agree. Pax Tharkas is where we should go next."

"Mog did not choose to come with us," Ogduan said to Tarn.

"Why not?" Tarn asked in surprise.

"He asked me to tell you, because he knew you wouldn't approve of his decision," the old dwarf shrugged.

"He's going feral, plans to lead a guerilla war against Jungor Stonesinger from within the kingdom."

"That fool!" Tarn snarled. "You bet your beard I wouldn't have approved. I gave my word that we would all leave."

"He has to follow his own destiny, Tarn Bellowgranite, just as you must follow yours," Ogduan said as he pushed away from the boulder. The North Gate had nearly closed. "You don't have to worry about Beryl anymore—the great dragon is dead. Go to Pax Tharkas. There will be elves waiting for you there, maybe even King Gilthas. There are other, more worthy challenges waiting for you also, Tarn Bellowgranite."

"How do you know all this, old one?" Tarn scoffed, raising an eyebrow.

"The world has changed since last you poked your beard outside the mountain," Ogduan laughed. "The gods have returned. Look for them. Meanwhile, make a new home for your wife and child. Crystal will need a safe place to have her baby." Saying this, he stepped quickly through the narrow gap of the closing gate and vanished from sight. Moments later, the gate silently sealed itself shut, and even those who knew it well could not distinguish its lines from the surrounding stone.

Tarn and Crystal looked at one another in surprise. "A baby?" Tarn whispered. She nodded, her gray eyes pooling with tears.

"But how did he know . . . ?" asked Crystal. Shaking his head, Tarn enveloped her with one arm and pressed her close, losing himself in both joy and sadness as he looked into the calm, certain eyes of his young son. Tor blinked at him and smiled his toothless grin.

Otaxx slapped Tarn on the back and pummeled his shoulder in congratulations. Then he stole Crystal away from the king and squeezed her to his huge, round belly. "Pax Tharkas is a fine idea," he shouted happily. "It has seemed more like home to me than Thorbardin for a long time. I can't remember the last time a dwarf child was born there. It's a good omen, I say."

Crystal shrugged out of the Daewar general's bear hug, complaining that she could barely breathe. "Well, after all, Pax Tharkas is close to my father's own kingdom," she said as she smoothed her tunic, "and we will be welcome there."

"Hill dwarves?" Tarn jibed as they started down the mountainside.

The War of Souls ends now.

The New York Times best-seller from DRAGONLANCE® world co-creators

Margaret Weis & Tracy Hickman

available for the first time in paperback!

The stirring conclusion to the epic trilogy

DRAGONS OF A VANISHED MOON
The War of Souls, Volume III

A small band of heroes, led by an incorrigible kender, prepares to
battle an army of the dead led by a seemingly invincible female
warrior. A dragon overlord provides a glimmer of hope to those who
fight the darkness, but true victory—or utter defeat—lies in the
secret of time's riddles.

The Minotaur Wars

From *New York Times* best-selling author Richard A. Knaak comes a powerful new chapter in the DRAGONLANCE® saga.

The continent of Ansalon, reeling from the destruction of the War of Souls, slowly crawls from beneath the rubble to rebuild – but the fires of war, once stirred, are difficult to quench. Another war comes to Ansalon, one that will change the balance of power throughout Krynn.

NIGHT OF BLOOD
Volume I

Change comes violently to the land of the minotaurs. Usurpers overthrow the emperor, murder all rivals, and dishonor minotaur tradition. The new emperor's wife presides over a cult of the dead, while the new government makes a secret pact with a deadly enemy. But betrayal is never easy, and rebellion lurks in the shadows.

The Minotaur Wars begin.